There are going to be new-consciousness books, and this is going to be one of the best; never sentimental or adolescently worshipful, always wise, exciting to read, hopeful and dangerous at the same time, as good myths should be.

SMILE ON THE VOID crackles, snaps and pops with the new, hopeful, intelligent, synthesized, holistic, right-and-left brain united planetary culture we are going to need to survive the 20th century, and everyone with an interest in that survival should read it to discover the options. It is a wonderful book.

ROB SWIGART,
author of *Little America* and *AKA A Cosmic Fable*

"A PARABLE FOR OUR TIME . . .?"
                                —LIBRARY JOURNAL

SMILE ON THE VOID

STUART GORDON

THE MYTHHISTORY OF RALPH M'BOTU KITAJ

BERKLEY BOOKS, NEW YORK

*This story is for
anyone & everyone
who doesn't believe a word of it*

Contents

Note:

The following account has been retyped and copied from the photostat of a typewritten manuscript which recently came our way. It is apparently the work of John Hall, sometime amanuensis of RMK. No definite claims can be made to the authenticity of the authorship. Nevertheless, the account gives strong internal indications of being genuine, and some of it may be of value in our struggle. Therefore we are making it available among those who may read it sympathetically and, we hope, take heart from it.

WARNING! Possession of this material will constitute a serious offense in many countries. Read it, make copies if you can, and pass them on—*but please take great care!* To take chances is part of our philosophy, certainly—but foolhardiness is not recommended under present conditions.

RALPH M'BOTU KITAJ LIVES!

> *Friends of the Hundred Thousand*
> *December 1999*

THE END OF THE BEGINNING
OR
THE BEGINNING OF THE END

"Counterfeiters exist only because there is true gold."
—Jalaluddin Rumi

1. IN THE SINKING CITY

Venice, 25 December 1992.

Christmas Day in the Sinking City.

At sunset the Transformation of Ralph M'Botu Kitaj takes place in full view of one hundred thousand people, as scheduled. It is a public event without parallel in modern times, possibly a turning-point in history, signaling an opportunity for change in our global consciousness and in our estimation of ourselves. It is an amazing event, a joyous event, enormous in emotional impact . . . but the aftermath brings controversy and persecution.

Were you there? If so, you will never forget. Do you remember the chill fog which blanketed the decaying, mournful beauty of the city? Do you recall the thousands of tiny boats bobbing up and down on the pallid waters in front of the floodlit eastern facade of S. Giorgio Maggiore, where it happened? Were you in one of those boats? Did you hold a flaming torch, were you among the Hundred Thousand? Did you see, with your own eyes, and did what you see change your life irrevocably, forever? And are you still alive today?

More likely you were not there, in which case you have no rational basis for belief in the Transformation, for there is no

1

objective evidence that anything happened at all. If you were not there, then all you have to go on is your faith and your sensation that there is more in the heaven and earth of the human being than is dreamed of by materialism. All you have is your courage, and your intuition that it is belief and will and imagination that move mountains and create history.

Even if you do not believe, whoever you are and wherever you live, you will have heard of the Transformation. The whole world has heard, despite the efforts to suppress this knowledge which has so undermined the OldStyle basis of power and scientific validity. You will have heard, and perhaps you would like to believe, but wonder why there is no objective evidence, and find it hard to accept what happened without some source of scientific proof.

So, why is there no proof? Why no film, no recording, no verifications other than whisperings and clandestine words of mouth?

First, even had such evidence been available, it would quickly have been denounced as a fraudulent superstitious concoction by almost every political and scientific authority in the world. It would have been seized, destroyed, and denied. This is not paranoid speculation. It is the fate of all other evidence relating to the myth and history of Ralph M'Botu Kitaj. In most countries he has been declared a nonperson who never existed. Any belief in Kitaj and in what he did is taken as evidence of a criminal insanity demanding the most rigorous and permanent cures which the laws and medicine of Mammon can inflict. The reason for this persecution is straightforward. Kitaj effectively denied the universality and power of the monster which oppresses this sadly shrouded planet. He is the Judas of the demon Materialism. He demonstrated the falsehood of many of the systems upon which we have been educated to depend. More important, he did so having climbed to the top of what he himself called "the shitpile." He became the richest man in the world, creating his myth of a modern Midas, fascinating millions—then, in the most dramatic way possible, he dismissed it all as worthless, destructive, and evil. He sacrificed himself in a way that means one can either accept or deny his example—there is no halfway house. Thus, from the viewpoint of our temporal rulers, there is no doubt that, alive or dead, Kitaj is the Devil Incarnate, and their rigid condition leaves them with no option but to try to suppress all of us who will no longer accept their description of reality, of life and its purpose.

Still, why no evidence? The event was massively publicized in advance. The whole world knew of Kitaj's intention. His actions of the previous year had made him one of the most newsworthy individuals who ever existed, and the censorship did not begin until afterwards. Kitaj made sure that everyone knew what he meant to do, and he made sure that the media were invited.

But I remember very clearly how at the time I thought, seeing the way he smiled when he signed the contracts for media coverage, that he had something up his sleeve . . . another shattering surprise of the sort he loved to pull.

So it turned out.

All that final afternoon there was bustle in the forecourt of S. Giorgio. Media crews, scientists, journalists, technicians, setting up their cameras and gauss meters and other devices for recording, timing, measuring, and proving; doing sound checks, vision checks, magnetic field strength checks; preparing all their equipment for the appointed hour, for the promised miracle . . . and the hour came . . . and Kitaj arrived . . . and the broadcasts began to all the world . . . and the Transformation began . . . and all the equipment failed, simultaneously.

The machines all jammed up. They all went dead. Meter needles fell back to zero. Tapes hissed blank. Cameras recorded only an intolerable glare.

No photographs. No proof. No timings, graphs, or charts.

The only witnesses of the Transformation were human beings.

This mechanical failure has never to my knowledge been publicly explained. How can it be explained? The event never happened so far as machines and politicians are concerned. It has no objective existence, while those of us who accept subjective evidence are not concerned with mechanical verification. By now there is a long history of failure and misunderstanding in the scientific approach to energy-phenomena which do not obey OldStyle laws of cause and effect. This is often regarded as indicating the fraudulence of the phenomena. I see it as indicating the fraudulence of the *approach* to the phenomena. But try telling this to anyone getting his paycheck from the systems of OldStyle. To some degree we all serve our own perceived interests, and rarely recognize to what extent reality is the product of our *unconscious* will.

Yet there is one media artifact which has become famous, in an underground way, as an apparently genuine survivor of the Transformation.

This is an amateur video recording, seemingly filmed out on the lagoon that night, amid the thousands of small boats. Genuine or not, it is an excellent aid to belief—its quality is so poor you can believe anything you like. The soundtrack gives the impression of an excited football crowd and is often interrupted by deafening surges of static—the same crackling roar which defeated every other attempt at recording. The video is equally vague, but contains odd effects which persuade some (those who need evidence) that it is genuine. It may well be. Of what happened beneath the arcade of S. Giorgio we cannot see or hear a thing on this recording. There is only a bright floodlit glare against which the heads of people and prows of boats in the foreground bob up and down, with many burning torches to add to the glare and visual distortion. But suddenly we see the black electronic blobs of people standing up in their boats, torches waving, the soundtrack roaring, the glare incandescent. Then it cuts out. Completely. It loses the Transformation, begins to record again only afterwards, with the white light gone, the static gone, Kitaj gone, and the people dazed in their boats. In fact it starts recording again at the point where everything and everyone, including all machines and the police, started to wake up again (or go to sleep) into "ordinary" reality.

This recording now fetches huge prices on the international bootleg market, though in many countries possession of it is judged a serious offense. People have died for it; and many who doubt their own belief, who were not at Venice, have made an icon of it, calling it *scientific evidence*. They regard it as a signpost to the Holy Grail. Others regard it as a signpost to Hell. Their rationality and the system say: *It was just another stunt, like Houdini or Evel Knievel*. They fear it was all done with mirrors, and that afterwards Kitaj slipped away into hiding somewhere in South America.

But the moon in them whispers something else completely.

Kitaj's vision cannot be stopped or even contained.

The reason for this is that he operated on the level of myth, and that on this level, which in most of us is unconscious and untrained, we all acknowledge the truth of what he showed us.

We know it, even if we can't admit it. Kitaj made sure of it, as sure as any human being could. Once he became aware of what his life meant, he organized his own myth with a skill unparalleled. He couldn't read or write words (or at least pretended that he couldn't), but he knew people, he knew what made people tick, from the gut to the crown.

The Transformation capped his work. It pierced our veils, changed our inner maps. Many of us have accepted this; have accepted that we and the world are not as we thought. But the emotional/mythic impact of the Transformation has been so great that many others find it hard to accept the way it makes them feel, the way it makes them question the value of themselves and their lives. They feel that their ego-barriers are under attack, and they are quite right. Thus, widespread acceptance, but also widespread denial, and ferocious war on those who believe.

But Kitaj's teachings won't be denied.

Every attack on us shows an inverted acceptance.

Now we near the time of Kitaj's promised return, in whatever symbol or form, and the disputes and persecutions rage more fiercely than ever.

"I'll be back," he said last of all. *"In seven years I'll be back, and hope to find you all through the Joke. Take a Chance. Why not?"*

Those are his last reported words.

After that only his smile lingers with us—Mona Lisa, Cheshire Cat, Black Hole Joke transformed. Since then we have been waiting and we have been working, and the permutations of the Joke perform all over the world.

The dark Joke of our idiocies, of our self-bondage.

Now the Seven Years are almost up. We are about to turn the corner into a new millenium—at least according to the Christian catalogue of time—and doubt is like a plague abroad in the world, in every land and at every level of society. Like a cancer this doubt is eroding belief in social values, self-identity, and existence itself; and it is generating great fear, which is one of the causes of persecution of those following paths called occult, such as the path of Chancing. Traditional religion is tottering, many governments have banned "mysticotechnic" research of the sort which Kitaj sponsored and which helped him towards Transformation. The demons of fear are writhing naked and unconcealed . . . but we should not make the mistake of assum-

ing that they are to be found only among those who attack us.
Fear also wears masks and subtle disguises. It can conceal itself
as hate, or anger, but also as self-righteousness, or as spurious
and desperate faith which will crumble as soon as put to the test.
Among us are some who think they believe in the myth of Midas
Transformed, but the truth is that they fear themselves, they
desire a leader, a symbolic hero-figure to take the burden of
self-responsibility from their shoulders. Others among us show
fear in their desire to descend into reaction by striking at those
who strike at us. Fear lurks in almost all of us. There is fear in
myself: you can see it in my choice of words. Why use such a
divisive word as "us," which necessarily implies a "them," if
not out of fear? The ambiguities of fear are coded into the very
ground of our language. Consider the word "host," which derives
from exactly the same root as "hostile." "Language is a prison," Kitaj told me once. "When you learn to read and write,
you gain the freedom of deciding which concept-cells you're
going to be locked up in. Words distort vision and perspective."

If we admit the fear among us, maybe we can deal with it.

How does it manifest most commonly? What form does it
take?

There is a question I have often been asked, amounting to this:
What if Kitaj does not return in some miraculous heavens-
splitting manner? What if there is no wonderful Second Coming?
What if nothing happens at all? Will our faith and energy fall
completely apart? Will the world end?

It depends. It depends on each and every one of us. It depends
how well we understand the Joke, the Black Hole Joke into
which it seems the powers-that-be are determined that we should
all be swallowed. It depends how poetically and multidimensionally
we learn to flow through this world of energy, this world of
mythreality. It depends on how much we want to stay the slaves
of fear, of convention, of OldStyle. There is no simple truth of
black and white, nothing is ultimately fixed or solid, but there are
always interactions and relationships. It is irrelevant whether or
not Kitaj returns in the solidity of the flesh, and it seems very
unlikely—although you never know. The final statement he made
can be interpreted any way you please, though I prefer to attempt
no interpretation at all. My experience of the man while he was
with us tells me not to take *any* of his words literally. And my
understanding of the truth of his return is this: Kitaj returns, time

and again, whenever we remember his example and put it into effect.

To deify Kitaj, as has been happening recently in some quarters, is a gross and fatal error, though perhaps inevitable, given the degree to which Kitaj himself played on myths of hero and hero-worship. But the man was not entirely the myth, as I hope to establish, and deification annuls the entire value of his example. He was a human being like the rest of us: it is his very humanity which stimulates us to hope, to work on. What he did, we can do. We can gain control of the forces within us. We can enter more consciously into the Great Dance. We can transform ourselves. It is a necessity. We humans are in an unbalanced condition, frustration weighing against unrealized potential. The scales may tip either way, and it is we who will tip them, either consciously or unconsciously. It is better that we learn to do it consciously, as Kitaj did. He demonstrated, in public, what we might be, what we might become. It is true that he was unique in his particular destiny, but no more and no less than each and every one of us. He was not a god, save insofar as we are all unrealized gods. For most of his life he was a tormented man, thoroughly confused by the interplay of so many forces within him, the chief creator and first victim of his own mythology. The power (and the ambiguity, at least to the fixed mind) of the patterns he bequeathed to us lies not least in his transcendence of this personal torment and degrading mythology of wealth, fame, and power. He sprang upon us out of Africa with tales of an impossibly mythical youth (tales which we will examine shortly), and he proceeded, at the age of forty-two, to become the richest man in the material world. He came among us selling commodities catering to the human appetite for self-destruction. He came among us with a grudge against humanity, selling death, and humanity, which has a grudge against itself, rewarded him by putting him right at the top. And when he got there he found nothing but the transparency of his ambition, of himself, of humanity. For years he did not know what to do about it. Consumed by boredom, disgust, and self-disgust, he became a global showman shaman, dicing with entertainments of life and death, a man filled with guilt who was challenging the world to call him out . . . but for the most part the world only applauded more enthusiastically. It was only in the end, and so very gradually, and in crisis, that he found the will and vision and direction to rise above this destructive confusion in such a typically flamboyant and startling fashion that, to this day, no two people can easily agree on what happened, what he really did, how he did it, where he went, what their senses perceived, how their nervous systems were affected, and how their lives were changed by the energies of Transformation.

Seven years have passed since then. Kitaj demonstrated what many have always suspected, but which few have succeeded in establishing so spectacularly. Before one hundred thousand "modern rational Western" human beings he proved that for the most part we are asleep to our true potential, that we make much less of ourselves than we might. How he did it we do not quite know, most of us, though there are theories and techniques which I will examine later. Where he went we do not know either, though of late there have been rumours of clairvoyant contacts with an entity that claims to be Kitaj. This entity, apparently related to the star-system of Sirius, has information which, if genuine, is of interest to us all, and in due course I will come to it.

First things first. We are living in the myth, and we are caught up in the Joke, and it seems time to render an account of that Joke.

An account of the life and myth of Ralph M'Botu Kitaj.

Who am I? What are my credentials? What do I hope to achieve by writing this account? It cannot be published anywhere. At best it can only be passed about, hand to hand, mind to mind. But perhaps that is good enough.

I am John Hall. I was with Kitaj much of the time between 1984 and 1992. I was his reader, his writer, his secretary, and I believe I was his friend. I was with him during the Disappearance (1985-87), and thereafter during the fraught period of the Black Hole Joke Shows, and again during the intense inner changes which brought him finally to Venice. Other people who were close to him during his latter years, Lenore included, are now either dead or in hiding as I am. Life since the Transformation has been difficult for anyone who was connected with Kitaj, and for a long time I have committed none of my memories to writing. Now I feel the need to break silence. I must write down what I know and believe and remember, hoping not to add more false myth to the great amount already generated. I want to try and clear up some of the confusion about the man and his motives, though my understanding is limited and there are other people who could probably do the job much better. At the very least I can put down a lot of information which is not generally available, and which may be of value to others.

Kitaj remains enormously obscure to many people, not least because they enjoy obscurity, and because they won't let go and relax. There is false intellectual conflict between the "historical" and "mythical" aspects of his life—false, because to Kitaj himself the two were essentially the same, and because people don't usually act on the basis of "what is," but on the basis of what they believe— "Fantasy is the ass that carries the Ark." Likewise I often encounter unnecessarily dogmatic conflict about his attitudes to such dualities as "Good & Evil," and "Truth & Lies," particularly as it's remembered how for a time he called himself "The King of Lies," rather like a latter-day Aleister Crowley . . . and there are many who were willing to agree with him, including the Pope who denounced him . . . many who were only too eager to take him at his self-denying word.

What is true, what is false? This is a game he was always playing, with ironic seriousness, acting out the question of his every word and deed, pointing the finger at himself, doing so I believe in the continual hope that other people would consciously look in the mirror which he provided and in it see themselves.

"History is the lie commonly agreed upon," he quoted sardonically at me once when we were holed up in Ireland during the Disappearance. He was mocking me for trying to persuade him to dictate his autobiography so that the world might know the "truth" about him. He claimed this epigram as his own. I fell into his trap. I pointed out that somebody else had said it first. He was hugely amused. "Surely," he said, laughing, "if I understood it, then it is also mine? Can people *own* words and statements, like property?"

Nevertheless the thought of an autobiography amused him. He saw possibilities for paradox and myth, particularly given his stated inability to read or write beyond the scrawled signature of his own name.

"So you want to write my autobiography?" he challenged. "What are you going to call my autobiography?"

"How about the *The Diary of Midas?*" I suggested.

"Rubbish!" He was contemptuous. "Who gives a shit about

Midas? That was long ago. This is *now*—1985. Come on, man, try again.''

"All right!" I snapped, stung. "What about *Liar's Gold?*"

He grinned. He gave me that great big smile that flowed all over you and lit you up inside. But his deep bright eyes, as always, stayed utterly level.

"That's better," he said. "That'll do. That's *truthful.*"

"So where do you want to start?" I demanded. "In the ghetto . . . or in the jungle . . . or," (I felt sarcastic) "way back when you built the Sphinx?"

"No idea," he said. "You're the truthful one. You tell me."

So I did. And so . . . here in John Hall's version . . . of the truth . . .

THE MYTH OF HIS HISTORY
OR
THE HISTORY OF HIS MYTH

"Every thing possible to be believ'd is an image of truth"
—William Blake

2. BIRTH AND EARLY YEARS

There is no hard evidence to support the claim made by Kitaj in his autobiography *(Liar's Gold,* Harper & Row, New York, 1988) that he was born of Polish-Jewish parents in the attic of a house on Muranovska Street in Warsaw, on 9 September 1942. If the claim is in any way correct, then it is amazing that he succeeded in being born at all, let alone in living through his first year. Muranovska Street was in the Ghetto, and the Warsaw Ghetto in September 1942 was deadly and getting deadlier. It was scarcely over a month since the deportation from the Ghetto by the Nazis of more than seventy thousand Jews to Lublin, Treblinka, Trawniki, and other death camps—many people going willingly to escape the disease and starvation in the Ghetto itself. The turncoat Jewish police of the Judenrat were charging their own people eighty zloty apiece for a loaf of bread; a tube of antityphus medicine cost several thousand zloty; the chances for survival of a newborn child must have been virtually zero. But Kitaj claims that he was indeed born in such circumstances, and that he did indeed survive.

The background to the claim and the evidence from which he deduced it are similarly rather unusual. For a long time he had admitted the total mystery of his origins, and in his autobiography he says that he had no hint of when and where he was born until late in 1978. In that year, increasingly troubled by severe nightmares which seemed to relate to his unknown early childhood, he underwent a series of Regression Therapy sessions at a private clinic in Berkeley, California, and it is through these sessions that recollection of his earliest days was apparently stimulated.

These sessions were extremely traumatic. Soon after I first entered employment with Kitaj in 1984, I saw the signed testimonies of three therapists present during the last two sessions in December 1978. Kitaj himself was always rather evasive whenever I asked him about these sessions. For a long time he would do no more than refer me to the signed statements—all known copies of which have since been seized and no doubt destroyed. But I read these statements, and made my own copies, which I still possess, and they tell an intriguing tale.

Through techniques of depth-hypnosis, and with the selective aid of certain memory-enhancing drugs (the hormones vasopressin and ACTH), and with the help of a sensitive guide (Lenore Springer, whom he married shortly afterwards), Kitaj was apparently induced to recall, in great detail, terrible events seemingly from the first eight months of his life. He was even induced to recall the names of people and places, though much of the information had to be reconstructed after the sessions from existing historical knowledge.

It will be asked how the mind of a newborn child could record any specific information at all, far less retain such knowledge to be recalled in depth some thirty-six years later. Yet the sessions occurred and the transcripts, which I saw, were made; and it is worth mentioning here the work done in the 1980s which to some degree bears out the theory that even "inanimate" objects such as stones possess a sort of memory—a capacity for recording into their molecular structure the subtle vibration of passing events. The difficulty lies not so much in establishing the existence of such memory, but in finding ways to elicit and draw it out. In this context I would refer you to the researches of Professor Vasily Novomeisky of the Kuchynka Institute in Odessa, except that these researches are now also no doubt under wraps, if continued at all.

So what is the tale that was reconstructed from these sessions?

Kitaj and his therapists claim that his true (i.e., biological) father and mother were named Stefan and Maria Dybowski, who both probably died during the final assault on the Ghetto by the Waffen-SS during April–May 1943. Stefan Dybowski had worked in Feiffer's Leather Factory in Okopova Street on the edge of the Ghetto, but after the mass transportations of July–August 1942 he joined the militant Ghetto organization Hashomar Hatzair, under the command of one Mordecai Anilewitz. When the final attack came in April 1943 both Stefan and Maria, along with thousands of others, decided to remain and fight to the end. But Maria made arrangements for the escape of their infant child. Curiously, during the sessions Kitaj was unable to remember his own Christian name. It seems that Maria made the arrangements with a cobbler named Szomanski—of whom no record now exists—who succeeded in escaping the Ghetto at the end of March 1943, taking the child with him.

As I write now I have the transcript of that particular session—the fifth and penultimate—in front of me on my desk:

GUIDE: Where are you now? What is happening to you?

KITAJ: I am . . . a man is . . . a man is holding me now.

GUIDE: Do you know this man? Who is he? Is he friendly?

KITAJ: I . . . I'm confused . . . what . . .

GUIDE: Sorry. My fault. What does this man look like?

KITAJ: He has a face like a knobbly potato. I'm frightened.

GUIDE: Why are you frightened? Is it the man?

KITAJ: I'm being taken away! He's carrying me away. They aren't stopping him! They aren't stopping him! They're letting him carry me away! I'm frightened. I'm crying but they won't stop him! I can't see them any more. He's taking me into a dark place. Too loud! Too loud! He's taking me down into darkness. Can't breathe! I'm wrapped up, something covers me, the light's gone, the light's gone, we're in the dark . . . it smells . . . there's

             water . . . he's got me in the water *(screams)*
             he's going to . . .
GUIDE: Okay. Okay. Relax. You're okay. Maybe
             he's a friend. I think he's helping you. Relax.
KITAJ: He took me away! He took me away!
GUIDE: He takes you so that you'll live. He's a
             friend.
KITAJ: Dark. It's dark and wet. Dark and wet. Dark
             and wet . . .

In the subsequent and final session it grew clear that this man
Szomanski, with the "face like a knobbly potato," must have
found a way out of the Ghetto through the sewers, and that the
recurrent nightmares which brought Kitaj to this therapy had to
do with this dangerous and unpleasant journey. He at any rate
was satisfied with this explanation, having previously consulted a
great variety of more orthodox psychiatric opinions, and having
refused to accept the orthodox interpretations of the dark wet
tunnel of his dream as a vagina, or as a descent into the unconscious, or whatever. It was certainly much more pleasing to Kitaj
himself to accept that the tunnel had in fact physically existed,
and that his dreadful dreams arose from suppressed memory of a
dreadful event.

And thereafter? Szomanski probably made contact with a sym-
pathizer, or with the Polish Underground Movement. At the end
of this last session Kitaj remembers a thick dark room with all the
curtains drawn, a very dim light glimmering in one corner, a
woman rocking him, and people coming and going all the time,
silently, and the name "Wlodek" being crooned, often, though
whether this referred to him or to some other child did not clearly
emerge. Such images tally with possibility. Nearly six thousand
Jews are thought to have escaped the Ghetto, and the Poles,
impressed by the Jewish resistance, did not offer the Nazis much
help in rounding up the refugees.

Of what happened to him during the two years that followed,
before the start of his definitely recorded history, there is neither
record nor memory. There is only the image of the curtained
room, and by the end of the sixth session he was in a state of
such agitation and exhaustion that the therapy was discontinued
as counterproductive.

None of it is conclusive. But Kitaj certainly believed that the

sessions had revealed the truth—or at least a meaningful lie—
about his origins. For a time he became obsessed with finding out
if he could establish facts. Twice in 1979 he went with Lenore to
Warsaw, seeking access to public records, looking for people
who might have known Stefan and Maria Dybowski, or who
might verify some of the harrowing details he claimed to have
remembered. There is no doubt it was important to him, as
Lenore later made very clear to me (at a time during which she
was less than outrightly hostile towards me), and on subsequent
occasions he submitted to further depth-hypnosis in the presence
of professional witnesses. They also signed sworn statements that
Kitaj, very agitated, described events that tally well with what is
known of the horrors in the Ghetto.

But his journeys to Warsaw were unsuccessful. The Ghetto
had been totally razed in the summer of 1943, and those who
might have provided corroborative evidence had long since died
or disappeared. The existence of the Feiffer Leather Factory in
Okopova Street was confirmed, as were other details of his story,
but nothing which could not already be found in existing histories. In his autobiography he mentions the obstructiveness of the
regime in power at the time of his visits, implying that his case
might have been proven had the Polish Politburo been more
inclined to help. It is of course no surprise that the Polish
Communist bureaucracy was unwilling to aid such a notorious
entrepreneur, particularly one who dealt in the commodities that
Kitaj then dealt in. It is also possible that the then-recent election
of a Polish Pope might have had something to do with this
unwillingness to help, for Kitaj was then already well known for
his hatred of and opposition to organized religion.

Thus in the final analysis there is, once again, no objective
proof, only strong implication. You may believe or not as you
will, but the myth of his origins in which Kitaj believed has its
own imaginative reality and gives insight into his character and
into his subsequent actions and activities.

Yet many people cannot accept this tale as myth, far less as
objective truth. Two points are worth making. First, there is
nothing intrinsically impossible about such an origin, although
Kitaj's incredible tales of later life in Africa have caused disbelief
in his Ghetto birth too, on the grounds that one supposed lie
proves another . . . yet such an attitude indicates no more than a
certain rigidity of approach. Second, many of us have been

educated to deny myth-thinking as part of the baggage of a
nightmare past from which we are now struggling to awake. To
pay heed to myth (as the Nazis did) can seem to mean a terrifying
regression back to a superstitious sleep from which science and
reason have but lately rescued us. However, the creative use of
myth can guide us in self-discovery and lure us to wider under-
standings. It need not mean abandonment of reason and common
sense; rather, it can lead to expansion and reorientation of these
faculties. It is an obvious illusion to consider this horrific era an
Age of Reason: if we deny our mythic and intuitive faculties we
will only plunge ourselves into worse confusion and disorder.
Two plus two do not necessarily make four; they may make five,
or seven, or nine. This principle, known to science as synergy, is
pre-eminently applicable to the inner life of the human being, and
we are in danger of self-destruction if we forget it. It was one of
Kitaj's aims that we should not forget it. Was he born in the
Ghetto? Yes. In the Ghetto of the World, as we make it.

At any rate there is little doubt that Kitaj's earliest and most
formative years were spent amid the destructive atmosphere of
Europe at war. It is very likely that he was in Poland until shortly
before the end of the war, and that during the final break-up of
the Nazi empire, amid the chaos of the Russian advance, he was
carried west by people who feared the Russians as much as the
Germans. It is not known what happened to these people or who
they were. It is however known that, upon adoption into the
wealthy Têtaurier household in July 1945, the child spoke only a
few words—in Polish. This has frequently been confirmed by
ex-employees of Château Têtaurier, a productive estate occupying
fine land between Cognac and Angoulême.

Maurice Têtaurier found the child in an Alsatian transit-camp
for refugees and war orphans. It is even known how the child
came to be in the camp. A Sergeant Daniel Buckley, of Madison,
Wisconsin, found him on the east bank of the Rhine in April
1945, in a devastated area which had just been heavily shelled by
the advancing Allied forces. The boy was starving, almost naked,
on his own and terrified, yet miraculously unharmed. He was
taken behind the lines and lodged in the makeshift camp, yet
another number with no name, and there he survived, in poor
health and half-starved, for some three months.

Enter Maurice Têtaurier. A melancholy man of material wealth
and strong spiritualistic learnings, he had spent the war fighting

out of England with the Free French and had now returned to France with his English wife Minnie to reclaim his lands and his business. They were a childless couple, approaching middle age, and no doubt they had discussed adoption before, yet it is not known what drew Maurice to visit this particular camp, far less what prompted him to select this particular child as an adopted son rather than any other of the hundreds of children in the camp.

Perhaps it had to do with the nameless boy's large, compelling grey eyes. They must have shone fanatically out of the thin white face. A photograph in *Liar's Gold* of a sombre child aged about five, which Kitaj said was a picture of himself taken by Minnie, displays an almost hypnotic brightness of gaze, and in the way the boy holds himself there is a distance, a reserve, a pride, indicating a mind of unusual tenacity and potential. It seems likely that Maurice Têtaurier, a sensitive man, always quick to be impressed by anything unusual, may have responded to the directness of this child's gaze. Or maybe it was simply that the boy looked like the son he wanted but could not have. Or yet again, perhaps it was some matter of destiny which I am not competent to probe—in later years Kitaj often told me of his guardian angel which had watched over him since his very earliest days. And who is to prove otherwise, particularly in view of his subsequent career and remarkable fate?

Whatever the cause, Maurice Têtaurier took this unknown polish boy with him back to the château, to the rich southern estate where for generations his family had grown the grapes for the famous Têtaurier brandy.

That the adoption was unpremeditated is suggested by what ex-employees of the estate have said: that to begin with Minnie openly showed her anger. She had not been consulted, and for some time she rejected this foster-motherhood thrust so abruptly upon her, particularly as it involved a final naked recognition between the pair of them that they were never to have natural children of their own. She was a gaunt and secretive woman, in mind as well as in body, slow to demonstrate affection under the best of circumstances, and she never entirely accepted the newcomer, who was eventually to pay back the dislike with interest. And that first winter after the war must have been uncomfortable emotionally as well as physically. The château, which had been used by the Germans as a regional Staff HQ, had been deliberately and severely damaged by fire during the German retreat.

The new family lived in a small house on the estate until the château had been restored. It was during that time that the child received the second of his many name givings; the first that he retained. Maurice and Minnie named him Ralph Armand Michel Têtaurier.

They proceeded to raise him as their own son.

For eight long years he stayed well dressed and outwardly cared-for at the château. He was never happy there. He made no friends. His foster parents refused to send him to the local school: instead they engaged a series of tutors (all of whom sooner or later gave up) and effectively imprisoned him in the isolation of their own social status and unfriendliness. He turned into an evasive and willful dreamer, with a vicious temper whenever he was crossed and a capacity for getting his own way. He was slow to learn French, and altogether unwilling to learn to read and write. All attempts to teach him failed completely. When chastised he would throw a tantrum or retreat into his inner world. If a pencil was put into his hand he would drop it or hurl it away. Sometimes he would condescend to draw fairly complex shapes, usually circles or squares with stick-figures of himself well protected within them—a clear enough indication of his state of mind. Yet, as if in compensation, he was unusually quick to learn and understand the dexterity of number and calculation, and though he would not read for himself, he soon showed a very deep passion for listening to stories—stories read or told him aloud by Minnie or his tutor of the moment, particularly heroic and mythical stories and fairy tales. He would listen entranced for hour after hour, the savage beast quelled, and before long he developed a most remarkable memory. Often after a storytelling session he would repeat the tale, word for word, astonishing his foster parents and anyone else who heard him, so that again they would try to persuade him to learn to read and write, and again and again he would refuse.

"I told them that if I learned to read I'd forget how to remember," he explained much later, in *Liar's Gold.* "The truth is I didn't want to be trapped any more than I was already trapped. I think I felt that words were only a way to make a cage of the world, and when they tried to make me learn about words I felt physically sick, and very angry. I didn't know why this was, I only knew I had to resist . . . and I did . . . and they couldn't make me do it."

On the face of it he had every reason to be grateful to his aristocratic foster parents. They had plucked him from a ruined world and given him every material advantage in life—good food, fine clothes, an education, the security of a home and social status, and the promise of an easy future. But it meant nothing positive to him. They were alien and distant, and so was the luxury in which they surrounded him. He was a wild child, a vengeful child, a war child, with an inner stress which later brought tragedy to his sad foster parents, and despite everything he never remembered Château Têtaurier with anything but the most acute dislike. "I was surrounded by walls and ghosts there," he said, "and there was nobody to talk to but the walls and ghosts." Thus when at last in the spring of 1946 they moved into the château (designed in the 1690s by Jules Hardouin Mansart), the boy did not find his vast new home at all comforting. When he grew older he would sleep outside as often as he could, under the stars, in the fields, or beneath the elegant trees in the woods which surrounded the château, where there were no walls to constrict him. The château made him very claustrophobic—as later did the conventions of human society—yet out of necessity he developed relationships with the phantoms, ancient and modern, imagined or otherwise, which thronged the great halls and long corridors. For him these phantoms hid in the suits of armor, behind the Gobelin tapestries, in the frowning eyes of the family portraits, in the darkness of the underground vaults, and in the little passages hidden through the highest walls. Most of all they hid in the spiritual gloom of the place, which was reinforced by the gloom of Maurice and Minnie, an unhappy couple, living in the past in a world of secrets, table rapping, and might-have-been. His foster parents were obsessed by a strange memory of which he did not learn until after his tenth birthday. Until then, the phantoms of the place were more real to him than the human inhabitants, and his mind took odd turns. He recalls old four-poster beds, the smell of mothballs, the enormous library with its rows of occult treatises by Albertus Magnus and Paracelsus, its musty religious tomes by Bossuet and Pascal. He recalls the little Catholic chapel at which weekly services were held. The chants and incense moved him deep inside, but the attempts to educate him religiously failed as completely as the attempts to get him to read or write. He would have nothing to do with organized Christianity, then or ever, associating it with hypocrisy and

boredom. But he was not irreligious. Far from it. His own more
potent, pagan, visionary tastes were soon to find expression. In
the meantime there were the ordeals of emptiness. He recalls
evening meals at which not a word was ever spoken. He recalls
few smiles and fewer visitors. Maurice and Minnie kept entirely
to themselves, and the ghosts with which the boy communed
cannot have been entirely imaginary, as subsequent events established. His foster parents never drank the brandy for which the
Château was justly famous; they showed little interest in the
running of the estate; they made no attempt to find playmates for
their adopted son. It cannot have been much of a life for a
growing boy. It seems there was no love in it at all—no warmth
other than in the reading sessions, no encouragement of any
outward interests in his education. He was left to invert. By the
age of ten he was firmly planted in a world of imagination and
growing resentment. The inner pressure grew severe: no surprise
that he preferred to sleep outside when the weather allowed.

What did he do in winter, or when the weather was bad? He
would slip away for hours on end, not to be found, to spend his
time dreaming uneasily with the ghosts that thronged the many
little attic rooms on the top floors of the house. The walls of
these rooms carried signs of a more recent haunting—messages
and memoranda, rosters and calenders, all in German. These
dim, dusty rooms were not properly cleaned out during the time
he was there, so the evidence of the German occupation remained.
He knew that these writings-on-the-wall were German from the
swastikas printed on many of them. They came to hold curious
fascination for him. In *Liar's Gold* he tells us how on his tenth
birthday (an arbitrary date of 21 September chosen for him by
Maurice) he underwent an unusual and terrifying experience in
one of these Nazi-haunted attics . . . one where a poster of
Hitler remained tacked to a closet door, a poster portraying Hitler
as a Wagnerian knight in shining armor. This experience is of
great importance, for it triggered many events, and we will
follow his own recollection, though some people have called it
overdramatic and not at all convincing:

"It had been raining all day," he tells us, "and it was nearly
dark, and the wind was rising. Because it was meant to be my
birthday there was going to be a special supper party for me. Of
course this meant just Maurice and Minnie and me. I didn't want
to go. I couldn't bear the thought of looking at him, with his face

like a sad old badger, or her, with her face like a bleached-out mouse. So I hid myself in the room with the poster of Hitler. The window rattled in the wind; everything was alive in a horrible way. I could feel the ghosts all round me; I started to get frightened as I stared at this picture of the armored man with the stern mad eyes. I knew he was the man supposed to have killed my parents and millions of other people; I knew I was supposed to hate him. I'd been told over and over again about how I'd been found, and how lucky I was, and what terrible people the Germans were, and how this Hitler had never been human at all, but a demon in human disguise. So there I stood as it got dark, fascinated by the eyes of this "human demon," and I got so angry and terrified I went into a sort of delirium. It wasn't just his eyes that did it: I had no proof that he was any worse than anyone else, when Maurice or anyone else told me of this devil incarnate their own eyes became just as cold and cruel. So that as I stared it began to seem to me that everyone probably possessed the same madness as this man Hitler. How else had he come to power? I saw that *everyone* had devils. Myself too. I could feel them in me. I stood trembling, feeling hot and red with the devils dancing in me. I started wanting to kill Maurice and Minnie. It terrified me. I felt so alone and helpless, like a puff of hot smoke; I didn't belong to myself; I had no control; I couldn't move; I was a red-hot hate wanting to explode but not knowing how or why. I stared at the man in armor wondering if he'd worn the armor to stop himself from exploding, and if it was why he'd had to kill so many people—so he wouldn't explode. My teeth were chattering. I couldn't stop wanting to kill Maurice and Minnie, because they were killing me, slowly. Of course they didn't know it, any better than they knew they were killing themselves. They'd adopted me for their own sad reasons; they'd never told me why; they'd never given me anything solid, just told me all the time I should be grateful for them and their kindness. But I hated their kindness! It was living death! I had nothing to call my own but nightmares and ghosts that were more real than anything or anyone I knew in the so-called real world. Of course there were the fields and hills and trees, but I didn't know their language, not then—so I stood there shivering until it was dark, until I could no longer see Hitler's eyes. I stood there until I could no longer feel or hear anything but the ghosts of the wind and the rain and the past, all round me, laughing and taunting. The pressure in me got to the point where I knew I had to explode. And I did. I think I fell down on the floor. I remember wild sounds coming out of my mouth. Something inside me was making them and I didn't know how to stop it. I was scared out of my mind. I didn't know what was going on. I didn't know what I was. It seemed like hundreds of voices were all bellowing inside me at once, and I was falling, falling down through myself, with no control at all, falling down through an endless lunatic darkness . . ."

Then, he tells us, he found himself trapped in a strange waking dream. He found himself trapped, as if physically and in full consciousness, in the dark wet tunnel of the nightmare which had afflicted him since his earliest years. He found himself drowning, with invisible animals chewing at him, eating him up, body and soul. He thought he was dying, that he was lost forever, and he gave himself up. Whereupon, he says, something, some inner tremor of intuition, made him turn round—slowly, stiffly, in acute pain—so that he saw a violet light.

The light appeared to be coming from an old, old woman who watched him.

She was hideously ugly! He was terrified and revolted! Her hair was white and scraggy. Her face was like a wrinkled nut. She was bent, and small, and scowling furiously. But the moment he saw her, he says, all the beasts eating him shrank back into the darkness—and he too shrank back.

"Why are you scared?" he says she cackled. "Don't you know that this is my home? Is this how you behave in somebody's home?"

"Who are you?" He describes his voice as having been a squeak.

"I am your mother. Don't you recognize me? Aren't you going to greet me? You have no manners! I call off my beasts and you reward me by shrinking away? Am I so horrible? Do you want to drown? Do you want to be eaten alive?"

He didn't know what to say. He didn't know what to do.

"How . . . how can you be my mother?" he stammered, still shrinking back. "My mother's dead, and you're much too old . . . I mean . . ."

He says he could feel the beasts creeping back, hopefully.

"How would you know how old I am? Aren't you going to

kiss me? Don't you think a son should greet his mother properly? Do you want to die forever?''

For a moment it seemed easier to die than to do as she asked. "No," he told her fearfully, "I don't want to die . . . but . . ."

"But what? But what?"

The beasts were growling and snapping, closer and closer. He felt their hot breath and hurriedly changed his mind. Shivering, he approached her, though appalled by her ugliness, by her rank smell. But he made himself do it. With a great effort he brought himself to kiss her on her warty raddled cheek.

The moment he did so, everything changed. Something inside him was made free. A bright light pierced the violet dimness. The old woman . . .

She was transformed!

She turned into the Angel! His Angel that he'd seen before, but only in the most distant dreams. She turned into the Angel, and the beasts all vanished, and the dreadful tunnel too, and without warning he found himself surrounded by her, protected by her, and her ugliness had become a towering column of every color, and of colors beyond color, shimmering and dancing, shot through by stars of purest warmest light, haloed by the incandescence of all creation, and she looked on him with a vast and dispassionate love. "You see?" sounded her voice inside him, above and below and all round him. "You shouldn't be taken in by appearances. You were scared of me because I didn't seem beautiful and kind, and if you hadn't overcome your fear you would have been drowned and chewed to pieces. But now my beasts will help you, and my waters will fill you."

Then, he says, he knew it was all right. It was like floating in an endless soothing sea, and through it he continued to hear her voice, telling him not to worry, telling him that soon he'd be going away for good, into another sort of life altogether, a life in which he wouldn't be locked up inside dark old mansions of the past—a life in which the lessons would be hard, but in which all would ultimately go well . . . unless he let himself forget that she was always inside him, because she was a part of him, and would appear in many forms, even if he couldn't always see or know her in these forms. "Forget me," she warned, "and you'll dry up and die inside; you'll never find your true homeland." He did not really understand. He said he could never possibly forget.

He asked if he could leave the château now. "You can try," she told him. "Go, and start to find out what you are. But you will have to come back here . . . for a while . . ."

"Then," says Kitaj, "the voice faded, and the glorious light too, and a while later I came round to find myself on the attic floor. It was dark, but I felt so powerful, so changed! I had to leave that house immediately . . . and I did!"

I remember very well the dark winter night in Connemara when Kitaj dictated this account. The wind was wailing in off the ocean as if it held all the banshees in the land. Kitaj was exceptionally animated. His eyes glowed like hot coals, he was perched tensely on the edge of his chair, leaning at me like a bird of prey, and his passionate words tumbled out so fast that later I found it hard to transcribe the tape. In fact it was hard to listen. It was like being subjected to physical assault. I became distraught. I had to stop him with questions. What did he mean by the "Angel"? Had Minnie read him tales where the hero's kiss transforms the crone-goddess into the beautiful lady? Such transformation tales, relating to themes of self-discovery, are common in world mythology, and I wondered if he might not have unconsciously incorporated such a tale into his vision. Then again, a commonly reported UFO curiosity which I also mentioned to him—it is to children most often that miraculous silvery "spacewomen," goddesses, the Blessed Virgin Mary, etc., make their appearances. Grown-ups on the other hands tend to report visions or sightings of adult males—little green men or giant blue men are the most common. I asked Kitaj what he thought of all this.

He was irritated by my desire to rationalize.

"How would I know? Believe what you want. Maybe she's my anima, or maybe an idealized image of the mother I never knew. Is it too hard for you to consider that there may be intelligent entities existing beyond range of our normal sensory faculties? Maybe she's from Sirius! She's real! That's what matters! I forgot what she said, I ignored her later, I became less than I can be—but now I begin to remember! That's what matters! Believe what you want!"

I made nothing of his Sirius hint—at the time. I knew nothing of those mysteries. I saw only that he was upset by himself, by his years of spiritual failure which (in his eyes) was measured by the extent of his worldly success. His recollection of what had

happened in the attic disturbed him greatly. Lenore blamed me for
stimulating such disturbances in him: it caused dislike between
us. But I have never doubted that these were necessary disrup-
tions, and that Kitaj·himself welcomed them as a means of
breaking down the internal dams which had frustrated and blocked
him for so long—or he would never have let me intrude on him
as he did. Nor do I doubt his experience in the attic. It happened,
and it was crucial. It triggered a new perspective in him, and it
triggered a series of bizarre, bewildering events. The bare bones
of these events, which culminated in the fatal journey to Kenya at
the end of 1952, have been proven historically, but Kitaj's
version of them has caused many people to feel very dizzy. There
is no sure ground to stand upon, particularly when we get to the
business about Tarzan, and at this point it is a great temptation
simply to quote entire segments of the autobiography, thus avoiding any critical analysis at all. But I must restrain myself, and
instead try to outline the sequence as matter-of-factly as possible—
especially as I want to complete this memoir by the end of the
millenium!

Thus as rapidly as possible we will move through the strange
circumstances which apparently preceded the African expedition,
but to lead up to these we must first consider the flight made by
the young boy from Château Têtaurier immediately after his
vision of the Angel. This episode gives rise to the important myth
of the "newspaper ticket," which once again confronts us with
the problem: *What is true, what is false—and why?*

When the thin and sallow boy at last picked himself up from
the floor and left the dark attic room he was still trembling, but
no longer with fear. He was possessed now by a sense of power
and immediate purpose. Quickly he went down the creaky narrow stairs to long dim corridors which he traversed until he came
to his own room on the second floor and west side of the
building. He took care not to be discovered, lingering behind
corners until voices calling him to his birthday supper died away
in some other direction. In his room he put on a sweater and a
coat and a pair of rubber boots, cramming the pockets of the coat
with objects which were special to him—a penknife, a glittering
lump of quartzite, a picture book of Greek myths, a rabbit's foot.
Also he took two apples. He was hungry, and it was wild
outside, but he couldn't wait, and he had no intention of linger-

ing. Down the wide main flight of stairs he crept, into the front hall, and he was almost at the doors when his foster father unexpectedly appeared behind him from the dining room.

"Ralph! We've been looking everywhere for you! Where do you think you're going? Don't you want your supper? This is really too bad!"

The boy's heart hammered. But the power was in him, and the determination, and he turned to face his foster father so abruptly, with such blazing eyes, that Maurice flinched, automatically looking down, and in that moment the boy knew he could do what he wanted, because for some reason *Maurice was scared of his eyes*.

"I'm going out," he announced coldly. "I don't feel like eating. I'll come back in when I want to come back in!"

"Don't be ridiculous!" snapped Maurice, who had not moved any closer, and who still could not meet the boy's eyes. "We're having this supper specially for you. You'll hurt your mother. Take your coat off at once!"

"I'm not ridiculous!" the boy replied in the same cold voice. "Minnie isn't my mother and you aren't my father, and I'm going out!"

And as he turned and opened the doors and ran out into the night, one of the servants, passing through the hall, overheard the last part of the confrontation, and later confirmed Kitaj's account, adding that for some seconds after the boy had gone Maurice stood as though completely, fearfully stunned.

It was cold and wet outside, but the boy did not feel the weather as he ran triumphantly, free, through the darkness, along the curve of the driveway to the road from Cognac. He started east towards the little town of Jarnac, three kilometers away, and he says that before he'd walked fifty meters a car came along, which he stopped by standing out in the road. At first the driver, a man, was angry, but the boy pacified him with his big scared eyes and pleading expression, and managed to persuade the man to take him "home to Angoulême, because I missed the bus, and my mother'll be so worried." So he got a ride all the way through Jarnac to Angoulême, further than he'd ever been on his own before—except that he wasn't on his own. He knew his Angel was with him, and he knew he could go anywhere he wanted; he felt strong and sure and very confident. In Angoulême he asked his way to the railway station where, sure enough, there was a train about to leave for Paris. Paris! He had no money in his pocket but nevertheless he got on the train, feeling in this wild rush of events that nothing could possibly go wrong. And for a while his euphoria persisted. He had a compartment all to himself, and he ate one of his apples with the sense that the whole world lay before him.

Then, he says, he heard the conductor coming down the corridor to inspect and punch tickets, and suddenly, everything felt different.

"I had to do something," he says. "I had to produce a ticket that I didn't have. The conductor was only one compartment away, and there was a horrible empty feeling in the pit of my stomach. What was I going to do? Getting my way with Maurice had been one thing, but this was apparently impossible. For a moment I was in a panic. Then I remembered the Angel and what I'd been told I could do. Something made me pick up a newspaper on the seat beside me and tear off a piece about the size and shape of a railway ticket. I stuffed it into my pocket and held my breath. When the man came in I was about ready to burst. He looked at me oddly and asked for my ticket. I was scared, but I made myself stare into his eyes as hard as I could. I handed him the scrap of worthless paper, holding his gaze, willing him with all the pressure inside me to accept it as a real ticket, command-ing him not to look down, commanding him to keep looking at me. My eyes must have been like searchlights! And it worked! For a second or two he turned the bit of paper about in his hands in an odd, faltering way, as if sensing something was wrong— but then, without once looking at it or away from me, he punched it and gave it back to me, and told me irritably to stop staring at him with such big scared eyes. 'You've got a ticket,' he growled. 'Why are you shrinking away like that?' And I couldn't say a word, I was so relieved. And that's how I got to visit Paris for the very first time!"

Certain questions must be asked about this episode. That Kitaj ran away from Château Têtaurier on his "tenth birthday" is established, as is the fact that he reached Paris by train and wandered round the capital for some hours, increasingly tired and hungry, before being picked by the police as a young vagrant and sent back home. And I (and many other people) can personally vouch for the fact that he possessed a mesmeric faculty which may well have begun to manifest itself as early as his tenth year. So what *did* happen when the conductor came round for his ticket? Is the tale another lie? Did he have a real ticket, or did the conductor perhaps take pity on him and pretend to be fooled? Or did it really happen? Possibly. My doubt about this tale arises from the fact that, long before I met Kitaj, I'd read an identical account of a young boy hypnotizing a railway conductor into accepting a ticket torn from a newspaper . . . only the boy was not Kitaj. This earlier account was told of and by the renowned psychic Wolf Messing, who had also escaped from Poland during the Nazi oppression, but as a man of forty and not as an infant, and east into Russia, not west into France. Had Kitaj heard this tale about Wolf Messing and decided to adapt it into his own myth? When I heard him dictate this story (which he did with the greatest liveliness and pleasure) I just had to challenge him about it. Whereupon he laughed, not offended at all, and he said something I've never forgotten:

"It's not a matter of what *I* believe, or of what actually happened," he said, "because I'm not telling this story for my sake. Don't you see? It's a matter of what *you* can believe, and how you let it affect you, and what use you can make of the information. Don't blame me if your idea of reality isn't the same as mine. Your belief or disbelief is your affair."

Which leads us neatly into the crucial tale of the African connection, which most people have considered to be a complete fantasy.

This tale, once again originating with Kitaj, has received only the most peripheral confirmation from other sources, or from anyone who knew Maurice and Minnie Têtaurier. But then, nobody knew them at all well during their later years. They allowed nobody close to them, except perhaps latterly their foster child, and it seems quite certain that they never spoke to anyone else about their emotional and spiritualistic secrets. People who had any dealings with them at all, including the employees of Château Tetaurier, have described them as discreet, silent, withdrawn, and devoted to living as though life were one long sorrow. They kept their sorrows to themselves, and once again there is simply no evidence any way, except whatever is suggested by the events as and when they occurred, and so, bearing in mind the dictum of William Blake that "Every thing possible to be believ'd is an image of truth," we must remain open-minded as to Kitaj's account of how and why all three of them went to Kenya at the end of 1952, with Mau Mau at its height, looking for a long-lost English cousin of Minnie's called Lord Greystoke.

So what happened? What can we reconstruct?

When the boy was located and returned by the police from Paris there is no doubt that he returned into a highly charged atmosphere. In the translation of an interview published originally in *Paris-Match* in June 1983, Mme. Marthe Hébert, of the nearby town of Saintes, who at the time had worked as an assistant cook in the kitchens of Château Têtaurier and who was married to Marcel Hébert, another of the household staff, gives us valuable information. She tells us how ''that boy stirred up a hornet's nest when he ran away. All of us thought him a strange lad, and I can't say that any of us liked him very much—he was always so grave and . . . creepy, somehow, with those big eyes that could make you forget what you were supposed to be doing—but none of us blamed him. If I'd been him I'd have run away. M. Têtaurier and his wife weren't unkind, or anything, but they didn't really belong to the world, and there was quite a strangeness about the pair of them too, and when Marcel told me later on about that ouija board I can't say I was surprised—it was that sort of atmosphere in the place, all the time, the sort that kept making you look back over your shoulder with the feeling someone was behind you, but there never was. Not so you could see, anyway, though dogs and cats couldn't stand the place. It was no place for a child, with nothing but shadows to play with. He wasn't encouraged to talk to our sort, and he didn't want to anyway. Always unhappy. So we weren't surprised when he ran away. The surprise was how M. and Mme. Têtaurier reacted. You'd have thought the end of the world had come. It was the first time I ever saw M. Têtaurier shout and get into a temper. He was so upset until the boy was recovered. Marcel saw what happened when the boy ran away out of the door, and said M. Têtaurier looked terrified, as if the boy had hexed him, or something. And Mme. Têtaurier too. She was always a bit slow and grey, not really there at all, but when the boy ran away she turned so white and haggard you really felt sorry for her. I'd never seen them show him any affection, like ordinary folk, but I suppose in their own way they were attached to him. Maybe they didn't know it themselves until then.

"And you should have seen the fuss they made of him when he came back. As if they were determined to make up for all the years of ignoring him. But it was an odd sort of fuss. As if they wanted him to do something for them, but were scared he might refuse, or that he might break into pieces. Marcel said that after that, all the time until they went to Africa, they used to let him stay up late, and often had him with them, shut up in that big room where none of us were allowed, where they tried to get in touch with the spirits, or whatever they did. None of us knew what was going on, but it didn't feel good. Mme. Têtaurier became feverish and tired, with big black rings round her eyes, and her husband got more and more nervous and excited. And the boy . . . he was so changed when he came back. He looked bigger, somehow, and much more confident of himself, and his eyes . . . oh, I never liked his eyes, but after he came back there was something about his eyes that gave me the shivers. I tell you, I didn't want to stay there; in fact Marcel and I gave in our notice about a month before they went to Africa, and I was never more glad to get out of a place. And I still think now that somehow they knew what was going to happen to them before they went. That child . . . he had the devil in him, and I hear he still has. It's not surprising, if you think of the start he got in life. Evil leads to worse, if you ask me."

That is the testimony of Mme. Hébert. It is very suggestive. But what went on behind those closed doors, in the room with the ouija board?

Kitaj tells us in *Liar's Gold* that Maurice persuaded him to act as a medium in attempts to contact the spirit, incarnate or otherwise, of an Englishman who'd once been more than just a friend to both Minnie and Maurice. This man had been an RAF pilot who had crashed in the central African jungle during the war, never to be heard of again. His disappearance was the cause of their melancholy. It seems that Maurice had been so impressed (as well as scared) by the boy's strong-eyed resistance at the door that he'd realized the boy might have useful psychic faculties. "He said I had eyes just like the eyes of the friend they'd lost,'" Kitaj told me drily. "At first Minnie was reluctant to involve me, but Maurice persuaded her that I was their only hope. They had to ask my help because their own experiments hadn't worked. It meant that sooner or later they had to tell me everything. That was hard for them. Before they told me about Greystoke, they wanted proof that I was worth it. I gave them their proof. I summoned up more than they'd bargained for.''

Astonishing. It seems to bear out the possibility that it was indeed a psychic link (at least in Maurice's mind) which had led him to adopt this boy. ''What did they get you to do?'' I asked him.

Not all that he told me went into *Liar's Gold*. Some of what follows derives from tapes I made which have never been published. This is another of the subjects about which Kitaj, for reasons of his own, was publicly and privately evasive. But one night (the same night that he spoke of the Angel) he was more than usually forthcoming with me, on the basis that I should not tell anyone of it, and that he should vet whatever went into the book. But all that is long ago, and hardly seems to matter now, and I feel I can speak of it.

He told me how one night soon after his return they took him into the big room into which he'd never been allowed before. It was high ceilinged and cold, this room, despite the roaring fire and closed windows and heavy full-length wine red curtains. They gave him a glass of cognac to drink, then Maurice blindfolded him with trembling fingers and sat him down at a round smooth-topped walnut table which (he saw before being blindfolded) had letters and numbers, in ivory intaglio, inscribed round the perimeter. Maurice steered the fingers of his right hand onto the chill top of a glass which rested in the middle of the table, upside-down. The fingers of their own right hands joined his. Maurice's fingers were cold and still trembling, and Minnie was breathing heavily. Tensely Maurice told him to relax and empty his mind and let his fingers rest lightly, and not to worry. He told me he wasn't worried, but that obviously Maurice was, and Minnie too. He told me he felt a sense of power, a thrill, running through him, and that, as they sat there silently, he began to feel tight with the same feeling he'd had in the attic before the vision of the Angel had begun—ready to burst with emotions he could not identify.

For some minutes they sat in a silence interrupted only by the crackling of the fire, by Minnie's heavy breathing. It was weighty, this silence, and the boy felt the pressure growing inside him. He knew something was going to happen. He was curious, intrigued, which was why he'd agreed to do it—not for his foster parents, but for himself. He felt sure that his future was in the wings, stirring in the pregnant atmosphere of the room. He felt nothing for Minnie or Maurice. He liked them no better now than before, and he was not flattered by their need of him. He waited, tighter and tighter.

After a while Maurice, in a curiously flat voice, began intoning words in some unknown language. Soon the boy felt the air behind his back stirring and growing yet more chill, and the glass trembling beneath his fingertips. Maurice continued with the invocation. A freezing draught began to blow. A log crashed out of the fire against the fender, and Minnie gasped. The boy felt the atmosphere gathering, stirring purposefully, and then, with an increase of the inner thrill, he sensed something like a cold intelligent fire, entering him, rushing through him, along his arm, into his fingertips.

The glass rattled and clattered on the table.

"Spirits of the Fire and Air," Maurice suddenly cried out loud, "are you here? Are you here? Will you speak with us?"

The cold fire in the boy increased. The glass began to slide crazily, all over the table, from one point to another, to another. Then it stopped.

"Spirits of the Fire and Air," Maurice cried out again, "we wish to find out if our friend is still alive. Will you help us?"

Now the whole room was freezing and heavy, and the glass started snaking so fast from one letter to another that they could scarcely keep their fingers on it. Like an electric wire the boy sat there in his blindfold, distantly hearing Maurice asking excited questions, with Minnie interrupting from time to time, and the cold fire inside him was consuming him, and enveloped him completely, so that he was hardly aware any more of who he was, and he started to get scared. But then he remembered the Angel and knew he would be all right. And with the corner of his mind that was not possessed he listened to Maurice and Minnie:

"Kenya!" gasped Maurice. "He's in Kenya!"

"He's alive!" muttered Minnie, barely audible.

"He's in danger!" Maurice whispered, the glass still sliding.

"He needs us!" said Minnie, her ecstasy unrestrained.

"We must go!" Maurice insisted. "As soon as we can!"

"Of course!" Minnie agreed anxiously. "But where in Kenya? Spirits of the Fire and Air, tell us where in Kenya we should begin our search!"

Then, Kitaj told me, the cold fiery entity must have taken him over completely. For a short while he became something else altogether. A voice that wasn't his voice burst out of him, an enormous voice, which he heard with such of his self-consciousness as he had left. He felt scared but not threatened; something told him that this entity, whatever it was, would do him no harm; would in fact aid him towards the destiny promised by the Angel, with which it was connected . . . and also he sensed that Maurice and Minnie were dupes for listening to it, for believing what it said, for they were only a means to its end:

"I AM IN THE ABERDARE MOUNTAINS!" it roared through him. "YOU MUST COME TO NAIROBI AND TRAVEL TO THE ABERDARES ROUND THE NORTH SIDE OF THE SACRED MOUNTAIN, MOUNT KENYA, ASKING PROTECTION OF THE GOD NGAI IF YOU ARE TO REACH ME IN SAFETY. YOU MUST BRING THIS BOY THROUGH WHOM I WILL SPEAK TO YOU AGAIN, AND YOU MUST BRING ALL THE MONEY YOU HAVE, TO BUY MY FREEDOM! YOU WILL FIND ME UNDER THE BLACK HILL WITH THE FIRGROVE ON THE SUMMIT. YOU MUST COME SOON! I AM WEAK WITH ILLNESS! DEATH IS APPROACHING! YOU MUST HURRY!"

But the Voice didn't seem at all weak to Ralph Armand Michel. Whatever it was that spoke through the boy had great power, and in addition possessed a dark humor which was evident to him even as it used him—the humor of an astral trickster. Yet apparently this aspect was not evident to Maurice and Minnie, who were simultaneously aghast and ecstatic. They believed. The Voice had told them exactly what they wanted to hear; and they were not critical.

Yet at the same time they got worried for their foster child. For, Kitaj told me, the moment the Voiced ceased, the entity had left him, and he collapsed unconscious. He did not revive for nearly twenty-four hours. Whatever had spoken through him had used up all his energy.

When he told me in Ireland about this experience, he was obviously very ambivalent about it, speaking of it dismissively. It referred to a part of his nature which for many years he rejected. When at the end of our stay in Ireland he began again to manifest such powers I learned, at first hand, just why for so long he had blocked off these activities of what sometimes he called the "oversoul," or the "Sirians." But all this we will examine in due course.

Upon the boy's recovery Minnie told him without reserve that she knew the owner of the Voice which had bellowed through him. "She said it was the voice of a distant cousin she had—John Clayton, Lord Greystoke," he told me sardonically . . . and then he related to me the strange tale which Minnie had given him.

Apparently this Greystoke had been an English nobleman with estates in the Lake District . . . though he had spent most of his life in Africa. In 1930 Minnie had met this man, had become his "good friend." That winter they had gone to St. Moritz for the winter sport and fashionable society, and it was there, in fact in Greystoke's bed, that she and Maurice had met for the first time. Minnie had not made this erotic connection plain to him, said Kitaj, but he had worked it out for himself later. Maurice, in his own rather mournful way, had seemed an attractive man-of-the-world, not yet entirely introverted, and moreover extremely wealthy, having just inherited the Têtaurier estates and business. She and Maurice had no sooner sealed their relationship than their lover Greystoke, who had probably instigated the whole thing deliberately so as to let this intense young woman down easily, had abruptly gone off back to Africa. It was obvious from Minnie's account that Greystoke was an unusual man with great sensual and physical appetites, and not easily to be tied down by any person or social condition. It was three years before he returned from Africa for another brief inspection of modern society, by which time Maurice and Minnie, feeling mutually let down in the vacuum of his energetic departure, had cut their losses and got married. But too late they had discovered the incompatibility of their blood groups: after two dangerous miscarriages Minnie had realized she could not make children with Maurice. They could have separated, but in every other way the two of them fitted each other excellently. They were similarly mystical and rather mournful in disposition, hardly sociable, with a love of old books and occult ways, and she knew she was not likely to make a better match. Most important of all, they were both in love with Greystoke. His memory bound them together, and in time came to give them their chief reason for living and for staying together . . . or so it seemed. In 1933, during his brief visit, Greystoke had temporarily united with the pair of

them again, further stimulating their sense of their own lack of
vitality with his loving which to both of them seemed almost
supernatural in potency and imagination. They implored him to
stay, but of course this was impossible. The jungle and its
freedom had lured him away again, and they had seen him only
once after that—at the outbreak of the war, when he had returned
to England to join the RAF. Because of his special knowledge of
the African interior he had been drafted out to Kenya. And there,
or further inland, they had heard, he had been shot down in
1942, reported missing and probably dead. And ever since then
they had been trying to get in touch with him, by means both
practical and spiritualistic, with no success at all . . . until early
in October of 1952, when Maurice had made use of his belated
realization that their strange foster child might provide the psychic link which they had been seeking all these years.

"And that's it," Kitaj told me. "That's why we went to
Kenya, so they could find Greystoke, believing it was Greystoke
who spoke to them through me. Maybe it was. I don't have
evidence one way or the other. You can believe what you like.
But whatever did speak through me, it was to me that it spoke,
not them, though they had to go so that I could go . . . and it
was to find Greystoke that I went, though I didn't really know it
then. I had to make that connection. Those stories that Minnie
read to me about him . . . she'd never told me that they were
true, that she and Maurice had known him. But he knew about
me, or something using his identity knew about me, and it was
my destiny to go and live like he had . . . though I didn't know
why, and I still don't . . . for when at last I found him, after all
those years, he denied and rejected me, he threw me into jail,
he'd forgotten himself and got corrupt like just about everyone
else. But I guess if I hadn't been thrown in jail I'd never have
had the chance to become what I am now. For what it's worth.
I'm still confused by it all. I still have a long way to go, a lot
of seeking to do, before I find out what it means." He shook his
head. "Life sure isn't simple."

He told me this in 1986, just six years before the Transformation. He was right. He still had a long way to go. He was
confused? He had me pretty confused too, and thousands of other
people, where this tale of Greystoke was concerned. Most people
have assumed that the entire Greystoke business was a deadpan
game of his, a metaphoric technique of fantasy he used deliber-

ately to wipe out distinctions between fact and fiction. And maybe it was. But if so, it was a game he never stopped playing.

He did believe in it. So I believe. Maybe that makes me the sucker. But my understanding is that he and Maurice and Minnie went to Kenya, right in the middle of the Mau Mau rebellion, and the man they thought they were looking for was better known to the world as . . . Tarzan?

It is as Kitaj himself tells us. At that age he had become entranced by the romances of Edgar Rice Burroughs, particularly those of Tarzan, which Minnie read to him frequently. Later he would barely admit to it, but her involvement with him had grown stronger and more affectionate over the years, and lengthy reading sessions had become and remained the closest point of contact between the boy and his foster mother. Minnie had introduced him to Tarzan . . . and Lord Greystoke, you may recall, was the title of English nobility conferred by Burroughs upon his famous fictional character.

It may well be that Minnie did have an English cousin who had been lost in the African jungle during the war. It may well be that the lonely boy, the dreamer who refused to learn to read or write, who had visions of angels and who had already learned how to manipulate the reality of others, who found no need to distinguish between fact and fantasy, preferred to call this cousin "Lord Greystoke," ignoring whatever real name Minnie told him, creating a hero in whom he could believe. But whatever the truth, Kitaj insisted all his life on the tale as given above, and did so with consistent seriousness.

Researchers who have checked the records—*Burke's Peerage* and other sources—can find no connection at all between Minnie Têtaurier (nee Caldwell) and any member of the English nobility, alive or dead. She was an only child, born 27 January 1909, to John and Mary Caldwell, of Bradford, in Yorkshire. John Caldwell was killed in Flanders in 1916; Mary Caldwell died of tuberculosis twelve years later. Minnie was at a school in Liversedge (between Bradford and Wakefield), which she left without distinction in 1924. Thereafter there is a singular lack of information about her life. No record exists in hotel registers for St. Moritz in December 1930 of anyone named Minnie Caldwell, far less "Lord Greystoke," though Maurice Têtaurier was booked into a place called the Hirondelle for two weeks of that month, so it is possible that Minnie and her unknown lover were booked into some establishment or other under assumed names. The marriage of Minnie to Maurice is, however, a matter of record: it took place in Cognac on 16 July 1931. Mme. Hébert (see above) mentioned local opinion that Maurice had married below his station, though nobody knew how or when or where the couple first met. In this connection it has been suggested that the fantasy of Greystoke originated with Minnie in compensation for her sense of social inferiority, that Maurice humored it, and that their foster child merely accepted what he was given to believe. More plausible to my mind is the suggestion that Maurice and Minnie developed the fantasy between them; that originally it may have had some realistic root; but that it got completely out of hand during their years of introversion, isolation, and spiritualistic obsession. Needless to say, there is nowhere any factual record of a "Lord Greystoke," though personally I believe that they did indeed meet in St. Moritz through a mutual lover who later died in the jungle.

Yet from our point of view it hardly matters. However the belief originated, Kitaj made it his own. In later years he elaborated this tale of Lord Greystoke to such a degree, confusing it so inextricably with his own life in and out of the jungle, that separation of myth from presumed reality becomes impossible and unproductive. Ultimately we are left with a myth more potent (in the effect it has had on events in the world) than anything which might or might not actually have occurred. Kitaj continued to believe in the factual existence of Tarzan (alias Greystoke) long after his own proto-Tarzan years were past and gone . . . long after he had attached Greystoke's imagined reality to a prominent white African politician, with embarrassing and dangerous (but far-reaching) consequences. Furthermore, in the years of his global wealth and power, with his own developing myth already subject to considerable fictionalization, he extended this strange obsession of his to the imaginative works of the American science fiction writer, Philip José Farmer. During the sixties Farmer wrote a series of ribald pseudobiographical adventures based on the premise that, in Tarzan, Burroughs had been describing a real person, only he hadn't been at liberty to reveal the truth behind his tales. In 1984, just before the Disappearance, Kitaj visited a World Science Fiction Convention held in St. Louis, Missouri, flying over from Rome upon hearing that Farmer would be at the convention as guest of honor. Farmer is said to have related afterwards, with wry amusement, how Kitaj was apparently unable to comprehend that Farmer's own interpretation of the Tarzan mythos was no more than a very detailed fictional joke. It also appeared to him that Kitaj was not willing to accept what both Burroughs and Farmer (in his definitive 1972 biography of Lord Greystoke, *Tarzan Alive*) made very clear—that "John Clayton" and "Lord Greystoke" were pseudonyms invented by Burroughs to conceal and protect the true identity of the remarkable man behind the stories. This man, apparently born on the cusp of Sagittarius and Scorpio (a potent sexual-physical combination) in the year 1888, would (if he existed at all) have been nearly eighty in 1965. And 1965 was the year in which Kitaj attached Greystoke's mythic persona to a politician who was very much younger than eighty—a politician who, moreover, had a perfectly clear past history of his own. But none of this mattered to Kitaj, and it should not matter to us. His beliefs were not bound by anyone's stories or by any historical logic at all. For him, the intertwining of mythic themes and facts elaborated by Edgar Rice Burroughs, Maurice and Minnie Têtaurier, himself, and later by Philip José Farmer, constituted a psychic reality of great importance to him. Any attempt in this context to discriminate between "fact" and "fiction" is simply irrelevant . . . and the problem (as Farmer appears to have understood) lies ultimately not with Kitaj, but with those among us who require fixed definitions of relativity, relationship, and reality.

"I went right along with him," Farmer is quoted as having said. "Maybe he's right. Who knows? What makes *you* think it's fiction? Do you need newspaper headlines to tell you what to believe?"

Exactly. We must step into the myth. Into Africa.

3. AFRICA

The heat. The smell. The tension of his dream. Years later Kitaj recalled these first impressions of the Christmas Day in 1952 when the three of them at last reached Nairobi. The parched heat of the dry season. The smell of the growing, overcrowded, angry city. The taut phantasmagoric tension inside him which matched the tension of the city. At the time of their arrival, thirty years of Kenyan racial stress had finally broken out into the open rebellion and violence, and Mau Mau activity had spread rapidly since the time of the ouija board session early in October. Excited talk of rampaging tribesmen and murdered whites had infiltrated every cocktail party in Europe, Kenyan atrocity vied in the news with Korean atrocity, and a state of emergency had been declared by the new governor, Sir Evelyn Baring.

All this was known to Maurice and Minnie Têtaurier before they left France. They were not wholly blind to the outside world. Before flying out they had anxiously discussed whether it might not be more sensible to postpone the expedition until a more favourable time. It was clear that a considerable amount of money, diplomatic subterfuge, and good luck would be needed to bring them safely into and out of the Aberdare Mountains, the wild woods of which were being used by increasing numbers of Mau Mau rebels as a refuge and base of operations. It was obvious that their lives would be in danger if they went. They knew of the situation. But how real and immediate was it to them? Real enough, Kitaj told me in Ireland. They had, after all, been through the Hitler war, in which many people they knew had died. Yes, the danger was real to them . . . yet they decided they must risk their lives on the slender evidence of the boy's mediumship, for only through the discovery and salvation of Greystoke could they hope to regain any sense of meaning and value in their lives. Demented? Insane? Perhaps, but courageously so. History is orchestrated by people who live and die for beliefs which other people consider mere self-deceit. Who is going to judge? What are we without faith? In their own minds Maurice and Minnie had no option but to go to Kenya immediately, taking the boy with them, believing as they did that the sick and imprisoned Greystoke had called them.

In *Liar's Gold,* Kitaj says that they were obsessed. So they were, and so was he. Since that night in October he had thought of nothing but Africa, and he didn't worry about the danger, knowing that his Angel would protect him, no matter what might happen to his foster parents. So, when at last they landed in Nairobi, the two weeks it took for Maurice to fool the authorities and mount the expedition seemed an eternity to the boy. But, like a snake, during that period he began the shedding of his European skin.

It seems that Maurice told the authorities he wanted to look over several tea estates with a view to buying one or more, having been advised that Kenyan tea was likely to be a profitable investment once the present troubles were over. The region in which he showed interest was the Rift; that great valley, extensively settled by Europeans, which lay northwest of Nairobi and west of the Aberdares. With the aid of his official introductions, some judicious bribery, and a lot of string pulling, he got the necessary travel permits, though these were subject to military endorsement and revocation at any point, and officialdom advised strongly against the journey.

At this point some background is in order.

May Mau was the recent development of a long-lived tension. For years the most numerous and powerful Kenyan people, the Kikuyu, had been growing increasingly resentful of European greed, incomprehension, and exploitation. *Gutiri mubea ma muthungu* ran the popular Kikuyu proverb—"There's no difference between a missionary and a settler." By 1948, the year in which the first Mau Mau oaths were taken, over thirty thousand white settlers employed more than one hundred thousand Kikuyu on the farms and plantations, hiring forty-five men for every woman, segregating the sexes, calling them "Kuks" or "boys," paying them a pittance, forcing the white Christ on them, detribalizing them and destroying their traditional patterns, forcing them into the towns and cities where thousands slept on the streets or in crowded hovels, where alcoholism, prostitution, starvation, crime, disease, and loss of self-respect were the consequences of the European way. For years the coming violence had been predicted by Kikuyu leaders, including Jomo Kenyatta (born Kamau wa Ngenga), who in 1946 had returned from abroad as the president of the Kenya African Union, to seek and fail to gain a satisfactory reorganization of the Legislative Council. The British would not compromise; inevitably, violence exploded to try to blow the blockage out. Early in October Chief Warukiu of the Kikuyu was jumped and murdered; the "Black Europeans" were the first to be attacked. Kikuyu militants began slipping out of the cities into the bush. On 21 October the British arrested Kenyatta and every other African leader they could lay hands on, thus ensuring a total communications breakdown and committing themselves to a policy of extermination by nullifying those who might have mediated the conflict. At the same time they failed to capture the real leader of Mau Mau, Dedan Kimathi, and further alienated those from whom the movement drew its strength—the uneducated and displaced Kikuyu who were inflamed by urban poverty, white intransigence, union agitation, growing nationalist consciousness, and by the large-scale theft of the land which, in their belief, could belong only to their ancestors, to the spirits of their dead, and which could never rightfully be sold to anyone. Witchcraft and pure fear also played a large role in persuading Kikuyu into the movement. In the months and years to come, thousands of Kikuyu who refused to join Mau Mau (the word perhaps derived from "Uma, Uma," meaning "Out, Out") were butchered, strangled, or buried alive. Thousands more were terrorized into taking the oath to kill, cut, and burn. The oath-takings were accompanied by rituals of the most degrading variety, so as through shame to root out all and any tendency on the part of those who'd thus sworn to return to western ways. The secret "oathing chapels" were decorated with intestines and gouged goats' eyes: the rituals involved such activities as intercourse with dead goats and the eating of human brains. The aim was to drive out the Europeans. It was before the days when African nationalist movements would seek the aid of the Russians, Chinese, or Cubans; it was informed by a traditional rather than superficially Marxist response to oppression. And to all this the reaction of the British was prompt and repressive. During Kitaj's early months in Kenya the concentration camps (in fact a British invention, during the Boer War) were being established; Kikuyu schools were being closed; any African found with a gun was killed on the spot; and soon the Lancashire Fusiliers, the Royal Devonshire Regiment, and the King's Own African Rifles (whose ranks included a certain Corporal Idi Amin) were busy shooting and capturing large numbers of Kikuyu who objected to "progress." Most historical accounts of the conflict available in the west (the British could never admit to it as a "war") are understandably one-sided, but the statistics speak for themselves: between the outbreak of the rebellion and its final flickering in 1956, over eleven thousand rebels were killed and a vastly greater number imprisoned, and a further two thousand Africans were killed by the Mau Mau themselves. Also, in keeping with the intent of the rebellion, a certain number of white Europeans were killed. How many?

About one hundred.

More than a hundred Africans died for every white.

Enough of this.

It was into such an atmosphere that Maurice and Minnie and the young Kitaj ventured in order to seek out the long-lost Greystoke.

Two landrovers had been ordered from Europe. There was further delay waiting for them to be delivered and driven up from Mombasa. When at last they arrived, both turned out to be painted brilliant red. This was unfortunate. Not only was the color unduly conspicuous; in due course it also proved attractive to an ardent male elephant.

By the time of their arrival Maurice had located two men who were willing to guide them, who said they could keep quiet about the expedition's true destination. Maurice had to pay them a great deal of money in advance, with a promise of more to come once the mission was accomplished. When Minnie met these men, says Kitaj, she was dubious and scared, and even Maurice had his doubts, though both of them insisted they knew the Aberdares well and that they weren't frightened of Mau Mau. Neither of them were Kikuyu. The first was a slender, tall, clean-cut, pock-skinned man called Thia, of the Turkana people—cattle herders of the northwest wastes. He wore a colored mud-pack in his hair and a two-inch wide wristknife; he looked barbaric and grim. He said he hated the city and was glad of the chance to get back to his own region. He turned out to be wholly unreliable, as did the other man Maurice hired so expensively: a grizzly old man in tattered western clothes who, it soon became apparent, was permanently under the influence of bhang—marijuana. He said he came from Somalia. His name, or nickname, was Hiti, meaning hyena, for this was what his face most closely resembled. With his roguish smile he assured Maurice that of course he could drive a landrover. Neither of them spoke French: it was necessary to get along in English, which allowed plenty of room for misunderstanding.

Kitaj says it did not look good. Minnie, who with the boy had been shut up much of the time in the safety of their hotel, grew depressed. She demanded a further session in their hotel room with the boy as medium to assure her that they weren't after all just setting out on a wild-goose chase. So far as she was concerned there was now a gathering air of unpleasant reality about the whole affair, and her belief became strained: in particular she found it hard to understand why the Voice which had spoken through the boy had demanded that they travel round the north side of Mount Kenya to get to the Aberdares, a huge detour in the wrong direction: "SO YOU MAY GAIN THE PROTECTION OF NGAI, THE GOD OF THE MOUNTAIN, WITHOUT WHOSE AID YOU WILL NOT FIND ME!" the huge voice again roared through the boy, again exhausting him, but convincing Minnie, so that, to Maurice's great relief, she consented to a start. For Maurice stayed determined in his belief that they would be successful, though his certainty held a desperation which he hid from himself, even if not from the boy.

They set out, all five of them, on the fourteenth of January.

"It went smoothly to start with," Kitaj records in *Liar's Gold*.

For a while after leaving Nairobi they drove through rich rolling country, but soon the landscape opened out into a vast, flat, brown, motionless plain. Dust billowed behind them, blending with the colorless sky. They passed herds of cattle guarded by skinny youths who eyed them expressionlessly. At Fort Hall their papers were checked by British soldiers who advised them to stay away from the west. They crossed the trickle of the Tana river and went through the town of Embu, where nothing moved. Soon after they were skirting the wooded southeastern flanks of Mount Kenya, and the boy, eyeing the pinnacled summits of Batian and Nelion, bursting tremendously up from the huge swollen base to a height of more than 17,000 feet, felt a strange urgent energy begin to grip him.

"The Turkanaman Thia sensed what was in me," he tells us, "and it scared him. He feared the spirits of the mountain. Later I saw him telling Hiti about me. They knew I had *bwanga*, or power. That first night we stopped on bare high land northeast of the mountain, where the forests ended and the grass began. We sat round a fire between the landrovers. A lion was roaring somewhere not far away. I stared at the stars, feeling strange, knowing I'd come to one of my homes. I lived one of my earlier lives in that part of the world—I knew it by instinct. I felt electric, and Thia and Hiti watched me, though they pretended not to. Maurice and Minnie didn't notice. They could feel something wrong, but it was vague to them, especially to Maurice. But Thia and Hiti sensed what was coming. They were sensible. They deserted us."

This didn't happen until the second night, by which time they

were well west of the Sacred Mountain, presumably now protected by Ngai. They had passed the dusty town of Nanyuki and
turned surreptitiously southwest to the gorges and fir-forested
heights of the Aberdares. This second day was more eventful, the
elephant incident occurring in the afternoon. By then, says Kitaj,
they had left any semblance of a road and were driving over the
high brown dry veldt, a near-desert stretching hundreds of miles
north into Ethiopia and west to the scarp of Uganda. From a
distance the surface of this plain—punctuated only here and there
by clumps of thornbush, by the flat umbrella tops of lonely
acacia trees, and occasionally by the movement of ostrich or herd
of zebra which kicked up clouds of the abundant red dust behind
them—gave the impression of flatness, but in fact it was often
broken by small gullies and dry riverbeds. While with difficulty
maneuvering the second landrover through one of these gullies,
Hiti got stuck . . . and it was the elephant that got him unstuck.
Hiti, who had Minnie for his passenger, had proved a competent
driver, but on this occasion he got the landrover firmly grounded.
The noise of his efforts to get clear attracted the elephant.
Frantically racing the engine, he tried but could not move the
vehicle with the interested animal moving closer and closer.

"Maurice and I were up on the further bank," Kitaj tells us.
"Maurice didn't dare shoot. The elephant tried to mount the
landrover . . . and pushed it right out of the rut. Hiti accelerated
away so sharply that the elephant fled. Hiti and Minnie were
really shaken up. Hiti wouldn't go on until a double-size dose of
bhang put the smile back on his face. Minnie refused to stay as
his passenger, so Thia took her place."

There was no more obvious trouble that day. They saw hardly
anyone as they approached the jagged Aberdares. There was only
the grey and brown, the rock and red dust. Mau Mau seemed to
belong to another world, as remote as Europe. But in the front
landrover there was acute tension. Kitaj mentions how Maurice
and Minnie frequently eyed him doubtfully, nervously, as if he
alone held the keys of life or death. That second night, when they
stopped on the veldt in the lee of a gnarled old baobab, Minnie
was very fretful. "Where do we start looking?" she kept asking
before they turned into the landrovers for an uncomfortable night.
"We need to know more. Where is he? It was all very well while
we were in France, but now we need specific information."
And, says Kitaj, she looked hard at him, "but I didn't want to

have that voice bellowing through me again, so I didn't meet her eyes. Yet I knew my destiny was very close. Thia told Maurice he knew a friendly village where there was an old man, a *murogi,* who would help us if we paid well. So Minnie had to be satisfied with that.''

Then they turned in, the three Europeans in one landrover, the two Africans in the other. ''It was a long time before I slept,'' claims his account in the autobiography (which we must examine shortly, in the light of the different version he told me much later), ''but when I did, I went into the dream-country, to a ravine under a black hill where horrible things happened. In the dream I was the only one who lived. I followed a scent, I met Njeru—he called me—and I drank the blood of the bull. My old life was dead. When I woke up I remembered it all.''

Also when he woke up he found Thia and Hiti gone with the other landrover.

Camp had been made at the head of a long gradual slope: the two men must have rolled the vehicle silently away, not starting the engine until they were at a safe distance.

They were not seen again.

Minnie wanted to turn back. Maurice, hiding his uncertainty, looked to the boy. ''I told them some of my dream,'' he says in *Liar's Gold.* ''I told them we would find 'our friend' near the black hill I had seen in my dream. I did not call him Greystoke. That would have been a lie. The name of the 'friend' was Death. It was what they were both unconsciously seeking. It was what they found. And I got to where I was going. It had to be.''

The fatalistic and self-seeking callousness of this account shocked me at the time. So too did the change of character he underwent when he began speaking of his African experiences. It requires examination.

When Kitaj spoke of his European childhood I always found him understandable, according to my own psychology, even if I didn't always believe him or take what he said at face value. But whenever he spoke of his African adolescence he turned into another being altogether—older, wilder, darker, less constrained by moralistic convention and supposition, as though abandoning the neocortex for the instinctual cortex, for the left, the sun the right, side of things for the moon. I believe the Voice that roared out of him during the ouija board sessions was in large part the product of this older witch-brain that exists in us all. The vision of the Angel, the episode of the newspaper ticket, and the process that led him to Kenya, to Njeru—all these indicate to me the activity in him of lunar, "magical" intelligence. And if frequently he seems like a chameleon, with different personalities for different circumstances, then perhaps it has to do with a natural capacity he had to shift at will the sphere of his mental operations, of his world-perception, from one brain to another, from left lobe to right, from gut to heart to crown, allowing him to deal with different people and societies at their own character-istic level, whether "primitive" or "progressive." Much confu-sion arises from the fact that for a very long time he was unconscious of this rare talent . . . a talent which seems now to be growing very common. To increasing numbers of us it is clear that the human race is undergoing a great and rapid Change of self-evolution. Kitaj was a harbinger and exemplar of this Change. For him it was a lonely, tormenting process. For many years he appeared as a veritable conglomeration of different entities uneas-ily united in the same physical frame: his self-integration did not occur until near the end, after a series of inner deaths-and-rebirths, and I recall what H. Rider Haggard wrote in one of his African novels about She-Who-Must-Be-Obeyed (based upon tales of the Lovedu rain-queens)—"Different personalities actuate us at dif-ferent times. . . . In one hour our desire is to kill and spare not; in another we are filled with the holiest compassion even towards an insect or a snake, and ready to forgive like a god."

I digress. We're concerned with the beginning of Kitaj's life in Africa; with his shift into an environment so much more primal, spacious, and intuitively connective than anything which crowd-ed, civilized Europe had to offer, and my distraction arises from memory of the *fierceness* of soul which he manifested in speak-ing of Africa. The alienated European orphan became a tropical dancer, feeler, lover, killer. Leopard-consciousness grew in him, and consciousness of nature. He took the Cuts and underwent rites which informed him more readily about who and what he was than an intellectual education would have done. He learned many of his strengths, though not all of his weaknesses, and he earned his new name, his soul-name, M'Botu. He earned it, then hid its meaning in a secret place, and would never tell me its significance. All he would say was, distantly, *"It's in the Tree."* By this I took him to mean that whoever discovered the secret of his name would have him at his mercy. Once in Ireland I put this interpretation to him, and he smiled like steel. "John, you're a good pagan Celt at heart," he said to me. "Isn't that what your living ancestors believe? Of souls hid in trees? Do you want to know what tree holds my soul?"

"Yes," I said, "I do."

"I'll tell you this," he said. "It was a tree that saved my life when the KAR caught us on Kinangop. A hollow sausage-tree, the cleft in its trunk just wide enough to take me in. Very narrow and hard to see in the dark. They missed it, even when they came down to kill our wounded. That's one place I left my soul. White officers and crazy blacks killing their brothers for Britain. Amin was there that night. I recognized him eight years later when he went wild against the Turkana. I was lucky again. A tree saved me again."

The meaning of his name was one subject which he avoided.

Another was the night when Maurice and Minnie died. Only near the end of our stay in Ireland would he talk of it at all, and then, in *Liar's Gold*, he gave a false picture, speaking as if he had deliberately led them to death, as if he were the conscious Hand of God, punishing them for their illusions. He spoke as if he felt no regret at all, and would not admit to any sense of guilt. "They deserved it," he said. "They weren't in touch with their feelings. They died. That's all." But the flatness in his voice gave him away. He wasn't as heartless as he liked to make out. Certainly he did not easily love or relent, there was a deep streak of bitterness in him, and he was capable of deliberate cruelty. But he was never heartless. He was not psychotic, as some have made out. Much of the problem of his public image arises from the urge he had to dramatize and disguise his self-disgust as pride. Invariably he made himself out to be much worse than he was, shackling himself by creating the image of one always aware of his destiny. Such an image implies foreknowledge and thus responsibility for the permitted murder of his foster parents . . . a heavy load for any child of ten. I believe he had intuitions of trouble. I do not believe that he foresaw it all with the certainty he suggests in his autobiography.

Before going to Venice for the last time in 1992 he admitted as much. By then he was relaxed, glowing with health and power.

"It all did happen," he said, "but Njeru was the one who knew about it."

"You mean you didn't know it all in advance, but Njeru did?" I asked. "So what about the dream of the black hill, of the death of Maurice and Minnie?"

"Listen," he said—but he was smiling that Smile of Njeru— "I'll tell you another version of what I knew. If you like it better, you can believe it."

It was then at last he told me about a boy who was not all-conscious Super Boy . . . just a boy, with doubts and fears, like anyone else.

Yet the tale was still amazing. Here it is.

After the desertion of Thia and Hiti the three Europeans continued alone into the Aberdares. Late in the afternoon they neared the high forested hills along a road of crumbling black cotton-soil. Minnie and the boy were nervous and unsure, particularly Minnie. The boy was still trying to remember darker details of his horrible dream the night before. "We'll find the black hill, and something beneath it," he'd blurted to Maurice that morning, "but I don't know what; I can't remember it properly." Now Maurice, his desperation still suppressed, insisted on continuing until, with the sun sinking, they found themselves driving up into a narrow wooded pass. It was then that the boy saw the dark conical hill above one side of the pass; then that he remembered all of his dream. The ambush! The rock! "No!" he cried out. "No! We mustn't go through here!" But Maurice, his face set like stone, incomprehensibly responded by accelerating up into the steep darkness of the pass, though both Minnie and the boy were shouting at him to stop and turn back.

Then it was too late.

It was hard afterwards for the boy to remember what happened.

The plunging rock, right on target, crushing the front part of the roof of the bright red landrover, followed by the shots, the spears, the blood, his violent retching, the shapes moving down the side of the crags—and then his panic flight from the back of the crumpled vehicle. Running, running, running! Ducking and dodging, gasping and running. Up over the rocks to the trees, not daring to look back, fleeing from death into the forest where death lived. There was blood on him as he scrambled up into the dense dark jungle that scratched and tore at him. He had forgotten the Angel, the Voice, his destiny: in terror he climbed through the ferns and wild banana as the light faded. Then, right at his heels, a gruesome screech. He jumped almost out of his skin. It was only a rock hyrax, but he didn't know that. Again he was violently sick, spewing up his fear and hopelessness as the darkness thickened. He was completely lost with the jungle on the move all about him; he started to cry and couldn't control himself. He stood, shivering, unable now to see more than a few feet, and suddenly there was a grunting cough. What was it? And again! Leopard? Or a signal between his pursuers? They were all round him; he knew it! Panic helplessness crept over him, froze him, rooting him. His resistance ebbed. He fled to his inner world. He fell down, down, down into the dark wet tunnel, to the deadly creatures which gnawed. No escape! The beasts were closing in on him. Silently he screamed to his hero for help—but Greystoke wasn't there.

"Use your *nose*, you fool!" The angry inner voice startled him. "Follow that scent you came here to find! If you stay here you'll die. Use your nose, find the scent, follow it, quickly!"

Then he remembered the Old Woman, who was also his Angel!

Sobbing, he recovered some of his wits. He wasn't entirely alone after all! For a moment longer he stood in the perilous darkness with head uplifted, seeking a scent that now he remembered from that terrible dream—a pungent odor, thick and fearful, but filled with life and power and a strange hope.

Cautiously, uncertainly, he started climbing again.

It was difficult and scary. He kept blundering into trees, into boulders. He feared snakes, leopards, most of all the men who had killed his foster parents. But he kept sniffing ahead, fighting off his exhaustion and misery, until quite unexpectedly he found himself above the worse of the jungle. Up through a belt of bamboo he climbed, to emerge out onto a wild high heath from which an ocean of grotesque head-high heather sprouted, surrounding him as far as he could see . . . for a fat yellow moon had just risen, away to his left. And the first thing he realized was that the moon had risen over the black conical hill which he had seen in his dream.

On top of this hill, against the moon, stood a grove of fir trees.

He saw torches flickering from this grove. His heart beat very hard. He stood staring and, as he did, he smelled—or imagined that he smelled—the thick and potent scent that drifted down to him from the grove on the hilltop.

Unexpectedly then he was flooded by certainty which brought a peacefulness. He was going to the grove, it was where he was meant to go, under the moon, and nothing was going to harm him . . . at least until he got to the grove. He felt light and dry and energized, as if by getting this fear he had already passed half of the test which some unknown force had put upon him. He stood, taking deep breaths. The moon showed natural paths through the heather, over thick humus and the acid-inky soil. He started towards the black hill, towards the grove of straight tall fir trees, towards the scent. Straight towards the moon he walked through the heather maze, the thick cloying scent growing stronger, sending shudders down his spine as he neared the base of the hill, which was not far away. What was this scent? Was he imagining it? Was it something that his nostrils were really picking up? It seemed very familiar; it lured him on; he knew what it was; it was a part of him; it scared him; it fascinated him; he licked his dry lips as he started up the hill in the silence of the still moonlit night, towards the flickering torches held high above . . . and the silence was so profound and peaceful that he could not really believe in the death of his old life left below him in the dark ravine.

Then, from the grove, the bellow of a terrified ox, and a great shout from many throats, followed by a single voice, ululating, silvery, dying slowly away on the enriched scent-breeze that shivered through the boy.

He stopped. The moon was so bright and personal. He looked round and saw a clump of heather shivering, maybe fifteen meters behind him. And something that might have been the glint of moonlight on metal, quickly removed. For a moment the nauseating fear returned. But his head swam with the rich, primitive scent. The scent of the blood of a sacrificed ox. He had to go on. But what would happen to him when he reached the grove? Still he paused, and now heard a low murmurous chanting from the voices in the grove, drawing him on, moving his legs with a sort of reluctant eagerness, so that he climbed and soon came to the outlying trees of the large grove. It was like a natural cathedral; the trunks of the trees were high and clean, and they bisected the moon as he crept from one to the next, towards the chanting of the voices, towards the circling of the torches . . . and it never occurred to him then to realize what a degree of risk

was involved in making sound and lighting fire in this country at
war, nor did he wonder why it might have been done.

Like a moth he approached the light.

He came to where he could easily see.

He saw the owners of the voices and the torches, and the man
in the middle who had cried out so wailfully, and the ox which
had been slain.

There were nearly thirty men and women and children in the
circle round the tree beneath which the sacrifice had been made
(the boy later knew) to God, Murungu, the All High, the Posses-
sor of Whiteness. These people, Kikuyu all, variously and rag-
gedly dressed or hardly dressed at all despite the chill now on the
night, were chanting very softly and intently, bent forward from
the waists, with regular gaps in their circle through which the
fascinated boy could see the strange old man who, in a bowl held
up in both hands, was busy catching the blood that still spouted
from the severed jugular of the ox, the white ox that lay, its legs
still feebly kicking.

The boy crept closer, the smell of the blood overwhelming.

The priest, the shaman, the *murogi,* the little old man with the
face round as the moon, he was attired most variously, in a
leopardskin coat and trousers, a colobus-monkey-skin hat, a vest
of tarpaulin, buffalo-hide gaiters, and a Boy Scout belt. His name
was Njeru, and he had a smile which was terrible and wonderful,
a smile which inspired his people and froze his enemies, and
knew that the boy was there. To the brim of the bowl he caught
the blood as the ox stopped jerking at last. He raised the bowl up
to the sky and then—with the circle scooping up handfuls of soil
and opening their lungs in readiness—he spilled a libation of the
blood, a little amount, onto the torch-flickering dryness of the
soil—and the soil was likewise dropped at that moment from
every hand, and there was a great shout:

"Thaai, Thaaiya, Thaai, *Haaaah!*"

Then all the torches were thrust into the ground and abruptly
extinguished, and there was moonlight, and silence, and waiting.

The boy knew they were waiting for him.

Trembling, he stood out with his nose to the scent which had
brought him here. He started to walk towards the circle, knowing
that two men now walked as openly as he, just behind him, and
for the first time he saw in the moonlight the gleam of the spears
and the guns which were stacked away to one side of the circle.

In that moment he remembered the rock which had crushed the landrover, which had killed his foster parents, his past. He stopped dead, an awful gulf yawning wide and black beneath his stomach, struck with a fear that had him half-turning as if to flee. But it was too late. He saw the tall shapes of the men who stood behind him, he felt the eyes reaching out to him, he smelled the blood of the slaughtered ox. The Scent! Scent of the Moon, Scent of the Bull, scent of his hidden selves about to be uncovered! The smell flooded through him, vitalizing him. He felt as crisp and dry and vulnerable as an autumn leaf about to fall. He felt as if sparks of electricity were flying out from him in all directions. He was almost at the circle, in the silence, in the moonlight. He had to go through. There was a subtle movement of the circle; none of the dim shapes seemed to move, but all of a sudden there was a clearly indicated direction for him to take . . . to the priest-man waiting with the bowl of blood.

His knees went wobbly for a moment—then he went through.

He walked through the moondance, into the circle, past the people. Their faces were carved sternness. Their foreheads were agleam with smeared fat. They stood motionless, watching. There was no sound. His brain didn't work. He was in a dream, in *the* dream, caught in curious déja-vu, with the sense of physically acting out what had already happened on some other level of things. And with a dreamer's inevitability he came and he stood before the priest-man, who was scarcely any bigger than he was. He stood there in the silence.

Njeru regarded the thin frightened white boy with discerning curiosity. For a moment there was annoyance in his look. That soon faded: the *murogi*'s round face dimpled into benevolence.

"*Tigai kuura,*" said Njeru softly. "Don't run."

Then, as he held out the bowl of blood to the boy, Njeru smiled.

The Smile of Njeru was famous, so famous that it had led the British authorities to put a high priority on his capture or death. It filled men with new life and confidence—or it pierced them like a spear. It was like the sun, it could burn or heal accordingly. It was dangerous, hinting at the abyss of high energies that shifted behind the apparent shape of things. It was soothing, suggesting that anything and everything could be overcome.

Now in the moonlight Njeru smiled at the boy, and the boy felt flooded by the radiance of that smile, so much so that he relaxed completely and took the bowl of blood without a tremble, and raised it up to his lips.

But then he paused. Blood? Drinking blood?

He felt disgusted. He felt eager. He could not decide.

"Idiot!" croaked his ancient inner voice. "Did you not see people drinking the blood of Christ in France, many times? This is the same! It is Communion! Drink, and go through the consequences—or the old man will kill you!"

He drank. He drank the bowlful of blood, at first slowly and hesitantly, then with increasing enthusiasm until, with Njeru still smiling upon him, he drained the last half of it down with one single tilt of the bowl to his lips.

The blood was hot with a power that dazed and intoxicated him. It made him feral and strong. His mind and body roared with the power of it, everything wavered, he nearly passed out . . . but the Smile of Njeru held him.

The boy breathed deeply—then shook like an animal, and screamed.

All about there was a muttering, a sighing, a relaxation. The boy screamed again with the violence and flux of life within him, but this time his scream was blended in the great shout that went up:

"Thaai, Thaaiya, Thaai, *Haaaah!*"

This was only the beginning of his rite of change. The murder of his foster parents and now this drinking of the blood had opened up a gate in him—and Njeru knew how to push him through this gate into the strange new personal and universal realms of self that lay beyond. The boy-animal stood, shivering and giddy, not knowing what was happening as the ox was cut up and the meat distributed to be eaten raw, all but the best portion, which was left for God. Njeru made sure that the boy was gorged, forcing steaming gobbets down him until the boy, the changeling, began to feel wild and hot and slippery, misshapen in knowledge of himself and his body, caught naked into a ferocious vibration of chanting and eating and dripping blood, turned into something dark and alien. He was plunged down through layer upon layer of increasing pressure, driven from the light of his mind, until at length he found himself again stranded in the black wet tunnel, preyed upon by the beasts—the sharp-toothed fishes, the hissing snakes, the devouring birds, the leopards, and the angry bull—which closed in upon him to gnaw upon him, to

eat him up and consume him as he had consumed the ox. The
pain began, and this time the old woman, his Angel, would not
appear to save him from himself. Through the agony of this
uncontrollable psychic dismemberment he could dimly sense the
presence of the old woman—but she would not help, she would
not dismiss the beasts, in fact she herself was the teeth and
purpose of the beasts—and when the pain became intolerable the
Voice suddenly burst from him, and he heard it as if from a very
great distance.

"ONE MUST DIE SO THAT A GREATER WILL BE
BORN!" it bellowed, over and over again, deafening him as he
dissolved and passed away.

So he died. Ralph Armand Michel Têtaurier died.

He ate and he was eaten by the beasts within him.

He ate and he was eaten, amid the blood and the raw steaming
meat, amid the blood and the death, according to the rhythms of
the moon and his fate, on this night of his passage from one life
to another.

It was very much later in the night that the nameless boy
feebly stirred, began to return to consciousness, to find himself at
last alone with his reluctant new teacher, Njeru, the shaman, the
murogi.

Through dense, painful veils he swam slowly back to his
senses to find the grove deserted and empty but for the two of
them, the old man and the boy, all the celebrants gone, melted
away, and only the moonlight slanting down.

He looked awkwardly, fearfully, at Njeru.

Njeru, who had been waiting a long time, scratched his bald
head as if he didn't quite know what to do with this white child
which Murungu had entrusted to him. The boy was a nuisance,
but it couldn't be helped, because obviously the boy had a
destiny, and God had spoken, quite clearly. Unsmiling, Njeru
shrugged, jerked a peremptory forefinger at the boy, and stepped
away.

The boy stood, weakly, and started to follow his teacher.

From the base of a tree Njeru picked up his spear, his divining
sandals, his pot, and the tasseled leather satchel which carried his
professional accessories, including several tubs of greasepaint.

These items, one by one, he handed to the boy.

"You will carry these," he said. "You will follow me."

Then he smiled, so that the boy understood and, doubtfully,

smiled back, at which Njeru, who was in a bad mood with this new burden on his energies, cuffed the boy—not hard, but warningly.

Njeru turned and left the grove without a backward glance.

Nameless, unknown to himself, the boy followed his teacher into the vast equatorial night, into the future of his myth.

So for the third time in ten years of life he came through gates that wrench the soul. The ghetto, the château, the jungle. Faced with such a history some people shake their heads. Voices, dreams, and messages from Murungu? Surely this is nothing but imaginative projection, movie reality. Why else would Tarzan be in the wings? Some people, hearing or reading Kitaj's tales, have been reminded of medieval stories of saints (usually composed hundreds of years after the supposed events) in which the budding sage or mystic is invariably guided at crucial times by the personal interest of the one and only Number One.

Yet first and foremost, history's about faith, will, energy, imagination, love, and hate. Without these, there are no "facts" to be misinterpreted. The external plane of history, its outer garment of dates and social/political event and change, derives from the inner pressure of the myths that we seek to enact— collective personal histories of our roles on the road. Whatever is taken as real and materialized started out as an imagining, a dreaming. There are psychic facts underlying the events they give rise to. The events can be anything at all, so long as they fit the psychic patterns being projected. We are not wholly conscious of what we project. Traditionally people have laid the blame for reality on externalized gods and devils that terrorize humanity. Individuals demonstrating god-powers have been dealt with in a variety of ways. Direct revelation is always a threat to any worldly interest that looks only to the world. Priests and kings rose to keep a community vision of the world playing. The priests were conspired for, not only by themselves, but also by all those who wished not to have look too far—who wanted Guardians of the Veils, not Revealers of the Mysteries. The Piscean Age has been hiding and divided.

These days, magic and science begin to make a marriage.

They always did. It just got forgotten for a while.

The myth of Kitaj is one road among many which we can scan. It is dynamic and alive among us, its details yeast and change; we make it how we see it, we see what we will in it, and laugh if we want, and learn if we can.

I don't know much, but I've got some hopes.

Kitaj could get distressed by hopelessness, by lack of imagination, not least because he knew these things in himself. People were always strange to him, as he was strange to himself. He appeared unable to understand why people disbelieved his talk of destiny, angelic guidance, and shaman teachers in the wilds of Africa. In fact I think he understood very well. There was a day just three months before he left us, during the latter stages of his world-tour medicine show, when he talked without ambiguity.

We were sitting on a bench amid the ruins of Roman Carthage, overlooking the brown blue of the filthy Mediterranean. He had perfected his art of not being seen. Bus-load crowds were all about, many people had seen the miracle show he'd put on in Tunis the night before, but not once all afternoon was he recognized, not even by the smart young Brazilian couple who sat down next to us for a minute, talking heatedly about Kitaj's performance.

"Of course it was all tricks!" declared the slim dark man angrily.

"You just don't want to see!" the woman scolded him just as angrily.

They left, still arguing, without once having looked at Kitaj. Meanwhile he'd been talking steadily, softly, about self-constriction and disbelief and the fashions of history. He talked of Blake and Swedenborg, dismissed as crazy for admitting conversation with their angels; and how Newton (seeking choirs of angels) and Kepler (seeking the Song of the Spheres) had discovered primary laws of science . . . which alone were remembered and worshipped. Then more recently, the parapsychologist Puharich, much respected . . . until he wrote a book about the alleged angelic or extraterrestrial contacts of the Israeli psychic, Uri Geller . . .

"But Puharich was quite right," said Kitaj. "So were the people who said he'd lost his senses, his scientific reason. So he had. Why stay in the jail of structure all the time, even if the structure is useful? You have to get outside, scout around, bring something back—doesn't matter if they call you crazy, doesn't matter what they do. You do what you must, and try to stand up."

Soon after this he began to talk about the night when Maurice
and Minnie died . . . which led into mention of something else
altogether.

"I thought I was responsible. The guilt got bad. It bred bad
acts. I persuaded myself that I had killed them, that I was a
killer. It was okay while I was with Njeru, but after Ruwenzori,
when I landed in the Congo, it all went ape. I turned against
everything I'd once found good. I would have nothing to do with
women, for every one of them carried the shadow of Iloshabiet's
face and reminded me of the curse on me; I knew I was damned;
I became a soldier so that I attacked and killed and was paid for
it, and gloried in it, thinking it was all I was good for, and the
circle grew more and more vicious . . . M'Botu the killer, who
despised everything and everyone . . . and the truth is I loved it,
darkly, I loved that guilt and hate, I came to love the treachery of
the world—my own treachery—so much that I shut away the
Angel, refused to hear the Voice, and locked away the magic
completely. I burrowed deep into the shitpile closed my fist and
mind on this world, and began to desire the wealth, the fame, the
power. What a mess. Now I sense that it all began that evening
when Maurice and Minnie died. All the time I was with Njeru I
never rid myself of that feeling of guilt. I felt responsible for
killing them . . . and after Ruwenzori I turned the belief into
reality. What a mess. What a tangle.

"But that night in Kenya I had only followed the destiny
trail—the Voice, the scent of Greystoke. The only control I had
was to follow it, or not to follow it. I was not in control of what
Maurice and Minnie did. They chose to believe what I had said,
what the Voice had said, but that was their responsibility. They
wanted to believe it; they denied what they really sensed.

"Now I'm back on the scent. I started to wake up again in
Ireland—you pushed me towards it, Johnny. You did that, and I
struggled against it, but the dam was well and truly broken that
night I talked about Ruwenzori. Now, I guess, I've taken responsibility, I've found my function . . . though I don't think you're
too sure about that, are you? You still halfway suspect I'm just
playing paranormal games and messing about with people."

It was true. The events so far of that last year had left me bewil-
dered. Ever since the Last Retreat, and the healing at Luzon in
March, and the start of the Medicine Show, I had felt more than
anything else like a gaping hanger-on, unable to accept entirely

the apparently miraculous realization of those faculties in him on behalf of which in Ireland I had argued so stridently—in which I had believed so long as they remained abstract.

I asked him again about Sirius, and again he shook his head.

"There's no point," he said. "The terms you employ in asking come from your mundane experience. They're sufficient for metaphor, but not for the actuality, because the actuality cannot be grasped in terms of experience in this world alone. If I say anything about it I'll only confuse and misdirect you, and probably do the same to myself as well. You have to leave it open, Johnny."

I grumbled. But he was adamant, saying no more, making me realize that I still wanted certainty and facts . . . even if it were certainty about uncertainty, and facts about fiction.

The next twelve years of his story provide us with no such difficulties of interpretation. Following his initiation in the grove of Murungu, we pass altogether into mythreality. Between 1953 and the end of 1965 the occasions when Kitaj's doings tie in with "known historical fact" can be counted on the fingers of one hand. We plunge into a maze, the Minotaur breathing down our necks, and no certain thread to guide us . . . for the myth of his life is a stage on which we all find ourselves acting. It is the perennial myth of the Nameless One seeking identity, meaning, and destiny. Thus most of the tales about him which flourish today are wholly independent of anything he ever claimed to have done. Many words and deeds originating with others have been attributed to him: most of the adventures are clearly mythic transpositions, in which Kitaj, as archetype, has had laid upon him the identities and activities of classical heroes such as Theseus, Cuchulain, Arthur, Roland, and (of course) Tarzan. In particular some of the tales of his early manhood amid the Mountains of the Moon are evidently mythic fantasies, of the sort one might expect to find in Tolkien or in the images of the Tarot. The reader may recall how during the late 1980s there appeared a flood of books and films purporting to describe Kitaj's youth. His reaction to these was consistently one of amusement tempered with a certain sadness. He knew that people have need of mythical heroes to explain and exemplify them to themselves, but it depressed him to think that he was the model upon which so many people based their fantasies. That is, it depressed him until he realized that the popular heroic view of him was more positive in its sense of his (and everyone else's) potential than anything which he had previously acknowledged as possible. Towards the end he found a great new freedom. For he learned, and we have learned, that he was what he decided to be, what we decide him to be . . . which is whatever we want to make of ourselves.

Some may find my approach to this twelve-year period disappointingly prosaic. I mean to stick to whatever Kitaj actually told me, and as far as possible to ignore the many tales invented or transposed by his mythographers, except where such tales tie in with ambiguities in his own account or teach us of something useful. I don't intend to spin out this period of his life any further than necessary. There is a lot of ground to cover, and I may not have much time.

It is always easy to make things difficult and complex.

It is not always so easy to discover simplicity.

4. THROUGH THE MOUNTAINS OF THE MOON

Njeru came for the youth M'Botu in the cool grey forest dawn of a dry season day that was going to be hot. It was a month since the youth had won his name during the Ordeal of the Cuts, and almost exactly four years since he had become the pupil of Njeru. It had been a tempestuous time. Many Kikuyu had died, many more rotted in jail, but Njeru and his pupil had remained free. Now, with the freshly healed scars of the seven slashes on the upper part of his left forearm, M'Botu had grown strong and fiercely self-controlled, yet with an angry pride and sense of difference in him which made him one of the most perplexing pupils that Njeru had ever known. M'Botu had power, but he was obstinate and hard to teach, and on that dawn when Njeru called the youth up the mountain with him, the old man probably felt relieved that his responsibilities were almost over. There was only one thing left to do.

"Come," he said in a peremptory voice. "There are things I

must show you. We will climb until it is nearly dark, and we will not stop.''

Without a word the youth rose from his sleep, took up his new spear and a water canteen, and followed the old man from the tiny wooden hut they had built in the depths of the forest on the eastern slopes of Kinangop. For the last month they had been here, fasting and dreaming, undisturbed by anyone else, and, though Njeru had said nothing, M'Botu had known that their relationship was almost at an end. He was on the verge of manhood now, and several times of late he had dreamed of a great journey ahead of him, on his own, without Njeru. The *murogi* had put aside many other matters to deal with the white boy entrusted to him by God, though in recent years matters had not gone well for his people. The rebellion was at an end; it seemed that the whites had conquered completely; there were more British settlers than ever in Kenya, and more Kikuyu than ever working on the plantations. Dedan Kimathi was dead, the spirit of resistance at an end, and those who had taken the Mau Mau oath abused by their own people. It had grown hard to stay free, even in the mountains, even in the secret depths of the leopard woods, even in the heather-forested heights where the giant lobelias grew. Njeru and his pupil had been on the run for a long time, and there had been many narrow escapes, and many of Njeru's people felt bitter, finding it hard to laugh now that so many of them were dead and the rest condemned as bloodthirsty savages. The strange white youth now called M'Botu had often been threatened by their bitterness and hatred: he had learned their language and undergone their rites, but he had never become one of them, and if not for the protection of Njeru he would have been dead by now. Yet, like it or not, and many did not, the white boy was the pupil of the great *murogi* Njeru—Njeru, who was like a mountain ever ascending into the clouds, who could read the future and the minds of men in his dreams, who smiled even when he questioned enemies by placing red-hot coals on their stomachs, who danced and who brought the rain, who sniffed out witches and destroyed them, who spoke with the ancestors, who had inspired opposition to the white men. M'Botu was the pupil of a respected man: for four years he had carried the spear, the pot, the divining sandals, and the leather satchel of his teacher; he had hardly once left the side of Njeru, and in return Njeru had taught him, Njeru had taunted and tortured him, Njeru had driven him very hard.

Once, after a year and a half, the rigors of education had become unbearable and the boy had run away, following a war-band of Meru who had fallen into ambush set by the King's African Rifles. He had only just escaped with his life, hiding in the hollow trunk of a sausage-tree . . . and after that he had gone back to Njeru, who had beaten him so soundly that he had limped for a long time, and who had refused to speak to him or smile on him for three whole months. It had been a stern and dangerous training . . . but his power and his strength and his character had been greatly increased, and many Kikuyu had come to respect the directness of his gaze almost as much as they respected the smile of Njeru. Frequently he had starved almost to the point of death, as much through the circumstances of war as through the methods of his teacher. More than once he had been fired upon by the guns of white authority, but he had never been hit. He knew that his destiny—his Angel with whom in dream he often spoke—would not allow that. Of course there had been the occasion on which a leopard had nearly killed him: what saved him then was not his spear but his wits—he had been running beneath the tree when his hackles rose, warning him, so that he had spun away and hurled himself aside of the trail just as the big cat leaped—then, instead of running, he had stood and charged the beast, screaming furiously at it, so that it had slunk away into the jungle, leaving him unharmed. When he had told Njeru about this the old man had smiled and said, "You think that you did it? What is that think you are wearing round your neck?"

"The claw of the leopard that you told me to wear."

"Why, so it is! Why do you think I told you to wear it?"

"Are you saying that the leopard ran from me because of it?" The boy, who had thought himself brave, was angry. "Did I not act well?"

"Yes, yes, indeed, what else could you have done? But what told you the beast was about to leap on you? What told you it was there?"

"I . . . I *felt* it there! My mind sniffed it!"

"Would you have sniffed it if not for the claw which is round your neck, night and day, scratching the soul-smell of the leopard into your thick head?"

"How can I answer that, and how can you prove it?"

Njeru had answered the boy's sulking with a broad smile.

"You still think like a white, with your head and not with your heart, and resist what your head cannot understand. I will count my work well done if when at last you leave me you know that your head is only a little pimple on the top of you. God laid the burden of your training on me, but you are obstinate and proud and difficult. Why teach you these ways of my world which is being destroyed by people with no heart? Will it bring the world much good? I cannot see it. Your head is very selfish: you do not truly live in the world."

"I *do!*" the boy had burst out. "The world is round, and I belong to all of it, and my Angel will take me where I go, and tell me what to do!"

"Maybe so . . . if you remain content to listen to your Angel."

"It was my Angel that told me of the leopard, not your claw!"

"Oh?" Njeru, smiling brilliantly, had stroked his chin. "Did you not once tell me that your Angel can take whatever form she wants?"

"Yes! So she can!"

"Then can she not dwell in the form of a leopard claw? Can she not dwell in my teachings that I give to you with no thanks from you?"

Once again the boy had found himself brought up short.

"I suppose so," he'd muttered, "and I do thank you."

"So you say. Now go and fetch that herb I sent you to get. Don't let any leopards jump you this time. I don't want to see my work wasted, and neither does God."

So it went for four years as the boy became a youth, strong and sullen and self-possessed, able to move silently and for many hours on end, able to live on very little, on nuts and roots and raw meat, able to live with hardship and without friends, gaining knowledge of the natural world, learning to listen to his dreams, walking in ways which were being destroyed by the powerful people of the world who had lost their heart. He learned about the spirits indwelling every natural form, every river and mountain and tree, every beast and bird and fish, every human being. He learned about fire and ghosts and visions, about pain and hate and fury. He did not learn about forgiveness or redemption. He would not learn about humility or self-sacrifice. Whatever he went through, including the rites of passage designed to bring a boy to manhood, he went through with some reserve, with pride, without full commitment. None of this, he knew, was lost on Njeru.

"I was a frustration to him," Kitaj eventually admitted to me. "He knew he could only steer me so far. I refused to open up completely to him."

"How did you feel about him? Did you like him?"

"I respected him. I was never close enough to him to like him. He was always distant. He had the universe in him. If I looked into his eyes when he smiled on me, I'd find myself falling through into some space of things that I'd never suspected. He was patient. When I fell through he'd spend days or weeks prodding and driving me to assimilate what had happened. Then he'd smile again, and I'd fall through into something else. That's how it went. Whenever I tried to face up to him, I fell through him. Wherever I pressed, he gave way as if he wasn't there at all. I never really learned that lesson: that he was solid because he was completely empty. He looked like a weak little old man, but he was stronger than anyone else. He knew Mau Mau would fail, yet he knew that the failure would lead to success for others. He didn't parade his knowledge. He wore disguises, especially when he dealt with Europeans. Once he agreed to meet some English, on neutral ground—I can't remember what for. It was hilarious. He dressed himself up and acted out the witch doctor bit for their benefit. He parodied their expectations of how he should be, and they were so rigid they couldn't admit what they knew—that he was laughing at them for thinking of him as a savage. They wanted juju; he gave the juju. He reflected their mentality, and they couldn't face his smile. Of course it did no good. It just made them hate him worse. He knew it. He chose it. He was only human. He had his pride, and he wouldn't crawl. He was a leader of his people, and he was partial to his way of life, and he inspired others to that partiality."

"How did you feel about the British?"

"The same as anyone else. Why get discriminatory about cruelty and self-interest? There's shit in everyone. There were times I got confused, though. I was white European, and everyone round me was black African. Then I couldn't understand what the hell I was doing there; I got lonely and scared and full of hate; I couldn't meet anyone in the eye. Njeru would just laugh and tell me that if I took the Cuts bravely, then I'd be as

good as anyone else, and why should I worry about where I'd
come from? He said that God had sent me and that was good
enough for him . . . so long as I did what he said and didn't talk
back and didn't get in his way.''

"Did Njeru give you the Cuts?"

"Yes. I was scared. They hurt like hell, but afterwards I felt
ready for anything. But I'm glad I didn't have to go through the
circumcision. They'd use rusty razor blades, anything. That's
one reason why so many young people were turning European.
They didn't see any sense of dying of infection just to satisfy the
elders and tradition. Don't blame them.''

"Why didn't you have to go through it?"

"Why do you think? My parents were Jewish."

"Would you have gone through it if you'd had to?"

"Maybe. But not if I'd been among Masai. Youths in Masai
circumcision ceremonies are sat down, arms out, legs apart, with
pellets of goat shit put on top of their knees and on the back of
their fists. If while being cut they tremble so much that one of
those pellets falls—that's it. They're killed.''

"I don't understand. What's the social value?"

"They're warrior herdsmen, very proud. If you live through
that—most of them do—you don't exactly doubt yourself thereafter. That's not all. With them it used to be that you weren't a
man until you'd tackled a lion head-on, armed only with a spear.
Not so much now, though—there aren't many lions left alive.
But the result was, nobody dared argue with Masai.''

"What about women?" I asked. "Didn't a lot of those tribes cut
off the clitoris? And the labia too? Why the hell did they do that?"

He sighed. "Why do you think? Cut up a woman like that,
you take away her pleasure in sex, you make sure she'll be a good
wife, meaning she won't roam and sleep with anyone else,
meaning you ensure your male pride and security." He was sad.
"Don't get false romantic ideas. I was among people who had
the same hang-ups as anyone else, just differently expressed.
Men fear women and don't like to admit it. Everyone of us
carries a mixture of maleness and femaleness, but an aggressive
masculine consciousness finds this hard to accept. I found it hard
to accept. I made mistakes which I still regret.''

He was referring obliquely to what happened when he was with
Iloshabiet in the Mountains of the Moon.

But that comes after the day Njeru took him up Kinangop.

*   *   *

Steadily through the day they ran up the slopes of Kinangop, the old man and the youth, and it was as Njeru had said: they did not stop. It was another test imposed by the *murogi,* the final test, and if it was also a test of the old man himself, he did not show it. Implacably Njeru climbed up, up, up through the forest, up through the bamboos until, with noon well past, they were high on stony ground, and Njeru still climbed, on and on, in a trance of easy motion. M'Botu, laboring far behind with flaming lungs, felt his pride of new manhood hurt and questioned, and he was parched and exhausted long before the sun began its sinking, long before at last he stumbled up a final high knoll to join his teacher, who was waiting, at rest, and who smiled gravely at him.

"It is hard and easy to climb," said Njeru. "You just have to join yourself with the air. You have to stop thinking and forget yourself."

The youth was gasping too deeply to be able to reply.

"Look," said Njeru pensively, his ancient round face wrinkled as he regarded the bloody wild beauty of the sunset. "The world is big. There are machines to make the world small, but the world is always big enough if you depend on your own energies. You go to one horizon and find another beyond it. You conquer one fear only to find another awaiting you. Discovery always begins. Now look to the west, tell me what you see . . . and give me a drink of water."

M'Botu, still panting, handed over the canteen, then looked down the mountain to the great brown valley of the Rift. He saw the diminished waters of the lakes of Naivasha and Nakuru, glinting red in the sunset; he saw far across the Rift to the distant scarp of Uganda. In a sullen whisper he described what he saw. Then he turned back to his teacher to find that Njeru had drunk all the water. Parched, beyond hate, he simply stared at the old man.

"It's a terrible thing to be thirsty," said Njeru reflectively. "I have often been thirsty. Soon you too will have to endure thirst, so you might as well start learning now. I mean last night I cast the sandals to show me your fate, and they told me that very soon you begin your search for the meaning of the power that haunts you. The search will take you many years and will fail unless you overcome your pride and your hate. In the first place you will go

west, in time to come to Ruwenzori, which whites call the
Mountains of the Moon. Here you may meet a woman who will
teach you things that I cannot. Good! But I see great danger! In
hate and jealousy you may one day kill another, without justification, and this error will cast you into darkness. Remember this
warning! If you cannot avoid the crime you will lose yourself in
wars and confusion, and shed more blood, and forget your
Angel. Be warned! You face strange years. You may become
rich in the world, and powerful, but not happy. You will abuse
yourself and others, and be hated as much as you will hate
yourself. There is power in you, but you are knotted, and the
cure will come only through great pain and doubt, through many
deaths inside. If you succeed, you will know the light and bring
benefits here on earth. I pray for you! I am an old man without
family; I have done what I can. Your journey will be hard. But
you are a man now; you must know what I have seen, even
though it is not pleasant. Perhaps you will profit from what I say.
If you find yourself in darkness, bring me to your mind, and I
will try to help. That is all.''

Then Njeru fell silent as the sun went down in blood.

M'Botu, alarmed by these prophecies, felt twisted inside.

"You must go and make your own fate," said Njeru gently,
"and prove that I am just a niddering old man. Now, we will go
down the mountain, and not stop until we are back where we
started this morning.''

Immediately Njeru stood and started back down the mountain.
For a moment the exhausted youth was flooded by loneliness,
fear, and self-pity. Then he remembered the Cuts and his name;
he set his lips and also started down.

It was a terrible night. Only with dawn already fingering the
east did M'Botu at last reel back into the hut. Scratched and
bleeding, he collapsed at the feet of Njeru, who had been waiting
calmly for over an hour.

Njeru smiled, but M'Botu did not see his smile.

"You cannot sleep yet," said Njeru. "There is work to do
before we part. Here, drink this drink I have made for you.''

He tilted a prepared cup to the lips of the prostrate youth.
M'Botu swallowed the thin, spicy, energizing fire. It revived
him. He felt an immediate rush of warmth and life. It did more
than revive him. It heightened him into a dizzy, hallucinatory
dimension. He looked up through writhing shapes and colors, he

looked up into the Smile of Njeru . . . and then, yet again, he fell into that Smile, through those eyes. He plunged into a visionary trance.

Years later he told me he found himself in a diamond-cold ice palace at the North Pole. In the vision he was dying, surrounded by beautiful women and grave young men, dying with snow in his veins, with people pointing big-eyed cameras at him . . . television cameras . . . which were the eyes of Njeru through which he had fallen. In Ireland he told me he knew this vision was of his future, and that one day he must endure the reality.

So it was to be.

For a long time M'Botu journeyed through this and other dream visions. He descended to an ancient underworld and did battle with unrecognized aspects of himself which included the beasts of the old woman. Over and again he was defeated, drowned, and destroyed until nothing remained of him but a tiny dormant spark. But once he accepted defeat his spark of life was nourished in the relaxation of acceptance. It grew into a flower of flame, of life-warmth. Slowly he awoke, knowing that the spirit, being energy, cannot die. He opened his eyes. A shaft of late afternoon sunlight was shining through the foliage, through the open door of the hut, onto his face. He awoke with a lesson learned . . . but he was to forget it. His pride would not easily let him accept any defeat.

He stirred from the hard earth floor. He knew that more than one day had passed, and that Njeru was gone. He sat up, naked but for the claw of the leopard round his neck. His spear lay beside him, and the water canteen, and food, wrapped up in banana leaves. And something else, left by Njeru as a gift.

Njeru's divining sandals.

M'Botu did not know his feelings. He was wiped clean. He stayed one more night in the hut. Then he started west, on his search.

It took him three months to reach Ruwenzori.

On the third day his clumsiness almost killed him. He had started without forethought, without clothing or much food, trusting in his luck, in his outer senses, ignoring heart-intuition which Njeru had tried to train in him. On the second night he was crossing the dangerous dry flatness of the Rift. He came to a farm near Lake Nakuru. He was cold. He tried to steal European

clothes from a washing line. A dog heard him and attacked him.
He killed the dog with his knife and got away, but without any
clothes, and not before the alarm was raised. The soldiers were
told that Mau Mau were lurking near Nakuru, and they came
after him, not knowing it was only one white youth they chased.
Throughout that night he ran, cursing himself. He could risk no
contact with Europeans, not even with their clothes. He was
angry about the dog too: he had killed it unnecessarily, wronged
it, and now it was another of the spirits that haunted him. When
the sun rose next morning he was hiding in the reed marshes
at the edge of the lake, which was diminished by the dry season.
The cover was poor. He was hungry. He plaited a rope of reeds
and snared a flamingo. He was eating the bird, raw, when the
helicopter came. He was so absorbed in his hunger that he didn't
realize the danger until almost too late. Frantically he dived into
the reeds and began wriggling towards the water. The movement
of the reeds was seen. The helicopter chattered close and low
above where he lay submerged in the muddy shallows. There was
a burst of machine-gun fire. The bullets missed him. A hippo
wallowing nearby was stampeded and almost trampled him in its
terror. Somehow he lay still. Eventually the helicopter moved
away down the lake. Gasping, he saw how it sent up swirling
pink clouds of scared flamingoes. He hated the men in the
helicopter. He wanted to kill them. He was wild and raw and
naked. He fled from the lake into the western hills. They were
bare. The whole world was bare. That evening he climbed the
dry brown slopes. He was seen by a herding boy, who ran off
and reported him. He must have been a weird sight, his bare
brown body caked with mud and powdery red dust. Only the
darkness saved him from the patrol that landed to sweep the
slopes. He moved all night, and all next day too, though he
found little food and no water. Njeru's training had made him
tough. But he was in a bad way, mentally and physically. When
night came again he half-slept in the scrubby umbrella branches
of an acacia tree. He had only the claw of the leopard, the
sandals, his sense of destiny, his pride, and his hate that life
should be so hard. He was frightened, and freezing, and he
shivered angrily in the tree, promising that one day he would be
the hunter and not the hunted. The stars shown down, and he
cursed them for being so beautiful and remote. He had the sense
of a terrific gulf, an abyss, and himself trapped on the wrong

side. Furiously he demanded forgiveness of the spirits that haunted him with ill luck. He invoked his image of Greystoke, fervently. He had not forgotten Greystoke. Then for a brief period he fell asleep. His dreams were bad. The spirits, unappeased by his grudging approach to them, plagued him. The dog he had slain came howling and snapping. Maurice and Minnie gazed sadly at him. Hitler glared from the door of the closet. The soldiers came shooting. The old woman too, shaking her head as she turned away. Worst of all, the unknown power, the power behind the Voice which had brought him to Africa. He felt it as a deep drumming vibration, building up in his dissatisfied haunted deeps. It was ready to erupt, and in his dream he knew that when it did erupt it would tear him apart, perhaps even destroy the whole world. It was a throbbing flame, huge power, coiled deep within him. He grew tense with fear. In his miserable sleep he clutched the sandals of Njeru and desperately called on his teacher for help. In the very nick of time he felt Njeru smiling on him. He found the strings of his dreaming the way that Njeru had taught. He caught hold of himself. He did not explode or freeze to death that night. In the morning, with the sun rising to warm him, he was still alive. This seemed amazing. Physically weak, very hungry and thirsty, but no longer demoralized, he continued west over the empty highlands. Before midday his luck changed. He surprised a long-legged gerenuk as it fed from the upper branches of a thorn tree, coming upon the spindly antelope from behind to spear and kill it where it stood on its hind legs up against the tree. He drank its blood, he ate its flesh, and the next night he wrapped himself in the bloody skin that he'd flayed off it.

So he continued towards Uganda, towards the rain forests of Ruwenzori.

Kitaj told me all this in Ireland, in the most matter-of-fact way possible, with none of the ambivalence or ambiguity which characterized his approach to other episodes of his early life. In a similar way he described his doings of the next few months. He underwent much hardship of the most banal and physical sort; he was too busy surviving to indulge in the heroic adventures attributed to him by some. He did not fight and kill a grown male lion single-handed on the slopes of Mount Elgon. He did not hypnotize three Ugandan policemen who caught him one day into taking off their clothes and tying each other up . . . though it

seems that, while in the land of the Dodoth people, in the
Morukore region west of Mount Elgon, he did have to hide from
the Protectorate police, who had received word of a strange wild
white boy in their midst, and he claims that once he did auto-
suggest a policeman who was staring right at him into seeing
nothing at all. Yet most of the stories are fanciful. He was not in
the habit of lurking round Dodoth households by night to play
trickster pranks on these people after the manner of the deadly
jests played by the young Tarzan on the cannibalistic people of
Mbonga. Far less did he ever lure beautiful young maidens of the
Dodoth away from their households to take his precocious sexual
pleasure with them. He told me, and I believe it, that he did not
gain his first sexual experience until he reached Ruwenzori, and
then under sufficiently odd circumstances to satisfy the most
bizarre in sexual-mythic tastes. Further, he told me that many of
the Dodoth (proud, tall, handsome Nilo-Hamitic warrior herdsmen
related to the Masai, often involved in rustling wars with their
neighbours, the Turkana) were kind to him, giving him food and
shelter when he most needed it, asking little in return. From other
sources it is clear that he lived among the Dodoth for a while
after his return from the blood bath of the Congo. By then rumor
was attached to his name, and many viewed him suspiciously,
but evidently his friends amongst the Dodoth thought well enough
of him to discount the worst of these tales. So it is apparent that
during his initial passage through their lands he could scarcely
have done anything to anger them. Rather it would seem that his
contacts among the Dodoth must have sensed the haunted power
of destiny that drove this bronzed European youth with the wild
strong eyes. Perhaps the directness of his gaze made them
dubious—prolonged staring may be taken as a sign of witchcraft
among these people—but also it is likely that among them were
some who took pity on his loneliness and unique condition.

Gradually he approached his destination. In a wide arc he
passed over the high plain of the Karimojong, north of Lake
Kyoga, through the lands of Dodoth, Jie, and Acoli. Over the
Victoria Nile he traveled past many scattered plantations of coffee and tea. He entered the volcanic foothills of Ruwenzori,
living on whatever he could find, a mood of great urgency now
upon him, a feverishness of soul mounting in him as he climbed
higher and higher through the wild unpopulated highlands towards
the massive range of misty wet mountains that straddled the

Uganda-Congo border. Into the fantastic forests on the slopes of Ruwenzori he struggled with the fearful sense of being bound upon the full discovery of a fate already half-revealed. He had begun to feel there was a curse on him, in his own nature, a curse subtly fixed and amplified by the prophecies of Njeru, and so he came to Ruwenzori with reluctant haste, the power throbbing dangerously in him, feeling like an Untouchable, an Unseen, a Ghost whose present existed only in the tremblings of the future. Thus at length came the evening as he walked in the high fantastic jungle when he heard the drum taps of Iloshabiet, the drum taps that matched the throbbing in him, and thus he was snared into his fate, high in the Mountains of the Moon.

It is nearly two thousand years since Ptolemy wrote of a source of the Nile high in a silvery mountain south of Ethiopia, in the heart of the Dark Continent, and hardly a century since the explorer Stanley, passing the white peaks of a huge mist-shrouded mountain on the equator, hailed it with the name that Ptolemy had mentioned, ''The Mountains of the Moon.'' In fact earlier explorers had named this great massif more accurately, if less romantically: Ruwenzori, from the local word, Rwenzura, the rainy mountain, a region with an evil reputation for rain, mist, hail, sleet, snow, and bitter cold. For more than fifty miles north to south Ruwenzori extends, some of its half dozen peaks rising up almost to 17,000 feet. It is not a volcanic mass like the other great Equatorial mountains, but consists of very ancient rocks, squeezed up from the depths of the planet, containing mica schists which sparkle like silver in the sun . . . when the sun shines, that is. There is no real dry season on Ruwenzori, and its many slopes are clad in forest which is dense, giant, nightmarishly prolific, while high in the secret recesses of the range there are hidden lakes surrounded by the sort of vegetation which might normally sprout only in the wilderness of an opium delirium. Especially the Nyamgasani valley is weirdly beautiful, magical, by turns fiendish or enchanting . . . and the events which befell M'Botu here, amid the lakes and black cliffs, were both enchanting and fiendish.

Years later Kitaj told me that the two years he spent on Ruwenzori with Iloshabiet now seemed to him like an incredible dream, particularly the conclusion, which led to his flight from the mountain. Certainly this period is another about which he was always very vague, and it is hard to piece together an account of his relationship with the witch-woman. This vagueness, of course, has proved to be a positive boon so far as the public imagination is concerned, and some of the most entertaining fictions about his life are set in this period. The most extravagant of these fantasies are evidently archetypal, and as such worth brief examination. There is the account which portrays Iloshabiet as a modern Circe, transforming unwary men into the snuffling hogs that she kept in a little pen outside her mountain cave. There is the tale, clearly derived from the myth of the Welsh earth goddess Ceridwen, which states that in her cave Iloshabiet had a pot containing an ever-bubbling brew, and that one day M'Botu had to flee her wrath when he denied her express command by tasting of this brew, which conferred deep wisdom and knowledge of nature. Slightly different is the story that M'Botu learned the language of the wild beasts by drinking broth made by Iloshabiet from the flesh of a white snake—a story that occurs in the dragon mythologies of a great many lands. Then there are the many versions of his crime, which I mean to approach only through his own account, and there are the stories of his meetings with other magical characters who lived in the Mountains of the Moon. Two of these are worth mention. Both of them, so far as I can tell, date from the late 1980s. In the first of these tales, M'Botu is said to have fought a magical battle of words and wits with a fierce old magician who lived alone atop the towering black crags of the mountain called Watamagufu. This forbidding person, referred to only as the Speaker, resented M'Botu's encroachment on his territory, and overwhelmed the youth by the power of word vibration, hurling M'Botu off his feet and leaving him suspended in midair over an abyss for fully twenty-four hours, before at length releasing him back to the lower slopes with a thunderous warning: "Never climb this high again until you learn to speak the truth with heart, for truth without heart is no truth at all!" What M'Botu had said to him is not recorded. Then again, there is the even more amazing tale of his encounter with another strange character called the Renewer, a cloaked and hooded being who carried a skull and who wore a loincloth with human teeth sewn into it, whom apparently M'Botu met during his furiously guilty flight from the mountain, and who challenged M'Botu to mortal combat. The story says that they fought for

seven days and seven nights, at the end of which time M'Botu
had slain his antagonist seven times, only for the apparent corpse
to blossom with miraculous new life on each occasion. Finally in
desperation M'Botu cried out: "What must I do to kill you? Why
have you not killed me?" To which he received the reply (from
the mouth of the skull): "Fool! Do you not know that life cannot
be destroyed, and that death is the guardian of life? 'Learn, you
idiot, or I will get the Speaker to suspend you over the abyss
again, this time upside down, as was done formerly—and there
you shall remain and rot forever! So learn to let your waters
flow! Now leave me!''

These last two tales, highly moralistic as they are, bear strong
indications of having been composed by an author versed in the
system and symbols of the New Tarot, also known as the Aquarian
Tarot. There are many cases of newconscious artists and seekers
adapting the Kitaj mythos to the requirements of their own
particular paths. I believe there is value in these approaches, so
ong as we remember the need to make up our own minds and not
let others do it for us, so long as we recognize that symbols make
good servants but bad masters, and so long as we do not drown
the original account beneath too great a weight of myth.

Thus, yet again, I turn to what Kitaj actually told me, recon-
structing the tale as best I can from the different accounts he gave
at different times. The possibility that Kitaj invented the affair, in
whole or in part, should again be borne in mind. Iloshabiet has
never since been traced—though her name was known throughout Uganda during the sixties, and there were rumors that she
died during Amin's reign of terror—and the man Remi, who
appeared a decade ago, claiming to be the son of M'Botu and
Iloshabiet, claiming his inheritance from Kitaj, was unable to
substantiate his tale to anyone's satisfaction. But Kitaj always
admired a good story and a bold nerve: it may be remembered
that he set up Remi with an expensive house in Mill Valley,
California. Remi subsequently established a lucrative practise as
an astrologer, which he maintained during the purges after 1992
by dint of denying everything he had previously claimed.

So it goes. There's no failure like success.

M'Botu heard the drum taps only just in time.

He had been two weeks on the slopes of Ruwenzori. He was
exhausted, losing faith, losing any sure sense of time and space,

falling ill. He had never been so high, nor stayed on the move so continuously, yet for days now he had lacked any sense of what he was doing. He had been following his nose, following the scent, but death now seemed the most likely destination. He was well dressed, in skins cut for him by his Dodoth friends, and his hunting had brought him a sufficient reserve of food, and drinking water was no problem . . . but his morale and health were very low, brought down by the cold of the mountain, by its damp mists, and by its unfriendly spirits which came upon him every night as he tried to sleep, jeering at him, promising him a lonely death.

Yet when he first heard the drum taps he was still climbing, dazedly following a stream that tumbled down from the mouth of a valley above him, the opening of which he could glimpse from time to time through breaks in the mist and in the jungle that surrounded him. In his exhaustion he was half-hallucinating and when he first heard the drumming he thought perhaps it was just the amplified reverberation of his own laboring heart, or maybe the audible writhing of the living jungle. For all about him the giant tree heathers loomed, some more than fifty feet high, their grinning fantastic interplay of sprigs making faces at him through the swirling mists. Giant groundsels, swollen and distorted, gaped at him. Huge lobelias speared their scarlet dimly up from the silent shadows of the lichens and liverworts which thickly carpeted the soil, the rocks, the trunks of the trees. Everything was huge, and silent, and very intent on watching him, so that the beating of his heart was the loudest sound he could hear as he clambered dizzily upwards, bound who knew where?

Then he felt the tappings of the drum.

He felt a rhythm, curiously familiar, resonating in him. Only when he stopped to listen very carefully did he realise that it came from outside him, from above him, and that he heard as well as felt it.

His heart began beating twice as hard.

"I was terrified," he told me years later. "I felt intolerable strain—that sense of the power inside about to erupt. It was worse than the night Maurice and Minnie died, when I came to Njeru. I felt sure I was entering a realm of the spirits, and that perhaps I was dying—I couldn't believe a human being was making that sound. It was unearthly, weird, very distant. But I had to find the source of it. It was what I was. The beat went on, and I climbed, remembering Njeru's warnings. I felt sick and hollow inside. Then I broke through the cloud into sunlight, and came to the valley.''

He just stood and gaped.

The valley was an amazement.

It was sweet and gentle, a delightful garden full of flowers, enclosed on three sides by steep ridges, with three rocky peaks at the head of it. In it were small grey hills covered with everlasting flowers, heathers, and groundsels. Little blue sunbirds flitted in the mellow late afternoon sunlight. The spirit of the place was fey, but kindly. There was no riotous jungle; rather, the sense of a decorous natural order, as if the elementals, happily unhindered by man, had been hard at work for centuries, creating an enchanted world.

In the middle of the valley, maybe half a mile away, was a little lake. It was blue, with green weed trailing round its verges. On the far side of this lake rose a steep pink rock, tangled over and half-concealed by vegetation, yet standing out clearly enough against the black mountain walls beyond it.

The soft drum taps appeared to be coming from the pink rock.

It took M'Botu some time to overcome his surprise. Cautiously he approached the lake, then detoured round it, feeling lightheaded, in a dream. The going was easy, and fairly dry, though with one marshy area where he had to jump between tussocks shaped like giant wobbly toadstools to avoid being soaked.

In this way he came to a grove of trees near the pink rock.

Before he looked past the thick bushes obscuring the pink rock, he listened again. He heard the low soft voice that accompanied the drum. A woman's voice. He shivered at the passion of her chant. Then he looked. The sun was sinking. He looked into the beautiful golden light. He had to squint. He saw the vine-screened arch of the cave, black at the foot of the pink rock. He saw smoke of the fire, curling gently up in front of the mouth of the cave.

He saw the woman who sat west of the fire, chanting, drumming, insistent.

He drew sharp breath. He moved closer.

She was young. She was beautiful. She was very black. She sat, but he could see she was tall. She had huge lustrous uplifted eyes, a high narrow head with very delicate features, a bush of hair tied with a violet ribbon. Protruding below her lower lip, an

ivory plug. He knew, from having seen similar decoration among
the Dodoth women, that her lower teeth would have been knocked
out to accommodate this plug. She wore many bangles and necklaces, and a beautiful robe of multicolored bird feathers. She
looked plumed, powerful; he stared, and for some time did not
reveal himself. He was scared and attracted. Who was she? She
looked like a witch. Was she alone here?

Then he realized she was weeping as she sang her drumming
song.

Soon, moved as much as anything by the responding drumming of his body, he stood out and showed himself, started
walking towards her, over flowers.

Her drumming and her chanting stopped.

For a long long moment she stared at him.

He stopped still and dropped his spear on the ground. Invisible
sparks flew. He saw her and she saw him. He looked small but
wild, brown yet white, strong but not quite sure. She saw he was
very young—in some ways. Shaggy long hair, tangled to his
shoulders. His face clean, but features already marked in subtle
ways. Clean and bold, but with an underlying shadow.

He felt hot and cold and eager and nervous, and he could not
take his grey eyes from the night depths and knowledge of her
gaze. He felt tremendous spirit emanating from her. Also, something in her that brooded . . . though he did not know what this
was.

Slowly she stood. She was a head taller and stood perfectly
straight. Slowly she smiled. Then she laughed—a peal of good
humour.

"Are you Her answer?" she cried out in one of the Karimojong
dialects. "I didn't think my request would ever be answered at
all! But *what* are you? Who? White, wearing skins of black?
Youth, walking like a warrior? Journeying up to this haunted lake
where people fear to come? Visiting Iloshabiet, whom people
fear to see? Don't you know who I am? Are you a fool? Answer
me!"

Her voice had grown imperious. Her smile had vanished.

M'Botu felt shaken. He pulled himself together.

"I had a teacher, Njeru," he called across the space between
them. "He has a famous smile, but I liked it not half as much as
I like your smile. I am M'Botu, here on a road of fate, following
the scent I follow . . ."

"What is the name of this scent?" Iloshabiet demanded.

"I don't know its name! It is the root of the power which moves all things. It has brought me a long way. I have been cold, I am hungry, I would like to be warm! So, smile on me again, please!"

His boldness pleased her. She smiled again, she laughed again, she beckoned him closer. She studied him with eyes that set him on fire, critical and sharp and warm and dark and very distant eyes. He could find nothing to say, nowhere to look but her eyes, in which he found nothing he knew . . . yet.

"I believe," she said very softly after a while, "that I need no longer sing the song . . . at any rate for a time. We will eat soon . . . then we will talk."

That night they sat across the fire, and they talked, and M'Botu frequently felt like a fool. But the stars shone down, very close and bright they seemed, and for the first time M'Botu found them not so much awe inspiring and terrible as friendly. He felt no agonizing gulf between himself and them; he felt light and high and free; he was a part of them, made of the same stuff. With Iloshabiet he looked up among the stars, particularly to one which she pointed out, a very bright blue white star, the brightest of all. From this star for an instant he had the sense of a message, a message he could not read, a transmission received in his bones, locked in the ages. Then, with the great eyes of Iloshabiet watching him curiously, impulse made him take the sandals of Njeru and toss them beside the fire. He tranced on the way they fell, on the flames in the fire, and again it was deep-rooted impulse that made him speak. He pointed up to the bright star, Sirius, and in a sudden strong confidence he said:

"One day I am going there, though not as I am. That is where we came from, and that is where I am going."

Iloshabiet stared very strangely at him. She seemed moved.

"That is the oldest secret of all," she whispered. "I have felt it myself. Now there is another old secret; you must learn it, and I will teach you."

Then, says Kitaj, his cock went stiff and told him what she had to teach him. They went into the cave, M'Botu willingly, excitedly, believing it impossible that he should ever fall into darkness the way Njeru had warned he might. In the flickering candlelit cave Iloshabiet drew off her robe of bird feathers and showed him her beauty. The shadows danced on her, long and sleek and full. M'Botu stood, consumed by the fire. She came to him and took him out of the muddy damp skins he wore, her hands stroking until he was trembling and naked. When she saw that he was thoroughly roused she sighed, she moaned, she went down on her knees, she took him in her mouth. He felt the huge serpent writhing and bucking at the base of his spine, fire roared through him, and he came, intensely. Then she took him down with her onto the bed of banana leaves. Thus, he told me, he began to learn about a new universe. There, the power began to flow between them, joining them, to flow between them for a thousand days and nights, until fear and jealousy and other forces which he could not control arose to destroy the circuit, ending the idyll, casting him from the garden into the outer darkness of the world. That is how he told it to me . . . and he was rapt with the ambivalent magic of the memory.

Who was Iloshabiet, and what is her place in this tale?

Kitaj told me she had been born of the Jie, the second tribe of the Karimojong Cluster, and that she had been exiled from her people on suspicion of witchcraft. She had been accused of casting spells of sickness on the cattle of a man who had rejected her in love. The dream of a holy man had in the first place revealed her as the witch responsible for the sickness of this man's herd, but nobody had wanted to believe it. She was of good household; her father was much respected; no taint of witchcraft had ever attached to her family.

But her behavior had grown strange and wild. She had taken to talking to plants and animals. She had taken to walking alone at night, especially when the moon was full and strong. She was seen sometimes when in anger to point directly at people to whom she spoke. Public suspicion mounted. Finally one night she was seen and identified lurking near the cattle compound of the man who had rejected her. She was naked and stepping widdershins slowly round the walls of the compound. She was chased, but escaped: it was said she had changed herself into a hyena to get away. The evidence, in terms of her society and its beliefs, was circumstantial but sufficient: she was lucky not to have been beaten to death. The case against her was strengthened by public rumor that this man who had wronged her had also swindled her father in a cattle transaction: she had every motive to hate him. There was sympathy for her, but the fear of witch-craft was greater.

Exiled, driven out with shorn head and smoldering heart, for months she had wandered without direction or aim, surviving by virtue of the caution she struck into the people she met along the road, for her strength of character was apparent in the flashing directness of her gaze. Yet for a long hard time this apparent directness hid an utter confusion. She did not know who or what she was. She did not know whether to hate herself or those who had cast her out. She did not know what to do, where to go. Often she slept beneath the moon . . . and she began to dream of Ruwenzori. She saw a hidden valley; she saw herself beneath the misty peaks. Several times the dream repeated itself until she knew without doubt that she was being urged to go to the rainy mountain.

She denied the urge. She didn't like the idea of Ruwenzori. Instead she went to Kampala where she began to learn about hanging onto the coattails of European culture. She set herself up as a diviner and fortuneteller, but she did not know enough. She told people what she saw, she told her clients the truth, and one night she was beaten within an inch of her life. Prostitution seemed the only sensible course to take. But somehow, before she was quite decided about this, she met and slept with an Italian film director who was in Kampala to make a Tarzan movie. He was captivated by her. She persuaded him to take her to Rome with him.

In Europe, under the name of Luna, she began a modeling career which promised considerable success. She made her invocations and for a time persuaded herself that ill luck was behind her. Her cool hauteur and mysterious beauty of unimaginable mystery were much in demand. She lived la dolce vita, and soon her face and form were appearing on billboards and in exotic magazines, advertising expensive attainability. But her dreams grew terrible with dislocation and psychic stress. The glittering gleaming luxury was not for her. She was confronted within by her spirits and told to get it right, or else. Thus, after a long struggle, she put off the Dior gowns and told her film director that she had to follow another path in life.

He was disconcerted but gallant. He bought her an air ticket back to Kampala, told her she could return to him any time. She refused the ticket and said she could never return, explaining that she had to find her own way. Then he was not so gallant: he lost patience, he spoke scathingly of the money he'd invested in her, and he kicked her out.

It took her more than two years to reach her goal.

She crossed the Sahara in a Peugeot truck, paying almost all she had to get safely through the war Algeria was fighting with France. She got stuck in Tamanrasset in the heart of the hot lands, the arid lands, the Ahaggar. In Mali by chance she came among the Dogon people. It was here that the connections and synchronicities began, for the Dogon have worshipped and held knowledge of the Sirius star-system from time immemorial. For centuries and longer they have known of the Dark Companion—a white dwarf star, Sirius B, invisible to the naked eye, only recently photographed, a cubic inch of which weighs about a ton—and they have worshipped Nommo, a fish-tailed being who, they say, came anciently to this planet from Sirius, bringing education and enlightenment.

Iloshabiet was not at the time very interested in this. She stayed a little while among the Dogon, then continued south, into the lands of the Yoruba in Nigeria. Here she came to the temple of a snake cult, and for over a year she served in this temple, handling the tame pythons, refamiliarizing herself with the magic worlds of moon and will, charm and dream . . . until she knew it was time for the last stage of her journey to Ruwenzori.

Through the Cameroons she came, over the high forest hills and into the Congo. She reached the Mountains of the Moon, but she was nearly dead of doubt and exhaustion when at last, high above the mists, she found the delightful valley and the cave at the foot of the pink rock.

She slept for a long time.

When she awoke, she knew she had reached her home.

Two years she lived there before M'Botu came. She grew beans, she laid snares, she invoked success for the hunting, and she survived. She endured the solitude and wild weather of this place which few others dared approach. The lakes in this part of the rainy mountain were said to be haunted, especially the higher lakes, which were bleak and glacial. The legend was of a tribe of supernatural beings who had once emerged from the waters and later returned beneath them, who if ever disturbed again would be violently angry. Iloshabiet did not believe the legend, not literally, but it was useful, insuring the solitude she needed in

order to discover herself and her purpose in life. Yet she found
this isolation hard to bear. Her last few years had been a whirling
delirium of glamorous misdirections, starting with her intuitive
sorcery against the man who had wronged her and her family.
Now at last she began to get it all into perspective. For months
she was angry at her fate, against those who had expelled her.
Only after a time did she begin to realize that all her wild
journeys were not a misfortune at all, but a necessary and valuable education. She had brought it all on herself. She had abused
her gifts in the attempt to harm another human being. Her fate
had been rough, but it was just, which meant it was in accord
with the direction of her will, which until now had been largely
unconscious. Now she began the task of making it conscious. On
her own in the valley she lived through a long first year of pain
and self-examination. Once she got through this, she began to
grow again. She began to learn more about the way that the
energies of life manifest. She began to learn more about the
depths that lie above, within, all about. She had always known
how to talk with the plants, with the animals—silently, intuitively. Now on Ruwenzori her conversations—sometimes stimulated
by the white-spotted red mushrooms that grew in damp places by
the lake—began to stretch deep into the earth, high through the
skies. She talked with the Mother, she talked with the Moon and
the Sun, she talked with those from elsewhen. She tended her
beans and talked with them too. For, despite all these conversations, despite all she was learning, she remained lonely. She
wanted a man.

None of the entities she met suggested that her desire for a
man was wrong, in itself. Nevertheless she had a vague feeling
that she would be best to stay on her own until she had absorbed
and understood more of the elemental powers. If she got a man
here now there would be danger to both of them . . . unless the
man was a magician strong enough to consciously harmonize
with her own as yet unruly and undeveloped forces.

Something in her did not want such a man.

There was a region inside herself that she could not enter. She
had only gradually grown aware that it had always been there.
Now she knew of it, but did not know who or what she was
inside it. From this region came desires she could not understand,
codes of demand that she could not break.

She wanted a man, but not one who would overwhelm her development by the influence of his own powers.

She took the chance.

During the evenings of the second year she began the drumming and chanting, her invocation and request, doing so throughout each waxing moon, for in this phase her inspiration and power flowed most freely. She breathed the shifting tides and at such times her dreams, she later told M'Botu, were so potent that often they invaded and overcast her waking self, convincing her of her former identity as a servant of Isis in a temple on the delta of the Nile—an initiate of the mysteries of the Sun behind our Sun, and of Osiris, the Dark Companion.

So Kitaj later reconstructed what she told him.

She invoked, though she did not know what she wanted. She invoked according to her dangerous need, and in time her answer came.

The white youth, the strong weak youth, M'Botu.

Kitaj's various references to his Thousand and One Nights add up to a very brief tale, and only once did he ever speak to me in any depth of what finally happened, of the misfortune which led him to abandon his high dreams and his Angel, directing him down into the darkness of the wealth, cynicism, blindness, violence, and power which preoccupied him for so many years . . .

For over seven hundred days and nights all went well.

When M'Botu came to Iloshabiet he was only a youth, though he had already been through more changes and trigger experiences than most people twice his age. He came to her partly awakened to the forces at work within him—those forces at work in all of us whereby, without necessarily realizing it, we create and structure whatever it is that we call "reality." He came to her bearing his personal inner trinity: the Angel, the Voice, and his image of Greystoke. But as yet he did not understand any of these forces which drove him, which played through him, and therein lay danger. He was opened, but not in control.

Nor, as we have seen, did Iloshabiet fully understand what moved her.

She was older than he, but not much, and wiser, but not much.

The first thing that happened between them was that she activated him sexually. She initiated him into the delights of Aphrodite, as we have also seen.

It is not certain whether, during the following year or so, she also tried to educate him in techniques of sex-magic. More than once he hinted to me that she attempted to teach him the difficult practice of Kundalini Yoga. This path of knowldge, involving release of the potent serpent energy coiled at the base of the spine, has many drawbacks, the main one being that too many people who attempt it lack the necessary health, experience, and strength of character to handle the forces thus released. They burn up. Kundalini, improperly invoked, without due training or safeguards, can intensify all natural pressures to an explosive and devastating pitch . . . and it is clear from his own account that M'Botu finally did explode, and in a very devastating fashion. To me it seems likely that the intensity of sexual experience between the two of them resulted accumulatively in a build up of tremendous emotional energy which ultimately the youth could not handle . . . but there is no need to invoke Kundalini to explain this. Emotional violence arising through sexual confusion remains among the most common of human tragedies, and the youth M'Botu possessed a lot of power, a lot of sexuality, and a lot of confusion. It also seems doubtful to me that Iloshabiet could have known very much—consciously—about Kundalini. She may have been initiated into Tantric practices while in Rome, and of course she had spent a year as a pythoness while in Nigeria, but the training involved in control of Kundalini takes a very long time, being not just a matter of mechanical learning, but of the most rigorous self-understanding and inner balance. From Kitaj's descriptions, Iloshabiet does not seem to have reached such a degree of knowledge at the time M'Botu knew her. Yet evidently she was a very powerful woman, as he was potentially a very powerful man, and the riot of their joined sexuality and subconscious natures probably provided all the fuel that was needed to cause a catastrophe. In later years, after Ireland, Kitaj definitely did become involved in Tantra and in Kundalini Yoga . . . but at this early point of his life it seems more likely that emotional confusion, not deliberate intention, was responsible for what happened.

Yet for over two years all went well. Their union seemed good and M'Botu knew contentment. Iloshabiet taught him about tenderness and the secrets of the moon. She taught him how to

travel in his dreams. When the mists closed in and the rain came
down there was much to learn and enjoy in the cave. When the
skies were clear they studied the stars, and the petals of flowers,
and grains of sand. They tamed a hyrax and a parrot. They
laughed a lot.

But like Eden it did not, could not, last. Perhaps they should
not have made a child together. Perhaps it was not the right time.
But after a year it happened. Iloshabiet gave birth to a healthy
boy. It was then that M'Botu began to get anxious, jealous,
possessive . . . and gradually love went sour.

Iloshabiet had known from the beginning it could not last.
Perhaps this contributed to M'Botu's fear of leaving, for she
knew he would have to go, sooner or later, to pursue his own
fate. He knew this too. But he grew dependent on her and the
child, he became dour and morose . . . and the tragedy came
when he tried to force Eden to last beyond its appointed time.

"She warned me," Kitaj told me bluntly, in Ireland. "She
said I would have to go, that I was young, with my own path to
tread, but that she had to stay in the valley and continue her
work. She said if I didn't go soon, the energies between us would
curdle and go bad, that I would start to hate her for holding me
back. But I didn't believe her . . . until it happened . . ."

Happen it did. He stayed too long. Their love turned into
conflict. But M'Botu, unable to imagine life without her and his
son, still refused to go. His confusion grew. He accused her of
bewitching him so he couldn't leave, because he wanted to leave,
knew he must, but couldn't. Soon Iloshabiet grew moody and
unfriendly, perhaps wishing that she'd never told him how, in the
first place, she'd doubted the good sense of her desire for a man.
He felt trapped, and perhaps she felt a little guilt. And so
M'Botu's confusion developed into an active hatred of the sort he
hadn't felt since reaching the valley. He refused to remember
Njeru's warning, though the Voice in him, the sense of dangerous power, became increasingly insistent. The old woman appeared
in his dreams, scolding him, but he denied her too. Greystoke
also appeared, telling him to get moving, and still he refused. He
was scared. Iloshabiet had his soul. The tension got so bad that
he started going off on long hunting trips, killing to ease the
pain, staying away for days or weeks. Several times he almost
broke the chains, almost went on . . . but every time he came
back, and every time it was worse. Each time that he came back

he did so in a futile agony of hope that this time it would be different, that this time he'd return to find the disease between them cured. But the disease was in himself . . . and finally he returned one time too many.

There are many weird and wild theories that try to explain why M'Botu did what he did that day. The "Kundalini explosion" theory, already mentioned, is among the most popular, perhaps because it touches an odd romantic chord in some people, and of course there is the myth, constructed probably by the same pen that wrote of M'Botu's encounters with the Speaker and the Renewer, which explains his action in terms of a violent attempt to overthrow the enchantment which Iloshabiet had put on him. Other versions rewrite what Kitaj told me in terms of a heroic battle in which M'Botu was not at all to blame, while there are psychological approaches which deny that the event took place at all, explaining it as Kitaj's fantasy effort to come to terms with his sense of guilt.

The "War in Heaven" theory has become very popular during the last few years, since the Transformation, after which Sirius speculation became explicit.

This theory states that the forces which tore M'Botu/Kitaj apart for so many years were not per se the forces of his own divided personality, but were the actual manifestation in him of opposing extraterrestrial (or extradimensional, or higher-level) intelligences which were fighting each other to control him.

Our planet, states this school of thought, has not only been under observation throughout recorded history, but has also been the subtle battleground of "Higher Intelligences" with an interest in human evolution. One side, it seems, tries to encourage our evolution; the other wants us to stay stuck and dumb in mires of self-destruction. On the face of it, this theory and its corollaries look identical to the old God/Devil dualism . . . but there is some evidence for it, if you seek evidence, if you seek a fixed structure of belief.

Some of those who hold this theory suggest that Kitaj was not born in Warsaw at all, that the memory was artifically planted in him, that in fact he was not even born in this space-time, but that he was what in other times would have been called a changeling, put among us by the fairies/extraterrestrials/Higher Intelligences, in order to act as an evolutionary accelerator.

This same general theory has also of course been used to account for Christ, Leonardo, Nikola Tesla, Roger Bacon, Kaspar Hauser, etc., etc. I suspect what is basically involved is a lack of imagination, also a kind of misplaced resentment that some earthborn human beings seem more remarkable than others. Yet this may be no more than my own chauvinism . . . for anything is possible. But to my mind the theory says more about those who believe it than anything else. Few of them can agree which side is which, or what means what. Consider the versions available. Kitaj was planted among us by the good powers that desire our evolution . . . or by the bad powers who want to keep us stuck. The bad powers . . . or the good powers . . . were always trying to spike him, stop him, destroy him. The good side (or the bad side) drove him to do what he did when he returned to the valley that day. The Voice, and the Angel were manifestations of one side, or the other side . . . or perhaps they were both on the same side, good or bad. The most popular theory is that Kitaj was terrified of the Voice, alias the baddies, and that it drove him to deny the Angel, alias the goodies. Greystoke is not taken into account by any of these versions . . . though some people postulate *three* invisible sides that fight for control of us. In addition, there are complex variants hypothesizing that people who influenced Kitaj (i.e., Njeru, Iloshabiet, Lenore, myself, others) were agents of one side . . . or another side.

The complexities are endless. Nobody agrees. There is no clarity in such theories. No useful light is shed. They reduce Kitaj to the status of robot or puppet, explaining his every action as the result of influence by other-directed forces, giving him no free will at all. The arguments advanced by one faction (good-bad) can just as well be employed by another (bad-good). Nothing and anything at all can be suggested by such dualistic and nonrelative thinking, and I submit that the purpose of such speculation is not to discover anything valuable, but merely so that people can keep themselves happy by inventing something to believe in. Whatever is really going on, it is not to be understood by any fixed or conventional mode of thought. "Convictions make convicts"—we are imprisoned by whatever we believe, and it seems that many of us want to stay in jail. In a sense we are all battlegrounds of cosmic conflict ("As above, so below") and I suspect there is indeed some truth, somewhere, somehow, in the "War in Heaven" theory. But dependence on such beliefs can lead to paranoia and irresponsibility: it is better to consider everything and believe nothing . . . for sure. The Unknown cannot contract to fit the Known. We have to expand.

M'Botu acted, it seems to me, out of fear and jealously.

"I came back to the valley," he told me that evening near the end of our stay in Ireland, when at last I got him to talk about it. "I came back and I found other people there. White people—a French botanical expedition.

"I came back furious because I was coming back. I hadn't killed anything while I was away. I was knotted with anger, tension, failure, self-doubt.

"From a long way off I heard voices speaking French. I thought at first they had come for me—the boy who had killed his foster parents then run off with the Mau Mau. My first impulse was to hide. Then I got angry at myself for being such a coward. I felt vicious, on fire inside. I ran towards the cave. From a distance I saw Iloshabiet. She was speaking with one of the white men. They didn't see me, nor did any of the other men, who were all some distance away, making a camp down by the lake. Iloshabiet and this man . . . they were laughing and joking together, speaking a mixture of French and Italian and Swahili. They were standing very close. When I saw them together . . . something burst inside me. I felt a terrible energy. I felt that I was choking in a sea of blood. I couldn't stop myself running at them, though I think through all this rage I was scared of what I was going to do, and I think for a moment I seemed to see Njeru. His face was very stern, and he was looking right at me. For a moment maybe I remembered his warning, and I might have been able to stop, but . . . just then . . . the man put his arm round her shoulders . . . and she let him do it! They were just flirting, but I didn't see it like that. I forgot everything. I was exploding! I ran at them from behind, without a sound, and I knocked him away from her, I knocked him down on the ground, hard, and then I shouted at him, I screamed at him, I challenged him to fight me to the death. But . . . he laughed at me. He shouldn't have done that, not for his own good. But he did. He got slowly up off the ground, wiping his mouth, laughing, and he called me a boy. He was a big man, sure of himself, or so it seemed. I wasn't quite sure. Not when he laughed at me. Iloshabiet . . . for a moment I thought she was laughing at me too. That

did it. It was like a huge horrible orgasm of hate. I threw my
spear at him where he stood. He was defenseless. I killed him.
Just like that. I killed him. I . . . chose darkness.''

That was what he told me. I was shocked to hear it. We were
sitting in front of a peat fire in a room of the cottage in Connemara.
I thought we were alone in the room. It was a wild afternoon,
near nightfall, but Lenore had cycled to the village to see if there
was any mail, and Isma'il, the phlegmatic Sufi-trained fourth
member of our taut little group, was also outside. Kitaj and I sat
staring into the fire. His eyes were as hard and bright as dia-
monds, but he was trembling with the shock of his admission,
with the shock of emotional return to that moment when, in his
own estimation, he'd cast himself down into the pit of the next
thirty years.

But he wasn't finished with what he had to tell me. There was
more. He had to tell me what Iloshabiet had screamed at him
before he'd run for his life.

Slowly, his voice flat and wooden and faraway, he told me
what he'd never told anyone else. He told me of the curse which
M'Botu believed that Iloshabiet had put on him, on his future,
and especially on his relationships with women. He told me this
. . . and all the time he talked, unknown to me at any rate, his
wife Lenore was there behind us, in the shadows, by the door,
come in from the cold, and she heard him tell me what he had
never told her . . .

For a long long moment after M'Botu had thrown the spear,
Kitaj told me, he just stood, frozen, numb, unable to comprehend,
Iloshabiet staring at him with horror as the friends of the murdered Frenchman started to run towards the cave from their
camp, revolvers drawn, shouting.

M'Botu could see nothing but the face of the man he had
killed. But it was not the face of the Frenchman he saw. It was
the face of Njeru. Eyes closed. The smile of a devil. The face
and the smile of death.

Then M'Botu saw his spear through the body of the dead man,
and knew it was his spear, and it was too late. He began to
recollect himself. Clumsily he turned, and saw the men who were
running to capture or kill him. They were still some distance
away. In agony he turned to Iloshabiet. Wild and rigid she stood

with pain, sorrow, disbelief. He took a faltering step towards her, but she stopped him by flinging up her arm, by pointing her finger at him so sharply that he too now felt speared; he was brought up short, stopped.

Iloshabiet shuddered with anguish.

Perhaps she was hating herself too.

"Oh, you idiot!" Her voice was faint. "Why didn't you go? Now you've denied your fate, you've denied your voice, you've turned into a killer, and you have to run. Did you really think you owned me? Will you rape and kill when inside you know much better ways? Oh, listen to me before you run! You've ignored what Njeru taught you. Will you forget what I have to say? It is this! From now on you'll find no happiness with anyone or anything, ever, until you admit that you cannot own the world, or any part of it, or anyone in it. Until you admit that, and know it in your heart, then you yourself are owned—owned by the curse of what you have just now done—and your act has also put a curse on me, and on your son. Now, you had better go!"

It was in this way that Ralph M'Botu, deluding himself that the curse had come from Iloshabiet, embarked on the trail that led to Ralph M'Botu Kitaj, the richest man in the world . . . and it was in this way and by this admission that, nearly thirty years later, he began to regain his soul . . . and lost his wife.

5. TO WINTERLAND AND BEYOND

M'Botu's murder of the French botanist—if it occurred as Kitaj later claimed—was a crucially regressive event in his development. It sank him for a long time. It took place, in fact or in his mind, probably late in the summer of 1959. I am one among many researchers who during the later 1980s attempted, out of various motives, to establish some objective evidence for this event which Kitaj reported to me. But all the trails ran dry. I was able to discover that there was indeed a French botanical expedition on Ruwenzori during the August and September of 1959, and that one of the expedition's members was killed while on the mountain. His name was Jean-Paul Barthelme. Late in 1988 I succeeded in making contact with one of the men who had been on this expedition. I am not at liberty, even now, to reveal his name or any details about him—he granted me the brief interview reluctantly, and on a purely private basis, and all I can say is that he is a man who enjoys a good reputation in his scientific field. When I talked with him, his mood was poor. It seemed I was not the first person to track him down and—as he put it—"pester" him with questions about "this lunatic Kitaj." Nevertheless, I asked him directly if he had witnessed the event which Kitaj reports. He denied it, flatly. He said that Barthelme had slipped and fallen to his death from a narrow trail high on a precipitous face of one of Ruwenzori's peaks. I asked him about the valley, about Iloshabiet. He said that the expedition had indeed come to such a valley as described in *Liar's Gold* (which had been published simultaneously in a great many countries about seven months before the interview) and that they had camped in this beautiful valley for some days. But he swore that the valley had been deserted, that they had met nobody else there at all. Finally, in some confusion, I asked him about Barthelme. Had he been a big man, fluent in Italian and Swahili in addition to his native French?

My informant was annoyed. "Yes," he said. "But so what? You can see that I too am a big man, and I too am fluent in Italian and Swahili. So what?"

"Well," I persisted, "how do you account for Kitaj's knowledge of your expedition? How could he have known about Barthelme's death?"

"It was no secret!" he snapped, increasingly angry, rising to indicate that my time was up. "It was in the papers. Even if your man can't read he could easily have heard about it. Perhaps somehow he even saw the accident and converted it into his fantasy. Either way it's obvious that his story's a fraud. Now, I'm a busy man—are you finished with your questions?"

But there was something in his attitude that made me curious. He was not only angry, but also seemed a little bit anxious, a little bit bothered.

"Just one more," I said, starting towards the door. "Would you be willing to take a lie detector test to verify all this? I don't want to be insulting, but this is really very important."

His anger increased. He took me by the arm and forcibly showed me the door. "If you ever publicly mention my name in connection with any of this I'll see you in hell!'' he warned me bluntly as he slammed the door on me.

Perhaps his reaction was only wounded pride. But sometimes I wonder. It is another mystery. Psychic events, physical facts. Where do the connections lie? Kitaj only grinned when I told him about this.

"Johnny," he said, "you should never have gone to San Francisco."

San Francisco. But I had gone there, and so had he.

It took Kitaj twenty years to get from the Mountains of the Moon to that collective fantasy called California, and when I first set eyes on him, then heard some of the tales about him, it seemed to me that he was just another con artist who'd swept into the Golden State on a magic carpet of impossible dreams, selling darkness, wealth, apocalypse, and instant enlightenment. More *Californication* . . . by then I'd been around long enough to know why folk further north in then Oregon and Washington felt the way many of them did about California . . . for California was always full of mindfuckers, and for long enough it seemed to me that Ralph M'Botu was no more nor less than a particularly accomplished mindfucker; a man who'd made his first ten million while still in his twenties, a man who'd survived the darkness that enveloped him after Ruwenzori, doing so however only by letting it take him over and by inflicting it on others, and by riding the back of the third man from whom he'd taken a name.

Ana Kanasay Kitaj, who'd got him out of Rhodesian jail in 1966. ". . . Presenting Kitaj & Kitaj, Your Majesty . . ."

Yes, by the time I first saw him he'd made it big, and the myths and confusions about him were already well developed.

But it was not all bullshit. By no means. His real purpose was still locked up in him, but the power he had was apparent to me the moment I first met his eyes that New Year's dawn at Winterland.

That meeting changed my life.

Who am I? Where did John Hall come from?

No, I'm not a changeling, I'm not an agent for the CIA or anyone else, I was not—so far as I know—put here on Planet Earth by Higher Intelligences with the mission either of aiding or of destroying Kitaj. No. The truth is that I was, and remain, no more or less alien than anyone else I know.

I was born in Scotland in 1947, the son of a farmer. My childhood was comfortable and not dramatic. When I was twenty-two I graduated from a red-brick English university with a degree in what they called Modern History. For a year I worked nine-to-five in London. That got depressing. I cut out and started writing stories, stories that began to sell. What they called Science Fiction. I had the usual emotional and economic ups and downs, went through the usual social scenes, tried the usual drugs, traveled to Turkey, Morocco and Amsterdam, pretended I wanted to give up ego, thought I was conquering the inner frontiers . . . just like millions of us were doing.

In the summer of '78 I was on the road in the States, belatedly doing the Kerouac bit. One blazing July day I hitched south from Ashland in Oregon, got a ride all the way to Sacramento through the burned haze of the San Joaquin Valley, took a bus and later that evening came to San Francisco with the vague intention of staying a few days then continuing south to Mexico.

But it was one of those San Francisco evenings, fog rolling in from the ocean to wrap itself round the multiple crests of the city, one of those strange misty summer evenings in the Bay when you might even find yourself shivering with the cool, an evening more atmospherically suited to the three witches in Macbeth than to a Big Mac burger . . . and I guess from the moment my bus came curving over the Bay Bridge and I saw those cloud-capped downtown towers and the curve of the waterfront docks, all so elegantly contained by the Bay, well, I knew I'd found the place I hadn't even consciously known I was seeking.

Within a few days I'd got a place to live, a room in a friendly international flophouse on Folsom and 20th—latino lowrider territory amid garages and broken glass and burrito takeaways down there on the hot side of town. I got a table and a chair and a mattress, put the typewriter on the table and started writing those tales which hadn't been working out during the previous two years I'd spent in poor and rainy Mid-Wales.

So . . . four months and a few days later it was the end of the eyar. I'd grown a bit sour with mental and physical cramp, with too many hours spent writing, and I needed a break. And on the night of the New Year, San Francisco's mythical sixties acid-rock band, the Grateful Dead, were scheduled to play what was to be the last rock concert at one of San Francisco's mythical sixties acid-rock venues: Winterland. The price of tickets for this big bash was pretty mythical too, $30 a head (breakfast included). Nonetheless, though muttering darkly about Money Vincit Omnia and how my next project would be called *GRAB IT!—A Manual for Personal Disimprovement in the Eighties,* I decided I was enough of an old hippy to buy it, and so with a group of friends and other strangers I went along to see the New Year in.

And it was there in Winterland, beneath the flashing revolutions of the giant crystal ball suspended above us, that I first saw Ralph M'Botu Kitaj.

And it was the first night of the last year of the seventies.

It's curious how few people can remember much about the seventies. It was the great nondecade of the century. Plenty happening, but almost all of it under the surface, under consciousness, deep in the ocean . . . but the ocean was getting wild as the eighties approached, and people, sensing this, were getting nervous again. Nobody talked about Peace and Love much any more, it was black light and leather and bodysnatchers now, it was occult ambition and disco andriods and fascist liberals who spoke in terms of meaningful relationships, and it was getting hard to tell who was going to do what next, and to whom, and why.

Many people had the end of the world on their brains.

Many people were looking for a war, or for someone to save them.

Enter Ralph M'Botu Kitaj . . . the world's new dealer-messiah . . .

In fact up till then Ralph M'Botu Kitaj had been too busy consolidating his wealth to spend much time calculating the effect of his style on other people. He'd been too concerned with himself, and was only just beginning to think in terms of deliberate big-time scene-making. He'd been in the Bay Area on and off during the previous three months, undergoing the Regression Therapy at Berkeley, antidoting the shock of that with a furious spate of transactions and takeovers. He'd had no time locally for the sort of fun and games for which he was already notorious on the Riveria; he was still formally in partnership with Ana Kanasay Kitaj and, though he'd gained a few mentions of his name in

Rolling Stone and in the *National Enquirer*, there had been many more references to him in the *Wall Street Journal*, *London Financial Times*, etc. And few people in San Francisco during early 1979 had much idea who he was, where he'd sprung from, or how he'd got rich.

In fact at that time Kitaj & Kitaj had investments in oil, arms, drugs, pornography, holography, transportation systems, electronics, nuclear power, biochemical research, and in a number of other lucrative areas. Their initial enterprise had been in Congo marijuana, subsequently heroin, then into the arms trade. Their business had snowballed rapidly. By January 1979, Ralph M'Botu was evidently the more powerful partner, and there were files on him and his doings held by many security organizations in many lands.

But Ralph M'Botu always knew how to cover his activities in the jungle. He knew when to stop, and when to start . . . and that New Year he was about ready to start. Recovering from the stress of the Regression Therapy, he was just beginning to check out San Francisco. He liked the city, and its beauty, and its energy, and he was thinking of buying a big old house on Nob Hill, to live in it, occasionally, and perform some . . . public educational functions . . . for a while . . . until public outrage got too hot even for his kind of money.

Edge-performances. Swinging-through-the-jungle-performances.

Ralph M'Botu Kitaj was ready to start playing the fool in a deadly serious way. The Regression Therapy had reminded him about his mortality. He had hits to make. But before hitting any place he liked to check it all out. He liked to choose his angle before making the kill, the leopard-claw was still round his neck, and that New Year's night he and Lenore had been through half a dozen other places before Winterland, to Fisherman's Wharf and the Hyatt Regency and Keystone Korner. He was sniffing the San Franciscan breeze, ready to start the Lunatic Dance, ready to stick pins in the Sleepwalker's Trance—but not yet out of any heightening or exalted motive; rather to establish the reality and basis of his disgust . . . for he was an angry and frightened man. He was trapped. He knew his motivations and present ambitions were nonsense, but he pursued them obsessively. He knew he was caught in a spiral of diminishing psychological options and returns. By treating this world and its inhabitants as a pile of shit he had got rich, but soon he'd be on top of this pile of shit, and then, he knew, he would have no more excuses. He would have to face himself again, rediscover whatever it was he'd once known, whatever it was he'd once been, whatever it was he was really meant to be doing. He would have to repay everything he owed, and he did not know how in hell he was going to do that.

Time was beginning to run short for him at the beginning of 1979.

Oddly, the Dead were playing a version of their classic piece, *Dark Star,* when I first saw him. Didn't mean much to me then, especially as it was almost five A.M. and I was almost asleep. But later I recalled this as another possible synchronicity so far as Sirius is concerned. Dark Star? The Dark Companion, Sirius B? I never did learn why the piece was so named.

Many people had already gone home. The floor of the hall wasn't so packed, there was empty space between the tables, but I was so dreamy where I sat that I'd been staring at the short sharp man in the orange djellabah at the next table for some minutes before I really began to notice him . . . to notice that I was noticing him, and to wonder why.

It was nothing obvious. Nothing external or immediately apparent. He was short, looked strong, with wiry build, dark tan, careless longish black hair, hook nose, thin lips, mid-thirties, sitting easily but giving the impression of impatience. European, I thought, though the djellabah and general appearance of him suggested the Middle East. With him was a blonde woman, beautiful in a severe way, hair long and straight, an inch or so taller than he. She wore jeans and a green smock, no makeup. They sat on their own at the table next to us. Or maybe I should say *he* sat on *his* own. Perhaps it was his distance, his reserve, that first drew me. The woman's right hand lay on his left arm, on the table . . . but he was separate from her too.

Yet, as I say, there was nothing obviously unusual.

Plenty of people there that night were curiously dressed. There were quite a few celebrities who emanated a more obvious charisma, who drew the eye more easily. But there was something about this man, something I sensed, and it bothered me, and I'd been staring at him some time before I knew what it was. The music was floating, Garcia's guitar lilting pure and high, and I was near sleep, in hypnagogic state, gazing at him and hardly realizing it, gazing at the strange, scarcely visible red and orange glow which seemed to flicker and fade about his head.

Then he sensed me. He looked at me, briefly, without interest. When his eyes caught me I woke up.

They were the sharpest eyes I'd ever seen. The deepest. His glance was utterly casual, but it pierced me so acutely that I had to look away, immediately. It was a shock. He turned away again.

Then I found my gaze turning, almost reluctantly, back to him.

He knew I was watching, I know it, but he did not look round again.

Several minutes later he and the woman got up and left. My eyes followed them out, until they were hidden in their exit by other people. I felt a bit spooked. I felt I'd been hooked, mesmerized, somehow enchanted. My heart was thumping. That red orange glow I'd watched flickering, playing round the head of the man . . . at first I'd assumed it was some oddly localized effect of the mutable lighting in the place. But not so. It stayed with him on his way out. It came from him.

In some states of mind, I knew, I could see the aura that people have.

Yet in this case I found it hard to believe. I'd never sensed such a vital and somehow confused and dangerous radiation.

Some years later, I saw a Kirlian photograph of Kitaj and recalled this first accurate perception I'd had of the man . . . his chaotic and uncontrolled vitality . . . the darker knots of ambiguous emotions surging through the aggression and energy and ambition of his unusually prominent corona . . . these, on the very threshold of my conscious perception, were what had attracted me.

It was a few weeks later, I recall, that I found out who he was. One day near the end of January I picked up a copy of the *San Francisco Examiner*. My attention was caught by the inner page photograph of the man I'd seen at Winterland. There was an article accompanying it which I read avidly.

The article said that some prominent local citizens were objecting to the purchase of an old mansion on Nob Hill by the entrepreneur, Ralph M'Botu Kitaj. They were objecting on the grounds of his known bad character. Reference was made (the article was written in a satirical style) not only to his flamboyant personal life (which had to be unduly flamboyant if people in San Francisco would object to it) but also to his alleged involvement with international Shady Deals and Commercial Conspiracies. It seemed that not only was he suspected of making huge profits via the Cambodian and French heroin connections, but that more recently and locally he'd been busy wrapping up billion-dollar deals in the Colombian marijuana trade. Colombian marijuana had become the number one turn-on for an estimated fifteen million U.S. users since the paraquat-poisoning of the Mexican crops by the U.S. and Mexican governments, and Kitaj apparently had got in early. The article insinuated without accusing. There was of course no clearly incriminating evidence—"of course," because Kitaj moved through a maze of front companies, and because he was already more than rich enough to buy the suppression of any evidence, at any level.

By 1978–79, marijuana was the fifth biggest industry in the U.S. so far as cash exchange was concerned. The tone of the article made it obvious that there would have been no objection to Kitaj moving onto Nob Hill had it merely been a matter of his business activities—business activity is business activity, and clean fingers are a matter of degree and public rectitude. The problem seemed to be that Kitaj was not the kind of person that any self-respecting society hostess could easily enter into her Blue Book . . . for he did not keep quiet about his criminality, his exploitations, his habits. He advertised them, openly. It was not so much that he was rumored to deal in hard drugs; it was his admission that he used them, himself. It was not so much that he and his partner were said to deal in guns, bombs, and other means of destruction; it seemed that he openly boasted that he had killed people, himself. His language, apparently, was often foul, blunt, and directly insulting. In addition, two of the various houses which he had bought in different parts of the world had burned down during the past year: the story was that he had burned them down himself. The *Examiner* article also mentioned the rumored occasion when, at a party in Paris a few months previously, he had not only stripped naked but then had proceeded to stand up on a table and piss on the pâté de foie gras, meanwhile bellowing a tirade against wealth and opulence.

In fact there were many such stories about him, hinted the *Examiner* article, of which those concerning his background and origins were the most extravagant. Evidently an uncommonly imaginative man, whatever else, and near the end of the article a well-known psychiatrist was quoted as commenting primly that Kitaj was "certainly unusual, if not actually abnormal . . . this man is very complex."

Finally mentioned was the boast Kitaj was rumored to have made that he meant to become "the richest man in the world by 1984."

I was intrigued, though rather against my will.

The objections must have failed, because Kitaj bought his house on Nob Hill, on Sacramento Street near Chinatown. Beginning in March he started to throw the parties which gave San Francisco something to talk about for the next few months. It seemed at some of them he was attempting to materialize the hysterical underworld atmosphere of a William Burroughs novel. For the first party, on the night of the spring equinox, he issued a large number of opulent R.S.V.P.'s to many of the Bay Area's leading lights—bankers, politicians, rock stars, artistes, columnists, professional Mill Valley elitists, and so on. He booked a famous band, a light show, professional caterers for the hordes. The theme of the party, which could be attended in fancy dress, was announced as "The Birth of Pan." News of some of what could be expected by way of the unexpected was leaked in certain quarters: he managed to engineer a phony black market demand for invitations, managed to make sure this got known about, thus boosting the interest value and insuring a full house. Great rocks of cocaine were hinted at, and wild pagan dancing in huge rooms electronically devised to seem like some ancient mountain moorland in another world—wind machines to send storms billowing through these rooms, all kinds of special effects and illusions which few had experienced. It was said that a menagerie of various animals had been installed, including a chimpanzee, baboon, and two leopards, and that the City Health Department had been bought into a blind eye. It was said that weird new cocktails which had never been tasted before would be presented, to the discriminating. There would be mazes and perplexities and "liberty-games" . . . whatever these were. It was all made most alluring.

"The Birth of Pan" . . . He left out the "ic" at the end of the announced title of the party theme.

On the night it happened—many full and various reports were

circulated afterwards; I read them all and agreed with none of them and none of them agreed with each other, which was probably what Kitaj had been trying to prove, if anything—on the night it happened Kitaj went to the streets north of Market, to the water and under the freeways, he gave out several hundred of his invitations to bums and gaunt-faced terminal cases.

Most of them came.

By midnight it was a riot anyway. Kitaj didn't really need to do what he did, but even then he was aiming to take things over the top.

The din was enormous. The effects were stupendous. With unaccustomed initiative I'd managed to find a way in.

For hours after that I was wandering lost like a babe in the woods through the worlds of the wealth of Ralph M'Botu Kitaj, through the crowded babbling rooms were the clash of bums and elite produced interesting hallucinations of communication, through a murmuring room like an underground grotto, past the green ghostly light of pulsing electric stalectites, to rooms of tables carrying anything you wanted to eat, drink, smoke, or otherwise cram into your system. Then a womb-pink room with an enormous red plastic phallus erected in the bare middle of it. The very worst of taste, etc. Kitaj could not at that time be considered a friend of the Woman's Movement: his approach to Pan was distinctly, deliberately male-aggressive-chauvinistic. Yet this big prick turned out to be another of his surprises: it was flimsy, like a balloon, the plastic not very thick, and quite a few outraged people, men as well as women, tried deflating it with nail scissors, whatever. I hear when it was finally punctured a grandiose drumroll was triggered by the deflation, the plastic slithered down into the shape of a bleeding heart form which the blood dripped slowly, and Shylock's voice whined out, "If you prick me, do I not bleed?"

Beyond this strange room I have vague impressions of entering new dimensions, some wild place on a mountainside, pipes skirling, dervish dancers whirling, and drums that beat the patterns of the heart. What happened here nobody can precisely tell, because everyone found their own worlds in there—it seems Kitaj had hired the dancers from Indonesia, their whirling interaction was mesmeric and the drums did not let up, there was an endless attraction in there and more and more people spilled in, all moving on a contact high, taken from themselves, in whatever element suited them best, so that I too found myself dancing (most unusual), moving on the numberless contrary complementary rhythms all available, moving on the wild windy mountainside as the day grew dark and the moon began its rise up the eastern wall, gliding through hundreds of other ecstatic tactile dancers, spinning like a cossack on some exhilarating Rimsky-Korsakov steppe, drawn by the drums and the pipes of hope into rites of spring's celebration with hundreds of people moving and weaving in vast mobile mosaic, not touching save on purpose, save according to the instructions of the music—one mind and soul and then—

Kitaj appeared at the door with a machine gun.

The music stopped as if it had been sliced in half. It had been arranged, but hundreds of people didn't know that. The music vanished.

Disorientation. Stunned silence.

Then the crazy voice, catching all eyes to Kitaj.

"Violence!" he screamed, gesturing with the machine gun. "We live in a very sick time, my friends. Do you think we'll live to see the New Age?"

Then he started firing.

They were blanks, but who knew that? Ripped from the Rites of Spring into clichés of modern mass murder. The last few months had seen the cyanide suicide of Jim Jones and the Peoples Temple down in Guyana, the assassination of San Francisco's mayor and a gay supervisor by a demented perfect All-American Boy, children going ape with guns, old people opening up from the rooftops, photographs of Rosalynn Carter shaking hands with John Wayne Gacy, the man alleged to have fucked and killed thirty-two men and boys—nothing seemed impossible. In about half a second flat I was on the floor along with just about everyone else. The ugly clatter, reverberating and enormously loud, seemed to go on a long time. I nearly shat myself. There was a lot of screaming, writhing, wriggling. Some few people stayed on their feet, hadn't moved—couldn't or wouldn't. "There was a man who stood there in front of me, shouting, baring his breast," recalled Kitaj years later. "He *wanted* me to blow him right into the headlines. I saw his face after I'd tracked the gun across him. He looked so disappointed I felt like apologizing that it wasn't for real."

Kitaj was lucky. There were no fatal heart attacks. Many

people said how crass it was—afterwards. In later years, of
course, it was considered by some as an early statement of what
later in the eighties became known as the Black Hole Joke. But
in the Black Hole Joke Shows, however, horribly, Kitaj was
venting his awareness, his own sense of horror—at this party he
was just shooting people with his spite and his power, and it was
not pleasant.

When the clatter of the machine gun stopped, it was followed
immediately by the sickening banality of huge laughter, amplified and distorted, pouring from a dozen hidden speakers as we
slowly picked ourselves up off the illusory side of the illusory
mountain.

The drums started in mid-beat, and the Indonesian dancers, as
though nothing had happened, as though a slice had been moved
out of time.

Kitaj was gone.

He was on his way to the airport already, Lenore with him, no
time to lose on new low tricks. I left his house with a sense of
unreality and pain. Like everyone else who'd been in that room, I
felt thereafter some kind of emotional relationship with Ralph
M'Botu Kitaj, which was disturbing, as it seemed that the man
cared for nothing but himself.

The machine gun event, I later learned, was what he called a
"liberty-game."

During the next month Ralph M'Botu Kitaj busied himself in
other parts of his global sucker-web, though first he went to
Warsaw, trying to check on his origins—as mentioned earlier.
His lack of success in this mission was one of the factors that
soured him into the uncompromising and vicious misanthropy of
the next deal he set up—what in 1984 became public as "The
Cold Cure Deal," of which more anon. Then to Tunis, where
Ana Kanasay had just sewn up the Tunisian olive oil market. Ana
Kanasay was too active for Ralph M'Botu's liking. Time the old
man was persuaded to retire. The public brawl between the two
men while visiting a Berber cliff village as guests of the Tunisian
government received prominent attention in San Francisco. In
Kitaj's absence the lawsuits were flying—so were the rumors of a
second party. Meanwhile the man was in Bombay—Ulan Bator—
Formosa—Manila—Sydney. Obviously he couldn't stop wheel-
ing. Obviously he had some kind of craziness. Rumor said he

would be back in SF for the second party at the end of April.
There was a lot of protest and angry talk. There was a lot of
reluctant fascination; there were many readers for the newspaper
diggings in the lurid goldmine of Ralph M'Botu's supposed past.
In particular, a series of articles purporting to cover the years of
growth of Kitaj & Kitaj between 1966 and 1979.

The articles were Hollywood, just what many of us could
believe—the sheer fantasy of reality, much stranger than fiction.
Myself, I'd reached a point of abandoning the fact/fiction barrier.
Whatever I could imagine, someone else was doing, had done, or
was trying to do. We were all following extraordinary patterns
and curves, imaginations springing into reality . . . melody . . .
or mass murder. There was not much control or comprehension,
since it was all out on some kind of edge. Anything is possible.

I read all this stuff and heard all the rumors with enthusiasm
and misgiving. I felt somehow that my interest had been annexed
by act of another will. Had I known then that I was to be living
cheek-by-jowl with this man for much of the next twelve years, I
would have left town right away.

"THIS IS NOT NECESSARILY THE TRUTH ABOUT
RALPH M'BOTU KITAJ!" announced the lead-off disclaimer to
every one of the articles I read. "It is an account gathered from
stories published in other papers round the world. This man has
not simply sprung out of nowhere. He has a past, like us all.
However, the early years of Mr. Kitaj are in doubt. There are
stories—myths, we would guess—which might make you seriously doubt his value to any community.

"But what are the facts?"

Nobody knew what the facts were—at least before 1966.
Kitaj's lawyers were hot and heavy if anyone started broadcasting
stuff like the story that he was the man who'd killed Patrice
Lumumba in the Congo in January 1961. The same went for
anything else he'd done or hadn't done up to 1967, including the
circumstances of his meeting with Ana Kanasay Kitaj . . . which
we'll come to soon. There were no stories, or hundreds of stories
that all contradicted. The articles began to unravel the confusion
only at a point when the partnership had already been formed,
telling how, with Ana Kanasay's contacts and capital, with Ralph

M'Botu's junglesense sharp-eyed muscle-hustle talents, they sharked in on the marijuana business in 1967.

To begin with they'd cut in on the middle. Before long they spread both ways. By 1969 they had growers in the Congo/Zaire and sellers all through Europe. By 1970 they'd sent feelers of control all the way down to street level in several large cities. This proved premature. Their home patch wasn't safe. With one hand they were paying their farmers, with the other they were bribing the police and military not to kill their farmers. It was unstable. As quick as they could they converted their currencies into Swiss banks and hired the best brokers (all of them personally checked out by Ralph M'Botu with his hypnotic eyes) who invested wisely in companies making guns, bombs, missiles, etc., and at the same time they began to diversify into heroin.

Their affairs began looking healthy, to them. They started living the Good Life. But then, it is said, the CIA moved in on their backyard.

Kitaj & Kitaj returned quickly and very discreetly from Europe to the threatened heartlands of their wealth. They found soldiers strafing their farmers and burning their crops. They took immediate steps to find out what was going on. They learned that the CIA and several other well-known secret agencies had been taking a friendly interest in Zaire just recently. It seemed that the new government was interested in acquiring an atomic capacity, plus a fair amount of direct cash support, from East or West, and that the CIA had got in first, promising that something might be possible . . . not officially, mind, the regulations are pretty tight, but . . . under the counter (these CIA agents were alleged to have said), maybe we know someone who might be able to help you out. Can't sell this stuff so easily back home because of the antinuclear bullshit. But you have to do it like we say. If anyone finds out, you say you did the deal with the Russians. And first you burn down that maryjane and do those other things we asked you. Then maybe you've got a deal. Maybe.

Now the experience gained and investments made by Kitaj & Kitaj paid off. They worked fast, dressed sharp, took their lives and their wealth in their hands, they came to a committee of generals and offered them a nuclear technology—in half the time and at half the price demanded by the CIA middlemen.

Meanwhile the generals were getting dubious about the way the CIA were interfering, making demands. Too many agents of too many governments trying to pull the strings, grab the pie, sell an ideological tunnel reality. So the generals sat down to dicker with Kitaj & Kitaj, who were uneasily aware of the guards all about, guards armed with businesslike Russian Kalashnikovs.

"We can arrange delivery of the major components for a lightweight water reactor within six months," promised Ana Kanasay, lying through his teeth with a charming smile.

"Can we make bombs with such a reactor?" demanded one of the generals.

"The plutonium extraction process is more expensive," said Ralph M'Botu, adding hastily, "but we have contacts in the U.S. Department of . . ."

"You have two weeks to provide proof. If we do business, you will pay us also 25% of your marijuana profits. Meanwhile, do not leave the country."

Of course Kitaj & Kitaj could not provide proof. They had no nuclear contacts then. But they got two weeks of breathing space. In that time the tide turned. It seems that the CIA were kicked out, that interest in a nuclear reactor was dropped, that Kitaj & Kitaj were allowed to keep half their business . . . but that they sold up and moved out of the Congo as fast as they could. That was about the time the CIA became popular villains with dirty noses, about the time they and ITT were busy overthrowing the Marxist government in Chile.

The newspaper emphasized that there was no proof for this tale, justifying the printing of it in terms of its popular currency, a demonstration in popular belief, a tale of the luck of Kitaj & Kitaj—evidence that they were in tune with the tide race of these rapacious times. For, following this period in the early seventies, they had not looked back. They'd bought themselves in, raced horses at Ascot and Kentucky, been received by the British Queen at Buckingham Palace in gratitude for unexplained services to the British economy. They'd moved into oil, opened offices in Abu Dhabi, by the late seventies had several tankers ploughing through the oceans. They'd sponsored charities and opened sales points not only through the so-called free world, but also in Peking, Moscow, Mecca. They lived rich and separate, and so did their hangers-on. By 1979 they had sewn up a lot . . . but relations between Kitaj & Kitaj were not good.

Ana Kanasay now desired respectability, even gentility. He

was said to be increasingly alarmed by Ralph M'Botu's violent extravagance.

Ralph M'Botu was said to be getting contemptuous and impatient with the older partner. So the recent brawl in Tunisia suggested.

This is as far as the newspaper mythology went at the time. There was a lot missed or insinuated. Nothing was said of the Regression Therapy in Berkeley during the previous few months. Possibly they knew nothing of it. Perhaps it didn't fit the image they wanted to establish—already, the mystical image.

It is noticeable how, throughout Kitaj's public career, *fact* was always forced into second place. So far in this account, *fact* has taken such a beating that one might conclude it did not exist. Nor does it, in the sense of any fixed or solid interpretations of events with which everyone can agree. Yet, very frequently, events which did occur have been thoroughly distorted by later mythologizing, and this is sometimes unfortunate. The *facts*, where they occur, are not necessarily as lurid and dramatic as the fantasies, not necessarily so much in tune with the desires of the collective unconscious, but on occasion they are more demonstrative and psychologically educational.

The second San Francisco party is a case in point.

Ten years later, at the height of the very lucrative Kitaj mythomania, this event was made the basis of the smash-hit musical, *Rich Man Poor Man,* which by now would have broken all box-office records if not for the curb put on all Kitaj material in most countries since the Discorporation, or Transformation.

Rich Man Poor Man is a composite of many fantasy-memories, neatly wrapped up in an eclectic sound-structure that manages to call to mind disco, Stockhausen, and the Ten Commandments all at once. It is pure fantasy cast at an archetypal level. Its casting calls for ectoplasmic actors to play the dead shades of Jack London, John F. Kennedy, Isadora Duncan, Aleister Crowley, Sid Vicious, Sylvia Plath, Pigpen of the early Grateful Dead, Mao Tse Tung, Marilyn Monroe, Janis Joplin, Rudolph Valentino, Trashman, Dick Tracy, the Fabulous Furry Freak Brothers, and a host of others, fictional-factual. Kitaj himself plays Mephistopheles and Faust alternately; Lenore is portrayed (she refused to appear in the movie) as Lilith and also as Eve. In concept and style,

Rich Man Poor Man is similar to another fairly recent mythic self-portrayal—*Renaldo and Clara,* Bob Dylan's 1978 projection.

Kitaj conceived it, put most of it together personally, cast himself in it as the Diabolic Dualist, the Demon King, who proceeds to spike all the opposition by the process of Divide and Rule. In it, he shows very clearly how this ancient power game works. You cut between people, break up their unity by exploiting their doubts and suspicions, get them to give you their energy, sell yourself to all of them as the only possible solution. This system works as well for Dracula as it does for anyone else who pursues paths of denial.

The theme of *Rich Man Poor Man* is Living Death, the material trap, and what it does to us. The music is wild and scary, but has a great beat. Much of the dialogue is occult, apocalyptic, but also witty, and conducted in down-on-the-street language which everyone can understand.

It is set in San Francisco during April 1979, thus presumably is supposed to represent the second party.

It is nothing like what happened at the second party. It is not really anything like any of the parties, though Kitaj told me that some of the dialogue is based on recordings he made of people at all the parties, especially the third one, the occult one, held in June 1979.

Though how can I say? I wasn't there at the second party.

It happened the night Kitaj flew in from Bangkok. It was all prearranged; all serious objections to it following the first bash had been overcome, though lawyers' fees had run pretty high.

On this occasion it seemed that the stakes had been upped. The invitations were mailed out to random phone-book addresses, a thousand of them. With the invitations came legal forms which had to be signed and returned with the R.S.V.P.'s. Signatures bound all guests to remain within the (locked) mansion until dawn, also absolved Ralph M'Botus Kitaj of any responsibility for whatever might happen to them while at the party. Booby traps and creepy trips were promised, and hired guards to keep the guests in and gatecrashers out. Phones and all lines of communication with the outside world were going to be disconnected, and guests would have to submit to being frisked at the entrance, to ensure that nobody was carrying anything that might shoot, transmit, record, or otherwise act sneaky.

"THIS IS A REELY-SHOW!" announced the invitation in bold black Gothic. "YOU CAN'T GO TILL YOU COME!"

It sounded dangerous, mysterious. This time the black market was genuine. There were cases of invitations exchanging hands at gunpoint. There were rumors that a renowned English New Wave rock band, famed for its explicit political obscenities, had been booked by Kitaj to abuse and infuriate the guests.

The invitations got into the hands of those who really wanted them.

Two hours before the party was due to start, Kitaj and Lenore landed at the international airport. There were police and press and a large crowd.

There was also a would-be assassin, waiting with his hands in his pockets, in the crowd behind the custom barrier. He never had a chance. Kitaj had a telepathic alertness to that sort of thing, could scent danger a mile off—it was why he was still alive. Long before Kitaj appeared, his men (never obviously with him) had got through customs and spiked the man Kitaj had described to them—hit him directly, physically, taken the gun from him, turned him over to the police. Later Kitaj told me this sort of thing went on all the time, and that it wasn't always so easy. Even then, plenty of people wanted to kill him.

Later still I found this out for myself.

It took an hour after the flight landed for Kitaj and Lenore to get into the city, to the big house on Sacramento. The street was packed. There were thousands of people, hundreds of police, a lot of motorbikes, a lot of black leather, chains, and shaven heads. Chaos. It took them half an hour to get into the house.

Inside, by contrast, everything was calm, everything was ready.

The musicians had been smuggled in earlier. They were waiting in the bare rooms to which they'd been appointed. Likewise the hundred Rentacops, who were standing around uncomfortably, twirling their sticks, scratching their heads, looking round at the strange arrangements and wondering what was going to happen . . . wondering if the five hundred bucks a head they were being paid for ten hours was going to be worth it.

Kitaj arrived with his small entourage. Lenore went to take a bath. Food was distributed and everyone was briefed. Kitaj was, as usual, full of energy. He checked the preparations. He checked every room. Every window had been curtained and shuttered. Windows with possible access to the fire escape had been booby trapped with alarms and with servoelectric arms which would grab anyone trying to get out. He interviewed the ten quartets of musicians, made sure they understood their instructions, told them the precautions which had been taken in case any of them might be attacked.

They smiled dubiously, wondering if the thousand dollars a head they were being paid for ten hours was going to be worth it.

The doors were opened at ten o'clock. The Rentacops went into action as the crowd surged forward. For a time all traffic in the street was stopped. For over an hour the Rentacops were busy with crowd control, keeping out the gatecrashers, filtering through people who held genuine invitations . . . also some of those who held forgeries. Kitaj had told them to let in up to five hundred people with fake invitations. Thus by eleven o'clock nearly fifteen hundred people had been let in, all expecting riot and mayhem.

Prompt at eleven the doors were shut. Kitaj told the guards to start keeping an eye on the guests, some of whom already wanted to get out.

Not because of terror, but because of boredom.

Kitaj had conned them all.

They'd come through the doors expecting bizarre marvels. They'd spread tense through the rooms of the mansion, meeting only their own reflections, wondering when this joke of bare rooms was to be transformed into terror, beauty, and strangeness. They'd circulated, more and more in every room, many bombed to begin with, ready in machine-gun alertness for the floor to open up at any point and swallow them—anything. Many professional paranoids had a great time that first hour or so, especially the police and other investigators among the guests.

But nothing happened.

Just the bare rooms—nowhere to sit, nothing to eat, drink, look at, play with, listen to . . . except for the weird sleepifying music that came from ten rooms consecutive to one another on the second floor—in each room the same dirge played by what looked like the same four elderly balding black-jacket-and-tie classical musicians.

Most of the musicians got very uneasy when the guests came to stare at them, examine them curiously, at first without rancor. Kitaj had given them plain instructions. They were to play the third movement of Beethoven's last quartet, the sixteenth, over and over again and all together until he told them to stop. In the event of threat of attack by enraged guests, he had told them affably, they should thumb the red-button pocket transmitter on loan to each of them. This would cause diversionary effects, also summon the guard.

In fact there were no attacks until well after midnight.

This surprised him, Kitaj later told me in Ireland. He said he'd had a bet on with Lenore that the fights would start by midnight. She'd said the only fights would be those he picked himself. "I guess she was right," he admitted. "She chose the music. Maybe it was too soothing . . ."

"That music's an enchanting as Lethe," I said. "You could only fight it as deliberate angry reaction to the peace it brings, equating the peace with death and rejecting death. You thought more people would fight."

"Maybe." He darted his glance. "I wanted to see what would happen. The violent publicity to attract the violent—then lock them in with the peace that passeth all understanding."

"You overdid it with too many warnings of a con," I said. "It was really just company for you, it was *your* reaction to the music."

"That music . . . it scares me . . . in a funny way." He looked at me, uncertain. "It goes deep. I can't just float in it . . . it takes you down, it opens you up and dissolves you . . . you're almost gone in its depths . . . then you see something in front of you—your door, your gate, your death, your hope of . . ."

He stopped there. He shut off. He could not yet admit the hope. He'd trapped himself into admitting a painful contradiction in himself.

"Whatever it is you hope for . . . ." he added harshly.

"Transfiguration," I said quickly, "Evolution, Transformation, Apotheosis, our common growth into the Garden, into the Song of The Spheres."

"Why do you give me crap like that?" he demanded, eyes hard.

"To remind you what you're trying to remind yourself about."

"What the fuck do you know about that?"

"You show it in everything you do and say," I said reasonably.

"That's what *you* tell me. My Higher Self, and all that bullshit. Why is it you that tells me this stuff, and not other people?"

"Because I'm the person you hired to keep telling you."

"You mean you think you're my conscience?" he sneered. "You think I asked you to come along to be a part of me that I've lost?"

I remember then I had a sense of vertiginous fear with regard to my own autonomy, my own identity. Somehow, Kitaj had swallowed me into becoming . . . an extension of his own internal war. I'd been hired as Devil's Advocate to his self-doubt. Seeing the way he looked at me, so mesmerically, so mockingly, I was suddenly afraid. This happened to me from time to time in his company. On this occasion, I drew back physically, showing my fear.

He saw this. He laughed.

"Don't worry," he said. "I'm not trying to suck your soul dry. I'm not trying to steal you from yourself."

"You don't know what you're trying to do," I muttered. "Sometimes you just don't accurately estimate the effect you have on people. You crash through every obstacle in search of the answer to your obsession; you don't think or feel for the people you knock over on the way. Those parties in San Francisco, they were for your benefit, weren't they? They were all in your head. You were trying to check yourself out, and using thousands of people for your cast. That Beethoven thing—you wanted those people to fall through themselves into violence. You wanted to prove to yourself that everyone else is just as dangerous to themselves as you are to yourself. You wanted to stop feeling lonely. You were disappointed that so many of them actually got off on the peace, on the beauty. Most of those people showed you something, didn't they? You'd angled for the most violent spectrum of society, you wanted another riot so you could drown and justify your own frustrations . . . but most of them accepted that the joke was on them . . . and they even listened when you got up and started your monologue about how you met Ana Kanasay in jail. They listened; they *liked* the story you told, all the weird Tarzan stuff. It made you more of a character. They didn't get mad; you got mad, with yourself; they told people outside; the story became part of the myth. You tried to tell yourself it was what you wanted, but it wasn't, not really, it only made you more lonely, removed you further from real communication with yourself or anyone else. It didn't work out as you'd hoped. I think you wanted people to get mad with you; you wanted them to find you a disgusting egotistic bore.''

"But everything you tried, people bought it, they cheered.''

I was furious. It pleased him. He grinned.

"I like it when you get angry,'' he said. "It's the only time you come out and tell me what you really think. Usually you're so goddamn polite and servile. Why don't you get angry more often? Listen—I'll double your pay if you can promise to get angry and honest on a regular, dependable basis. How about it?''

"Sometimes,'' I told him flatly, "I can see why you dislike yourself so much. You only get off on the misery of others.''

I was trying to hurt, but at the time it was true.

So the Beethoven party didn't work out quite as energetically as Kitaj had hoped. The wild boys he had lured with such pains into his snare did not go berserk when confronted by endless repetition of the third movement. There were arguments with the musicians, but few fights. The red buttons were hit only twice, bringing the guards running, setting up an intolerable electronic scream which dazed guests and musicians alike. There had been some struggles at the door with the Rentacops, a few people had tried to force a way out, there was one broken window . . . but Kitaj had overdone the arrangements. There was too little incentive to riot. Not everyone was as complicated as himself. Most people, accepting they'd been suckered, accepting they were in for a night of boredom if they tried to stay awake, sprawled down on the floors as best they could.

Thus the deep dreamy River of Lethe flowed through the bare halls of Kitaj's house . . . and by two in the morning almost the only disturbance in it was Kitaj himself. Silence and Beethoven reigned until he could stand it no longer. He began stalking from room to room, waking people up, barking angry questions how come they were all asleep. He provoked a few fights. Finally he pulled himself together and changed the focus. He stopped in the middle of a crowded room. He told the musicians to stop playing, and without preamble he started the untold tale of how he'd met Ana Kanasay Kitaj in a prison of the country then known as Rhodesia, now Zimbabwe.

It was a wild tale. He was a natural storyteller. He was angry, on fire, he was shaking loose, he ranted like a shaman, he peddled incredibility, but belied it by the fierceness of his eyes

. . . which, some said later, caught you if you so much as
thought a hint of disbelief. Soon he had everyone crammed in
and listening. Later I read and heard several eyewitness accounts
of Kitaj's mesmeric passion on this occasion.

"I didn't really want to listen," a friend told me afterwards.
"Just wanted to sleep with that music—but he cut out the music,
he just . . . *hooked* everyone in. He believed it. Either that or
his act was perfect. He put it so deep into me that after a while I
thought what he was telling had happened to me. Some kind of
ability of mass hypnosis. Got me so stoned I forgot I was sober.
But it was scary. It got so I felt I'd have to listen until he stopped
talking. I felt he was holding me there. I started wanting to
object."

This feeling grew common. People who heard Kitaj tell this
tale on this and other occasions usually ended up feeling battered.
For one thing, in it he vented his feelings against Ana Kanasay.
For another, at certain main points of the tale, which never
varied, his passion became terrifying to some . . . though at
other points he often added or subtracted minor details of color
and romantic invention . . . which hardly disguised the rawness
of his sense of betrayal.

"What was that about Tarzan?" I asked my friend disbelievingly.

"Don't know." He shook his head. "Says Tarzan betrayed
him."

I laughed. "And Godzilla saved him, right?"

In his alleged soul-baring at this party and on other occasions,
Kitaj said nothing of the years before he came to Salisbury. At
this time and for some years to come he had referred to his early
life only when apparent evidence and acquaintants came out of
the blue of the past—for example, the Marthe Hébert interview
published in *Paris-Match* in 1983. He said very little at all about
his life before the loss of faith, before the thumbs-down on
Ruwenzori.

He never mentioned Njeru, far less Iloshabiet.

Before the Disappearance he said nothing to anyone but Lenore
and Ana Kanasay of his doings in the six and a half years
between Ruwenzori and Salisbury.

When the myth was beginning to roll worldwide in the early
eighties, many people claiming to have known him between 1959
and 1966 came forward. They were mostly from Kenya, Uganda,

and Zaire, and they were mostly on the make. Remi, possibly Kitaj's son, has been mentioned. There were many others who came claiming he was their father. His lawyers were kept very busy at this time, dealing with these and other claims that people put upon him. His response varied. He insisted on meeting everyone who came forward claiming to have known him, or to have indulged in acts with him, or to have observed him indulging in acts. Many of the claims had more than a touch of the flavor of blackmail. But none of them provided good independent corroborative evidence. If they did, he probably bought them off. It's hard to tell. He met them all personally, and his reactions seemed arbitrary. Some he kicked out, others he paid off, others still he took out on the town and spent time with, admitting old friendships, plying the drink and roaring with laughter.

The strange thing was, most of the people he kicked out seemed to be the people who really had known him, while the ones he admitted and paid and had a good time with seemed (to met at any rate) to be the obvious rogues whose stories were filled with holes.

But not so strange, really. He paid liars with liar's gold . . . or sometimes he rejected them . . . and vice versa with those who told the truth . . . so much so that nobody else could tell. The myth and his legal security were preserved. The claimants mostly contradicted each other; Kitaj advertised the claims but not his own inner reactions, so that the mosaic of his myth was increased as many tales about him grew out of the public imagination.

It was not until late in our relationship that he gave me a very brief summary of this period.

1959–1966.
Degradation. Prisoner of a warring self.
Was he the man who killed Lumumba on 17 January 1961? Henry Kaninga, one of Kasavubu's Katangese secessionist forces, apparently one of the men who kidnapped and later saw to the death of the leader whose vision was too farsighted, came forward in public in 1981 to claim he recognized Ralph M'Botu Kitaj as the brother soldier who had actually done the dark act.

Kitaj denied it pointblank and to me he would later say nothing about it at all. He would only say that this time was the worst—after Ruwenzori, in the Congo, in the blind angry heartstruck years. He said he felt like an unsheathed sword all the time. He said that bad luck and trouble followed him everywhere, that rumors accrued to the various names he had to use, that there were times he had to lie low, other times he had to move very fast. He said it was like Mau Mau all over again, "only it was happening inside me, through me."

Whatever he did in the Congo, he left that land as fast as he'd left Ruwenzori. He no longer had Njeru's divining sandals. He'd left those on Ruwenzori along with his hope and much else. He came back among the Dodoth. But he gave out a dangerous negative energy; he was brooding, angry, and quick to violence in easy offended pride. He provoked fights, and soon he was driven out. And early the next year he was hanging onto the edge of a Turkana encampment. He witnessed the murder and torture when Lieutenant Amin came with his soldiers.

"I got away, but I was shot in the leg. Splintered bone. It festered, I nearly lost it. Idi wasn't court-martialed—politically inadvisable with Ugandan independence so close, and him one of the only two black officers in the King's African Rifles."

He spoke to me vaguely of a refuge he found until his leg was healed. What happened after that, between 1962 and 1966, is not clear. The stories, the claims of others, and his own short account are very tangential, impressionistic. He said he looked for Njeru, but didn't really want to find him, and his wish was granted . . . for he never saw the *murogi* again . . . in earthly form. It seems he spent time in Mombasa, hustling affairs that never worked out, deep into opium, too confused and bitter to gain any perspective or purpose. He said he had no idea how long he was there, except that just before he left he heard on the radio a song by the Beatles—"Can't Buy Me Love"—which was first released, I remember, about April 1964. So M'Botu was probably in Mombasa at least until summer 1964, leaving on a new quest before his twenty-second birthday. For by then he was desperate.

He went looking for Greystoke. That is what he told me.

For nearly two years he wandered over Africa, seeking the only man (or image) he could still admire. Through Somalia, Ethiopia, lower Egypt, as far west as Nigeria, through Cameroun to Uganda, down towards Tanzania . . .

Towards Rhodesia . . .

Ralph M'Botu did not reach Salisbury until some months after

the Smith government's Unilateral Declaration of Independence
on 11 November 1965.

Many people would add, "Nor did he arrive in his right
mind."

He never retracted his apparent belief. To the end he insisted
that the man he'd identified as Greystoke *was* Greystoke, alias
Tarzan. Perhaps it was all a cynical fantasy, a deep trick he
played on himself—to tell himself that all heroes were dead,
devolved into ordinary beings with ordinary, corrupt, self-
interested motives . . . like himself. Maybe. There are many
theories available. That M'Botu desperately sought a father figure. That he just meant to embarrass the man with a blackmail
demand in which he alone believed. That (as usual) it never
happened at all, or that he was crazed by the devil, by drugs, by
anything you like. In fact Salisbury records state that a man
named M'Botu was held in jail on suspicion of attempting an
assassination. The intended victim and the circumstances are not
made clear.

In his rant at the party Kitaj indignantly denied such bloody
motives.

Likewise he denied insanity on his part.

He denied it, yet appeared to demonstrate it.

With apparently furious conviction he told his guests that for
years M'Botu had sought the man whose real-life exploits had
given birth to the myth of Tarzan.

Years later he admitted to me that thought of Greystoke had
not in fact returned to his mind for a long time after Ruwenzori.
"He came back to me in Mombasa," he said, "when I was using
a lot of opium." Which at any rate seems believable as a source.
But it does not explain how he maintained such a belief. He was
not, after all, smoking opium all the time. Even now I suspect
that the entire Greystoke affair was a private joke, never admitted
as such—something he maintained as a continuing comment on
the ridiculousness of life.

I asked him once: "If Greystoke obsessed you, then what
about the Old Woman and the Voice? Did they never appear
during those years?"

His grin was taut. "You know they belong to a different order
of things."

"You mean they're fact, to you, and Greystoke is only a fiction?"

"You're a dirty duelist, Johnny." His grin stretched wider. "You want to spike everything on your fork and divide into two, into opposites, into categories of explanation. For someone trying to sell me on mythreality you're not doing so good. Tarzan Lives!"

Thus he maintained at the party in San Francisco. With burning eyes, he spoke of the dream which had told him that the man he sought, whom he wished to respect, had grown tired of the jungle and had faked his death during World War II . . . and that this was the man who subsequently, with new identity, as premier of the rebel Rhodesian government, had announced UDI to the world.

It is hard to imagine any connection between Tarzan and Ian Smith, but this is the discovery that Kitaj claimed as the truth.

"Some people started laughing when he said this," another of the people at the party told me. "He glared so mean that they shut up. It sounded serious."

He told, speaking with intensity, of how M'Botu had gained clandestine entrance to Greystoke at his office desk. This was in April 1966, most likely. But sadly, when the strapping young savage met the harassed politician, it did not work out. M'Botu was seized and slung into jail.

Kitaj told his guests he understood Smith's motives.

"There's evidence that one of Greystoke's uncles was Jack the Ripper," he told them. "This knowledge haunted him all his life. He was scared he had bad blood, and that one day it was going to get too much, he was going to go all atavistic and start slashing and killing the wrong sort of people. It's not mentioned in the stories, but he became obsessed by this fear, and finally it dragged him down from jungle nobility to clenched-teeth scenes of white supremacy. He faked his own death during the war and took on the identity of another RAF pilot who actually in fact did die—the original Ian Smith. It worked pretty well. Nobody suspected him . . . until I turned up.

"I turned up at the wrong time. He wasn't in a good mood. He'd heard that the UN Security Council was about to ratify the oil sanctions which the British government had slapped on his rebel government. Maybe at no time did he want to be recognized for who he was—but certainly not then. He was armored and defensive. I alarmed him the way I evaded his guards so easily and came stalking right into his living room. I was all muddy and barefoot and I must have looked pretty wild—hardly even white—in fact just the way he looked before he got tired of being aped by all that clean-cut bullshit Johnny Weissmuller stuff, before he settled down to respectable modern statecraft. I managed to get about half a dozen words out of my mouth, starting to explain who I was and who he was and how I knew—but before I could get any further he'd hit the panic button and his men were all over me.

"I put up quite a fight. I was furious. He betrayed me! I was thrown into jail—worked over and thrown into solitary—and in time he'd have had me killed on the quiet, I know it, only it didn't work out that way."

This treacherous betrayal by Greystoke was the last straw. It deepened Ralph M'Botu's already deep despair and anger. His violent cynicism began thickening into the desire for revenge on the whole human race. For months he rotted alone in prison, without light, without exercise, without any companionship . . . and he made a vow . . .

"I decided," he told his guests in a very sharp staccato voice, "that if ever I got out of that stinking hole alive I'd let nothing, I mean nothing, ever get in my way again. Not even the ideals I'd thought I still held. They were all just ways to trip up, ways for people to club you over the head. I'd been through the whole thing; I'd seen just how people are; I'd seen I was just as bad but maybe a lot sharper. So what would you do? Seek *nirvana?* I made a vow to myself it was time to stop losing—I was going to get out and get to the top of this bloody pile of betrayed ideals we call the world today. And that's what I'm doing now. I'm going to the top. I'm going to do it. I'm going to taste and hold and own it all. Then I'll find out . . . what?"

He hurried on to tell how the chance to escape came.

For months he festered alone. Meanwhile the jail was filling up until it became necessary to start doubling up on solitary cells. There was opposition to the new Rhodesia not only outside the country. Yet not every new arrival was black and political. One stinking hot night in December 1966, M'Botu's destiny was suddenly pitched into his cell in the shape of Ana Kanasay Kitaj, a middle-aged Tamil merchant imprisoned for the murder of a competitor.

Ralph M'Botu's account of this meeting varied while his partner still lived, but took fixed form thereafter, and I have reconstructed it according to the version in *Liar's Gold*.

"It was my cursed enthusiasm," it seems the fat new arrival complained when M'Botu hoarsely demanded to know his crime. Sullen, the merchant paced uneasily round the small dark cell, M'Botu's eyes glowering on him. M'Botu's eyes were adjusted to the perpetual dimness, but for a time Ana Kanasay could see nothing at all. Yet he could sense the odd, powerful, dangerous magnetism of M'Botu. "I loved Ali like a brother," he continued, gesticulating as he stalked about, "but we got too excited in our efforts to corner the market from each other. Such a good game—but one in which the blood grows very hot. I have been an idiot! Life will be so dull without Ali to compete with!"

The merchant needed to talk. M'Botu needed human contact. They fed each other, immediately, and M'Botu was amazed to find his introspection penetrated. He had thought that never again would he find interest in another human being, but now he heard his rusty unused voice asking Ana Kanasay a question.

"What did you do?"

"I cut off his head." There was mournful pleasure in Ana Kanasay's smooth voice. Slowly he sank down in the corner of the filthy cell opposite Ralph M'Botu and wiped his sweating brow. "We were arguing—he was undercutting me on the sale of certain items. He called me 'pig' and I called him 'dog,' and he menaced me with his ivory swordstick, and I was so distressed that I snatched up a ceremonial *kris*—one of the items in question—and sliced off his head in one clean sweep. I didn't mean it—of course I was only gesturing the way I do when I get excited. In fact I was more surprised than he was! His head bounced in the corner, rolled upright, and faced me. He just had time to raise one eyebrow in amazement at my enthusiasm—and the other in horror at the sight of his headless body falling in front of him. It must have been a very strange sight to him. Then his eight seconds were up.

"I did what I could. I recited what I remembered from the *Bardo*—for when I was young in India I loved a girl from the north, from the mountains, and very philosophical she was, so to please her I flirted briefly with the Mahayana. I did what I could for Ali's shade—yet still the idiots accuse me of murder!"

"How did they catch you?" Ralph M'Botu demanded.

"I made it hard for them. I made it very hard!" Ana Kanasay smacked his lips with grim dissatisfaction. "They would not have caught me at all if not for politics.

"When I had done what I could for Ali, I collected myself; I considered what I should do. Then I took a false passport; I took addresses and recommendations and whatever I could take; I went to the airport without telling anyone, not even my wife. There was no trouble leaving the country . . . but the police were waiting when the plane landed in Rome. They held me on evidence of a photograph transmitted through, even though I had evidence that said I was someone else. I regretted that I had not taken the time to alter my appearance. I was confident I could bribe my way free. But they were not interested in what I offered. I could not believe it! Never . . . but this time . . . no! They were still not interested even when I offered them everything.

"Then I found out . . . it is political. It is complicated. My case has become a matter of great political delicacy. What I think has happened is that the English government is secretly paying the Italian government to make sure I am sent back, as the English Prime Minister is about to have talks with Mr. Ian Smith, which they want to do more than he wants to do, so the English do not want him to get angry at such a delicate time. Somehow my case is known, that I escaped through what is called 'lax Rhodesian security,' so that my trivial and momentary error is inflated in importance, and Mr. Ian Smith wants very much to have me back. So here I am!" Ana Kanasay sighed gustily, with massive sad emphasis. "The weight of our collective karma is most distressing. I face what some would call just execution, though captured and brought back only due to mockeries and trickeries of fate . . ."

He sighed again, more sadly and vastly than before, throwing up his arms as he did, so that Ralph M'Botu began to feel irritated.

"This is a most embarrassing predicament," Ana Kanasay continued in the same doleful vain, "but I have arranged that it should turn out to be embarrassing for someone other than myself."

Ralph M'Botu, who'd been about to shut him up, pricked up his ears.

"With much difficulty and expense," Ana Kanasay went on in a more intimately cunning voice, "I have arranged to escape from Rhodesia tonight, since I do not mean to be executed as a common criminal.''

Ralph M'Botu said nothing. He knew when to keep quiet. He could feel Ana Kanasay leaning forward at him now, sending the breath of some need of his own.

Ralph M'Botu did not like the scent of that breath . . . but he knew when to wait and listen.

''Surely you are interested?'' asked Ana Kanasay after a long pause. ''Is the world going mad? Police who won't take bribes, prisoners who don't want to get out of their cells? I could almost doubt my scheme!''

''I can escape with you? What do you want in return?''

''Nothing—a mere trifle—a compliment I wish to bestow upon you, because I sense you have fascinating talents which are being wasted in here.''

''I have told you nothing about myself!''

''On the contrary, your reactions to my tale of woe have been instructive.''

''What do you want?'' demanded Ralph M'Botu, his voice steely.

''I want to make love with you.'' The words were soft, but Ralph M'Botu saw the brief, strained, haunted smile . . . and he began to wonder. ''It is three weeks since I had a woman, and something would be better than nothing.''

''Thank you for nothing! Who do you think I am? I am not just a thing you can use and dominate to satisfy your lust!''

Immediately, sensing withdrawal of interest, M'Botu feared.

''Well, it is nothing to me, but—how long have you been here?''

''Too long! Many months!''

''How did you get into this terrible predicament?''

''I learned the truth about a man who does not want the truth known, even to himself.''

''Is he a powerful man?''

''He is the man who had you brought back here.'' M'Botu wiped sweat away. ''His real name is Greystoke. Tarzan. Tarzan did not die!''

''Of course not,'' agreed Ana Kanasay easily. ''But soon you will. You are an embarrassment; you have no power; you cost money to feed. No doubt also they think you are crazy. Crazy prisoners are always expendable.''

Ralph M'Botu breathed very deep. He too feared this.

"Then impress me with details of your foolproof escape!" he growled angrily, uneasily. "Explain your friendship with better reasons than your mad greed for a stranger you haven't seen properly or even touched. Why do you want to help me? What is it about me?"

"Because if you don't come along with me the guards will have to kill you immediately so you can't talk." And Kanasay sounded disgusted. "It is too bad! I should have had a cell to myself. Now I must include you in my arrangements or have more blood on my hands—why do you force me to speak so nakedly? —so in return for my trouble I want to fuck you. If I don't fuck you, you will be shot or clubbed to death in about one hour, when they come to take me out. It is simple. It is up to you. Freedom does not come free!"

Ralph M'Botu pondered. He had to make his act good.

"How have you arranged all this?" he asked sullenly.

"My money was no good in Rome . . . but here it works well . . ."

"Then I will do it," grunted Ralph M'Botu. "I don't mean to die yet. Do what you want. But don't try to betray me, and don't get the idea that you own me . . . because I am not a fool."

"You are ungrateful and too defensive," murmured Ana Kanasay, sliding forward on the beam of M'Botu's strangely feral magnetism, the attraction of which had increased to an intolerable pitch. "My need for you is inconvenient and hard to explain, but we must be philosophical. Satisfy me now, and I will give you freedom, and after that, we will see . . ."

Ralph M'Botu waited in his corner, and Ana Kanasay came to him, and he controlled himself savagely when Ana Kanasay grasped him. This was not at all to his personal taste—but evidently Ana Kanasay had been sent to help him fulfill his personal vow. The vow of his damned and urgent desire to get to the top, to escape from this dark pit and climb on those who climbed on him. So he did what Ana Kanasay wanted. He did it, and in the darkness an unpleasant symbiosis began to form—the partnership of Kitaj & Kitaj—born in mutual degradation, born of the mutual need to dominate—born of need itself. M'Botu did it, and he let him drown in the odor of Ana Kanasay, who for many years had been feeding his body the oils of delight. This odor was thick, and variable, containing many fascinating influ-

ences, but predominantly musky, curious, and very acquisitive
. . . and it imparted unknown new flavors to the half-formed
darkhearted dreams of Ralph M'Botu . . . Kitaj. He learned no
love, only another lesson about power and consequences, and there
was no longer any hint in him of the Angel or the Voice. Perhaps
he remembered Iloshabiet, and the long list of betrayals and dark
acts which had followed . . . but in *Liar's Gold* he says that,
during his submission in the cell, he was thinking about *Need!*
This unexpected and potent need which the merchant had for
him—on former occasions people had developed infatuations
with his energy, if not his character, but never so opportunely—
was obviously his connection to the wealth and power at the top
of the dungheap. Need! Need plus the Stimulation of Need!
Create addiction in others, supply the satisfaction—but never
enough! Maintain the addiction, get rich, get powerful! The
beautiful equation that summed up society more honestly than
any manifesto or constitution.

Obviously Ana Kanasay could teach him the niceties of exploitation. Ana Kanasay could teach him how to fuck the world. So,
take it now! he urged himself. Get your own back later. Let him
ride you now—you'll ride him later!

It was after midnight that they "escaped" in a limousine, near
dawn when they crossed the Zambian border, on foot, with
money and false papers. Then the sun rose where they stood in a
thorny wilderness, and for the first time they both saw each other
clearly. Ralph M'Botu saw a fat little man, perhaps in his
mid-forties, sallow-complexioned, with heavy jowls and slick
black hair and a beak of a nose, and close-set black eyes which
seemed very bright, very cunning. There was confidence in that
face, yet also a little fear, for the need was on Ana Kanasay, the
need for this thin hard filthy young man whom he'd rescued, and
the young man had the coldest and most rapacious eyes Ana
Kanasay had ever seen—eyes that studied him without a trace of
emotion or gratitude, eyes which seemed as if at any moment
they might grow huge, start spinning hypnotically, and swallow
his mind entire. In fact perhaps they had already done this, in the
darkness of the cell the night before, for Ana Kanasay could not
understand his hungry desire to be with this obviously dangerous
individual.

The older man did what he could to bind the younger to him.

"You are not the same as Ali. But perhaps you are like a son.

Perhaps we can work together and improve our fortunes by helping each other.''

Ralph M'Botu stared very steadily for some time before answering.

"Perhaps you are like a father. Where do we go from here?''

Ralph M'Botu was ironic and freezing inside. Ralph M'Botu was aimed. Ralph M'Botu Kitaj was ready to hit the Need Complexus of the world.

When at the second party in San Francisco he described this meeting he was interrupted and heckled for the first time since starting the tale. Several women and gays of both sexes and straight sympathizers began protesting his connection of sexuality with domination and wealth and power. They called him uptight and moralistic. One woman called him a fascist. Another, a liar.

There was some tumult. But he regained attention. He launched into a furious, passionate diatribe. Later I heard or read several versions of this rant, and what follows (unfortunately and yet again) is a composite, constructed on the whole from a magazine piece which I have retained since that time, and rounded off by Kitaj's own later recollections.

"You're right!" it seems he shot at his angry audience. "You're right! I'm fucked, because I want to fuck everyone. I'm really fucked, because I mean to get to the top of the pile, and when I get there I'll probably find nothing at all—but who knows. I've told you how I decided that Kitaj was the key, sent to me, so I started to turn that key. But it's still not fully turned; I don't know where it goes, yet. I haven't seen it all the way through. Somebody here have a fully turned key? Somebody here know the Way Through? Or are you all just the same as me? I think you're all just as fucked as I am. I think you're all stuck in the pit as well, and I think a lot of you are in a worse position, because you make excuses all the time, you look for money and power and the best fuck and you tell yourselves your reasons are really good—enlightened, New Wave, modern, expanded consciousness reasons. So how come you came here? How come you let me stand here so long, selling you this bullshit, listening to it, lapping it up, until at last I say something that strikes your conditioned social conscience? Jesus Christ! Don't you know what I am? Don't you know what you're doing? I've killed and I've stolen and now I'm so rich it makes me sick, and you bloody people—all of you—keep on making me richer! I shit on you, and you buy my shit and make me rich! The gas in your cars, the dope that you smoke, the guns and missiles that you pay for in taxes that you agree to pay—everything—I'm selling it to you, to the people you elect as your representatives! You should tear me apart for your own health, and you would, if you really thought I was wrong. But you don't! You listen! You applaud! You buy! You admire me! You admire me, because I'm a Nazi, and because you're all Nazis too! Don't you understand? *The Nazis won that war!* They were beaten physically, but they fed their ideas into the world, and none of us have escaped the plague! Now the party's over. The Third World War started years ago, and we're in the middle of it right now, and *most of us are fighting on the wrong side!* We're fighting ourselves and each other, and I am your enemy, and you are your enemies too! If you want to live, get the fuck out of here right now, and never buy anything from me again! That's it! Otherwise, don't complain, don't come on holy, because I can see through you. Don't blame your government, don't blame the police, don't blame the Russians—don't blame THEM, whoever your THEM may be—just take a good look at yourselves and work it out!''

That was it. The part was over. Kitaj stalked out, and the doors were opened, though it was still well short of dawn, and gradually the guests drifted out into the dark deserted streets to their cars, which were made by companies doubtless owned by Kitaj, or by people like him.

But who cared?

Not I, said the fly.

Not I, said I, and I, and you, and you.

Because Ralph M'Botu Kitaj went on getting more and more rich.

THE HELL OF NEEDS
OR
THE NEEDS OF HELL

*"In wartime, truth is so precious that she
should always be attended by a bodyguard of lies."*
—Winston Churchill

6. PANIC STATIONS

The tidal wave swept everywhere. By 1982 everyone in the
world was living and re-enacting all recorded and unrecorded
history in the present, in the NOW, though by no means everyone had acknowledged or recognized what was happening. We
were catching up with ourselves; we had caught up with ourselves; we were staring our Doppelgängers in the faces, staring
straight through the distorting mirrors of subconscious creation.
The walls of separation had grown very thin in this time when
there was more individual separation than ever, the invisible
worlds approached visibility, the UFOs were landing, we had
been creating unconsciously all along—now we were becoming
aware of it—now all we'd created started landing back on top of
us, RETURNED TO SENDER, price to be paid—NOW got
faster and faster and weirder and weirder from month to month in
whirling frantic cycles of new wars, agreements, treaties, depres-
sion, reflations, new fashions that mixed all the fashions and
philosophies of the mass media era—people picked up every
possible mask, tried it on, discarded it for another—the eighties
were a time in which everything ever imagined was happening all
at once, merging and juxtaposing and breaking apart into fresh

formulations which in their turn broke apart, faster and faster. There was cancer fever in the system, everything proliferated madly, the heat rose, the weather went wild, Mother Earth and the human mind generated more and more strangeness until we all seemed strangers to each other, to ourselves, until the definitions of insanity, reality and conformity all collapsed, until the OldStyle dualistic models were quite broken down. It got rough if you tried to stand up straight and rigid like an oak, like a totem pole or an iron girder. The wind was whipping through the world, through every mind, and it was an idiot wind or an inspiration wind, depending on how you chose to react. It changed you from the inside, armor was broken, the fortress walls all cracked, but building societies still tried to sell security while the cities burned, while the volcanoes erupted, while countries changed hands, while coastlines (in some places) changed shape. The only way through was to go with it like a flying sapling, gliding on the gale, bending this way and that, changing shape where necessary, with no fixed concept about anything on the earth at all. Fixed concepts were under a death sentence. In the eighties, people were crucified on their fixed concepts. It was a long hard labor and we're still not altogether born. Long and hard, but it was a creative chaos, though sometimes this seemed difficult to believe. It was as long and hard as human negativity could make it, because we inherited all the tendencies of the past; we found we had the task of transforming everything in order to survive. In just a few years we had to work through centuries of developed social misdirection. To some this seemed impossible. To some it still does. Collapse and total destruction—THE END—was as far as some people could see. THE BEGINNING, which required the rebirth of us all, seemed impossible, because DEATH stood in the way, and DEATH was stigmatized as fearful and undesirable.

Fear and Need flourished.

Like drowning creatures many of us grabbed desperately for the sedative straws—TV, insurance, Law & Order, ideologies, isms, enemies, gurus, higher wages, heroin, valium, librium, military security—dope of every sort.

It was hard to know who or what to believe, or whether to believe anything at all. The appearance of solidity was falling apart in front of us. We looked at ourselves and each other and saw fields of crackling energy. The future lay in crossing an unknown number of incomprehensible gulfs, collectively and in every mind, gulfs hither-to veiled, now naked, yawning enormously, appearing vampiric to some. Fear made them seem like that.

Fear creating need creating demand creating dealers.

The buying of Illusion got frantic and murderous.

The burning bridges were packed with people going nowhere.

Crowds thronged the halls of those who sold sleep. The dealers were everywhere. The times were such that many of them had to, chose to, come down out of their offices onto the dirty streets. The dealers showed their faces. Many of them were hated by people who hated themselves for their bondage in need. Sometimes they were mobbed and killed, martyred, executed, assassinated, snuffed out, sacrificed on the hungry angry altars of Need—Need which wore many different faces in different lands of different economic situations—but essentially it was all the same thing. Need of Sleep, Need of More, Need of the Easy Way that didn't exist. Need. The dealers were needed. They could be killed, but they always reappeared—different faces, but the same products.

Head-in-the-sand products for the ostrich mentality.

Of these dealers, Ralph M'Botu Kitaj became the most famous, the most hated, the most perversely loved, the most . . . needed.

This was because he alone among the Dealers of Need told us exactly what he and they and we were doing to ourselves:

"I AM KILLING YOU AND YOU ARE KILLING YOURSELVES BY BUYING THIS SHIT."

Kitaj knew what he was talking about. He had well-known needs of his own. He was no remote Demon of Vice. On the contrary, in many ways he appeared just like me and the same as you. Yet obviously he wasn't. He said things that anyone might say . . . but the things he did, not anyone could do. He turned himself into a famous public question. He did this at a time when all history, all reality, had become a naked question. He had come out of very tough circumstances—nobody could accuse him of being an effete intellectual or an aristocratic patrician who didn't understand common folk—and he had got rich by dealing in and playing on basic human needs. He felt himself to be criminal in a time when a lot of people, at least unconsciously, felt the same. In a time of great doubt and cynicism he expressed the basis of the doubt and cynicism. He blew away the glamour of wealth—from the inside. He got rich, like millions of people believed was their own heart's desire—but at every point he was overturning the applecart to show that the apples were rotten, because they weren't being eaten, they were being stockpiled. The false economy of greed. He screwed people, he screwed the world, he screwed himself—and at every point he was throwing up his arms and demanding plaintively, publicly, with utter disbelief, how come people hated themselves so much that they bought from him. He couldn't hit anyone without telling them he was hitting them. "I sell to you because you think you need to buy." He showed his contempt, he made it all very clear—at least, as far as he understood it himself, for he didn't work out the whole Need Equation until after the Disappearance—so that, time and again, those who bought direct from him stumbled away wondering how come they let themselves stay so hypno- tized, so dumb, so much in need of stuff that was doing them no good at all. Meanwhile, Kitaj was wondering the same thing about himself. Why was he so hypnotized by his own obses- sions? Why couldn't he lift his head through the ceiling to what he knew existed beyond? Six times in a row in 1982, he says in *Liar's Gold*, he got the Fool, the zero card, as the final outcome of Tarot readings Lenore did for him. This irked and worried him with a sense of the abyss which he knew he was refusing to face. He knew he was treading the precipice path and that soon the path was going to stop short.

The abyss.

The closer he got to his chosen material goal—richest man in the world, remember?—the greater his sense of time and hope running out, the greater the pressure of his self-disgust and the nightmares which told him he was still running from Ruwenzori, from Njeru's Smile, from Château Têtaurier and the Ghetto. By the beginning of the 1980s his ambition to hit the top and trample the human race, which in 1966 had seemed such a safely impos- sible ambition, which had required no introspection at all, was at the shocking point of realization. He had to face it. He was about to bump his head on the unexpectedly low ceiling of his second- rate purpose which had arisen only because of his sense of damned failure in other more valuable arenas of existence. He was going to run out of excuses, defenses, and reasons.

The richest man in the world. He felt more like Humpty Dumpty. Between 1980 and 1984 he spent many nights worrying

if he was over the humpty and about to be dumptied. Uneasy lies
the head, etc., and Kitaj's head got very uneasy once he began to
acknowledge how thoroughly he was trapped in the chaos logic
of his programs, his image, his fame. He knew he was going to
have to break out or be destroyed eternally—dissipated through
his·own nothingness.

This became clear to him in 1979.

His response was to pursue his empty ambition even more
assiduously, with more frantic mockery.

In the latter half of 1979—a Year of the Goat, a Year of
Pan—he butted out his partner, married Lenore in Istanbul,
bought robot factories in Newark, New Jersey, set up the Cold
Cure Deal, looked into the possibility of buying up Britain, and
caused riot and complaint in many parts of the world. Immediately after the third San Francisco party, in June 1979, he went
down to LA, where he financed, produced, directed, and starred
in a hard-core movie which was released later that year as *Jungle
Rape*. This utterly explicit and cynical production, with its many
graphic scenes of Kitaj fucking his way to wealth and power, was
panned the world round by critics and moralists. It was called
Gross, Bestial, Evil, Utterly Without Redeeming Merit. The
world public flocked to see it during the next few years; there
were many arguments as to whether the permanently virile
member—the chief star of the movie, the symbol of perpetual
blind greed—in fact belonged to Kitaj.

It didn't matter.

Jungle Rape increased Kitaj's wealth and fame.

Gross? Yes. A huge gross. At the end of 1980 he followed it
up with a more ambitious production—*The Sex Life of Adolf
Hitler*. In this riot of apocalyptic perversions Kitaj played Hitler,
had women shit and piss on him, recent psychohistorical research
having indicated this was the Führer's main means of sexual
release. Beforehand Kitaj approached many famous actors, from
Brando and Paul Newman to Olivier, to play the roles of Goeb-
bels, Goering, and the rest of the gang. He offered seven-figure
contracts for five-minute roles. He approached well-known politicians, told them publicly to get their pants down and show what
they were really made of. He suggested publicly to Margaret
Thatcher, the Snow Queen of English politics, that she could
play the part of Eva Braun pretty well. Finally, amid uproar, he
cast a crew of unknowns, and the movie went ahead. When it

came out it was banned almost everywhere. Kitaj was irritated by the ban—but as usual it turned out to his advantage. The movie became a hot underground item. As usual it looked as if the human race was conspiring to lift him to his sordid summit. Whatever he did, it increased his momentum. The joggernaut of his myth was gathering speed. "It got ridiculous," he told me later. "No matter how gross and disgusting I got, people still bought it."

With an increasing sense of desperation and unreality he played the part of and called himself murderer, pervert, thief, vicious pusher. In August '79 he got married—and immediately thereafter began a rakish life of calculated sensation, mostly with other people also in the public eye. Invariably when questioned about their marriage neither Kitaj nor Lenore would comment, but several of Kitaj's lovers in particular were not so reticent, selling graphic ghost-written stories which, along with *Jungle Rape* earned him the ambivalent loathing of millions and the desire, the captured interest, of millions more. These stories and the movie portrayed him as a sexual capitalist, a power addict, a dangerous loveless fucker who didn't care which or whose orifices he penetrated so long as he came in them. So long as he sold and dominated.

Many hungry people believed and admired this image and came after him, came to be victimized by the brute animal magnetism of this mysterious new jungle despot. Locust hordes of people pursued him everywhere he went, wanting him to take their money, their pride, their virginity, their soul—whatever loads they could not bear. "It was everyone taking everyone for a ride," he said one night in Ireland to Lenore and me. "Lots of warped intelligence and insect lust. Lots of calculation. Lots of strange complaints and complex fantasies. Decadence de rigueur, right there on the hunger/greed line. I made sure I was needed. People got right down on the floor for me, and I got down with them, because if you don't keep it personal you lose touch, you can't sniff it out any more, you dissolve, fade out like a starved vampire. And that's no way to go."

"Can vampires feel any love at all?" I asked suddenly.

He gave me a funny self-reflective smile.

"They can love and hate their need," he said. "That's all."

Lenore cut in then, and her voice was very tense.

"Do I have to be a vampire to know you?" she demanded. "Is

that what you still think? Can you only see things in terms of need?''

Only a week afterwards the matter of Ilsohabiet's Curse came up between the two of them. They had been married seven and a half years.

After their riotous departure from Turkey in August 1979, Kitaj told the media that their marriage was "a whim we had one afternoon on a boat on the Bosphorus.'' In fact as usual he disguised his true motives by appearing to reveal them. Neither he nor Lenore had been married previously. The bridge, thirty-two, of Irish-Norwegian-Hopi descent, retained her name. The ceremony was conducted by a skid-row mullah in a seedy hotel near the Blue Mosque. The reception, in the Pudding Shop, turned into a riot involving travelers, tourists, streetboys, pick-pockets, two fatal stabbings, police, finally soldiers. This was the final straw so far as the Turkish authorities were concerned. Kitaj's week-long stay in Istanbul had already proved sufficiently embarrassing. They suspected him of being in the city to orga-nize a new heroin/opium route to the west. In public he had been insulting. He'd talked of buying up Topkapi and Hagia Sophia, tearing them down, erecting plastic fun-fairs instead. Lenore too had made a nuisance of herself, talking to a foreign correspon-dent about "Islamic male chauvinist piggery—these men won't know what hit them when *their* women decide to get it straight.''

The newlyweds were advised to take the next flight out of the country. At the airport they walked into a prearranged trap. They were subjected to a very thorough search by Customs. A search-ing hand planted then found a bar of black hashish in Kitaj's pockets . . . in front of hundreds of tourists. Very embarrassing. They were interrogated at police headquarters, and accusations were made.

Kitaj refused to take it seriously.

"Prove it,'' he said.

It was impossible. The police knew it. They had hoped to scare him, to get their own back, maybe even to set him up on trial.

Very quietly Kitaj told them just exactly what would happen to the Turkish economy if they gave him any more trouble.

They let Kitaj and Lenore go. They had to. Photographs and stories of the arrest appeared in papers all round the world—but as usual this did nothing but increase public interest in Kitaj. In addition, it gave a new idea to Kitaj. Frequently during the next few months when going through customs barriers he acted furtive, trapped the officials into searching him. Each time they found hashish or heroin or cocaine. Each time he bought, blackmailed, and lawyered his way out of trouble—then made the whole thing public. "It shows what money can do when you've stolen enough of it," he bragged on TV. "I'm doing stuff that would land anyone else in jail for ten years, twenty years, life. You all know it, don't you?—one law for the rich, another for the poor."

It was only after a while that the bureaucracies of the world got wise, gave their customs people instructions that never, under any account, no matter what the provocation, were they to search Ralph M'Botu Kitaj.

It was this dangerous, paradoxical honesty which made him into such a unique folk-hero, which later in the decade led to the apparent contradiction of movements of mystical anarchism (the Spreaders, the Chancers) which drew much of their inspiration from his words and acts. Whatever he did showed something or someone up, because he was not afraid to show himself up, to portray himself in the worst possible light. But during this period his tricks were essentially negative. He was full of contempt and drew no inspiration from his own behavior. Nor did he draw inspiration from anyone else . . . save perhaps, in an oblique way, from Lenore. Yet the aggregate effect of his theater in the early eighties was influential and important, for every deal he made he advertised publicly his personal failure to come to terms with the inner pressures and fears which had brought him to his present cloudy eminence. Invariably he made it clear that there's never a seller without a buyer, that nobody can escape responsibility for what they do, and that the choices we were making collectively were disastrous death-wish choices. Philosophies of escape and priestly solace he regarded with loathing. "The fault, dear Brutus," I often heard him quote, "lies not in our stars, but in ourselves."

Lenore's influence was apparent in this attitude, also in many of his actions at this time, including I believe in his overthrow of Ana Kanasay.

*   *   *

Lenore Springer appeared to ride through the tumult of the early eighties with magnificent poise and calm. She seemed able to handle all the trips and traps and games that always went on round Kitaj. She had her own center and did not often show it when she felt perturbed or upset. She was emotionally resilient and had a wry humor. They were well matched in a mutually freewheeling way . . . but during the Disappearance (apparently her idea—one that she came to regret) the forced continual proximity and boredom caused great friction between them. She and Kitaj had no children together, though during the period of their marriage Kitaj fathered at least three children with other women, one of whom was the punk-rock star Gloria Mundi, of Gloria and the Hellholes . . . a liaison interpreted by many as Kitaj's attempt to get all the way into the teen market.

Lenore didn't seem to care. She accepted it, saying she didn't want to have any children in this particular life. She said she'd had fifteen children during her last life as the wife of an energetic Spanish grandee in the sixteenth century. "Fifteen's enough for at least two lives." She'd smile when she said it, but the smile would be slightly tight. Certainly, there was a strong maternal and protective streak in her love for Ralph M'Botu. She regarded him as a child more often than not. She was a serious, intense, intelligent, devoted woman, speedy and sharp by nature, able to juggle beliefs, able to match his moods, with strong inner certainties which meant she was not absorbed by him. She claimed her maternal grandmother had been a Hopi Indian—one of the prophetic, visionary tribe. Maybe so, though with her pale complexion and long ash-blonde hair she looked much more Scandinavian than American Indian . . . save perhaps in her impassive, proud, high cheekbones. Yet her conscious approach to the state of things in the eighties, the state of things and their possible outcome and solution, was Indian, and she knew a lot about Indian philosophies. On occasion she would speak softly of the Five Ages, and of how these Five Ages were now coming to an end with the end of the lesser period known to the Aztecs as the Nine Hells—the nine consecutive negative fifty-two-year cycles which had been inaugurated by the conquest of Cortez 1519, which finished in 1987. She would speak too of the Hopi belief in the Purification of humanity, of the time of great war to begin with the Saquasohuh Kachina (The Blue Star) "dances in the plaza."

To me this sounded as typically vague as most prophecies, but she insisted that the Blue Star was already dancing.

"We can feel it in our bones!" she would insist. "The body of the earth and the bodies of humankind were made the same way. Now everything is shaking and vibrating, in everyone, all through the world—that's the dancing of the Blue Star. What it means is that we have come to the end of this phase of our evolution, we have to move the energy up to the next chakra, we have to learn how to deal with the brighter, fiercer energy. We can make it harder or easier for ourselves, as we choose . . . but we have no option but to go through it."

Once in Ireland I tried to find out with her if this tradition of the Blue Star had any connection with Sirius traditions.

But she and I found it hard to communicate sympathetically. I think we ended up arguing about something else . . . probably about Kitaj.

I believe I've made it clear already that Lenore and I were never good friends. She regarded me as an interloper. Over the years we arrived at a sort of truce, at reluctant mutual admission that we were both after all in the same boat . . . but this came about only after Kitaj had moved beyond the understanding of either of us. For several years she and I contested with our different images of what we wanted him to be, to become. To a degree in Ireland we each lived vicariously through him, trying to find our personal meanings through his existence, so that between us stood fear of the loss of something that neither of us owned. During the Disappearance she thought I was drawing him away from her and her ideals with my notions of mythreality, which she called egotistic, megalomaniac, and dangerous—just what she'd tried and failed to steer him away from—and it took us a long time before we could acknowledge that we'd both been barking up the wrong tree.

We were both concerned for Kitaj, but our interpretations and the nature of our self-interest differed. I was never his lover; I don't think I was exposed to anything like the degree of hurt and pain that she had to put up with. Yet it had been her choice to be with him, just as it was mine. To start with she had been a trained therapist who had happened to help him through a difficult period. *Happened*. She believed that they had met inevitably, that between everything and everyone there is a fatal link, and that certain stars, or human wavicles, are bound to come together.

There is no doubt that she helped to earth Kitaj so far as he could be earthed at all during the craziness of those years. She loved him . . . but his attitude to her was too often one of petulant . . . need. His feelings towards her were very ambivalent. He used her emotions, he drained her, and by the end of 1984, when I became his secretary, she knew she would never mold him according to her own fixations and preconceptions. She knew it had been her own ignorant expectations which had led to her emotional exhaustion. In certain crucial respects he always remained completely alien and distant. Throughout their marriage he remained egotistic, self-obsessed, acquisitive, rapacious, and frequently cruel. He had no warm love to give her, and he continued with capitalizing patterns which essentially she despised. Increasingly he demeaned her by trading on her love, on his magnetic hold. He ignored her while at the same time demanding her presence when he wanted it. She told him what she thought of this behavior, she scolded him, but he did not change, and for a long time she remained patient.

Some people say that she stayed with him so long because of the money, the power, or because she was weak and attached to him by her own patterns of need.

Hardly so. With such motives predominant she would never have stuck it through those hard twenty-one months in Ireland. The way she saw it, I think, was that she had a function in Kitaj's life which nobody else could fulfill—essentially an ethical function—and despite all his negativities she thought sufficiently highly of him to keep on plugging, sacrificing her private interests to the hope that he might yet wake up out of the pit . . . and when she came with us to Ireland I don't believe she expected any personal happiness. She underwent the plastic surgery, the alteration of her appearance, without complaint, and likewise for a long time she put up with his coldness, with the brutal unpredictability of his moods. By the time of the Disappearance the connection between them was not at all sexual—most of the time in Ireland the two of them slept separately. In fact she came as often to Isma'il and to me as she did to him. This she accepted as her role—the earth-priestess, if you like. Kitaj accepted it too. For him at that time, women were still either on a pedestal or in the pit. He could be unrealistically reverential and cruelly cynical almost in the same breath. For a time he nearly smothered her heart entirely . . . though her heart was not easily smothered. She put up with a lot. It was her decision. And his cold attitude was not unconscious or accidental. He felt threatened by her love. He feared it might melt his armor. He feared that the monsters and abandoned dreams of Ruwenzori might flood through and drown him. These horrors he preferred to approach via the sparring intellectual techniques which I provided, through symbols of mythreality—gradual roads of reconnection with his deeper self which he'd tried to deny. Heart-love was then too hot and direct for him . . . even on that cold Irish moor where we needed all the love we could get. The Wasteland and the Wounded King . . . he protected his wounds, kept them open . . . and the tension between them grew extreme until in time she knew she had to go her own way again.

The break itself, the final straw, came that evening when she overheard him telling me about Iloshabiet and the "curse."

That was in February 1987. And the break was a new beginning.

"The fault, dear Brutus . . ."

Yet everything interconnects, micro- and macrocosm mirror and interact, the large-scale astrological background to the period 1980–2000 is as informative in its way and much more concise than any cataloguing of political and geophysical events during this period. In the sixties and seventies the "Mother of Sciences" was resurrected as a subject for scientific study. In particular it gradually became apparent that much valuable knowledge—ever-subtler interpretation of our electromagnetic environment, of our minds and bodies and of the body of the earth—might be gleaned from precise study of planetary motions and interactions. And during the convulsive eighties there were millions of people who learned to modify and regulate their own attitudes by comparing these with tendencies outlined in the psychological mirror provided by their birth-charts, thus preparing themselves for the wild times breaking and wilder times still ahead. Which is not to say that superstitition did not also flourish in this borderland, nor that the rapprochement between science and intuitive discipline was easily or quickly accomplished. It was not, and is not—not by any means.

But let's do a quick breakdown. Between 1975 and 1996, energy radiating from that area of the galaxy covered by Scorpio was very influential. Late in 1982 all the other planets in our system were lined up in opposition to Earth within a 60-degree sweep of the zodiac. There had been no such configuration since the time of Columbus. Many people cite this conjunction as the beginning of the period of cataclysmic change—the time when the Blue Star truly began its dance. (Some also mention the presence of Neptune in Sagitarrius in the years before 1984—the planet of the subconscious in the sign of the higher mind—as an influence shifting world consciousness from rigid dogmatic cultural forms towards more intuitive and personal approaches . . . but if so, there were also many more obvious influences at the same time.) And between 1984 and 1995 Scorpio housed Pluto, then at its closest point to the sun and Earth, going through its fastest motion and dipping inside the orbit of Neptune, and many believe that during this time Pluto, planet of violent upheaval of every kind, had its maximum impact on physical and psychic processes of life and death. Such belief is not quantifiable—but Kitaj's major changes and the Transformation took place within this period—in fact we all underwent our own transformations, or we froze solid, we died.

Between 1982 and 1988 all the outer planets were approximately aligned with our galactic center at 26 degrees Sagittarius—prime directional source of cosmic energy—energy which the resonating lenses of the planets stepped down and focused through to us. This was arguably an additional cause of energetic convulsion, likewise the pull, such as it is, of the planets themselves. It was certainly during this period that the rate and nature of change seemed fastest, sharpest, most cruel. By the mid-eighties most of us in the world who were capable of coherent thought consciously found ourselves caught irresolute between the deadly mires of the old world and the apparently horrifying abyss of the new. The purification and changes demanded by the situation seemed much too severe.

But that was over ten years ago. Now here we are, 1999, still on the planet, still going round the sun, alive, though millions of us are dazed, for the changes and devastation, especially during the last two years, have been more than anyone can easily assimilate. But the worse may be over. We may be about to tiptoe into better circumstances, with Pluto in Sagittarius, Uranus in Aquarius, and already there are optimists speaking yet again of the "New Age." And this may be . . . but on the other hand there are still income tax inspectors, secret police, all the apparatus of patriarchal bureaucracies and OldStyle organizations which stubbornly refuse to cut their own throats. We have witnessed many great and transforming events . . . but the old world refuses to sink beneath the waves with the convenient speed and totality of an Atlantis. It remains with us, in our bones and blood and actions, and many generations will be needed to complete the intended changes in our DNA, in the fate-programs of our inner constellations.

In the meantime there is the matter of Kitaj's "return." And there is the matter of Sirius. It looms ever larger, at least as metaphor, and since reception of those odd signals in 1990 the entire affair has been under a cloak of tight international security and obfuscation. We "ordinary" folk are not supposed to know of it, but it seems likely that the U.N. (wo)manned planoform expedition which left for the Sirius system last year will physically reach its goal. Yet to many of us this expedition seems to be based on a materialistic misconception. Why send people all that way, so expensively, simply to visit the intelligence coded in our own unconscious constellations?

As Above, So Below. The mysteries of the relationship that the Egyptians coded as Isis, Osiris, and Anubis have their practical foundation as equally in the physiology of our brains as in the highest and most distant heavens.

It is true. There really is gold the other side of the rainbow, the other side of that brainy bridge, though naturally it is guarded by a Dog.

BEWARE OF THE DOG! BEWARE OF THE DOG-STAR!

Yes. But only if you hate and fear Nature.

Last night the dogs were howling.

Last night I dreamed and in the middle of the dream I awoke and there was a man in black in my room who'd come to kill me . . . and kill me he did, stabbing me through the heart, and down I fell, down through endless night, through crushing tunnels and into a sphere of radiance which . . . and it was only then I realized I was still dreaming, and I awoke—I awoke—but it was hard to trust my senses telling me that this time I was _really_ awake. I sat up in bed in the dark thick room, I was soaked in sweat, the heat was stifling, there was no air, and no wonder, for lately I've been keeping the shutters closed even at night. Call it paranoia if you like, but I can feel them, I can feel them coming, it's inexorable, though there's no logic to say I've been identified or found out, it's purely intuitive, I don't even know who THEY are . . . THEY might even be the protesting functions of my own body, unhappy with all the alcohol and all the stimulants I've forced them to deal with, calling on the Shadow to come and stalk my pounding heartbeat, calling on the Old Man to come and tear scars in my liver . . . it doesn't matter how, I know there isn't much time left, I have to hurry to complete all this, I must have it all written out and duplicated and dispatched into the world before it can be seized and destroyed. That's all. I don't have to worry about anything else, not any more. The tremblings of the earth and the plans of the plutonian crews are of no more interest to me.

So last night I sat there in the darkness wondering if I was really awake, truly alive. And for a time there was no sound, nothing, nothing but thin bars of moonlight trembling through the slats of the shutters.

Then the dogs started howling, all round the village.

Maybe it means another earthquake. Or maybe a UFO.

Kitaj didn't take me on until September '84, a full five years after he'd hooked me at the third and last San Francisco party in June '79.

Earthquakes. What he did was wild and indefensible. To begin with there was nitrous oxide, or something like it, coming through the air conditioning. That was okay, I guess. After an hour or so all the open-house guests, overflowing through every room, all masqued and in costume, were caught into a total merriment. Then he pulled his dirty joke. The moment that midnight struck the house began to shudder and shake. There was chaos. Just above everyone thought the San Andreas Fault was making its big move at last. In fact the explanation was the Kitaj had installed a subsonic generator in the basement. Immediately after the shock, with people still screaming, being sick, and picking themselves up off the floor, I reeled straight into the arms of a little old man with incredibly piercing eyes. He was garbed as an Indian shaman, I thought he was Don Juan, he grabbed me, shook me, told me to stop wanking, start taking chances. I didn't know then it was Kitaj. He cut right through me with his eyes, his words; I left that party and went home in a state of shock. For three days I stayed in my room, not sure who or what I was any more, caught in a nightmarish waking dream. Out of this fugue I came to find myself obsessed with my image of the potential of Ralph M'Botu Kitaj. I didn't know how or why it had happened, I'm still not sure what he did to me that night, or if it was me that did it to myself—but what happened was this:

I stopped trying to write the great soulful novel, half a million words long, that laid bare the dilemma, the painful conundrum, of modern existence.

Instead, during the next six months I worked furiously, wrote six short novels full of foul people and foul situations, full of existential need and greed and putrefaction, full of drugs, desperadoes, sex, black magic, international Illuminati conspiracies, political insanity, UFOs, sharks, full-bosomed victims, mad scientists, mindwarp, germ war, cancer, catastrophes, earthquakes—everything. They were cynical, and all the sex was unnatural, by which I mean that nothing was born out of it. Likewise the philosophy was unnatural, by which I mean the same.

They were written and sold. And they sold and sold and sold.

You'd have thought that by 1980 people were sick of the same old negative life-destroying shit. Not so.

These stories (*The Venus Plague* was a typical title) sold a few millions all round the world. Two of them were turned into movies. Not quite up to Harold Robbins, but enough to let me do what I'd decided to do.

I became a student and follower of the Kitaj mystery.

Between 1979 and 1984 he was my tunnel-reality, my focus, my way of coping with the craziness of the eighties. Most of this time I spent in London or San Francisco. I kept myself informed about where he was, what he was doing. I became an expert on his burgeoning myth. Early in 1981 I got to interview him in Detroit, on a magazine assignment. From my point of view that was a disaster, but it hooked me deeper. My obsession increased. Thereafter I planted myself in front of him whenever and wherever I could; I loitered in the lobbies of hotels and airports through which he was expected to pass; I was arrested three times on suspicion of being a mad bomber . . . and had eye-contact with him on just four occasions. Each time I got the total brush-off. Each time he swept on to another continent, another boardroom, another deal. Each time I walked away, already planning the next such futile encounter, determined that sooner or later he was going to listen to my ideas about him, determined that some day I was going to write the definitive biography of him.

During these years I wrote him many letters in which I detailed my ideas about mythreality and his potential to move the world positively. There was never any reply. I was not shaken. With blind determination I kept on planning, pursuing, writing. He became my whole purpose. I lost touch with my family, my former friends, my former sense of reality. I babbled a lot about Kitaj and was frequently avoided. It didn't bother me. I felt no need for ordinary human company, not even my own. I lived ate drank slept and dreamed Ralph M'Botu Kitaj until in my mind he seemed like some chimerical monster, an angelic beast or bestial angel, a mythical being who fitted my mytical preconceptions. I should have grown discouraged—but I was crazy—or maybe not—fo. I did not want an easy goal which would be disappointing in its attainment; I wanted an almost impossible goal which would preoccupy me entirely and thus distract me from the madness of a world in which nothing seemed too wild or monstrous any more. Over the years my dedication became more absolute, more confirmed, until in my mind it had attained the dimensions of something sacred and spiritual. Kitaj was the mystic castle in which the Grail I sought was hid. I felt that in San Francisco and again in Detroit I had gained the opportunity to glimpse the Grail, even to free the Keeper of the Grail—but each time at the crucial moment I had failed to ask the right questions. So the mad years reeled by, snow falling more thickly as the Ice Age returned, and still I persisted.

Maybe you remember those years. Maybe you acted crazy too.

Detroit. By 1980 Kitaj had overthrown and (some said) killed his partner. He was contemplating the horror of the Cold Cure Deal. He was thinking about buying up Britain, cheap. He was trying to corner the world grain market in the knowledge that fifty years or so of fine weather and good harvests were over forever and that—for a while anyway—American agribusiness could hold the world to food-ransom. He was fascinated and appalled by his fortune. He was up on his own on that lonely mass media height, rich and famous, with his horns dangerously close to piercing the ceiling of the realm he had created—the ceiling of his fears. Like a knight in chess he was jumping about in patterns that his competitors never appreciated until it was too late. Yet for him the board was too small. He could never quite hide from the past. From Ruwenzori. Ruwenzori was a permanent dangerous growl at the back of his mind. The flashbulbs, the fame, the easy flesh could never quite expunge it, nor what had gone before it. The old woman. The Angel. The Voice.

Only Greystoke remained moderately safe to him.

The entities connected with his higher and deeper self he had transformed into monsters that pursued him, against which he fought, contradicting himself as often as he could, asserting his self-hating self to the hilt.

In 1980, for the first time he began to exhibit what looked like paranoia. It was self-conscious, public, and he exploited it to the hilt, but nevertheless what he did constituted a genuine *cri de coeur*.

He got himself a heavily armored private estate in a suburb of Motor City, also procured a new bodyguard—a Quasar robot—designed to electrostun or roll over its victim at a neat, steady thirty-five miles per hour.

He made himself a concentration camp of this estate. He was the concentrate, and Lenore refused to join him in it. For three months he sat alone (save for a succession of starlets) amid this razor-sharp self-reflecting jail of glass and wire and electric notoriety. Not only the robot but also Taser-armed human guards bristled round him. Searchlights played on the courtyards and withered rose gardens. Barbed wire spat from the not-quite-elegant fake Georgian red brick walls. These walls, enclosing the entire three-acre estate, were fifteen feet high, forming a square, with towers at the corners. Two of the towers overlooked a freeway. He had a struggle getting the permits to install ZSV radar-controlled machine guns in the towers. It wasn't the cost of the permits— only a hundred bucks a time—the trouble was that he couldn't legally fix them in the towers, not even in America.

Out of this self-mocking public retreat he roared to rage publicly against this defamation of the rights of the individual.

One day in December 1980—the same day *The Sex Life Of Adolf Hitler* was refused any license at all in the U.S.—he went downtown, stalked into City Hall to argue his case. He had called in beforehand. When the media closed in he pulled out and openly brandished two Tasers. Nobody wanted to get wired up to 20,000 volts. He cleared a path as miraculously as Moses. I saw

it on TV. But the police in the hall stood up to him, stopped him.
He started to rant and look dangerous. He was more than a bit
demented; he wouldn't put the Tasers away, and he almost blew
it, because the police were ready to kill him. One cop was
actually going for his gun; he told me later he could feel it down
his spine—"I thought I'd mistimed it . . .''—then . . .

There were shouts and screams from the main door. The
crowd, which had flowed together in his wake, again did the Red
Sea bit, with even greater alacrity this time. The cops all froze.
So did Kitaj. But he smiled . . .

The Quasar robot came crashing through.

Detroit jaws clanked downwards when they saw what Kitaj
had done by way of modification to the factory model Quasar. It
looked like a *Star Wars* monstrosity, with waving rubber tenta-
cles, whirling antennae, and big red bug eyes atop its gleaming
conical seven-foot height. The future, come to roost at last.
Through the appalled crowd it glided, "breathing" with a metallic stertorous sound like it had some terminal disease. Three feet
in front of Kitaj it came to an obedient halt. In a grating fake-
Nazi voice, both servile and threatening, it said into the mesmerized silence:

"Master, you sent for me. Who do you want me to kill?"

"Use your own discretion!" Kitaj snarled.

Then with the robot at his heels he stalked past the police, and
nobody moved an inch.

He got the permits. Or seemed to. From the freeway next day
could be seen the black silhouettes of machine guns in the
towers. Within hours the local CB and two-way cablevision
channels were full of anxious chatter and complaint by the citi-
zenry. What if the Man went crazy during the Rush Hour? From
these towers he could sweep the freeway clean.

The police and the TV people arrived about the same time.

Kitaj was ready. He was naked but for loincloth and turban.
Expansively he revealed that the machine guns were only wooden
replicas. The interviewer, a sharp young woman, summoned up
her righteous indignation as Kitaj goggled his lunatic grin close-
up into the camera.

"Mr. Kitaj, what's the point of all this?"

"Give you some adrenalin when you drive," he intoned, voice
sepulchral. "Give you all a shot in the arm. Metaphorically
speaking."

"Okay, so where are the *real* machine guns?"

Kitaj looked puzzled. "Have you seen any dogs?" he asked.

Wild looks between the crew. "*Dogs,* Mr. Kitaj?"

"Yes, dogs . . . Dobermans, Alsatians, German shepherds, wolfhounds . . . dogs like that. Nasty, dogs like that. You know every year in this country over a hundred thousand people get bitten or mauled by dogs. Mostly children. People use big dogs as extensions of their own failed instincts. Would I do that to a dog?"

"There are no dogs or machine guns on this estate?"

Kitaj shrugged. "Dog backwards is God, you know."

"Mr. Kitaj, what are you doing here? Why this set-up?"

"I'll show you," said Kitaj slyly to the TV crew, "but only after each of you takes down your pants onscreen. Why should I expose myself if you won't do the same? Is it fair? Is it right?"

This was typical. During the following month he gave a lot of interviews, but in none of them did he give any straight answers at all. More often than not he humiliated the questioner. So that when word came through that he would give me half an hour on behalf of the West Coast magazine, *Torch,* for which I was freelancing, I felt pretty nervous.

The weather was terrible when I landed in Detroit with a stack of prepared questions. It was January 1981. I dared to hope I'd get the scoop, that I'd get under his skin. I was met by a limousine, led into the stronghold, past the barbed wire, through the 400-pound glass doors which opened only when the ID card of the blackshirt guard escorting me was slipped into a wall slot and recognized by the computer. I felt I might never get out again. The place was lurid Gothic. I was taken along glaring guarded corridors to an opulent room with seventeen-foot ceilings and spectacular abstract tapestries. Kitaj was lounging at his ease with a starlet called Mary Hari to one side, a huge world globe on the other. He gestured at a hard-back chair; the pair of them sipped at frosted glasses of piña colada while I stumbled through my questions. They gave each other languid reptilian looks and fondled each other extravagantly. I felt like a slave at the foot of the throne of Darius. I did my best. For some minutes he answered me more or less directly, his eyes mocking, but soon he got tired of my stock questions about pornography, cocaine, oil, his dealings in world food supplies. I tried to draw him round to the question of his myth, but he was obviously distracted and

bored, beginning to ignore me, stroking the world globe posses-
sively. Then, unexpectedly, he asked:

"Mr. Hall, did you ever hear of a man called Le Petomane?"

"No." I felt awkward. "What about him? Who was he?"

"He made himself famous farting on the stages of France."

I felt lost. I fell back to another prepared question:

"Mr. Kitaj, Andrew Carnegie once said that, quote, *Surplus
wealth is a sacred trust to be wisely used for the genuine good of
my fellow man,* unquote. Do you have any comment to make
about . . ."

It was the wrong question.

"Bullshit!" snapped Kitaj. "Why don't you ask me where my
wife is?"

I shrugged and fell in. "Okay. Where is she? Why isn't she
here?"

"Don't worry about it. What else do you need to know?"

"Ana Kanasay," I said with difficulty. "He died, almost a
year ago, and there were rumours that . . ."

"I stabbed him in the back. Certainly. He was old. It was time
he was out of the way. So I got rid of him. Everyone knows
that."

There was an odd look on his face—a mixture of pleasure and
pain—and for a moment I sensed the man's acute physical and
emotional tension.

"What exactly did you do?" I asked, haltingly, uncomfortably.

"Belladonna in his popadum!" Kitaj cried dramatically, his
eyes bugging out, sending Mary Hari off into giggles. "You
know they call me the Borgia Jew. He walked out of a window.
Now . . . I fear his ghost . . ."

I flushed, feeling hot and numb in his presence, burned by his
siren-red aura and by his contempt. It was hard to think. I tried to
pull myself together. Borgia Jew? Belladonna? He was talking
murder and hate, riddling me with his mystery, his sense of guilt.
With difficulty I met his eyes.

"Surely you're afraid of enemies more solid than ghosts? Why
all these guards and walls and robots? It looks to me like you're
dramatizing your real fear."

"They're for fun." He sank back lazily beside his sexy starlet,
his eyes half-lidded, unreadable. "They're all toys. Useful toys.
I needed a rest, but right now I have to stay in the world's eye. I
do it like Salvador Dali, but he was never a dealer like me. I

can't be too careful. Millions of people need me. Need creates
anger, greed, hate, danger . . .''

For a long moment he studied me. The heat grew.

"What's *your* need?" he rapped suddenly.

"To know what makes you tick," I heard myself say without
any premeditation, needled into honesty by the slice of his stare.
But then, in 1981, I could not clearly articulate the nature of my
fascination. Clumsily I added, "I want to write a biography of
you. I want to . . .''

I was interrupted, thrown into silence by his bellow of laughter.

"Listen," he said, once he'd subsided, in a chilling voice.
"You want to know what it's all about? Listen. Once I lived
among people who understood the value of rites of passage for
their children. Know what I mean? Growth ordeals to tell you it's
time to grow up and drop childish needs; time to stand on your
own two feet and stop leaning on other people. Hah! But in this
world now, self-responsibility of that sort is subversive. Capitalizing economies depend for their survival on an addicted population. It's not just that deadly infantile needs persist—they're
encouraged—so that shits like me can get rich. Children that try
to step outside, they get called criminal. Rites of blockage. Most
people feel so bad about themselves all they can do is drag down
other people into feeling as bad as they do. I'm like that. It
makes for company in hell." His eyes glittered on me; I could
not look away. "It should make you want to puke. Instead there
you sit, gaping at me like I'm your hero, telling me you want to
know what makes me tick, saying you want to write my
biography—really? Do you mean it?" His laugh was strained.
"Do you think you need it? Will it bring you satisfaction, will it
bring you any meaning, will it bring you peace and joy?" Slowly
he shook his head, and I could not look away. "I have enough
suckers hooked into me already. Do yourself a favor—go away,
live your own stories, write your own life, forget about Kitaj,
because he'd only suck your soul dry."

He got up. That was it. The interview was over. I didn't know
what I'd learned. But before I left he beckoned me over, his
expression ambivalent with that pleasure and pain. He offered me
a couple of tracks of coke.

"Pure uncut Colombian. You'll never see better."

"Thanks," I snapped, "but no thanks. I don't!"

"Oh yes you do," he said sadly, wagging his finger like an

admonishing teacher. "I can see you . . . and you don't stand up so straight. You walk with a bent spine too. You'll be back for more. Too bad."

He grinned fiendishly and Mary Hari giggled as I turned away.

"Oogy Wawa!" he called after me—an ironic Zulu toast.

"Shlante!" I shot back in Gaelic.

But he was right. Of course.

With the bizarre interlude of Detroit behind him, with the books and movies beginning to proliferate, his myth grew ever more sensational. In June 1981 he was denounced by the Pope as an agent of Antichrist. This added greatly to his fame and popularity. Details about him, no matter how trivial, were ever more eagerly sought. Up to then he had seemed more of a playboy than a competently ruthless capitalist. In '81 and '82, via dozens of lurid magazine articles (mine included), the scab-scratching world thrilled to be told that Ralph M'Botu Kitaj was more mean, mysterious, and elementally glamorous than Getty, Hughes, and Onassis put together. It was learned that he believed in mucus-free diets, carrot juice, psychic surgery, and that in addition to heroin and coke he was killing himself with two packets of unfiltered French cigarettes every day. It was learned that he was sentimental about dolphins and whales, and hated killing them, which he would do only for profit. It was said that he was in contact with beings from outer space, that he possessed occult and mesmeric powers, that he had refused to teach himself to read or write, that his memory never let him down. It was said that at any time he could recall every deal he'd ever made, with whom, where, when, and how much, plus all the small-print details. Fifty-page contracts had only to be read to him once, it was said, and he would store every word away in his mind, with total recall whenever he required it.

This at least was absolutely true.

"So what's the big deal?" he grumbled to me one time in Ireland, dismissing this talent. "There was a guy in Lithuania called Rabbi Elijah who memorized twenty-five hundred books, completely, including the Bible and the Talmud. So what? And that Vatican library curator a hundred years ago—Cardinal Mezzofanti—he had a hundred and eighty-six languages and seventy-two dialects under his belt. Likewise, so what? Look at

me. I can't even read. I just get off on causing other people pain.
It gives me pleasure."

"You get off on causing yourself pain," I said. "It makes you
feel real. It gives you connection with that stuff you've spent the
last thirty years trying to ignore and forget. The spiritual
dimension."

"Fuck that," he muttered, looking away.

"No way," I said. "It's you that fucks yourself. You're not
really a masochist. You're just trying to remind yourself about
what's real. That's why you knocked over Ana Kanasay and
made a big deal about your guilt."

"I don't want to talk about that," he said.

Pleasure and pain. In October 1979 the retirement of Ana
Kanasay was announced, "for reasons of health." In March
1980 he was reported to have died at his estate in Tuscany. Of
cancer. Very fitting. But unlikely. I suspect that he simply faded
into the grave—a vampire whose partner would allow him no
more of the blood of the world, the blood of need. For some
years thereafter Ralph M'Botu publicly relished the cloying sweet-
ness, the sickly pleasure, the grim poetic justice of having betrayed
the man who had buggered him on his way to worldly success.
Mythically and psychologically, the act was inevitable—the "murder of the father," according to the gospel of Freud, the myth of
Cronos.

Often in Ireland I saw Kitaj pick up and return burning coals to
the fire with his bare fingers when he could have used tongs or a
shovel. The look on his face at such times was the same look as
he had whenever he referred to Ana Kanasay—pinched, an ambivalence of pain and pleasure—guilt triumphant.

I never met Ana Kanasay and I have nothing more to say about
him. You must seek other sources if you want detailed information about the man, about the partnership. Many books and
articles were written about Kitaj & Kitaj while the parnership
existed, and a biography about Ana Kanasay was written after his
death by one of his associates. This biography attacks Ralph
M'Botu almost as viciously as Ralph M'Botu customarily attacked
himself. Yet the attacks are unnecessarily wild and inconsistent:
once again we find ourselves in a situation where an author has
been overwhelmed by the paradoxical nature of the myth, so that,
far from reducing Ralph M'Botu's power, the attacks serve only

to increase our fascination with the man. This was recognized at
the time by many critics, and the book was poorly received,
particularly since Ana Kanasay never attracted anything like the
same degree of public interest. Yet for a while it was extensively
in print, and was used as fuel by Ralph M'Botu's enemies. Now,
of course, it has been suppressed and you may have difficulty
finding a copy. It is called *The Fat Man: A Memoir of Ana
Kanasay Kitaj,* by Lorenzo Lopez . . . yet in fact it is more
concerned with Ralph M'Botu than Ana Kanasay.

If there was any one event which brought home to Ralph
M'Botu the absolute psychological and practical need of the
Disappearance, it was the Cold Cure Deal. For with this he
nearly went too far. He stuck his neck out, almost caused world
war . . . or perhaps he diverted it. The whole thing seemed
suicidal.

This was almost the case. Deliberately in 1984 he loaded the
risk against himself, playing grimly with the chance of a total
self-destruction.

"When Hitler realized the Russian campaign was lost, in
December 1941," he told me mordantly, in Ireland, "his prompt
response was to declare war on the United States, though for
months he'd been ordering that America must under no account
be provoked. From the same psychological space and at the same
time he ordered the extermination of the Jews."

"You mean when you decided to go through with the Cold
Cure thing you'd already decided you'd lost your war, that all
you could do now was achieve a catastrophic failure, demonic
fame worthy of your historic greatness? Come on!" I was sardon-
ic. "You were never Hitler. You've just got pretensions in that
direction. You're not a world destroyer. You're a creator, have
been all along, you just got fucked up along the way."

Kitaj smiled.

The Cold Cure Deal was pretty nasty. It demonstrated a corrupt genius. Wolfgang Heinrich Overath was the originator. Late
in October '78 Herr Overath made what at first to him seemed a
useless discovery. He was a biochemist in the Koln research
laboratory of Schmutzmayering—the German pharmaceutical sub-
sidiary of one of the octopean European arms of Kitaj & Kitaj.
Overath was alone in the lab one night, working after midnight,

burning midnight oil with only a black cat for company, seeking solution to the enigma of his existence . . . and he synthesized something.

He was another hungry man. What he synthesized turned out to be the Cure, but not his solution. He had just been refused a raise, among other disappointments. He needed something that would set him up, break him through, make his name—something with a commercial function.

He stayed in that lab all night. He exercised his talent. He worked backwards. He started from the Cure.

He invented the Cold.

To start with he experimented privately on rats and rabbits. The tests proved positive. He thought of experimenting on his colleagues, but decided against it. There was too great a risk of discovery. In addition, he did not want the Cold to spread before he was in a space to market the Cure. The isolation procedures at the laboratory were very efficient, but he could not be sure. There was only one solution. He infected himself, reported himself sick, and went into total seclusion to observe the course of the sickness.

One week of misery he spent in bed, observing headache, sore throat, streaming nose, upset stomach, plus intervals of hallucination.

When it became too unpleasant he applied the Cure to himself. Within twenty-four hours he was up and about again.

He was elated. The concept was viable!

He was sensible. He said nothing until he got the chance to take the idea straight to the man who might like it.

Ralph M'Botu Kitaj.

Overath came to Kitaj early in 1980.

Kitaj was appalled, amused, fascinated. He ordered tests to check the concept. The tests proved positive. The Cold was nonfatal but very nasty. The Cure was uniformly effective. Obviously it could be very profitable.

"I felt naked then," Kitaj told me in 1992. "The ceiling wasn't after all about getting rich. It was about the limit of self-disgust. I knew I was set on it. But it took me four years before I found myself doing it."

The consequences were almost cataclysmic. The cover-up Kitaj put out placed blame for the Cold on the Russians at a time when they were playing bully. There was nearly full-scale nuclear war.

What happened?

There are many versions. In January 1984 I was in Rome when the Cold was first released in ten European cities, including Amsterdam, London, Paris, Rome, and Zurich. It was another extremely severe winter; the release of the Cold coincided with a week of blizzards, food shortages, fuel shortages, and acute industrial unrest. The sniffling and sneezing began. Soon millions of people were sick. Existing social chaos was exacerbated. The story began to creep around that the Cold had been artificially and deliberately induced, though to begin with there was no clear idea who might have done this, or why. Meanwhile, Kitaj's plan had been that the Cure should be "discovered," mass-manufactured, and rush-released onto the needy market within six weeks of the start of the Cold. Discovery and production of the Cure was set up through yet another new front company which, registered in Switzerland, was also to receive the profits. The Board of Directors of this company were all unknown and anonymous men. Kitaj was not to be associated in any way at any point with the Cure. "It wasn't part of my image to appear philanthropic," he later told me, very caustically. Overath had been bought out and pensioned safely off to South America. It all looked as if it was going well.

Then the problems began. The rumor started that the Russians were responsible. This perhaps could have been foreseen.

"I never got more irresponsible than that," Kitaj later admitted.

For the Russians, threatened by American-Chinese alliance, began boosting their uncertain self-respect by threatening Europe. Throughout January there were massive troop movements and maneuvers in several East European countries, and growing fear that the Kremlin was considering invasion. The rumor seemed very believable. The Russians were using the Cold to soften up Europe. By the end of the month, accusations were on the wing. The Russian denials were too virulent: nobody believed them. Next, the armed forces of France, Germany, Italy, and Austria were brought to red alert when the Russians refused to withdraw their armies from Hungary, Bulgaria, Czechoslovakia, Yugoslavia. For some days it was eyeball to eyeball. Only gradually did the tension slacken, maybe diverted by a fresh outbreak of Middle Eastern chaos, by bloody revolution in South Africa, but most of all by the terrible snowblitz that swept northern and central Europe during the first week of February.

The Cure was rushed onto the market two weeks ahead of schedule.

"I got scared," Kitaj admitted in Ireland.

By March he'd made a few more millions. But the affair did not end there. It had gone too close to the edge. The Russians demanded a full investigation to clear their name. During the rest of 1984 the international inquiries got to the point where Kitaj himself was threatened with exposure. Then he needed all his leopard instinct, his jungle sense, to stay clear. Most of all he had to fight his own urge to self-destruct. In this business he had made several blunders, all of which can in retrospect be seen as his hostile moves against himself. Yet as soon as he found himself threatened from outside he brought all his energies to bear on self-defense, denial, evasion, obfuscation.

"Richard Nixon was too self-righteous to know how to lie effectively," was his comment, in Ireland, with the memory still hurting, "and his intelligence system wasn't up to really effective blackmail and murder. He just didn't do it right according to the fucked-up rules of that particular game."

It seems that Kitaj did. But only just. Overath's complicity was discovered; Overath himself was tracked down and extradited from Brazil to stand trial in the same court where Andreas Baader had once stood. Kitaj was within an ace of exposure. But Overath never reached the courtroom. When they came to take him from his cell, they found him poisoned to death.

That was November 1984, a month after I joined Kitaj, at the time he and Lenore began planning the Disappearance. He was tangled in the ceiling of madness.

The postscript? Recently it was established that the Russians had indeed been on the point of a European action. If not for the Cold scare and its consequences—which almost caused war—there would have been war. By his greed and lies, Kitaj quite probably saved the world. Very paradoxical—but no more so than the principle behind much immunization—fight poison with poison.

"Do you think that always works?" I heard Lenore ask him in Connemara. "Can the liar find truth through lies? Can good come out of selfishness?"

Kitaj just raised his eyebrow at her and went out for a walk.

I made the crucial connection with Kitaj in the lobby of the Dorchester hotel, Park Lane, London, on 2 September 1984.

The previous few weeks had been frustrating, insane. I no longer had a clear idea what I was doing. The Golden Fleece of Kitaj that I pursued now looked very muddy to me, yet still I pursued it. In July, while attempting to track him, I got caught in a riot in Kingston, Jamaica, which cost me a broken arm. Some weeks later I was waiting for him to show up in Mexico City for talks with Jiminez. He didn't arrive, but the earthquake did. Somehow by the beginning of September I got to Brussels where he was expected to be making a grain deal with the EEC Commissioners on the evening of the first . . . and there, while crossing a crowded plaza, minding my own business, I was blasted by a bomb planted by resurgent Flemish nationalists. Five people were killed. I was mildly concussed, I missed Kitaj, but while receiving attention in a Brussels hospital I saw a TV newscast: he was already gone, to London.

I took the chance. I knew when he was in London Kitaj usually stayed at the Arab-owned Dorchester, despite his alleged Jewish background. I had the feeling that if I didn't make connection this time, I never would. The three and a half years since Detroit had tested my faith and my funds to the limit, and I feared that soon I might give up. Feverishly I discharged myself from the hospital and caught a 4:00 A.M. flight to London. The flight took half an hour . . . but then it took more than three hours to get from Heathrow to Hyde Park Corner: the Piccadilly Line tube broke down in the tunnel. I looked and felt dreadful when at last I emerged into the morning rush hour and walked the few hundred yards up Park Lane to the hotel. It was 8:10 A.M. when the new automatic doorperson at the Dorchester denied me entry despite the battery of ID cards and credentials which I always carried with me, but just when I was beginning to despair (conscious of the dangerous looks I was getting from the armed human porters) the door clicked open in unexpectedly positive response to a Conservative Party membership card which had expired two years earlier.

My luck felt good. I went in. I had no evidence that Kitaj was here, but it felt right. To allay suspicions I went straight to the desk, told a tale of being caught in the Brussels bomb-blast and how I had a breakfast rendezvous at the hotel with a business associate. They bought it, but I was aware of eyes on my back as I went to wash and clean up. As nonchalantly as possible I set myself at a table in the ground-floor restaurant, near the door, with a good view of the lobby through which, I hoped, Kitaj would soon pass on his way out. Of course I had not asked if Kitaj were in the hotel.

I lingered forty-five minutes over that breakfast, stretching out the bacon and eggs until, at long last, hotel security staff took up positions in the lobby, and I knew my hunch was correct. I watched them carefully, and when I saw their eyes flick towards the elevators, I knew my moment had come.

Very casually, I stood. Silently, grateful for the soft carpeting, I approached the door . . . then moved quickly through it and into the lobby before the staffpersons on guard could stop me.

My timing was perfect.

Kitaj, with Lenore, and four sharp-faced grey-suited men with them, was striding rapidly towards the main exit. He was just feet away, the other side of a large potted aspidistra. He was wearing a golden-threaded royal blue silk djellabah. Its billowing folds seemed oddly inappropriate on his truculently purposeful frame, yet his dynamism was obvious, electric, and for a moment I felt taken aback, unable to move. The moment almost undid me. The staffpersons had noticed me, were closing in behind me, and Kitaj's own guards had also seen me. I responded positively. The frozen moment passed: I knew what I had to do. I estimated Kitaj's brainwave frequency as very fast, approaching twenty cycles a second. I moved quickly towards him, and as I did I tried to tune into his attention with a carefully visualized flood of dynamic, aggressive, thrusting success images.

They worked. Someone was grabbing me from behind, one of his men had a hand on my chest, pushing me back, when abruptly Kitaj stopped.

He turned, stroking his neat Van Dyke beard, and eyed me.

"You again," he said mildly. "Still at it, eh? Why?"

There was a lump in my throat, butterflies in my stomach.

"Tell these goons to take their hands off me," I said harshly.

He was amused, though Lenore wasn't, nor anyone else.

"Let him go," he said. "Let him speak. He's worked for it."

Rapidly I babbled at him that to me he symbolized an important mythology alive and evolving in the world today; I told him he hadn't realized his own true potential; I tried to explain why I followed him.

"I've got no sane reason," I said quickly, keeping my eyes fixed on his face. It looked more drawn, more haggard than it had. "The chase I guess had become its own reason. It's taken me so long to catch up with you that you've turned into my yoga, my oath, my Grail, my purpose—my means of growth. I've had to sharpen my consciousness to impinge on your attention at all, you've walked past me so often that . . ."

I stopped in mid-flight. His head was cocked.

"What the hell are you talking about?" he asked. Before I could answer he turned to Lenore. She was scowling at me. "Can you make it out?" he asked her.

"Just another nut," she said bluntly. "Don't waste time with him."

"I'll tell you," I said quickly, for the bodyguards were about to start pushing me out again, and I was finding it hard to keep my center. "It's like this. You have mythreality. You're not aware enough of it for your own good. You feel like a modern Midas. Everything you touch turns to gold, but it won't feed your heart or soul. You don't have any answers. You see the destruction, but you can't see how to create. You told me once about rites of passage, but you never made it through your own rites. Now you have to start! These days we're walking tightropes; we have to learn to walk them well, or soon we'll all fall into the pit. You can influence our balance—I can tell you how!"

He clapped his hand to his head in mock amazement.

"You're really something! You run round the world after me for four years just to tell me this bullshit?"

I felt it slipping away. I got angry. I shouted at him.

"You talk about bullshit? You're terrified! There's a black hole in your heart and you don't know what to do. The money and power are just substitues that make you sick, but you don't know what to do. You're scared you killed yourself years ago, you want to wake up, but you don't know where to start! So what do you want? Life—or death? Healers—or more killers?"

It was corny but strong, and it caught him.

There was a silence which lasted until he broke it.

"Okay," he said very slowly, and his eyes grew so brilliant that I had to look down. "You leave your number. I'll get in touch."

The call came a month later. I could hardly believe it. But I was ready. I flew to Rio de Janeiro to meet Kitaj. He was with Lenore and Isma'il al Azhari, the quick-witted Sudanese who

was his secretary and reader. He sat me down alone with him in a
room and had me talk to him for twenty-four hours without
stopping, until I no longer knew what I was saying.

Finally he raised his hand and stopped me.

"Isma'il's complaining that I give him too much work," he
said. "It looks like I need someone else along . . . to do my
letters, stuff like that. You're crazy, but you're an interesting
crazy, and you say you can type as well. So, if you'll work thirty
hours a day and four hundred days a year, you've got a job.
Okay? Just one thing—if I ever suspect you're telling me less
than the absolute truth of what you believe, I'll probably kill you,
because I'm sick to death of all the lies, mine included. You just
tell me about them—right?"

So I was hired . . . much to Lenore's displeasure.

Eight months later the Disappearance began.

The Disappearance confirmed the power of Kitaj's myth. Before
it, he was famous. During it, in his absence, he became a legend.

He did not announce his true intention publicly. Only Lenore,
Isma'il, myself, and a few others knew what was going to
happen.

In May 1985 he bought up TV time all over the world and
gave warning that during the next two years he was going to take
over . . . everything.

Yes, *everything*.

Then he disappeared. Completely.

For the previous five years or so he had been every day in the
public eye, the epitome of the crazy eighties, almost comforting
in the constancy and dependability of his excess. Then . . .
without warning . . . he was gone . . . completely.

Between June 1985 and March 1987 he vanished more thoroughly than Howard Hughes had ever managed to do . . . and
he scared hell out of the world. Nobody could find a trace of him
anywhere, and soon the myth of him—his origins in the Ghetto,
his jungle years, his Tarzan belief, now his intension to take over
the world and his Disappearance—became more newsworthy
than his presence had ever been. The industry of Ralph M'Botu
Kitaj proliferated enormously in his absence. Books were written, movies were made, debates were held about the possible
whereabouts and motivations of Ralph M'Botu Kitaj. Secret
agencies sent out their spies to search him out and track him

down. Politicians and businessmen everywhere got very scared with the threat that Kitaj was somehow invisibly in the middle of their activities, unknown to them. Governments took the opportunity to submit major companies in many countries to compulsory audit. Many foul deeds crawled out of the woodwork—but not a trace of Kitaj. Everywhere his unknown activities were denounced, and particularly in Europe and America there was Kitaj-mania. Those dedicated mystical anarchists who called themselves the Spreaders propagated his myth for their own purposes. "Kitaj will be back!" announced a manifesto they issued in 1986. "One morning we'll wake up and find him coiled all round the world like Ouroboros, snaking all through the system and its holes. We'll wake up to find that he's the man who sells us our news, delivers milk to our doors, sends us our mail, puts the tax demands in that mail, provides the bus that takes us to his work in his factory in his city in his land in his world. One man? You think it's impossible? Do you think it's illogical? Then take a look around you. Who owns what?"

There was riot and arson and assassination throughout Europe when governments agreed to outlaw Spreading, which involved total dropping-out from the remains of nine-to-five society. Once outlawed, the movement spread like wildfire. It spread through the formerly conservative middle classes which realized that they too were now totally screwed economically. By 1987 it involved so many people who refused to pay taxes, who took over entire towns and districts, who burned down churches and banks and police stations and halls of justice, that clearly the social fabric in an increasing number of countries was shredding completely. Spreading spread to Russia and the east, from the United States it spread down through Mexico and into South America—very few areas of the world remained entirely unaffected by this new wave in the twentieth-century process of mass rejection of OldStyle hierarchies, beliefs, and chains of command.

It spread and spread and spread. There were civil wars. There were massacres. There was bitterness and hope. There were increasing numbers of people realizing that the future could be won only if past patterns of social assumption could be unraveled and reconstructed into new policies involving a more general self-responsibility . . . an undoing of centralized authorities into more cellular structures of interacting regional autonomies.

But of course it was not so easy. For every individual who

realized the requirements for social union and integration, for new community through individual self-responsibility, there were ten, fifty, a hundred others who felt only the desire to bury their heads ever more deeply in the sand, or to grab what they could for themselves while there was still something to grab.

Nor would it be true to say that Spreading arose entirely out of Kitaj's negative example, out of his Disappearance . . . but the Disappearance was one of the signal events. For, though Kitaj was then in many ways a reactionary symbol of the Great Global Screw-Up, he had also become a (r)evolutionary symbol. The formerly invisible or socially approved tendrils of infantile need and commercial greed which had drawn us ever deeper into the grip of the Black Hole Joke were growing increasingly apparent . . . at least to citizens of the commercial Coca-Cola nations . . . which by 1985 were most of the nations. In a way that was rationally inexplicable but which was becoming intuitively obvious to great numbers of people, the spectacular nonpresence of Kitaj made tangible the channels and nature of the system he'd sworn to take over . . . so that in the wrecked streets people started shouting "Kitaj!" as the key and the sign of their new understanding—an ironic rejection.

Agents of the powers were seeking him everywhere.

But his organization and its loyalties were sufficient . . . and all the time he was living simply in that cottage in Connemara . . . that dilapidated little cottage, with Lenore and Isma'il and myself, near the black lough.

The black lough . . . the lough of the *peiste* . . .

THE PHILOSOPHER'S STONE
OR
THE STONY PHILOSOPHER

"All knowledge is ultimately personal."
—Michael Polanyi

Note:

What happened to Hall? How did this ms. reach us?

When we got the photostat, we found inserted into it by unknown hand (at exactly this point of the narrative which we have now reached) the following duplicated page.

Written on a different size of paper (quarto), and with a different typeface, it appears to be part of a recent field report made by agent(s) of the International Security Organization. We have since learned that the ISO headquarters at The Hague, Northern European Community, was infiltrated on 31 October by Chancer elements. It is probable that this following page, and the entire photostat, were liberated from the ISO and subsequently "placed on our doorstep."

The fragment, if genuine, throws light on the fate of John Hall, secretary to Ralph M'Botu Kitaj.

INTERNATIONAL SECURITY ORGANIZATION

. . . did not resist nor attempt to flee when we entered the single room in which he was living. Following orders we engaged in no conversation but terminated him as soon as positive identification was made. We then searched the room thoroughly. A complete carbon manuscript was found, but no sign of the top copy. It seems therefore that we were too late, and we suspect that copies reduced to microfilm may already exist. Every attempt must be made to seize and destroy. Preliminary inspection of the material suggests an inflammatory work which could lead to serious consequences.

When we made an entry Hall was engaged in burning loose sheets, apparently discarded first draft. He looked unwell. He was not surprised to see us and apparently knew who we were. He stood and said calmly: "You're too late, you can't stop it now. Why not take a chance, and . . ."

Neurorecording of the termination of Hall is also submitted with this report, and we will now proceed in search of the . . .

*   *   *

At this point we must repeat: there is no sure proof that this book is the work of John Hall—and there is no sure proof that this ISO report is genuine. "Convictions make convicts"—we must take care in areas such as these where we may too easily be misled by our modern susceptibility to the irrational, the charismatic, the apocalyptic. We are dealing here with a dynamic mythology which can aid us in our growth—but we are slaves if we believe it literally, if we long to abnegate self-responsibility by seeking salvation from "superior powers" or "space beings." *We* are space beings.

Concerning Sirius: the author has already hinted that the solution to this is internal. We speculate now that much of the recent focus on "intelligence from Sirius" is part of a deliberate blind perpetrated (along with much

UFO activity) by a group or groups unknown upon this planet, their purpose perhaps to trigger evolutionary change in human consciousness, using "Sirius" as reinforcement mechanism.

This may seem fantastic, paranoiac—but what if Kitaj belonged to or was an agent of such a group? What if even now he is alive and well and living in South America? And what if in fact it was Kitaj himself who wrote this book?

"It's a matter of what you can believe, and how you let it affect you, and what use you can make of the information."

So said RMK when Hall called him a liar—so TAKE A CHANCE!

THE DREAMS OF BABYLON
OR
THE BABBLING OF DREAM

"I've always wanted to be picked up by a UFO . . ."
—anon., quoted by Jacques Vallee;
MESSENGERS OF DECEPTION.

7. THE LOUGH OF THE PEISTE

Halley's Comet came back in 1986. In Connemara we hardly saw it. For months, day and night, the skies were clouded. The four of us had our work cut out just staying alive and getting on with each other as best we could.

To start with, the change from international city pace was a shock. We found ourselves voluntarily stuck in a cottage in a fold of a wet, windy, brackish, wild, underpopulated, and impoverished moorland. There was little protection against the storms that came wailing in off the Atlantic. The cottage was thatched, whitewashed, solidly built of stone, but it was cold, in bad repair, and without gas, electricity, or running water. The perfect hide-out for a rich man known to love luxury, within yards of the reed-fringed verge of one of those innumerable little black Connemara loughs associated with the *peiste*—apparently a close relative of the better-known Loch Ness Monster.

In fact it was a place with a tale and atmosphere not so very different from that of the haunted lakes of the Mountains of the Moon, which is one reason Kitaj chose it. He was always fascinated by wild watery places with legends of creatures in the dark depths. In such places he found a geographical analogue for his own rather fearful inner processes.

We were three miles from the nearest village, a tiny place consisting of a pub, post office, general store, church, another pub, and little else. It lay, this village, in a rocky and more-or-less sheltered inlet of the sea, on both sides of the humpbacked seventeenth-century stone bridge which spanned a small fast river. The local people were fishermen or subsistence farmers, most of them elderly. There was nothing to keep young people there. Our transport was a bicycle. We had arrived in the old landrover for which after January 1986 we could get no fuel. Later on we got a gray mare, who was steady enough pulling the peat-sled, but nervous with riders, except Isma'il, and so usually, when it was my turn to go into the village for supplies and any mail, I took the bicycle or walked. It was almost as fast to walk. Surfaced road came only half the distance to us from the village, and it was often flooded during the time we were there. Between us and the road, a mile and a half away, lay the roughest of tracks, alternately rocky or passing through mires.

We were emphatically isolated.

The occasional letters we got were addressed to Robert or Sheila Carr (Kitaj and Lenore), or to John Morrison (myself), or to a Mr. Pauwels (Isma'il). For the most part they consisted of inoffensive gossip from imaginary friends. The gossip was meaningful to us; we would reply in a similar way—we took great care. Our cover had been created with precise attention to detail. The subtle plastic surgery had only been the start. Before arriving in Ireland we had coached each other in very prosaic personal histories—ex-urban back-to-earthers, increasingly common in the transitional countrysides of Britain and Ireland. It would have been a strain, maintaining this pretense, except that we hardly ever met anyone. To the locals we made it as clear as we could that our interests lay in the potato patch, the compost heap, and the weather. At the start we had a few "casual" visitors, checking us out, some giving good advice, even help, others openly amused by our inexperienced rural fumbling. So that, after a while, we were pretty well ignored . . . and by the time we met other back-to-earthers, we could talk about compost with the best of them and, if we seemed peculiar in our setup and personalities, then our peculiarities were less suspicious than no peculiarities at all.

The upshot was, we were the only people who bothered us.

The world was being turned upside down by people looking for Kitaj . . . but Mr. Carr's cover was never tested during the twenty-one months we were in Ireland . . . except by Mrs. Carr, Mr. Morrison, Mr. Pauwels, and by Mr. Carr himself.

It was what the Disappearance was all about.

There is a day I remember in mid-March '86. Windy, the light cold and pure, high wracks of fast grey cloud. I was in the kitchen, making a lentil broth. Through the window I could see Lenore, bending in the meager garden. Isma'il was up on the roof, repairing and rebinding black thatch torn almost completely away in the most recent gale. Kitaj—Kitaj was out on the moors somewhere. For weeks now he had been roaming, wildly, seeking the lost locked gates to his pre-Ruwenzori soul, bound entirely in his self-interest. He was approaching the wilderness, the desert, the dark night.

On this day he was gone again. From where I was I saw how Lenore so often lifted her head from her work, scanning the dark undulations of moor for a sign of him—then shaking her head in sharp irritation at her own concern.

That night he wasn't back; she slept with me; we argued.

Lenore would sleep with each of us, but occasionally, almost ritualistically, preserving her distance. Three men and one woman—for reasons of his own Kitaj had chosen this, and each of us had assented. We began with tacit understanding of the potential difficulties of Lenore's position—for her and us. There was no room for power games or gonadal mind-fucks. She had to keep her perspective. Mostly she did. She had. Her sexual mediumship was delicate and sympathetic. Yet for a time the situation had bothered me.

"It's a pity," I said to Isma'il one morning, after several months, in autumn '85. He was planing wood; I was trying to shape some stone. "We haven't had this triangle-quadrangle thing out in the open. We haven't talked about it."

"If you need to talk about it," he said, "maybe you'd better."

I talked, then went away and thought about it, after which I felt easier. Lenore was being practical. But she needed our help. Sometimes she felt she couldn't handle it. Then she would go off on her own, as each of us did sometimes—into the healing of the Old Religion, of moor and stream and wind, earth and elementals. Her face, alienated by the plastic surgery, grew wry and strong and personal again. She had heart, and she was generous.

Yet she was distressed by Kitaj's distance. She knew he had secrets. She suspected he'd begun to tell them to me.

With Isma'il she found some peace, good humor, the release and earthing of her emotions; they did yoga and meditations together.

With me she found troubled stimulation, and only sometimes a physical loving empathy that brought us above our usual state of thinly veiled competition.

By March of '86 we were all impatient, fretful for spring, and that night, with Kitaj not returned, with black wind rattling the windows, we argued, and she told me what she thought:

"I believe in evolution. Things don't have to happen all at once. I hoped the countryside would help him to do it, naturally, gradually. But he brought you along—and you believe in revolution and apocalypse. He's a volcano, and you're laying dynamite in him! He lets you close so you can punch holes in his hang-ups. Now you believe in hammerblow enlightenment, you say we don't have time to fuck about, you walk on thin theories you never tried out, and maybe you mean well. But what happens if you punch a hole in the wrong place? Do you know what you're doing? How will *you* cope when the volcano explodes?"

She had a point. I thought about it, then I sought Isma'il, and said, "I wish I had a better idea what's going on. I keep feeling unreal about being here. What the hell am I? Psychoslave of a crazy rich man? Sometimes I think I'm playing the Fool in this pack. Sometimes I sense chasms underneath us that I can't quite see . . . but I've had dreams, and . . ."

Isma'il eyed me steadily, quizzically.

"If you're the Fool, then what is Kitaj? And Lenore? And who am I?"

"Kitaj's been playing the Devil for years," I said carefully. "The Prince of material power, hating the way he loves his own chains. But now . . . that bondage is cracking, and . . . I sense the fertility of the Star . . ."

Then I remembered dreams and must have looked troubled.

Isma'il leaned on the spade, searched me keenly.

"What is it?" he asked quietly.

"A few nights ago," I said tensely, "I dreamed I saw clean-picked rib cages on a battlefield, and Death passing through. But

green grass was sprouting between the bones, and the bones were
shaped like dragon's teeth . . .''

"I wonder what that means," murmured Isma'il, staring at the
restless fast clouds, giving me the impression he knew perfectly
well.

". . . Then the dream changed," I went on. "There was a
star so bright I couldn't look at it with my ordinary eyes, and we
were standing under it, the four of us, and its light was like liquid
fire, flowing through us . . . changing us . . . and I couldn't
recognize myself, nor you, nor Lenore . . . and where Kitaj had
stood, there was a pool of melted gold . . .''

"We'll know about these things," said Isma'il again as if to
himself. Then he shook his head, and took the spade, and turned
over another clod.

"Kitaj is starting to change," I said tersely. "So are we all.
It's going to get drastic; it means death of the old. That's okay,
but I keep wondering about our set-up here. Lenore says I'm
punching holes through his hang-ups; she asked me what happens
if I punch holes in the wrong places.''

"Who is Lenore?" Isma'il asked. "Why is she here?"

I shook my head and breathed deeply, in and out.

"I don't know. I'm not sure if she does, either. Sometimes I
think she's the Priestess, the Isis, except she's not confirmed or
happy with it." Then a sudden dizziness of apparent insight
struck me. "She has an unfulfilled Persephone role. She hasn't
yet crossed her own Styx. She hasn't yet gone down to the
Underworld. She knows she must. That's why she's here. Kitaj
is her gate. The shock will come through him—for all of us.
There's such great *power* in this situation! Kitaj's energies will
become increasingly focused—and sometimes I'm scared of what's
going to come through, because the three of us are here to help
him bring it through. But . . .''

I shook my head, couldn't go on.

"You don't want the responsibility?"

"I don't *understand* the responsibility," I said. "All I can
sense is it's a large one, and that taking it on will mean . . . the
destruction of everything I hold familiar, including . . . all my
ideas about myself . . .''

Isma'il shrugged, went on digging.

"Sooner or later we all have to make that choice."

"But if we make it in blindness, how can it be a good one?"

"The blindness is never total," he said over his shoulder.

"You mean I'm hiding what I know from myself through fear?"

He looked round at me, friendly, directly, engaging.

"Are you still concerned that Lenore sleeps with us?"

I shrugged. "Maybe I've got ancient notions about marriage."

Isma'il laughed. "Maybe not ancient enough. Excuse me, but I think you like to tie yourself up in knots. The work we have right now is enough."

She had a point, and he had several. Isma'il al Azhari was in his middle forties at this time. His people were from Libya; he had grown up in the Sudan. He was a lithe, energetic man, with a continually darting air; with a fondness for Sufi ways and writing, particularly Jalaluddin Rumi, and a great store of Nasrudin tales. He never spoke much of his past or his attainments. He could be sharp, he was always direct but gentle, with a tolerant humor, and whatever happened he remained methodical, with open eyes, both amused and serious about his curious involvement with Ralph M'Botu Kitaj. "I was in Teheran when Khomeini came. One day I saw Kitaj walk on the street in the crowds when all the western connections were getting out or hiding up. I liked his style, and something made me approach him and tell him so. We kept in touch."

When all else failed, Isma'il remained constant. We all turned to him at one time or another. The cold northern weather must have been troublesome to him; he joked about it. He was one of those people whose remarkability is so understated that you realize it only when they're gone.

His face was keen, mobile, a bit lopsided, with a scar across the right cheekbone, and a nose which had once been thoroughly broken. It was the face of a man always active but never hurried, almost always easy-humored. He'd dig peat, wash dishes, go to the village, empty the shit-bucket when nobody else wanted to do these things. He worked steadily on various personal projects. By 1987 he had, on his own, built a concrete outside bathhouse, and a small barn where we had the mare, hay, chickens, and two goats which he milked.

Also he planted a great many trees in the poor soil round the cottage, hardwoods, the growth of which we'd not live to see.

"Trees are like people," he'd say with a grin. "I talk to them, and sing to them, and they will grow strong."

Which was the nature of Isma'il's card. Strength.

Throughout that springtime Kitaj roamed, spending days and nights away on the moors, often returning abstracted and strange. He had recovered physical health; imaginative health was also returning. He had cleaned himself up. In the first nine months he had worked to discard factors that supported what he defined as illusions. He had gone cold turkey on all the drugs. In Ireland there was only Guinness and whiskey. The first weeks of the Disappearance had been a hell of withdrawal for him. He'd drunk like a fish, been sick much of the time, gone days without speaking, but from all this he'd emerged, with other drugs also discarded. Like the need of money, luxury, speed, thousands of people to say yes all the time. His life had been a long-maintained and deliberate superficiality. Now he began to seek the courage to go deeper again. For the most part he sought it on his own, speaking on something only after he'd thought about it maybe for weeks. He was coming together. But there were drawbacks and difficulties. There were fears and blocks.

"You're a country boy at heart, aren't you?" he'd asked me casually one day in New York. "You like digging ditches and seeing waters flow, don't you?"

The relationship between Kitaj and myself took time to develop. It was hindered by mutual suspicion and self-suspicion, by my mythologizing of his personality. It was hard for me to get spontaneous with him. He forced me out of my awestruck reserve by baiting me continually until I lost my temper and started shouting back. Thereafter our interaction was more productive.

So I found myself in Ireland—in a vacuum, a morass of indecision about what I really sought. For years I'd been rushing after Kitaj, hardly thinking.

Now I was stuck with him in the back of Ireland.

It was a shock to learn I didn't know my motives.

Lenore was right: I couldn't articulate my image of his future. It was an ideal, not an assimilated experience, personal to my sense of reality. Whenever I went on about newconsciousness, mythreality, about Midas Evolved, I had no more practical idea than he did what I really meant.

In time it didn't matter. In time we got in tune, developed a strong correspondence. My past mental life, and some of the thoughts I had, proved complementary to his life-drama, his own search. Increasingly in Ireland we teased each other with shadows and insights, a dangerous game . . . so that trust and suspicion grew mutually between us.

We were rarely joined by Lenore or Isma'il for the long night talks in which the autobiography began to take shape.

But as and when we could the four of us shared our activities. Usually we ate together, sometimes went for walks. There were music sessions round the old black stand-up piano—Lenore played a pretty mean honky-tonk style.

And there were the play readings.

We spent hundreds of hours at these. Shakespeare, Shaw, Brecht, Wilde, many others. Kitaj was invariably the most immersed and word-perfect. His favorite, curiously, was *Macbeth*, which seems to argue that there was in him then a certain sense of doomed fatality. Lenore did not relish playing Lady Macbeth, for reasons made clear in February 1987 . . . yet by then Kitaj's knowledge of western dramatic roles was considerable.

"You'd have made it as a bard or *filid* among the old Irish," I told him. "It took twenty years to be recognized as a bard—a druidic training—you had to have at least five hundred stories in your head . . . and in your heart."

"The Word had power," he murmured, "before it was caught onto the page."

The Word. That winter and spring I read to him copiously. I'd brought many books, and ordered more from Dublin. I read him much that he already knew and liked, including all twenty-four Tarzan tales, which drove me crazy. So far as I could I read him information, not romance. For a long time it had to be information disguised as romance, and I read him a lot of science fiction, I read him Carlos Castaneda and *Illuminatus*. Later, *The Romeo Error*, *The Shaman's Doorway*, and much of Joseph Campbell's vast work, *The Masks of God*.

Also we went deep into the Irish tradition—Flann O'Brien, and *Puckoon*, and *The Crock of Gold* by James Stephens, and Joyce's multilevelled babelhouse of games for saintly whores. Kitaj enjoyed these, especially *Puckoon*, yet most of all he loved the wild and ancient magic sagas; the *Tain*, and the tales of the Tuatha De Danaan, and the stories of giants, heroes, and gods. He was fascinated by *The Voyage of Bran*, especially the bit where the sailors, back at last from the far-off western Land of Youth and Happiness, from Tir nan Og, return to find not five, not ten, but a hundred years and days passed by since the hour they left; to find that they cannot set foot on land without crumbling to dust . . . for they are out of time, from another space, no longer mortal.

This tale caused a crisis between us.

"When was that story written?" Kitaj demanded when I was finished.

"I guess it was written down by the monks maybe twelve hundred years ago," I said, "but it's probably much older than that."

"The time change in it," Kitaj mused, "sounds like a relativity effect, as if they were star travelers, not Irish sailors, and . . ."

"Maybe Tir nan Og really means Sirius," I heard myself saying. "There's a lot of weird stuff about Sirius in the old . . ."

I stopped dead. Kitaj was staring at me with horror. I didn't know why I'd said it; we'd never talked about Sirius; there was only that dream I'd had, the one I'd told Isma'il about.

I asked Kitaj what was wrong. He refused to answer, and soon after went to bed. Next evening he insisted I read him more Trazan.

"I'm sick of bloody Tarzan!" I protested. "What's this thing about Sirius? You looked as though I'd spooked you. What was it?"

He lost his temper. I was amazed.

"Don't talk about it!" he yelled. "Some things you just don't understand, do you? Leave off! Forget it!"

"You told me to tell you about your lies!" I answered angrily. "This sounds like one of them. You're evading something. What is it?"

He looked away. There was petulant grief in his eyes.

"Some other time," he said, his voice very low. "I want Tarzan."

For the next two nights we compromised with *A Feast Unknown*, one of Philip José Farmer's more brutally explicit jungle escapades. Kitaj seemed to find it gloriously funny and heroic. But by then I could see a little way into him, and I knew he was brooding . . . about Sirius. It was a mystery.

"That's right," he said sharply, cynically, after I'd read the last page of ultraviolence and closed the book. "Just like it was when I was in Africa."

"You're not there now," I objected. "You're here."

"The past's in the here and now!" he shot back. "You think I'm so dumb because I don't read or write. You talk of my expanded preliterate consciousness and my powerful aura and my destiny—you get as bad as Isma'il with his *Parliament of Birds* and that Jellyludo fellow." He eyed me warningly. "Don't try changing me too fast; don't go fishing out of your depth. I like your line, Johnny, but don't push it—okay?"

He fell silent. I said nothing. I was a little scared. Not for the first time I wondered just who he was, where he was going. We sat. We listened to the wind, to the sound of Isma'il hammering nails into the table he was making in the next room. It was only after a minute or so that Kitaj looked at me with a wide-eyed, painful expression, and asked:

"Do you know what I am, Johnny?"

I stayed quiet, thinking he was going to tell me something.

Then I realized: he was asking me if *I* knew.

That was in May '86. It was a turning point. In mentioning Sirius I'd touched on a dimension of Kitaj which he hadn't shown anyone, perhaps not even himself—something buried deep, lost on Ruwenzori—and thereafter I was a hunter of his secret. On my own account I started reading about and meditating on Sirius, though to Kitaj I said nothing further about it. I was willing to wait . . . for my own sake too. Some things I hardly felt ready to learn about, and always with Kitaj there was a sense of the threat of explosion.

There was no explosion that summer. There was steady progress. Kitaj started opening up about his early life. By September almost all the early episodes of *Liar's Gold* had been recorded, and for the first time I heard about the Angel and the Voice. Thus, bit by bit, he faced and revealed the inner life which he'd denied and, as he did, the blood came back into him, he relaxed and laughed more often, and his magnetism grew powerful and clear.

Yet it was sometimes a battle. Advance and retreat, advance and retreat, three forward and two back, admission then elusiveness, and frequently still he went tramping on the moors, each time returning with something new resolved inside him, with an increased receptivity in his face.

None of us talked about it very much. The months passed; we were not discovered; we survived. But then came autumn, and then, the second winter.

The potato crop in Ireland failed. There was blight, and terrible weather, and this was common throughout the world. There were food shortages in Europe. We found ourselves faced with a threat of starvation. This seemed ridiculous. Then it hit our bellies and became real. By November the old man Jessup who ran the village store was grimly rationing the last of the flour, and there were no greens to be had at all once our meager garden supply was exhausted. And over the radio as we huddled round the fire we heard of the deaths of millions of people in Africa and Asia; we heard endless political denials that international weather engineering and industrial activities had led to the storms; we heard of plans to harvest tiny protein-rich crustaceans called krill from the oceans, "thus depriving what whales are left of what food they have left," Lenore commented sharply. And Kitaj, whose bank balance included the blood of whales, was silent. Much of the winter he was silent, withdrawn and thinking deeply, spending days painting crude and childlike pictures in which, sometimes, a brilliant star would appear. "It is not the comet, and it is not a star of ill omen," was all he would say.

The comet. That year the comet was blamed for many things. The collapse of governments, the dissolution of borders with starving populations on the move, the power blackouts and epidemics in many cities, and in Europe the specter of the fourteenth century. The Ring of Fire was active from Chile to Alaska to Japan and New Zealand; a huge tonnage of volcanic debris was swirling in the atmosphere, blocking the sunlight and reducing the temperature still further.

The rain lashed continually through the last half of the year. There was only one night when we saw the comet clearly.

"A Plutonian time," Kitaj murmured as we gazed up at the visitor. "A pulverizing time."

We drew in our belts, conserved energy, grew lean.

Meanwhile in the outside world that abstraction, Kitaj's wealth, was still growing. In his absence his managers went right on dealing for him, upping the price of grain by withholding, and on the radio we heard the condemnations of Ralph M'Botu Kitaj, and of how in many countries his interests were being seized, nationalized, and annulled.

In December Kitaj reacted when an old woman in the village died and was determined to have died of starvation. She hadn't eaten in two weeks. Kitaj mailed a coded letter giving orders for the distribution of food in the Sahel (the Sahara's southern edge, where the Dogon were among those who were dying) and in other parts of Africa, in India, Europe, and Ireland. He said nothing about it to us. He remained apparently abstracted and withdrawn. In January on the radio we heard of this "gift" which could come only from Kitaj; we heard of the fleet of grain ships assembling in U.S. ports despite a barrage of legal, commercial, and political opposition. And by the end of the month we were hearing of the bloody riots and corruption at nearly every port where the grain arrived. Most of it got into the hands of those who were already well fed, nowhere near the bellies of those who needed it.

"What else?" said Kitaj. "It's the way things are."

His voice was flat, but his inner turbulence was nearing the boil, and, as if seeking to temper the heat of his conflict and irresolution, many nights that bitter winter he spent listening to tapes of Grieg, Nielsen, Sibelius. He'd lie down flat on his back on the floor, with only the coals or the peat on the fire for light, and spend hours slow-swimming those depths he'd denied so long. For a time he and Lenore were close again, almost playful; they'd float together in the clarities of Grieg's mirror-surfaced pieces, and for a while everything would seem peaceful. It was calm before the storm, and it endured while the weather was most vicious and our bellies emptiest, throughout January 1987. We spent long evenings together, the four of us, avoiding seriousness in play readings, stories, and frivolities. But there was an edge on us, all the time. It was transitory, like a prelude, and we could all sense the unexpressed energies that were building up in Kitaj, in each of us.

This peaceful taste in music didn't last into February. I think he found himself drifting too close to precipices which as yet he was unwilling to confront . . . and it was in the last week in January that he and I got into an argument about his motives for setting up the second party, the Beethoven's Sixteenth Quartet party, in San Francisco back in 1979.

He expressed doubt. He spoke about his door, his gate, his death, his hope of . . . and then he stopped.

There was no more symphonic music after that. During the following week, with a growing passion that sometimes he found hard to control, he started telling me about Ruwenzori . . . about Iloshabiet . . . and at the same time, as if now decided to let it all come through, to let the heat of remembering take him through chaos or destruction or anything, he started wiring himself up into machine-kill. Orwellian rock by Mammon, Genocide, the Rotten Review, bands like that—fast three-chord autodestruction, more efficiently selective than the medical brand of electroshock. After talking to me he'd clamp himself into headphones and sit there sometimes muttering or even shouting the words of nihilistic and disgusted songs.

The atmosphere became very tense. Lenore accused me of trying to drive him crazy. ''You're chasing the goals of your own ego!'' she snapped, and I snapped something back at her, and it got so we were refusing to cook for each other, and for a week or more Isma'il was doing it all, patiently, his face thoughtful and unrevealing, taking time to speak to Kitaj I think when both Lenore and I were out of the way.

Yet Kitaj persisted. He had grown sharp and edgy, apparently brittle and ready to break into something else.

Then came the evening he told of murder and curse . . .

Elsewhere in this account I've described something of what happened that evening. How Kitaj and I were sitting by the fire in the front room, how I thought we were alone, with Lenore gone to the village, and Isma'il outside talking to his trees. The wind was rising, making the walls creak and the windows rattle, and the two of us were cocooned in the dim tent of firelight with a bottle of Scotch for inspiration. The tape recorder was running. It had been recording almost two hours, and much of the tape was blank, for I had asked many unanswered questions before he had begun to speak directly about Ruwenzori and Iloshabiet. Other questions he had answered in ways that cut me. These sessions were always hard on both of us, and this was the hardest of all. For months I'd been probing him, and often I was unhappy with the questions I had to ask . . . but they were part of my responsibility, my function. Usually I was in deadly earnest, a slightly paranoid hunter of his hang-ups, and frequently he laughed at my clumsy approaches. He would trip me up and riddle me with my own inner conflicts until I could not tell his red herrings from his reality. But on this afternoon there had been no laughter. He had evaded, I had persisted, until we were both tense and tired. He had spoken of how he came to Ruwenzori—fleetingly he had mentioned Sirius, had shown me something of himself, and I hadn't dared take him up on it, for fear of making him clam up completely. He knew it. He knew what I was thinking. He'd talked on a while longer, about Iloshabiet and her history, and of the two years Iloshabiet and M'Botu had spent together. Then we'd hit a difficult space, a silent period, during which we both stared into the flames and reduced the level of the whisky bottle by a few inches. Finally he looked up to me and said, with a twisted grin:

"You just want to prove what a shit I am, so you don't have to feel so bad about yourself. You want to know why I ran from Ruwenzori, what went wrong between me and Iloshabiet. Fine. I'll tell you. See if it makes you feel any better to know."

It hurt. But he was hurting too.

His face taut, his eyes clouded, he told me of the murder that M'Botu committed—the murder of the French botanist. The wind was swooping down the chimney, the light outside was thickening. I listened with the utmost attention, straining to hear him through the racket of the storm.

Maybe, if not for my focus on him, I'd have heard her come into the room behind us. Perhaps Kitaj heard her. His senses were very acute . . . but I just can't say. Nor can I guess when precisely she did come through the door.

He spoke of the murder. He judged himself, then fell silent, his eyes lost in the fire. I watched him, utterly disconcerted, but willing him to speak on. She must have been there by then. Standing in the cold shadows by the door, brought home early by the storm, which by then was so cold that when Kitaj's lips began to move again I had to bend close to hear him.

To start with he was almost inaudible, mumbling in an African dialect, his eyes lost, his face rigid. But soon his voice began to rise. It became very clear. And his words were Iloshabiet's words.

"Oh, you idiot!" She was sad, angry, faint. "Why didn't you go? Now you've denied your fate, you've denied your voice, you've turned into a killer, and you have to run. Did you really think you owned me? Will you rape and kill when inside you know much better ways? Oh, listen to me before you run! You've ignored what Njeru taught you. Will you forget what I have to say? It is this! From now on you'll find no happiness with anyone or anything, ever, until you admit that you cannot own the world, or any part of it, or anyone in it. Until you admit that, and know it in your heart, then you yourself are owned—owned by the curse of what you have just now done—and your act has also put a curse on me, and on your son. Now, you had better go!''

Then I was doubly shocked, by the sudden stripped nakedness of Kitaj's face as he stated at me, and by Lenore's laugh, out of the shadows.

"Filthy lucre!" she said sardonically. She stormed between us at the fire, blocking off its heat, its light. "Rafe, I have never heard this story from you." She gazed down at him intensely, windswept and wet, firelight flickering on the tightness of her profile. "I would like to know from you now if this story you have never told me did really happen. Or is it merely an invention to dramatize your confusion and sense of guilt?"

He looked up. He was not smiling.

"John's got the tape recorder running," he said.

She ignored both me and his statement completely.

"When you and I married," she said to him with steely composure, "we made the promise to be honest with each other. Now I want to know from you about what I've just heard. Did it really happen? Did you kill that man? If you did, and if you have known all along that your way of life is cursed, why did you never tell me about it? So, did it happen, or not?"

"It happened," he told her, his face glassy, impenetrable. "I've told John because he wants to know. But you never did. There are some things about me you have never wanted to know, because you don't want to lose the image you formed of me, that I'm a basically decent human being who might still be reformed by your faith, redeemed by your hope. But don't take it personally. This is something I just could never talk about before, in any case."

"No!" she said sharply, moving from the fire. "No, Rafe, I never thought I could 'redeem' you, and if I feel protective of you, then that's my folly. But I don't like hearing you making excuses like this, drumming up stories to explain your guilt. It makes me lose my respect for you."

She was back at the door, she swung round, pacing.

"What worries me," she went on, "is how you sit here night after night and let this man persuade you to spin romanticized yarns that only feed your inner poverty and self-pity. You could be behaving much more positively." She was at the fire again. Its light flickered on the dull straggling gold of her hair. "How long does this go on, Rafe? What's the point of this empty-bellied soul-searching? What's the program? Right now you could be out in the world using your influence to good effect instead of lurking here with whisky and delusions. You're not well, Rafe! You'll crack uselessly if this goes on!"

His face was blank. She was scared too. I sat tensely, wanting yet not wanting to leave. Just then Isma'il came in. He sensed it, stood quiet, said nothing. Nor did Kitaj speak. I felt his confusion. The chasms were close. Lenore must have known it, but she'd had enough, and it was also to do with her own compulsive inner journey, her ambivalence of desire and fear for those Persephone depths of death and rebirth . . . for she was not willing to stop.

"So tell me: why are we here?" Her voice attacked. "How long must we wait for you to reach the great conclusion?"

"What is that?" His voice was hardly audible.

"That this Iloshabiet, whether she lived or not, was quite right. There is no 'ownership' of life. You have to let go and relax, Rafe."

"I know!" His voice rose. "I always did!"

"Then are you saying you are compelled by this 'curse,' that you're not responsible for the life you've led?"

"I am responsible!" He rubbed his brow. His voice, getting louder, was shaky. I felt tension flowing through my body. "And we won't be here much longer. It's coming. Can't you feel it? Don't you hear the wind?"

She said nothing. She bit her lip. He stood, eyes wild and hot.

"Listen, goddammit! It's breaking through! Now!"

Then it happened. The tension broke into inexplicable drama. For as he said "Now!" there was a crash, a cascade of sparks from the fire. I jumped. A big stone, dislodged by the storm, had plunged down the chimney, rolled into the hearth, a gust of wind swooping down after it and scattering more sparks. We stared at it, frozen. Then I sensed the growing chill. Not just the cold of a draught: something more icy. We were all standing now, and instinctively we drew closer into a circle with Kitaj the distraught focus. The energetic tension that flowed through or from him had me utterly tight. Something was happening. I watched Kitaj's features, and they were shifting, seemed to be undergoing rear-rangement as he eyed each of us in turn. Then I realized this also went for my perception of Lenore, Isma'il, myself—of the room and everything in it—and for a fleeting instant I recalled the dream I'd had nearly a year before, with Kitaj as a pool of melted gold.

Then I heard the Voice.

I swear his lips never moved. Equally I swear I heard *his* voice, in my mind. *His* voice, clearly so, but not familiarly so. Resonant, potent, sounding in me telepathically, with absolute definition . . . containing character and knowledge with which Kitaj didn't fully integrate until the last year, 1992:

"Who are you? Who are we? Time to find out. Time to step out!"

It rang through me. I was dazed. In its wake came another savage gust of wind, attacking the house. When it fell away, the moment snapped. The tension suddenly fell away. Perception returned to normal . . . almost. Kitaj slumped oddly, as though spirit had gone out of him. He fell back into the chair. His face was ghastly, tight and jaundiced, with eyes alone ablaze.

"I don't know," he whispered after a while. "I don't know what it is. Not yet. I always had it, but I turned it off. I'll work it out. Don't push me."

He reached for the whisky. His hand was shaking. We were silent. Lenore sat heavily. So did I. Only Isma'il remained calm.

That was the beginning . . . of the end . . . of the beginning. That was when the strangeness really began, the naked knife slicing old pretenses into ribbons.

I did not get to sleep until late. The storm was wild that night, the whole house moaning; there were poltergeisty bumps and bangs. I lay in bed like a small boy frightened of ghosts. The storm and the evening's events made it clear: Kitaj's critical hour had come. I felt we were watched, not by police or intelligible human agency, but by something lurking deep and vague and dormant in us all; something which in Kitaj was now starting to activate, for better or worse. I lay, shivering. That stone, and the dissolving of appearance, and the voice . . . and Kitaj's collapsed condition afterwards . . . if all his life he had been a natural medium for such power, no wonder he had blocked it off.

But he could no longer block it off. His time had come.

At length the storm dropped. I lay, cradled in a deep noumenal silence. Then, very far off, a dog barked, once, twice, three times, stabbing that age-old silence with a new note. I thought then of Sirius. It was hard to breathe. And when at length I did sleep it was to fall into restless dream of another world, of a great purple ocean rolling under an ultraviolet sky that burned with intelligence, and of a sleek black barque with a serpent prow. It was rowed by beings who had no faces. At the prow stood three women in black. One was a hag, one a mature mother, the third a virginal girl. They were somber and powerful, returning to our modern world, to the domain of the cerebral cortex.

I sank into the ocean, into the unconscious depths.

In the morning, we found that Kitaj had gone.

"He went before first light," said Isma'il. "He has answered a call. If he returns, he will return changed . . . and the change will change us . . ."

He had taken a pack, a tent, and food, and the primus. But it was a wild cold week, raining every day. I was fearful. Every night I dreamed vividly. We all did. We did not speak about it. We said very little at all that week. We worked. Lenore dug the garden. Isma'il repaired the roof. I transcribed the tapes. And I read about and contemplated Sirius.

This I did uneasily, with the sense of an abyss just inches below my feet. I felt at any moment the floor, the earth, might dissolve, revealing an utter emptiness. It seemed that nothing in the world was left of ordinariness but a thin and very fragile membrane of past custom and habit which at any moment now might finally snap to reveal . . . what?

Though perhaps it had already snapped.

Sirius. The Dog Star. The brightest star in our skies, 8.6 light years away, in system with a collapsed white dwarf invisible to the naked eye.

For millenia on this planet there has been knowledge of the Sirius system. The origin of this knowledge is an ancient mystery. Earlier in this account the Dogon of Mali have been mentioned. Their knowledge of Sirius B, the invisible white dwarf—its existence, its mass, the fifty-year period and eccentricity of its

orbit round Sirius A—was first known to the modern western
world in the 1950s, when they were anthropologically examined
and their strange creation myth revealed. This involves a fish-
tailed being, the Nommo, who came down among men with the
teachings of civilization. Their rites also told of a third sun in the
system, Sirius C . . . which remains unadmitted in the limited
reality-scope of hard science . . . though many now accept that
the Third Sun exists in a supersensible, etheric range of formation.

In the late sixties a Fellow of the Royal Astronomical Society,
Robert Temple, published a book tracing the knowledge of the
Dogon back through the last six thousand years, connecting the
Sirius mystery with the myths and coded tales of many ancient
cultures and philosophies, finding, for example, that the fifty
oars of the good ship Argo probably referred to the fifty-year
orbit of the invisible Sirius B. Back through Greece to Egypt,
beyond the rites of Isis and Osiris he traced this road, to the time
of the Sumerians, and their myth concerning the repulsive (to
human eyes) fish-tailed being, Oannes, also called Ea, the Divine
Man-Fish, who—according to the fourth century B.C. Chaldean
astronomer-priest Berosus—"wrote a book on the origin of things
and the beginnings of civilization, and gave it to men." Berosus
tells how this Oannes came out of the sea by day to give lessions,
and how "when the sun went down," the "monstrous Oannes
used to plunge back into the sea and spend the night in the midst
of the boundless waves, for he was amphibious."

Was Oannes also the Nommo of the Dogon? By "the sea,"
did Berosus mean the wet, physical, water-type sea? Or another,
more spacy and mental sea? How much did he know? He died
over two thousand years ago, but between him and the time of
the story he reports lay at least three thousand years. There is no
dependable factual precision here, any more than in the history of
Kitaj. This Oannes, like Atlantis, lurks behind history, possibly a
metaphor for mental evolutionary change that took place, possibly an actual visitor, perhaps both. There is nothing to put a
dogmatic finger on. We are dealing with vagueness; it would take
a von Däniken to insist on it as fact.

That's what I found myself wanting to believe in Ireland.

Yet I knew very well that magical and occult traditions about
Sirius are strong in many cultures, over several millenia, suggesting not only some singular physical visitation *x* thousand years
ago, but a continuity of two-way connection conducted through

the developed human consciousness in every age, with images in the traditions to suggest that this third-eye connection with Sirius, a road of wisdom, is not yet fully explored, that an understanding of it lies on the road of human destiny. On the Qabalistic Tree of Life Sirius is associated with Daath, the Sephirah or sphere which as yet, on current charts of reality, has no number, no symbol—the recently added and shadowy world of mind, beyond which division cannot penetrate, one of the virtues of which is said to be confidence in the future.

I felt no such confidence that fraught wild week in February 1987. I was worried for myself, for Kitaj, for the world, in that order, and secretly I feared his returning almost as much as I feared the permanent loss of him. My dreams disturbed me; I felt psychically imperiled and naked with too little functional knowledge of these new frames of reference which were being manifested. The change was general in us. Whatever was happening in Kitaj was triggering us as well, and I spent that week in a frame of mind I had never known before, one in which the symbolic completely overwhelmed the material appearance of things, in which every cloud was a beast of particular disposition, every shape a face or form frozen in act of gigantic play that stretched between many unseen and unknown worlds—everything resounding with meaning that I could sense but hardly fathom without letting go.

Five days passed, then six, and the weather was still severe, and still the three of us hardly spoke our fears to each other. But it was there in our faces. We walked the moors independently, grimly, further and further afield, but there was no sign of him, and when the seventh night came we sat bleakly in the kitchen, staring into cups of black tea.

"I see him!" said Isma'il suddenly. "He's on his way here."

We sat round that table all night, waiting, until we slept, and the dawn came, and Kitaj with it, entering the house unheard by us, so that when we awoke it was direct to his face.

To the smile on his face.

He was filthy, covered in mud, clothes torn, pack and tent missing. He was gaunt, the bones in his face standing out sharply, with a new coherence.

I awoke to the warmth of his gladness to see us. I saw the energetic, youthful stranger who smiled at us where we lifted up our heads, blinking, and for a moment I was confused, wondering who this was—then there was a shift, a blur in perception and definition, and I knew this was Kitaj.

But where was the darkness and weight?

He said something. I don't remember the words. He embraced us in the way that he stood. I remember Lenore and I met eyes, both dazed, yet both of us in that moment of revelation admitting that our egotistic hostilities were redundant and negative. Lies of ownership were exploded there.

The rest of that day he slept. The rest of that day it was hard to do anything at all. For the first time in weeks the weather was calm and clear. The sky was pale, infinite. It felt like a corner had been turned, that Kitaj had thrown off the pressure which had kept his eyes in the mud so long, that he had found and attracted into himself an abundance of that vital energy which imbues, to greater or lesser degree, according to the health of the organism, all living things. His mind had cleared, he had reconnected with that free flow of power which only the knotted body and the blocked-up mind can reject and prevent in itself. So it seemed to me, and all that day I felt like a sleepwalker, conscious of mystery, grace, new hope.

Yet also there was nagging doubt. Kitaj had found means of rejuvenation. What next? What would he do? Would I find myself left behind?

That day I got dangerously close to becoming a devotee.

That night Kitaj blew out any such possibility, for he was not out to become a god or even a guru . . . at least not in his own eyes.

It was dark before he came down from his sleep. Lenore had cooked a meal of black beans; we ate together in a friendly, energetic, expectant silence, and Kitaj's smile embraced us all with its ease and relaxation. Yet he said hardly a word until after the meal. Then he looked at each of us with the energetic sparkle and the daring, impish humor of a youth.

"It's a lovely night," he said. "Let's go for a walk."

By the light of sharp stars and a declining half-moon the four of us went west from the cottage. Through the silence and stillness we tramped towards the ocean, over the sodden heath, until we came to the top of a low bare hill overlooking the black lough, the lough of the *peiste*. Here Kitaj stopped, and Isma'il spread the groundsheet, but for a time we stood, side by side, facing south, night-entranced. Below us on the waters gleamed a silvery thin road of moonlight, and, at some distance the other side of the lough, the twin dim lights of a cottage. Briefly we heard voices murmuring from that cottage, soft and low, carrying clear over more than half a mile. The night was very intent, as if waiting. I found I'd been holding my breath. Then I found myself starting to shiver, though not through cold nor (yet) through fright. There was a natural energy in this place; energy to unfreeze matter and set your every atom dancing. I felt it rising up into me through the soles of my feet, stronger all the time, making me want to jig . . . and it brought to the mind the awesome sense of being at a vortex of power—serpentine, spiraling power that flowed between earth and sky, bringing pantheistic images to my mind of all nature in one vast interacting dance. It occurred to me that this bare hill was, in older terms, a fairy mound, a hill of the *sidhe*. Also it occurred to me that Kitaj beside me was a focus or lens of this energy.

Why had he brought us here?

Maybe fifteen or twenty minutes, maybe longer we stood there, silent, the three of us waiting for Kitaj, and Kitaj waiting for . . . what?

The moon set. It became very dark but still Kitaj stood in silence until, in the southeast, the brilliant blue white star began to rise.

I felt the shivering in my bones increase. I felt I was dissolving.

Then I felt Kitaj turn to Lenore, and I heard his voice.

"Did you bring the thermos?"

"What?" Lenore hesitated, unsure how to react. Then she laughed with a quick nervousness. "Yes, I did. Tea."

Kneeling, she snapped on a light. I saw Kitaj smile at Isma'il.

"Can you think of a prayer for us?" Kitaj asked. "For this night?"

"The Mothers are here," Isma'il murmured. "This is an old strong place, a nerve place." Then he added: "I dreamed of them the night you went. In a black boat, in a purple sea. I will ask them to smile on us."

I started. I was shocked, remembering my own dreams.

"Johnny," said Kitaj wryly as he sat, "how were your dreams?"

"Uncomfortable." I sat stiffly, clutched the mug of tea that Lenore gave me, clutched it as though its warmth would save my life. "One night," I went on reluctantly, "I dreamed I saw you in the middle of an old stone circle. You were talking with an old man. He looked like a tramp, but . . . I could see right through him, and his face was a blur of light. You turned and beckoned me into the circle, but I was too scared. I turned away. The dream faded."

"I had the same dream!" Lenore was fascinated, maybe fearful.

"We all did." Isma'il sounded ironic, as if we were discussing the obvious. "Also other dreams we haven't talked about. Isn't that right?"

"Where have you been?" I demanded of Kitaj in a sudden impatient rush. "What's happened to you?"

"You know where I've been," he said mildly. "You just told me."

I stared at the star, at Sirius. Its light was quick and fast in me. It was hard to think; I was shaking with the stress of hidden extrasensory familiarities I didn't want to admit as familiar, for such an admission would mean that the boundaries between myth and the solid world were entirely gone.

"In that circle?" I asked wildly. "With the stone men?"

He chuckled. "They're not all men," he said. "Not at all. As Isma'il says, the Mothers are here too. You need both male and female inside yourself united to get the three in one of unity."

I couldn't bear this riddling.

"Tell us what happened, for God's sake!"

"Did you bring the tape recorder?" he asked.

"Yes." I felt embarrassed. "I did."

"Good!" He spoke with relish, with humor. "You'll be able to write a great last chapter for that tale of Kitaj you're doing."

But in *Liar's Gold* I found it beyond my skill and courage to render accurately the spirit of what he proceeded to tell us, and the effect he had on us. Words themselves are cold bare things, but also they can serve as disguises, and that is how I used them. I could not face the implications of his account, I could not accept my own realizations. Instead from his words I constructed a romantic drama, the emotional climax of that liar's tale which sold fifteen million copies round the world.

That was twelve years ago, and I still have the scratchy tape I made that night beneath the blaze of the bright star, and I admit how much there is about Kitaj and events connected with him that I still don't understand, and maybe never will . . . at least, not through logical, linear, left-lobe processes, for the structures of mythreality are associative, synchronous, and magical. I can write down words that were spoken, recall the outer shape of events that may or may not have happened, but the meaning (if any) is in every case a matter of personal interpretation and responsibility. My reactions, insights, dreams, and memories don't necessarily make a good guide for anyone else. You must decide for yourself what makes sense . . . and it may be that, if you feel you have to believe or disbelieve, there is nothing for you here.

Watch TV instead, if you like, but you'll find the same problem.

Because Kitaj's account turned into more than a tale. It became for each of us an intense personal experience, the flesh of the dreams we'd had, and what Kitaj described became our own experiences as he talked, and the culmination frankly terrified me.

Kitaj began, his voice hypnotic-soft in the dark, with that evening on which he'd admitted murder and curse, when the Voice had burst through the shreds of him, after which, he said, he'd collapsed onto his bed, to lie there feeling great pain of self-contempt, and pressure of inner explosion, but unwilling to let go and pass through the long-locked gates. For hours amid the storm he'd tossed and turned, voices and shadowy visions tormenting him, so that he'd feared to fall asleep.

Yet eventually, sleep he did.

The journey had begun.

He'd found himself on a bus full of tourists—apparently on a package tour of the Middle East, visiting battlefields and holy places. On the bus were three other people with whom he felt connection. To start with he was traveling with a blonde woman for whom he felt great affection. Some of the time this woman was Lenore, but mostly she was simply and closely his "sister."

In the seat in front were another man and woman with whom Kitaj and his "sister" developed close but increasingly ambiguous relationship. This other couple seemed Egyptian, and there was something very old, wise, familiar, yet threatening about them. The man especially, with his enigmatic hawk eyes and his questions which Kitaj could not or would not understand, was a threat, particularly to Kitaj's "sister," for she found herself increasingly fascinted by him, yet not pleasantly so, while Kitaj found himself tense, weak, and self-restricted in this man's presence.

The other woman was always silent and oddly vague, as though veiled, and he never succeeded in making out her features clearly.

The crisis came at an old temple in Egypt. The dark man persuaded Kitaj and his "sister" to accompany him to a part of the temple which nobody else knew about. They stepped through stone doors released by hidden levers . . . and through time . . . and into a place of utter horror.

This secret inner chamber of the temple was a golden charnel house—a place of human torture and sacrifice. It was shadowy, red, lurid. From hooks on the stone walls hung recently severed human limbs, and human carcasses were being roasted on spits above fires in pits in the floor. The smell of boiling blood and entrails made Kitaj's gorge rise, and his "sister" was terrified.

The dark man—the other woman was not with them—turned with an odd, dangerous smile, ignoring Kitaj, and said to Kitaj's "sister":

"I am the priest here. Everything must end to begin again. The old gods stir hungrily in us. This is why I have brought you here."

Then his eyes grew so strong that she could hardly stand. Kitaj knew he should intervene, but he did not. He simply stood as the dark priest took control of his "sister," plagued by fear, and by a strong and increasing sense of personal identification with the dark hawk-faced man, and he did not care to examine this closely. For a moment his "sister" tore her terrified eyes from the priest and beseeched him, but he did nothing to help her; he could not move. He stood, and the priest took possession of her for sacrifice, and when the situation was quite clear the priest turned to him at last:

"Do you know who I am?"

Kitaj shut his eyes and shook his head.

"No!" he forced out.

"Do you know who this woman is?"

"No!" Kitaj repeated, and it was all he could say.

"You are a coward and a fool," the priest told him flatly, "and your answer betrays us all. But if you find the courage you can buy her life."

"Money?" croaked Kitaj. "How much do you want?"

Implacably the priest raised up the sharpness of his knife.

"This is the only means of purchase admitted here," he said. "Give yourself up to the knife, save her, and learn what you cannot yet admit!"

A tremendous unreasoning panic seized Kitaj.

"No!" he gasped, for the third time, in agony, and could not meet the eyes of his "sister," far less those of the hawk priest, and as he spoke everything began to spin and whirl. "No! I'm going back to the bus!"

"This is not possible." The priest's voice held calm, reflective regret. "You have lost your way, and condemned us, and you must start again."

The spinning and whirling swallowed Kitaj completely. His "sister" and the priest, and the bloody ancient temple were obscured and torn away, and Kitaj fell, it seemed forever, through distortion of many dimensions . . . until he found himself . . . drowning . . . too solid and real, too leaden and helpless . . . in a vast purple ocean beneath a glaring, much too bright violet sky . . .

When I heard this voice in my mind and found myself in the sea again I stiffened, afraid for the walls of my personality. The horror in the temple I could not understand, yet knew that Kitaj's account was somehow appropriate to my own inner processes, and likewise with Lenore and Isma'il. Frozen I sat there on the hilltop with that hypnotic voice echoing as if from my own dreams levels, not at all from an external other being called Ralph M'Botu Kitaj—and it was only just begun, beneath the bright star, in the deep night . . .

He had failed. He was drowning. Twice he'd been down and was starting down the last time when the black boat came, gliding over the sea at a great rate, straight at him, so that he thought it would hit him and make an end. Then the ocean threw him up on a sudden swell, and he saw her, standing by the serpent prow of the black boat, looking down, and there were three of her, which he did not understand. But he knew it was her. His Angel, whom he had not known since the murder and spiritual suicide on Ruwenzori. And he sensed such anger from her that for a moment, even as he cried out for rescue, he nearly preferred to drown. Yet as the black boat raced by, something struck, stunned, seized, and wrenched him up . . . onto the boat. It was like a giant invisible fist, not gentle, and it deposited him before the forms of her.

He stood there squeezed, shaking, choking, like a guilty tongue-tied child, with no easy way to look or turn, for wherever he looked she faced him, as hag or mother or virgin, with the faces of women he'd known flickering continually through her faces, and the faceless crew rowing, and the violet sky flaming.

He felt terrible. He was sick. His stomach heaved.

"You idiot!" snapped the Old Woman when he'd finished puking over the side of the ship. "You've been murdering yourself and everyone else. You've been chasing money and making a mess. Why did you abandon yourself like that? Why did you forget where you come from and what you're for? Now you're down to one more chance, and you must take it, now! Listen! When you wake up, go, and find the place where the serpents meet. There you'll find the well, and a key, and the chance to go through and rediscover your proper direction—if you look for it, you'll find the help you need. Remember Njeru! Remember that I am in you, and remember that you'll find nothing at all if you can't let go!"

Then the spinning seized him again, and he fell, and fell, and fell . . .

He awoke in his bed in the house in Ireland before the dawn, but his waking was also a dreaming and he couldn't be sure he was really awake, really in Ireland until, clumsily, he walked into a door and bruised his head.

"Then I knew I had to go, immediately, and find the place where the serpents meet . . . whatever that meant. I knew I had nothing to lose, or everything to lose, and that I would have to let my feet guide me, because my brain was ignorant. So I dressed, I packed, I left without waking any of you, and when dawn came I was already on my way, in the rain and the fog."

So he went on the dream trail. All day long his feet took him northeast over the moors, steering him wide round farms and any hint of human beings.

The rain was continual and the going was hard. Yet much of that day his mind was in Africa, on the hot dry plains, returning to the heart-routes which Njeru had tried to teach him . . . and it began to seem to him, the longer he went on, that his feet followed a subtly undulant course of energy that pulsed up out of the earth. It was like walking the back of a serpent! For a while he felt good. He was on the right track. He lost caution. The next thing he knew, he was up to his waist in an Irish mire, freezing and wet. He continued more soberly. And he came to the place just before night fell.

It was slightly raised, a natural mound amid dark wet moorland. Two low hills rose to north and south. There was a stone circle on the mound. Half the stones were missing, others were out of their original alignment—but the place was still very much alive and functional.

The rain was drifting heavily when he got there. The stones loomed black and huge, distorted in the twilight. He arrived nervously, realizing this was his destination. There was just enough light to pitch his tent in the lee of the mound, giving slight protection against the bitter rising wind.

Starting to shiver, he crawled into the tent, into himself. He could not eat or drink. He sat there in the darkness and the shivering got worse, until he realized that it was caused not only by his fear and the cold, but by the serpents—the energized underground waters—that writhed and warred in their meeting under the mound. Leviathan, Typhon! He sat there, superstitiously horrified, scared in the outer eddies of that natural energy-well which he'd come to find. His fear increased until he wanted to get out and run far away. Then he made an effort. He sat and thought. He recollected what he knew about places such as this. How animals and dowsers and gauss meters pick up the prickle of increased electromagnetism above the crossing of underground waters, how this energy mediates between earth and sky in spiral form, its polarity dependent on the phase of the moon. He remembered my telling him how once societies had grown and developed through understanding of this power, how to places like these large stones with special properties had been brought and erected in particular geometrical configurations, in order to store, amplify, and tap the power, and to predict the seasons in the skies. He remembered that the stones are often rich in quartz, which is piezoelectric, meaning it expands and gives off voltage when charged and under pressure. No surprise, therefore, that in the thirty-five hundred years or so since the death of these united megalithic cultures and their science, the legends of dragons, hauntings, strange powers, and magical ''stone men'' had developed around these places, bringing them to Christian condemnation and destruction . . . though many churches were sited on just these nodes of natural power, people refusing to have it otherwise.

All this Kitaj told himself as he sat there shivering. But he could not understand why he felt the power so strongly. He could only think that he was still in dream, prey to dream intensity and sensitivity, with intuitive rather than rational focus on what he had to do.

His task was clear enough.

He summoned the courage to do it.

He walked up the mound and entered the circle.

His nervous, energetic shivering increased. With flashlight in hand he stood there giddy, lightheaded on the midnight vortex of the power station, and the continual shaking in his bones produced exhilaration and instinctive reverence. Then, almost ritualistically, he began feeling his way round the inside of the circle's perimeter, touching each stone, coming to sense that each stone was, or represented, an archetypal human individual or faculty. He simply knew this in the touching, and in his lightheadedness began talking to the stones, not feeling foolish, ignoring the wind and rain which, though they penetrated the circle, were no nuisance or threat but an expression of nature.

Then everything was changed.

His trial began when he got a shock from one of the stones.

''It was like being stung by a bee. I jerked my hand away. It changed my attitude. It seemed like a sign, a warning, and I stood back, shocked, realizing I was in a spooked place with no good idea what the hell I was doing. As soon as I thought that the giddiness got bad. I felt huge shakings in the earth below me. I was scared then, and I tried to get out.

''But I couldn't. I couldn't leave the circle. I couldn't walk straight; I didn't understand; I fell into total confusion. It was like that Buñuel movie, *The Exterminating Angel*, where the guests gradually discover they can't leave the room—no obvious reason why not, no physical barrier—just, they can't leave. They try, but they get into arguments, or forget what they're doing, or walk about in habit circles—it was like that. My feet wouldn't do what I told them, or I couldn't tell them right. I couldn't get through to myself to get out.

"It was unpleasant. All night I just . . . wandered about inside the stones, snapping my fingers, biting my tongue to stay awake, singing—stuff like that. Didn't dare stop moving because, you know, I started thinking there were goblins grinning behind me. I started thinking the stones were my guards."

When the half-light of day drizzled up he was still staggering round in ever-smaller circles. At length he lifted up his head and saw the tent, only yards away. His stomach started grumbling about breakfast. It seemed simple now. The giddiness was almost gone. The power was almost quiet. Back to daytime normality and straightforward physical need. So it seemed.

He started out of the circle. But before he crossed the perimeter he stopped. He could see now that obviously there was no barrier at all. Just a few old stones, wide spaced and askew, like single lopsided teeth. It was a puzzle. All night long he'd thought that something or someone had stopped him leaving. But at its widest the diameter of the circle was no more than twenty-five yards. Within this limited area he'd been walking for hours in the darkness, and not once had he managed to cross the perimeter.

What was going on? What had stopped him leaving?

The answer was obvious, or seemed obvious.

He had stopped himself leaving.

"I stood in the drizzle and very unhappily admitted that my only positive way out was through the well. I knew if I walked out now I'd have thrown away my last chance, because nothing on earth would drag me back into that circle. I had to do it. I had to stay, whatever the consequences. I had to go right through, all the way."

He couldn't let himself leave. But he was terrified to stay. A conflict of voices started up in him. He stood in the rain and imaginary people argued in his head without reaching any conclusions. Hours passed. It was near midday. Kitaj was in poor shape. He fell into panic and fury, forgetting his resolution. He made enraged efforts to break out. He took long runs, building up momentum to smash through whatever barrier it was—but every time he managed to trip himself up a few yards short, or forgot what he was doing and stopped to study the patterns of the rain instead. His conscious desire was no match for his unconscious will. He got exhausted, and tried logic.

"I tried to think my way out. I assumed I was in some kind of mental maze, and that I couldn't see the angles or right passages because my third eye wasn't open enough, or because there was no Ariadne around to give me a thread. None of it helped. Eventually I still stood there, shivering, trying to be uncaring and Buddhistic, but that didn't help much either."

By then it was dark again. He started his second night in the circle. The stones and the well they defined seemed more energetic. He felt caught in a web of intelligent interplay. He felt the serpents shaking underneath. He was deeper in the well. It roared up round him, through him, spiraling, snaking up to the sky. He felt himself drowning in the purple ocean, and now he knew that all he had to do was abandon himself to it, go with it, wherever it took him. But still he was unwilling to lie down and let go of himself. Throughout that night he walked round and round in an increasing delirium, clinging to his personality, babbling with ghosts which jeered at him, swimming through his life and seeing his mistakes with a merciless clarity.

The second day came. The weather was worse. Everything was worse. He was starving with food only feet away. He lapped at the rain. He was delirious. His ideas about space and time were collapsing. He felt sick and hopeless. A trapped rat in his own maze. For the first time in years he babbled prayers and cried. Nothing happened. Nobody came but ghosts from his past.

When the third night came he was no longer on his feet.

"I was flat out on the ground. Hardly conscious. Soaked and sick. I remember staring with the last of the light at the stone which had stung me. I knew it as The Judge. It stared back, its face a perfect pitiless balance."

Then, at last, he let go and slipped into the well.

The music.

A faint distant piping in his darkness was what drew Kitaj back to a level of self-consciousness.

Slowly he opened his eyes to find he was flat on his back on an indeterminate ground, the night total all about, nothing at all to be glimpsed . . . but for what seemed like two glimmering, coiling, misty wraiths that twined together vertically above him. He blinked, and the form of the wraiths grew more clear. Two tall, slender, energetically luminous serpents, swaying above him in the night. They were beautiful—coral and diamond—and they were scintillant.

And they were watching him, waiting for him to move.

The music.

Vast, plumed with subtle fire, the two serpents watched him, to see what he would do, and the music was very faint through their interested hissing, but he clung to it, like a drowning man to a straw, and shortly found himself standing in that illimitable darkness, as insubstantial as a feather in the breeze, and starting to drift after that alluring tendril of music.

It was siren music. Pied Piper music, so familiar yet strange that it tantilized him utterly, and he needed no reason to follow it; it was reason in itself. It was high, sweet, wild, fast, light, free, then so poignant, then deep, and full of hints and questions. Away from the serpents through the darkness of this strange inner world he followed it, lured by it into a journey without sense of time or references of space. He followed, and followed, and sometimes the music grew so faint that he feared he would lose it altogether, then it would sound unexpectedly close, so that ahead of him in the mistiness of this unformed world he would sense a moving shape, the shape of the musician, so that he never quite lost hope, and these glimpses became more frequent, and the music more specific, so that this world in which he moved gradually took form according to the specifications of the music.

Eventually he was drifting over a haunting moorland with the sound of the music and the shape of the musician ever closer in front of him—a shape that kept shifting, but which seemed more and more manlike—until at length the music stopped, and the shape stopped moving, and turned, and waited for Kitaj to catch up.

He approached. He stood before a rippling bright blur. Then he sensed the sly, potent, familiar smile that came out of this blur.

And he knew who it was.

On the tape at this point there is an interruption of Kitaj's measured voice. The interruption is the voice of John Hall. My voice. The voice is very agitated, speaking in a fast shaky babble, away from the mike, so that only a few words are caught, and they make no sense. It is a babble of fear.

I still have blocks against remembering that night. I was reluctant to let go and plunge all the way into Kitaj's journey, even though I'd spent years talking about mythconsciousness, even though I'd spent the last twenty months arrogantly trying to push this man through his own inner barriers.

"How will *you* cope when the volcano explodes?"

Lenore had asked me this. Now I was finding out.

It is nearly thirteen years since that night. My own final rite of passage approaches, I hear Kitaj's soft voice as he interrupts me, gently:

"That's right, Johnny! It's okay! You're right! We're all in this together. No way out the side, or by sitting on the fence, or by pleading flat feet. Too late for that. We all have to take chances now—many of them. There's no security. There's no soul-insurance. Just calculated chances we have to take, and not worry about ourselves . . ."

It was Njeru. Also it was not. The Smile, which was deepening, taking human form amid the blur, was certainly that which Kitaj remembered from the teacher of his youth . . . yet also an expression which has indwelt many human beings with the power and knowledge to realize and carry it. It was that question at the heart of all things human, that Mona Lisa Cheshire Cat which lurks beneath the skin of appearance . . . that gentle understanding which shines in the face of Einstein in the famous portrait by Karsh of Ottawa . . . the understanding and acceptance of relativity and uncertainty in all things.

But Kitaj fixed on the image of Njeru that he remembered, and that was the image that formed—the little old brown Kikuyu shaman.

Yet there were anomalies which Kitaj had not consciously wished.

For, out of the blur, Njeru materialized in the garb of a down-at-heel Irish fisherman. He wore patched Wellington boots, a shabby once-white cable-knit sweater hanging from his neck to his knees, and an ancient buttonless raincoat loosely tied round the waist with a frayed length of tar-blackened string. And a curious thing was that water oozed apparently out of the soles of the Wellington boots, so that the apparition always stood in a pool of water that traveled with its movements. A further curious thing was that in his left hand Njeru held three sticks of ash, straight, with fire-hardened tips, like fishing poles, and they splayed out of his hand in such a fashion as to form a trident.

And in his gnarled right hand he held the pipes which had haunted and drawn Kitaj from afar.

Njeru thickened into form.

His smile grew positively goatish.

"It is the man who forgot his name. Now what would you be doing here?"

Kitaj was detached from himself, and standing straight.

"Looking for what I left on the mountainside," he said, but then he grew less certain. "I don't know its name," he said, almost testily, finding it hard to meet Njeru's eyes, "but I know I'm sick of drowning. Any more bullshit and I'm through, I know it."

"But you like dancing to the music, is that it? Well, now, what do you think you are facing?"

"I put the face of Njeru onto you," said Kitaj hoarsely, "the upper slopes of which I never saw properly: they were always hidden to me, in the heights, I don't know what I face: it is a confusion still, what lies through the gates, because thirty years ago I stopped going through them and turned back to fixations. But now I have to go through."

"You are the sword to cut your own knot? But when you were in the temple you would not take the knife for yourself!"

Kitaj grimaced.

"Do you know everything about me?" he demanded.

Njeru, saying nothing, fingered the pipes, meaningfully.

"You led me here," Kitaj went on. "I followed the music and found you here at last. But I want to know if I can now go on, or if this is just a dream which will bring no positive changes at all."

"It is no dream," said Njeru severely. "Nor is it a fever. Nor is this Ireland, or Africa. Nor am I altogether what you see me as. Nor are you whatever you think you are. Now, you say you'll go through *any* gate?"

He was raising the pipes to his lips, his smile was mocking, and his form was beginning to blur and dissolve. For a moment Kitaj felt constricted and afraid and could not make the dedication he knew he had to make in order to go on. Then he swallowed, and overcame himself.

"Yes," he said, "any gate."

"Then," said Njeru, "you'd better take your chance now, hadn't you?"

*   *   *

Kitaj did. He stood square as the pipes met the lips of the Smile, as three high, clear, identical notes trilled from the shimmering whirl of the Smile. And the music stripped away the appearances. For an instant he saw his body, crumpled in the circle of stones. Then light flooded him, and fire, and the world of the well started to rock and sway and dissolve him as the shape of the piper turned away, capering and dancing into the brightness of the light, growing fainter and larger, fading brightly as the music too began to fade and distort. Kitaj knew he had to follow, now, or miss his chance. He stood poised on the instant of choosing different future fates. His feet wanted to move, but his brain held back. Then for a flash he was back in the bloody temple. The priest, about to kill his "sister," and himself standing by. But both priest and sister were aspects of himself. Of a sudden this was clear. Now he was ready. He offered himself willingly, though fearfully. He offered himself up to the knife. He stepped forward, into the core of the light, following the music that dissolves. And in the last moment he had the sensation that he was walking into a mirror, straight through his own reflection.

Then he walked through, and the mirror shattered.

Which is exactly what happened to me.

I don't know how Kitaj did it, pulling us so deep into his experience, somehow persuading us as he spoke to re-create in our own minds the critical elements of his tale, but I remember, distinctly, like one clear flash, how as his words resounded in me I saw that mirror, and myself, and how I walked into that mirror. It cracked into a thousand shards. My reflection, my self-consciousness, was destroyed.

"It was like being in an earthquake. Lurching, total gut panic. Knifed and dissolved. The scrambling of all dimension into a chaos."

He (you, me) was ripped apart, shattered into random numbers with no cohesive relationship between them—no progressions or exchange of information. For a moment we felt his tied, locked-up, knotted personality flying apart. The personality screamed with fear. Then we no longer existed.

Only scattered numbers, hydrogen drifting between the stars, a strange and latent exaltation, as of a song hidden, demanding materialized expression.

A dream formed, like a veil of gas on the deep, consisting of tentative relationships between particular numbers that sought this hidden song.

In the first place the numbers were random. In the search came relationship, meaning.

Shards and splinters flew together again, and there was new form.

"Hunka Hinka Shamba Aum Alhim!" cried Kitaj from the stage of Madison Square Garden during his last world tour, in August 1992, after he'd been healed at Luzon, after he'd begun the demonstrations of "miracles" and the laying-on of hands. He stood there in his bright bird-feathered robe, his face made up like a Pierrot clown, and he resonated each apparently nonsense syllable with a deep and powerful clarity. "Hunka Hinka! What are you? What am I? Why are we here? What must we do?

"Well, speaking for myself, I am here as a lens, as a resonator, as a focusing agent. For a long time now information has been streaming into this world, into our varied minds, important information, from sources beyond our planetary system. The information itself is clear enough, but reception here has been poor. We have been picking it up in confused and incomplete form. One person intuits one part of the jigsaw, another picks up another, but few realize how the pieces fit, and false religion results.

"Now it is nearly midnight at the ball. Our names were called out long ago. We have taken many partners. We have danced many dances. We have made many patterns and worn many disguises—but now it is time to take off the masks and integrate, for the bell is tolling, we have little time, we have now to form a new realization of what we are and act on this realization—or we will die uselessly, and the planet will dance no more. We are here to stand as individuals, we are here to admit and harness the powers that flow through us . . . for we are the Transformers of this world, and can decide the shape of things on earth.

"We are Transformers. We must decide on the Transformations. *"Every man and woman is a star."*

Kitaj found himself in a maze.
Lenore found herself in a maze.
Isma'il found himself in a maze.

I found myself in a maze, and it was dark.

How about you? Did you ever go through K-Therapy?

K-Therapy (for some time nobody knew or even suspected that it originated with Kitaj, nor that the first time it was consciously practiced was on a hill in Connemara in February 1987) is generally regarded as a heavy treatment for harsh times—a crash course, a freefall jump into the psyche without any kind of parachute . . . meaning you have to materialize a parachute before you hit. The triggering technique is by means of subliminal verbal clues—the power of "The Word"—and heightened emotion; but most of all it is stimulated by transfer of energy from the human lens, or focus, to the human subject, who is a person scattered and unfocused on his or her purpose. A series of jolts are provided, to spin the mind through a minotaur's maze to a level much deeper and more integrated than one might normally reach either through dream or intellection or meditation.

Then you're left to work it out, to evolve through the trials of your hang-ups via symbolic dramas in which you, and you, and you, are the hero.

It's just like being born, only we forget.

"I stood in a sort of shroudy illimitable darkness. I could hear nothing and sensed no movement other than drafts of air which suggested the opening of passages close by. I did not yet realize that everything here was image of my own projection, personally created . . . though I do think also that the race unconscious is involved, as well as the conscious work of many explorers, for many have traveled this road, and a guiding groove is worn through the fatal maze—the groove of tales, of myths like maps, which remind us where we are. But as I stood there I knew no stories at all; I had no sense of order, no real sense of self. I was a point amid darkness and vagueness, with no purpose until from one direction I thought I heard the ghost of a rhythm.

"It was like the beating of a drum . . . or a heart . . . and when I heard it I knew that the heart was what I was looking for."

He took a chance. He took a step.

Years later, the last time I met her, in 1994, Lenore asked me if I'd ever realized that, after the shattering of the mirror, the four of us on the hilltop were holding hands, linked in a circle, which surely aided the transmission of Kitaj's imaginative authority. In fact I had never realized this, and I cannot to this day remember the precise sequence or nature of my own inner journey that Kitaj stimulated through projection of his own. But Lenore, trained in these matters, remembered what she went through, and so did Isma'il, and since then of course there are the thousands of accounts of those who have been through K-Therapy. What emerges is that no two journeys are duplicates, just as no two human beings are duplicates—not even clones are perfect duplicates. But just about every journey shares certain symbolic features with just about every other journey. In almost every case there are the arid wastes to be crossed, the chasms to plumb, the false images to kill, the goal (the boon, the benefit, the confirmation of new power) to be won—and the return to be accomplished.

"We were lucky that night," Lenore told me. "Rafe didn't really know what he was doing. He didn't realize quite how much power he was projecting. He could have burned us out. I think it was Isma'il who kept control and somehow stepped down what was coming through to you and me. Otherwise we could have ended up dead."

He took a step. He started along the passage from the depths of which he sensed the beating of the drum, the heart. It was totally dark, yet he had a sense of familiarity, as though he had been this way before, many times, and knew this maze as intimately as he cared to remember. There was a thread in his mind, a subliminal whispering, he was tugging at some knot which had to be undone to release . . . what? He would not know until he had released it.

He felt his way along the tunnel until he came to a drafty place where the passage split into three, forking away, like the trident sticks which Njeru had held. Here he sensed mutable glimmerings of color and sound—fragments of the music, broken. From the left fork, a dim but vibrant orange glow, a faint fast pulse. It excited thought in him, a flow of fantastic images—matter-annihilating theorems, tremblings of words of power, beautiful hermaphrodites with winged sandals who gazed seriously at him. And from the right fork came a suffusion of emerald, rich and clear and beautiful, hinting at sweet distant sounds, like fruit, which grew ripe in his mind, producing a sensual sexual languor . . . yet also the hint of feral nature, of tooth-and-claw danger, of the corruption as well as the beauty of the flesh.

These passages he ignored. Without pause he kept on the straight way, for along the central path he sensed the tantalizing drum beats, the particular mystery. Violet and indigo flashed in the darkness before him, he thought he saw a pale moon, pale flesh, ancientness, and he thought he heard lilting siren laughter, the murmur of running water, the roar of crashing tides. So he continued. But soon he began to feel heavy, morbid. Then the illusions and chaos began. His mind manufactured freely. Bloody headless children scuttled grotesquely past him, and women, dragged screaming by ancient patriarchs. He saw the flaring comet, shedding ghastly light on a frantic world whose people could no longer read the signs written in every leaf and stone and organic cell. He passed jackals, snarling at him as they tore at bloated corpses . . . and now the drums were multiple, sounding loudly . . . and he knew they were the drums of war, of the anxious divided heart, throbbing through him, in him, as at last he came out into a dim gigantic cavern-world . . . where, without warning, the drumming of a sudden ceased.

It was a place of still dark lagoons, of rocks fantastically carved, and the only light was lunar and pale in diffusion. Unquiet he walked a winding stony path between those dark lagoons, a nightmarish expectancy in him . . . and passing through a ravine found his way blocked by a strong naked man who wore the head of a bull, who carried a club. And the minotaur challenged him.

"We must fight. Only one can live. This is the Law."

The Voice resonated in him with bellowing familiarity. Kitaj hesitated. There was no way round. Then desperately, suddenly, he charged at sure death.

The minotaur offered no resistance at all. He collapsed the moment that Kitaj touched him. The bull mask rolled off his head. Kitaj was shocked.

It was Greystoke. His image of Tarzan, of macho identification.

"Okay." Tarzan grinned bleakly. "Kill me. Do it! Now!"

Instinctively, the moment his opponent had collapsed, Kitaj had snatched up a large rock. Now he stood, gaping stupidly, unable to act.

"Tarzan dies," insisted the image hoarsely. "Get on with it."

Slowly Kitaj raised the rock above his head . . . and as he did, the features of Tarzan slowly slid into . . . the face of Kitaj himself . . .

Kitaj went numb, but he understood.

With a curse he hurled down the rock, accurately.

The flare of crashing pain tore him into a new, naked condition. It was some time before, blinded and in agony, he was able to crawl to the edge of the nearest lagoon. He bathed himself in the deep black waters. The pain swiftly receded, as if opiated away. After a further period he found himself standing, still in a daze, not knowing himself, yet feeling curiously light inside.

Then he smelled the perfume, the scent.

It led him to a grotto where the light was green and warm, where flowers grew, where a woman sat on a rock, naked, her feet trailing idly in the water.

"Iloshabiet!" he exclaimed, fear and delight sparking in him.

She looked up at him. The dimensions of the grotto wavered, grew insubstantial, so that he thought himself back in the valley on Ruwenzori.

"In the Green World," she said gently, "curses can be dissolved . . . but courage and firmness are needed of you now if you wish to go on."

She picked up a mirror and gave it to him. Trembling, he took it, and he looked, and he cried out with shock. For the bloody face of M'Botu stared at him, and the blood ran from the mirror, thick and viscid, over his hand, down his arm. He gazed wildly at Iloshabiet and in her sad eyes saw the grossness of his thirty years of killing reflected. His breath caught short, he tightened, he was filled with horror and rage, and he started towards her, dropping the mirror as he did, not knowing what he meant to do.

Before he reached any decision she produced something else.

The spear. The bloody spear with which he'd killed the Frenchman.

It was too much. Shivering, for a moment he clutched the shaft of the weapon, the smell of blood overpowering . . . then, in one sudden motion, he turned and flung the spear far away, out over the waters of the lagoon, the lake.

An amazing thing happened. The instant before the spear plunged into the waters a hand appeared up out of the depths and grasped the weapon. Kitaj stared, his heart pumping frantically. For the hand was followed by the arm, and then the head and the body, of the Frenchman whom he had killed.

Kitaj stood, unable to move, as the pallid corpse came at him out of the waters, holding the spear pointed at his heart, the eyeless sockets fixed on him. For a moment he managed to tear his horrified gaze away from this ugly nemesis. He saw Iloshabiet, sitting motionless, watching him.

"You can run again," she said, "or you can accept it, and go through."

He found that his limbs were free. The murderous corpse was only feet away. A terrified inner voice urged him to run. He almost obeyed it. But, fighting the sick churning of his stomach, he steeled himself, and stood where he was.

So the corpse came, and speared him through the heart.

The lilting of a distant music brought the function called Kitaj round to a new self-consciousness. He stirred slowly, without memory, to find himself alone on a bleak and arid wasteland. Like a disembodied ghost he rose and began to float across the dark, apparently endless plain, following the ever-receding hint of the music. Gradually, memory and identity returned, and he knew that yet another obstacle had been overcome. The curse had been neutralized, and his lightness was increasing . . . yet he knew that there was still much to be paid for and answered. So he floated, drifted, for what seemed like centuries, with the hint of the music so faint and intermittent, and hope flickering low but never quite abandoned. It was an evanescent landscape, with no sure fixed forms, nothing solid, and things there dissolved the moment he tried to fix or define them. He met phantoms which riddled and tricked and cheated him. They all turned out to be himself. He wandered without nourishment, stripped even more bare of illusion and beliefs, following petrified rivers to frozen sources which did not feed. He came to a shattered red landrover with two bodies there which he had to face. He came through ghosts of France, and after that into a red world of feverish war where armies clashed by night, endlessly, meaninglessly, trumpeting patriotisms and false heroics. He was killed yet again, shot to death by a Nazi firing squad, and fell to the black watery underworld where the Old Woman's beasts chewed at him. There were soundless explosions, sunderings in him; there was agony and grief and self-condemnation. Then he was in a vast hall of judgement where he passed sentence on himself with the utmost impartiality as the images of those he had abused and exploited paraded before him. After this he came to a Hall of Records. The clerk who wrote out his account had a birdlike face and wore the emblem of the winged serpent.

"You've come a long way," said the clerk. "You have further to go."

So it proved. His wanderings through these levels continued, for a long time, and they were bleak, and filled with painful adventures . . . yet increasingly in him developed the sure sensation that he was following a specific and purposeful trail of self-sacrifice, leading to a goal of transformation, of a self-controlled new condition. And always he followed the hint of the music, which took him through whatever deaths confronted him, so that his lightness and feeling of essential immortality increased . . . and sometimes now he thought he glimpsed the piper in the distance ahead of him.

He began to climb. He climbed through great rolling forests, through wild and beautiful lands, in time to cross a great plain which ended in a deep abyss.

The other side of the abyss rose a sky-piercing golden mountain.

From the far summit of the mountain a figure seemed to beckon.

The piper. The piper of transformations.

Steady, now, sure of his goal, with confidence in the spirit that dwells in him and in all of us, he searched until he found a very narrow bridge across the abyss. It required firm balance to make the crossing safely, but now he had that balance: there was little weight left in him. He crossed. And with the gulf behind him he started up that mountain to the summit, no longer tired, for he was absorbed in and enriched by the general vitality of this sphere of things, in which he now shared, and the music of the piper drew him up, thrilling him with its energy and sense of worlds beyond. Up, up he climbed, through dry golden summer grass, seeming as he did to hear the roaring of lions, the laughter of children who played with the lions . . .and the potent sun shone all about, its light weaving, flowing, pulsing, dancing to the song of the piper which he had followed so far, through such long confusion and disturbance of soul. But now at last he knew he was close to resolution, to an integration in himself of elements which had formerly eluded him . . . and so, peacefully, in light, he climbed to that radiant mountain peak where the shining figure of the piper waited; a figure which as he entered its field of

life had him smiling with understanding, sharing . . . and as he
smiled he saw that once again the form of the piper was the form
of Njeru, whom he joined now, on the summit.

"Don't waste time congratulating yourself and gaping at me!"
the old man said sharply. "Look beyond! What lies beyond this
peak?"

Kitaj looked . . . and his jaw sagged.

For beyond the summit of this golden mountain lay another,
much greater abyss. It was so black and deep and wide that he
could sense no end at all to it . . . and he knew that it stretched
beyond all worlds of form and time and space. He stared, his
eyes fell into it, he was overwhelmed, and at first it was an
awesomeness which he could not plumb or contemplate. Then
the music encouraged his mind into making a leap—a jolt I
remember, which I could not follow, which almost stopped my
heart with the shock of its abruptness and energy—and with new
scale of insight he understood the gulf to be like some huge
empty upper room of mind, full of potential, but with little of
that potential as yet manifested or realized by earth-human
consciousness.

"It's the future," he whispered, not knowing what he meant.
"What are we doing there?"

"Look deeper," said the Smile, the *murogi,* the spirit of
adventure.

Kitaj did. There was another jolt, a gearing-up of focus and
intensity. He opened himself. His mind plunged into that apparent emptiness until, at one point in the gulf, he sensed a swirling,
a grayness, an activity as of wind driving a tunnel through depths
of cloud—a piercing, spiraling corkscrew of insinuated movement—
and from the further end came a light, at first vague, silvery
gray, but growing brighter, more pointed and specifically defined,
until the silveriness was very intense, a star, its light driving deep
into his mind, striking inside him with bright dynamic patterns
which danced and seemed alive with intelligence . . . and the
music to which these patterns danced was the music of the piper.
It all sounded within him, and so he stood amazed, forgotten to
himself, absorbed by these patterns which (he later said) were
conscious, were living entities, were mutable musical equations,
expressing ever-changing relationships, forming structure for self-
evolution that flowed down through him like quicksilver, exciting

every level of him, triggering new thoughts, triggering gland secretions which began a work of chemical and neurological change in him, so that, as he continued to absorb the light of this star astride the abyss, increasingly he knew that he was a part of this stellar intelligence, increasingly he knew that the patterns were communicating with him, proposing courses of action for his future which he could choose to follow, or not. He felt dissolved, transported, transformed by this liquid fire that burned all through him . . . and for an instant he sensed himself spread all through the living gulf, the intelligent universe, looking back down on the familiar planet earth with the perspective of those entities—those dynamic agents of universal evolution, in whose mind we share, though as yet unconsciously—that we perceive and admit or deny as angels, or flying saucers, or whatever form into which are able to cast them according to the extent of our present understanding. And so for that instant Kitaj traveled the higher reaches and saw the patterns of a potential creative future which we can still choose.

Then, without warning, the music stopped, the patterns faded, Kitaj found himself standing on that mountain top, dazed and amazed in the face of the void.

"You can't stare forever," said Njeru. "What do you see?"

"Something that will not become real until we take it into ourselves and choose to live it on our earth," Katij muttered, abstracted.

"And what is that?"

Kitaj indicated the star, the hidden world inside us, outside us.

"Somehow," he said, very quietly, "we are there as well as here . . . and the patterns of that star are coded into us, into our very structure, into our DNA. We have star-selves which we haven't fully admitted yet . . . though our star-selves have been visiting us, publicly, visibly, for many years now. And so long as the mass of us continue to see these visitations as something external, apart from us—as the churches have trained us to think of God—then there will be no good communication, only fear and hostility. For there is gravity that holds us onto the physical earth, making our thoughts and bodies heavy . . . and there is fear that stagnates us. Few of us have the perspective to see that we are already there as well as here. We are part of a universal organism, but most of us think our only business is on this planet. And we are destroying ourselves and the planet with this attitude. We have to educate ourselves into the wider perspective. Star-perspective. We must go to the stars. But we'll never do it by machine technology alone. We can send spaceships beyond the outer planets, but the human crews will all go mad . . . unless they are people who have admitted that the void is in themselves as well as outside. There is a Styx, an abyss, a river of death that we have to cross. There are inner mental barriers which have their analogues in outer space, and the road is in us. It always was and always will be. To go to the stars, to bring the stars down to earth, we have to turn ourselves into something else. If we can't do that, then we'll fail, and life in this planet will have to start again.''

"Very well. What do you mean to do about it . . . in the world?''

"However I can demonstrate what I see,'' said Kitaj, facing the image of his old teacher, "I will do it. I will try to find the middle ground.''

"Your idealism is rewarding,'' said Njeru drily. "You have realized something about yourself at last. But what response do you expect from people?''

"I expect nothing,'' replied Kitaj, after a pause. "The world is not in good shape. Millions of people are too bound up with survival and pleasures and selfishness to deliberately want to reorient or rethink themselves. So we do what we can. We don't turn back. There's nothing to lose. We work for racial transformation. It won't come overnight, and it may not come at all—but it certainly won't come if we don't take a chance and try for it.''

"It will come.'' The Smile grew very brilliant. "The Joke is on you if you let doubt or cynicism distract you. Because beyond the warp and death of the Black Hole lies the White Hole. But now . . . you must go down and start.''

Then Njeru lifted the pipes again, and the first note sounded: his form dissolved wholly into the Smile, into a radiant field of spiraling light; and for an instant Kitaj felt the Old Woman through him too, smiling too—then tremendous rings of fire swooped, enfolded, and consumed him.

Through the Black Hole. Into the Smile.

The Smile of the creative void itself.

Willingly, at last, he let himself go.

* * *

When he found himself again he was stretched out, soaked, in the stone circle, in Ireland. It was night. Without pausing to consider the logical fact that he should have been starving and weak he stood, stretched, left the circle, and started back to our cottage by the black lough, walking all night, energetic and renewed, not knowing where he was bound, with the Sirian patterns come to consciousness in him.

But I did not understand this.

Meaning: I did not want to.

They are closing in.

I can feel their approach, but I think there is time.

It is hard to write sensibly about this. The structures of our languages are insufficient, and my fear has been persistent for years. After that night on the hilltop I fled from Kitaj and remained in hiding for a year thereafter. In fact I was hiding from myself, terrified at the experience of otherness which Kitaj stimulated in the three of us. I blamed him for attacking my consciousness. I feared to associate politically with the directions and chances which clearly he now meant to take. And until recently, save in peak flashes, I never recalled what happened in me that night.

Yet lately my dreams have been vivid and concise, returning me to recollection of that night. I play the tape and hear the strangeness of his voice and recall how, when he spoke of his vision from the mountain top, I too sensed those dizzy living patterns, flashing from the bright star which we faced, coruscating with intelligence in my mind, speaking of the need for a sacrifice of personality which then I could not face. They made the choice known. Personality can accept death and transformation into wider condition—or it can curl up into hedgehog ball of false security and self-limitation.

I tried to go both ways at once. I tried to let go while still hanging on. It didn't work. Of course not. I ended up hanging by fingertips from the edge of the precipice, unwilling to let go totally, unable to climb back.

And something else. The patterns showed the shape of things to come. A premonitory shivering in the bones which laid out in the imagination a range of variables, of possibilities . . . possibilities which through the power of human will might be converted into the events and facts of a particular road.

The road I saw through Kitaj was an archetypal road.

Long Live The King. The King Must Die.

In my negativity I foresaw only the darkness of persecution
and death—the Black Hole. I did not realize the Smile that lies
beyond.

The Joke was on me. That night was my Ruwenzori. Soon
after, when we left Ireland, I fled to Edinburgh, into the conventions of the past, hating Kitaj for my bent spine, unable yet to
shed the old skin.

Lenore and Isma'il? He alone remained with Kitaj. He understood and gave himself to Kitaj's new direction without reserve.
She went to live alone on Vancouver Island. For nearly two years
she lived amid the forests, working out and integrating her own
sense of shock and change from that night.

And Kitaj returned to the world with a program.

The shattering of the mirrors of conventional self-definition.

Now it is a long time since I made my choice. Nearly thirteen
years since that night when the die was cast, almost seven years
since Venice. Now they are closing in on me. The agents of
those who wish to maintain conventional blindness in earthbound
human society. They will kill me when they find me.

But this will be completed first. It will be done. I choose those
patterns which say it will be done, and soon. Then function will
be fulfilled.

We who live now are the people of the Transition, and as yet
we can only grasp hints of the song that our children will sing.

Our individualism, our existence as separate mental/biological
units, is one of evolution's deliberate processes. The purpose of
separation is to end all separation.

I know this, even though I don't completely understand it.

I know it. During the last five years, Kitaj demonstrated it
. . . and finally offered himself up to it . . . though the route he
took seemed circuitous . . .

MIRROR IMAGES
OR
SEGAMI RORRIM

*"There are good grounds for the awesome theory
that scientific discovery is the projection into
matter of the exploration of the human mind . . ."*
—Lawrence Blair, Rhythms of Vision

8. MYTHONAUTS

Kitaj's return was engineered as a babble, a deliberately bad and banal act. For over a week the hype went on. He was "discovered," dressed like a bum, drinking ouzo on his own, in the dark back room of a Piraeus waterfront bar. His Stanley went by the name of Jane Moonlight. She was a professional American media psychic who claimed to have followed a "trail of hunches, hints, and dreams." She happened to have a TV crew with her. She plowed through the bar crowd and came onto Kitaj with utmost certainty, not put off by his disguise and changed appearance, and challenged him by name. I saw it on TV, on the Ten O'Clock News. Fights broke out between her TV crew and people in the bar; the police arrived promptly; the bar was cleared, but soon it was full again, a chaos of people representing many powerful interests, Kitaj's included. The game went on all night beneath the spotlights. The ouzo-drunk bum was positively identified as Ralph M'Botu Kitaj, but, though he was questioned all night by the world press, he gave no straight answers at all about where he'd been or what he meant to do now that he was

back. He acted drunk, flippant, and incompetent, as though he
had no clear idea at all what was going on in the world. The date
was 1 April 1987, just two weeks after the leaving of Ireland. It
was a well-chosen date.

Thus began a week or so during which his every reported act
and word seemed empty and farcical. From Athens he toured
through a dozen cities accompanied by an entourage of anonymous hard-faced men in business suits. On TV he seemed out of
tune, out of touch, almost diffident, bluntly avoiding important
questions rather than playing with them as he'd used to do,
looking unkempt and nervous even though he too had changed
into a suit after the first night.

None of it rang true. It was an utter disappointment. It seemed
that he had nothing spectacular to do or say. The people he met
were bureaucrats and businessmen, financiers, politicians. He
spent his time in boardrooms and exclusive clubs with the managers of his interests. Soon the word was out that he owned an
estimated ten per cent of available global assets. He was, in fact,
the Richest Man In The World. But, so what? It was nothing
compared with the myth he'd become during the Disappearance.
He had returned . . . with what? Only money and seeming
paranoia. It was a lousy letdown for millions. KITAJ BUBBLE
BURSTS! headlines were soon declaring. Soon he was being
threatened and derided whenever he appeared in public. He
stopped appearing. He stayed behind closed doors all that summer, meeting with those who'd been his enemies. The wars and
oppositions developed in his name began to fade and die. The
Spreaders and other radical groups who'd fed on his mystique
lost momentum. It seemed that he'd lost his nerve, that now he
sought tame respectability, looking out only for himself, still
dealing in death, concerned only to fight the international movement that developed to bring him to trial, to nationalize or seize
his interests and take away his power. Evidently his webs and
connections were efficient, for by the end of summer 1987 this
movement had failed.

The public contempt deepened. Kitaj had slunk back into the
human fold with nothing in him changed. He was not a hero. Not
even a villain.

Just Getty, Onassis, or Hughes on a super scale.

Nothing mythical or born-again about that.

I didn't understand. Obviously more was going on than met

the eye, but I didn't get in touch. In July 1987 I finished *Liar's Gold* and mailed him the manuscript, anonymously, with no return address.

"I had to avoid hero-worship," he told me a year later when I rejoined him. "Too many people looking for someone to turn up and save them from themselves. I had to stop them laying their lazy bullshit on me, like New Hope of Humanity, or Great Scourge. So I came on like a mean banal cop-out. They despised me for not being mythical, for failing their apocalyptic expectations, and they began to forget me . . . and I got space to start work on the *real* story."

His grin was a dance I found hard to return.

"What's that?" I was tense, unsure of myself.

"You know very well," he said. "Come on!"

"You mean . . . the projects?" I asked cautiously.

"What projects? What projects are those, Johnny?"

"Well," I muttered, "Isma'il says you're operating on several levels right now, and that the Black Hole Joke Shows are just the . . . like the basement . . ."

"Right." He beamed. "The bargain basement. In which I wear the mask of having stripped off all my masks. You can call it a diversion."

He was full of diversion. That first year of return he acted as he did not least to insure his own safety. He was a lone wolf, an outsider, and had many enemies among the world's power elites. Those belonging to what he generally referred to as "The Club" wanted him dead. The Club consisted of people whose interests and ownerships were adversely affected by Kitaj's influence. By the time of the Disappearance many of them had noted with alarm how, in his role as clown-demon prince of capitalism, Kitaj had begun to undermine not only their wealth but also their social base. His self-condemnations also condemned them.

Socialist condemnations were one thing. Betrayal from within the ranks was another. Kitaj had become a threat to many. During the Disappearance this threat had increased, with millions of rebellious have-nots drawing inspiration from him. The totality of the Disappearance—which made clear the effective complexity of his organization, the loyalty of his mostly anonymous managers, and the extent of his power—had emphasized the threat.

So that now, having returned, he was in great personal danger.

The danger would have been even greater if not for the protective strength of his organization and alliances. Few of these alliances were public. "When I started getting rich," he told me, "I knew I had to protect my ass. I hired a lot of investigators. I learned a lot of things about a lot of people. I built files on the individuals who mattered in every country in the world. Over two thousand names, and in time I had something on almost all of them."

Blackmail was one game he could play better than his enemies, for most of them, unlike him, had to maintain the guise of respectability.

This did not make those generals and presidents and directors in The Club like him any better. There were many people out to nail him, permanently.

"I had to buy time. I had to play it tight. I couldn't be seen in public too much, or get predictable, or outrageous, or give any hint of my real goal. So I put on the face of boring respectability. Ralph M'Botu Kitaj, a changed man, no longer out to cause shock and horror, willing for the first time to deal with his buddies at the top of the shitpile. Of course the people who were planning to hit me didn't believe it. But they were greedy enough to hope that maybe I would deal with them. They were curious to find out what I was really up to. So they didn't hit me when I was most vulnerable. They wasted time and energy instead, trying to buy me onto their side . . . and I had to pretend to go along with it until I was ready to play my hand. You know. I flirted with joining a consortium that would have trimmed my wings. I was seen in the right society and made the right noises at the right times . . . and didn't let on I was dumping all those arms interests." He laughed. "It was tricky as hell. Transferring funds from death to life and making out I was still staunch on the side of respectable death and exploitation. Had to watch it, because they were checking me out all the time. Had to assume that every room I entered was bugged, and that everyone who shook my hand was bought.

"It made things hard. But I got by. Had some advantages they didn't know about. And they couldn't focus entirely on me. They had a whole lot of other problems. You know. The world . . ."

The world . . .

In 1987 the world was in strange condition. In general it was a time of fuck-up and repression. Mechanical fascism was in power all over the place in fearful reaction to the world's growing nervous breakdown. Rigid walls of convention and brute force were being desperately erected against the flood. Military dictatorships in many half-runned countries were trumpeting slogans of expediency, making and breaking alliances with and against each other, but for the most part mutually supportive against their own starving and angry populations. There was common cause against Spreaders and other newconscious radical movements who spoke of self-responsibility and independence. In this struggle to maintain existing social concepts, the old "democracies" openly joined forces with the most vicious despotisms.

The fury of the Third World War was increasing.

It was not always a physical war. It was war in which as many of the combatants were being blown up by evolutions in themselves as by the shells, bombs, or rockets of some outer enemy belonging to different economic class, nation, sex, color, or religion. It was (is) war to realize that external physical war results from internal emotional/mental war.

In the meantime, pending mass enlightenment, there were many mass conflicts of a conventional sort, in which convention was flouted only by the lack of subsequent global escalation. Nobody wanted to go over the edge. In October 1987 the Chinese started to "civilize" India from Tibet and Burma and Sri Lanka simultaneously: the rest of the world pretended not to notice, or found reason to approve. In June 1988 OPEC announced cessation of all oil supplies to the west on grounds of dwindling domestic supplies: Pentagon hawks were said to be in favor of aggression. But then occurred a series of events in the Middle East that shocked anyone still capable of being shocked by human lunacy.

The Israelis used a version of the Mindwarp Field.

This followed a Palestinian bombing campaign in selected Israeli cities. When, despite warnings, the campaign continued, the Israelis retaliated in a horrific manner. Employing Mindwarp at the slow Sleepbeam frequency (2–4 cycles a second), they broadcast suicide commands into the sleep of thirty military officers and politicians of surrounding Arab nations. Next morning all those selected and thus struck (a list of names had already been given to Reuters for subsequent confirmation) were found to have cut their own throats with a perfect efficiency.

It did not prove as conclusive as the Israelis had hoped. Tactical nuclear warfare broke out. Several cities and their populations were reduced to hot radioactive ash, though Jerusalem was spared because of its religious importance to both sides.

The rest of the world managed to keep out of it. Everyone had their own problems. Nobody wanted to push any buttons. The U.S.S.R. was preoccupied with "liberalization," made necessary by internal conflicts and secessionary disputes. The U.S.A. was also suffering from internal problems. Many Americans were wondering if they could possibly survive in a horse-and-buggy society. Washington, Oregon, and Northern California were on the point of abandoning the Union to form a separate republic . . . while Southern California (by 1988 more Mexican-Spanish-Catholic than WASP) was agitating to become part of Mexico. To the acute embarrassment of the President Jane Patchen, herself a Catholic, the Papacy entered the fray on behalf of Southern California's Third World Catholic majority . . . while the Mexicans, oil rich, were carefully saying very little at all, while building up their armed forces against a possible invasion by the U.S.A.

The Catholic Church. In some ways it was more obviously powerful than ever before in its long history. Enormous numbers of confused people were turning for meaning to the authoritative rites of Rome, for all definitions were crumbling and props were needed by many. For every new Spreader or (soon) Chancer willing to step forward through the gates of change, there were two or three new Catholic converts . . . and every earthquake or rise in inflation brought more. The churches were full again, and the Jesuit order swelled with a new breed of militant. Likewise with Islam and other old and institutionalized religions. With increasing care barriers of orthodoxy were being defined to exclude and condemn all varieties of uncomfortable new knowledge which suggested that humankind, not God or the Devil, was responsible for the mess. Inevitably, the witch-hunting mentality began to take root.

It looked bad.

"Listen," Kitaj told one of his audiences in 1992, "this situation is what we make it. Why are people talking doom and despair? We still have day and night, the planet still goes round the sun. What more do we want? Blue skies? I tell you, if we get through this lot in one piece—and we will—we'll know how to *manufacture* blue skies. This time is a necessary breaking-apart. It's twenty-three skidoo. It's tough, but it's the only way. We'll make it . . . though we can't stay the same as we were. That's the point. We have to go through the fire. The Old World is dying. We have to transform ourselves into something new—and we can do it! But if you keep looking back over your shoulder at what you were, you'll turn to stone. I mean, good God, did you ever hear a caterpillar complain about turning into a butterfly?''

It wasn't all bad. Of course not. It just looked that way sometimes. There was horror and tragedy, yes, but also business as usual. In that year of 1987, Chubby Checker's "Let's Twist Again" hit the top of the British hit parade for the third time in thirty years. The Boston Red Sox won the World Series; Liverpool, Munchen Gladbach, Juventus, Celtic, Barcelona, and St. Julien were the Cup Winners in Europe. Meanwhile, amid holocaust and hurricane, the world also thrilled to the daring, gravity-defying exploits of a ten-year-old Korean gymnastics star, Wi-Ha-Yo. Public interest in this amazing young girl soared when charges were made by disgruntled older competitors that she was a cyborg; that she had brain implants—neural stimulators—to improve her performance, and that likewise much of her muscular system was artificial. Proof that this was true led to the scandal that many world-beating athletes, at least since the early eighties, had been wired up in this fashion.

The 1988 Olympics were declared open only to "true biological humans."

More to the point: Newconscious research, the marriage of science with the occult, was developing rapidly in many world centers.

In October 1987, at Rio de Janeiro, where the magnetic field strength of the planet is lowest, an immensely influential conference was held. It was an all-out effort to integrate disciplines which never previously in public had been considered in relation to one another. Delegates included biologists, electrochemists, physicists, astronomers, astrologers, historians, spiritists, parapsychologists, poets, yogis, psychologists, theologians, numerologists, financiers, statisticians, pure mathematicians and practicing magicians. It was organized and financed by an unrevealed private interest operating through a trust, and lasted over a month. It was an intellectual assault course, and quite a few delegates dropped out, exhausted or confused or furiously rejecting information that denied their beliefs. But those who stuck it out melded a lot together. Following the conference was published a long report. It became known as *The New Level*. It carried the signatures of over seventy delegates, including five Nobel Prize winners, and it was authoritative in areas where formerly nothing at all had been authoritative. It issued guidelines, detailed summaries, and holistic viewpoints covering many new directions of newconscious research, including social/ethical/poetic projections and perspectives. It was a revolutionary scientific document, for the matters it discussed were principally those formerly excluded by science and religion alike . . . and, because of this, it soon ran into trouble. Many interactions and possible developments of human consciousness were discussed, from the unified viewpoint that, without relationships, there are no objects—without values, and value structures, and respect for the creative potential of every life, no worthwhile life to live.

Some of the papers I remember dealt with:

(1) Life-fields. Effects of electromagnetism in the growth of tissues, organs, consciousness itself. Schumann waves as carriers of psi information. A general study of correlations between geomagnetic fluctuations and states of consciousness, with reference in particular to connection between atmospheric ion levels and the level of serotonin in the brain.

(2) Consideration of nature, effects, and predictability of other planetary, solar, and stellar-galactic radiations on Earth activities and consciousness. Consideration of Earth as intelligent organism, with humanity the expression of that intelligence. The myth of the "Closed Planet." Examination of reports of "intelligent signals" from stellar sources. Examination of possible psychic-physical correlations in UFO phenomena. Conclusion: "The human race is a self-modifying organism at present in a state of acute self-examination. We recognize as much as we are willing to recognize. We can choose or not to join a wider community. But before we can do this we must first set our own house in order."

(3) A paper examining means—yogic, alchemic, and technologic—towards self-control of the cerebral hemispheres and the emotional centers of the hypothalamus. Discussion of the Leary "Eight Circuit" model of the human nervous system. Circuits 1–4, located in the active left lobe of the cortex, relating to mechanics of terrestrial survival. Circuits 5–8, in the right lobe, only partly activated, concerned with the evolution of consciousness to the eighth, quantum-level circuit: a "god-state" beyond matter, space, and time.

(4) Cyborg technology. Human/machine reflections and interfaces.

(5) High-voltage photography. The aura. Acupuncture. Psychic healing. Energy transfer. Reorientation of medical practices and attitudes. Chinese aphorism: "The superior physician cures *before* the illness is manifested. The inferior physician can care only for the illness which he was unable to prevent."

(6) Discussion of a proposed project to cross-reference the mythologies and folklore of the world, in order to develop new lines of approach (metaphoric and functional) to the inner conditions of human consciousness, to develop reflection and decision with regard to the nature and solutions of current human dilemmas and self-blockages.

(7) Development of biological receiver-transmitter systems. Exploration of plant, reptile, and mammal brain levels in the human being. Development of closer interaction with aquatic mammalian intelligences: whales, dolphins, etc.

(8) Discussion of value failure as modern disease. Cancer as expression of value failure at the organic level. Maslow's positivism useful in search for social psychological reorientations, but ". . . before we can send humansoul to the stars, we have to get our feet back on the ground . . ."

What this hinted at was taken up by the last of the forty-seven papers, which dealt with the possibilities of the phenomenon generally known as "astral travel," or "Out Of Body Experiences."

It was this paper that caused the uproar; this paper which, some state, has led to the reactive persecution of newconscious research by churches and states during the last decade. It was a speculative and poetic statement, with very radical implications. The authors made it clear that they regarded the existence of the astral or "bioplasmic" zone of consciousness as firmly established. From this controversial and didactic standpoint they proceeded to deliver a cosmopolitical manifesto for Planet Earth.

Here is some of the text. No doubt you will have seen it elsewhere, but it is worth repetition.

> We on this planet are in trouble. Through our ignorance we have created for ourselves certain problems which presently appear insoluble, not least because we lack the perspective to see the problems as a whole.
>
> We cannot clearly see the nature of the problems because we are stuck in the middle of them. We are the major problem. We must find a way to gain perspective. We must step outside of ourselves and our environment.
>
> To go to the moon is to remain within the same sphere of age-old effect. Likewise the planets, within whose wheelings we exist, while the sun, though giving us light and life, is also the very image of our imprisoning ego.
>
> We must go to the stars in this time.
>
> How do we do this?
>
> It grows apparent that interstellar travel and communication on a purely material or mechanical basis is not possible. Relativity effects and quantum paradoxes, plus the evidence gleaned by inner journeys into the mind indicate that, though material philosophy is an appropriate response to certain levels of earth-bound existence, it is inappropriate, and its laws nonfunctional, at higher levels of space-time integration.
>
> Our material technology is a reflection of our own mentality, and as such is important in seeking solutions, but secondary. Of primary importance in this time is the marriage of the scientific attitude to the exploration of certain human faculties which traditionally have been termed "Magical," "Occult," etc. We

must come to understand that the road to the stars is
already written within us. Our nervous structure, our
electromagnetic environment, our consciousness which
is a mutable flux within this electromagnetic environment—these are influenced and formed by the "signals" and variable fields of energy through which this
planet spirals (the "Song of the Spheres").

This is to say that we are already, and always have
been, star-travelers. It is also to say that we already
possess within us the means to shift at will our frames
of reference within the stellar continuum, and that it is
now time to explore and develop these long-realized
inner means scientifically. For the chief difficulty is not
one of technological complexity, nor of expense, nor of
the vastness and incomprehensibility of the universe,
but of our own belief in and understanding of ourselves.

Astral travel can come to mean no more nor less than
what the name implies. There are close analogies between
the Inner and the Outer: one does not exist without the
other. Development of the potential of "inner journey"
techniques, leading to appropriate methods for the controlled projection of the mind, will open the human
door to a psychotechnology of space-time travel more
efficient, economic, and genuinely profitable for everyone than anything envisaged by solid state material
techniques.

The sound of one hand clapping on itself.

With global dedication to an improved understanding
we will soon be able to visit former cultures on this
planet—they are within us.

Mythonauts will spin out the silver cord to visit
dwellers of many wheres and whens, many stars, for
they are coded in us, and we in them.

The roads are not new. Throughout our brief recorded
history there have been those who visit and those who
go visiting, leaving or restructuring their bodies and the
somatic physical continuum in order to do so.

It can be objected that to date there is no hard
quantifiable proof of this. Likewise *there is no such
proof that consciousness itself exists.*

The roads always exist, in every conscious mind,

and thus they can be owned or taxed by no one earthly
force or agency. We ourselves are the basis of the
technology. We are our own permission to travel. We
are the continuum. We are the key. The only passports
and tickets required are those of courage and will. The
only laws we need to recognize are already written in
us.

But wake up! It is getting late. Wake up!

When I first read this, early in 1988, I was reminded and
began to feel ashamed of my flight from myself on the hilltop in
Ireland. I read it, and sensed Kitaj's influence, but not until later
in the year did I learn that he had been behind the conference in
Rio. He had organized it, funded it, and done much of the
persuading required to bring the delegates to it. Yet he assured
me that he had brought no influence at all to bear on what was
decided and written in *The New Level*.

"Johnny, you have a problem," he said. "You tend to see
everything in terms of personalities. You see me as a leader or
something. But all I'm doing is trying to bring focus to ideas
which are spreading through millions of people. I'm trying to
synthesize, dramatize, coordinate. I'm feeding cash where it's
needed. These are my functions. I have my own talents, yes, and
I'm developing them further—but there are many people much
more competent than myself to do the actual work. Many people
on the ball. Unfortunately, there's also the inertial mass of
millions more who've been educated and driven into total lack of
faith in themselves. And the OldStyle interests who want to stop
all this. It means much of the work has to be clandestine. Too
bad."

This was in 1989, a year after the shock of the Black Hole
Joke Shows, and Kitaj's intentions were no longer, whatever he
said, clandestine.

Yet what showed publicly was only the tip of the iceberg.

How had he gone about it?

For almost a year, until the publication of *Liar's Gold* in early
'88, which he used as a springboard for the Shows, Kitaj had
kept a low profile, flirting with his enemies, acting as though his
only interests were materialistic. He used this period to set up the
programs. He transferred a massive fortune into newconscious

research and managed to keep it secret, funding many groups and individuals all round the world. In many cases none of the work was put down onto paper, or onto tape: it circulated between those involved in it, outside the scientific establishments.

"It arose through people knowing people," I was told a couple of years ago by a man I met, a neurologist who at the time had been connected with the Abolish Death Committee in Berkeley, California. "When the New Level thing was published after Rio a lot of us realized the shit was about to hit the fan. The New Level said pointblank that there's no realistic basis at all, no justification, for conventional government and religious institutions. It provided the basis of a scientific approach towards breaking down the entire money-leader society and opening up something new. Already the FBI and a host of other people had been trying to infiltrate groups seeking new approaches, so that after Rio it was clear that the power merchants had two ways to turn. They could try to take over these new areas themselves—identify with and try to control these fields that deny their authority altogether— or they could, as usual, try to bust the whole thing. Bust the Gnosis, set up the Inquisition, establish limits, control the mind. Nothing new. But embarrassing, because for a long long time scientists themselves had performed these acts of self-limitation, had stayed willingly within the social structures, had built the bombs and served convention. But after the sixties a lot of us were coming out of the closet and standing on the streets with everyone else. I mean I got my imprints in the campus riots, and a lot of others too, which made it hard to find work in the seventies. The universities weren't hiring radicals. Which meant the best minds just got more radical, in time for the eighties.

"You want to know how Kitaj's thing came through. Well, I got the word one night from a guy I'd known and respected a long time. He said there was a particular problem in my area—self-control of cell regeneration—that I might like to work on, privately, relating it back to nobody but him. He said he in turn was in touch with someone else, and that a pattern of research development derived from Rio conclusions was being distributed secretly from an unknown central source. He said some more and I thought, wow, we've got a conspiracy here, just like the Illuminati . . . so I started wondering who was pushing what, and why, and which side I was on. I said I needed more information—you know, I had a family, and I couldn't take that sort of chance without knowing more. My friend just grinned and said he'd asked the same thing. 'Now I'm telling you what I got told,' he said. 'The Word is: is it what *you* want to do? Can you sneak that lab time without anyone finding out? If you can, then just trust your heart—and Take a Chance!' So I did. That's exactly what I did. And that's how I got involved.''

This man (for obvious reasons I can't identify him) must have been at least fifty when I met him, but he looked a good twenty years younger than that.

But in 1988 the Demon Prince returned.

Kitaj put off his respectable mask and put on that of the Devil. So at first it seemed. He began the new game in February, a month after *Liar's Gold* came out, riding the crest of a wave of renewed interest in him, launching his most uncompromising series of attacks yet against what he saw as global complacency and dishonesty.

At first, from my musty book-lined lair in Edinburgh, I thought this new role to be nothing but a crude fake. In fact it was more like a crusade. The Black Hole Joke Shows were the main medium. They involved infuriating, terrifying, goading, pushing, tantalizing, and otherwise trying to stimulate millions of human beings to take their chances and step through their own inner gates before everything inside them got fatally blocked.

Caligula might have been proud of the Shows. Parts of them would have been unbearably horrible if not for the self-mocking dark humor which characterized them. Indeed, many people did find them unbearably horrible. The flood of righteous protest became so intense that, after the third show, the so-called Snuff Show, there were few broadcasting companies anywhere willing to put his productions on the air. So, instead, they went out on pirate or on viewer-sponsored cable channels, and videotapes were extensively bootlegged, and Kitaj wielded his scalpel to such effect that soon it was generally clear that the disappointment of his Return had been a legitimate phase of his still-developing myth.

There is down as well as up in life.

And sometimes the King Must Die.

If there was a main connecting theme to the Shows, this was it. In each of them Kitaj played aspects of the Everyman Monarch, uselessly self-degraded and self-constricted by trivial concerns. His technique was to take and expose an issue by presenting himself as the well-known archvillain, making the deadly possibilities clear and dramatic.

With the early Shows came the public introduction of a new technology, on a limited scale, in the wealthier parts of North and South America, Europe, and Australia. This was a species of telefactoring. Suitably equipped viewers (there was a considerable advertising campaign beforehand, but only a few thousand of the adapted sets were sold, at first) could see, hear, smell, touch, and experience the Show from Kitaj's point of view. He was wired up and his responses were projected through the networks, to be reconstituted via headsets into the minds of the viewers. It was primitive, and not very successful.

Yet when I heard of it I again remembered that night on the hilltop, and my doubts grew. I still blamed him, and I was uneasy about this concern of his with direct projection of his attitudes into the minds of others. I was not the only one. "Total Identification," he called it, and it caused as much uproar as the Shows themselves. Accusations of fascism, power mania, and corruption of youth hit him from all sides. In March there was an assassination attempt on him in London, after the second show, the "Miz Universe" show. There were fresh moves to stop him "legally," all of which failed. His web ran deeper and wider than anyone had suspected, it seemed, and there was talk of the presidents he had in his pocket.

Yet he had his finger on the pulse of the daily world again. Few people tuned in via Total Identification, but millions watched, and millions were also reading *Liar's Gold*. And when, later in the year, the Israelis struck with Mindwarp, Kitaj's attitude no longer seemed quite so ridiculous and excessive, and the morality of his intention, at first denied by all but a few, became more apparent.

In the first show he appears on a bare stage, wearing bright red radiation protective gear, followed by two similarly attired technicians, who wheel out a trolley on which sits a fat black box. They do so very carefully.

Kitaj motions a halt. He stares at the box for some time.

Silence from the live theater audience. It is in New York.

"What's in this box?" Kitaj asks quietly.

Voices shout from the audience—raucous, imaginative. After a few seconds Kitaj cuts them off with a half smile, a negating wave of his right hand.

"In this box," he says, "there are samples of plutonium stolen from reactors in six different countries during the last month and a half. I am responsible for the thefts. The governments and energy commissions of the nations involved have naturally kept quiet. They don't want you to know! But it is true! Here, tonight, now, every one of you in this theater is faced by . . . by active particles of . . . *plutonium!*"

Groans, boos, screams, disbelieving jeers.

"Then I'll prove it!" Kitaj laughs—funny, mad, metallic. His face cannot be seen through the visor of the radiation suit. "I will open the box! Why not? We all have to go down to the Plutonian halls sooner or later. So why not now? Why not take a chance?"

The pandemonium is considerable.

"Very well," says Kitaj, pausing. "Of course you don't believe me—but you can't be sure, can you?" He shrugged. "But most of you don't want to take the chance. You don't want me to open the box. Okay. I won't."

And he did not, so that nobody ever knew, for sure.

"People have a healthy fear of Pandora," he told the press afterwards, "but sooner or later they'll always open that box."

In the second show he masqueraded as the chauvinist male clown-judge in a Miz Universe beauty contest. It was mounted with glitter, razzmatazz, and sparkling lights. There ended the resemblance to a straight beauty contest. The contestants appeared naked, and Kitaj interviewed them with political questions. It was straightforward until the Israeli contestant, who went by the name of Ms. Sophia Yetzirah, grew angry at his attitude.

"Mr. Kitaj," she declared, her eyes flashing, "this show is a farce. You stand here in your armor and your masks, thinking you make a fool of me and the audience, and maybe you think, and maybe the audience thinks, that *I* am the only spectacle here. It is true that I am willing to degrade myself by standing here naked on this unpleasant sexist scaffold, because you are paying me a great deal of money—but if you want to discuss serious matters, then you too must take off your clothes, and we will face one another as equals!"

"Well, of course," said Kitaj, visibly impressed, for Ms.

Yetzirah had flashing eyes and she was very lush, with Titian hair and tinted nipples. And with great decorum Kitaj stripped down to socks and suspenders and thick black oxfords. "Do you believe in God, Ms. Yetzirah?"

She looked him up and down with immense hauteur.

"You are too squat and hairy," she said loftily. "You look like a biological throwback, and I do not believe you are thinking of God at all."

For by now he was physically clenched and erect, his condition censored in the broadcast I saw by a little black blob, an electronic loincloth. But the play was not censored. He was furious, obviously could not stand to be bested by a woman. He growled like an ape. He ran and leapt at her. With cool and ease she karate-chopped him to the floor. There was a spontaneous burst of cheering from the audience. He crawled painfully up to his knees.

"God couldn't have meant that to happen," he muttered, perplexed.

Ms. Yetzirah exited to wild applause. Kitaj was booed all the way back to the rhinestone-studded rostrum. There he met the Finnish entry, Ms. Hargitta Lemminkainen, a slender ash-blonde person with skin as white as snow. Ms. Lemminkainen was an articulate ex-disco-queen sex-changer who'd become politically committed and militant on behalf of all sexual don't-knows.

". . . But also I am here," she breathed, "because it excites me to think that at this very moment millions of people are looking at my body."

"Thank God for that!" exclaimed Kitaj, and lunged again. This time it was a knee that met his belly, an elbow that met his nose.

"We are on television" Ms. Lemminkainen rebuked him primly.

The contest was "won" by Ms. Juanita Ventura, a Brazilian bellydancer. It was she who, afterwards, tried to kill Kitaj. She cut him in the shoulder with a knife, and there was quite a struggle before she was overpowered. Later on the news she said how sorry she was that she hadn't managed to kill him. "It was not a fake, like some people say," she claimed. "I meant to kill him. It is five years since his dealings in Brazil coffee made the company where my father worked go out of business. My father got no more work. When he fell sick we could not afford the doctors. He died in pain. Kitaj is responsible for that!"

What is true, what is false?

*   *   *

There is no doubt. The shows were diverting. Watching them,
it was hard to imagine that this man could have anything positive
in his mind, and the third show, the Snuff Show, confirmed the
opinion of millions that he could be nothing but a beast. It caused
uproar. Moralists and many others protested the opening scene in
which Kitaj, bathing in a bath apparently of human excrement,
received his checks from powdered and periwigged eighteenth-
century flunkies. Witches objected to the farcically dangerous
misuse of a potent rite of Pan which followed. Animal lovers
were furious at the sacrifice of a dog, a goat, a chicken. But as to
the main event, the climax of the show, there were few direct
protests or charges. The TV critics uniformly copped out by
trying to deal with what they'd observed in aesthetic terms. Few
could truly believe that what they'd witnessed had really happened.

Maybe it did. Maybe it didn't. Personally, I don't think it did.
Either way, there was no evidence afterwards. No body.

Yet Kitaj's potent Total Identification fury (I tuned into a tape
of the Show a year later to check it all out again) seemed insanely
genuine, and so too did the strange sense of ritualistic reverence
that seeped through the fury when, artificially bloody, dressed as
an Aztec priest, he plunged down the obsidian knife and tore the
heart out of the young man, the sacrifice, who lay stretched out
and wide-eyed with fear on the "altar."

Blood gouted, in close-up.

Total shock.

Gory, slit eyed, Kitaj stared into the camera.

"Nothing is true!" he ranted. *"All is permitted!"*

I recognized this. The philosophy of the Old Man of the
Mountains, Hassan i Sabbah, father of the Assassins in eleventh-
century Persia.

But what came next was a much greater shock, at least for me,
though I'm sure it meant nothing to anyone else.

For of a sudden the dissipation fell away from him.

His eyes grew wide and clear; they fixed on me, personally.

"Johnny," he said, "maybe by now you know what's what.
Once you told me that these days we're walking tightropes, that
we have to learn to walk them well, or we'll all fall into the pit.
So now don't you go falling into the pit yourself. Why don't you
get in touch? Or maybe I'll give you a call."

Just like that.

* * *

For the next twenty-four hours I was in total confusion. So much for my belief that he didn't know where I was. I slept badly. In the morning I went from my flat on Leith Walk up to the Princes Street Gardens, where I spent most of that cold blustery day pacing back and forth, trying to face the questions I'd been avoiding for a year. Why was I still in hiding, still using a false name, buried in libraries, pretending to be writing a history of radical religion from the year dot? Why? Fear of Kitaj? Fear of being publicly associated with Kitaj? Or fear of what I'd become if I returned to Kitaj? Clearly after Ireland I'd decided to take no chances, to stay on the fence, being utterly scared to commit myself to that road of self-sacrifice which I'd sensed in the patterns from the bright star. After all, what business was it of mine? I was a writer, not an occult activist. In addition, I tried to tell myself as I paced, I could rally an honest ethical doubt. Essentially, I felt, Kitaj's intentions were benign . . . yet his effect on me that night had been like a razor blade, slicing my personality so deeply that even now I had no real belief in the way I was living. I reminded myself as I walked of Bakunin's credo that *"the urge to destroy is a creative urge too"* . . . but this I found hard to apply to myself. The extremity of the methods of healing he envisaged, and this new craziness of the Black Hole Joke—did I really want to be in the company of such a man? Surely it would be better to forget him altogether, to leave the phone off the hook, to return to the ancestral home in the highlands and bury myself in the past . . .

I went back to my flat in the early evening.

An hour later the phone rang. I dithered with my hand on the receiver. If I picked it up, I knew, there would be no going back.

I picked it up.

"Hi," he said. "Do you want your job back? Isma'il's going to visit his folks for a month and I could use your help. How about it?"

"The thing is, I need you to make me feel bad once in a while," he said, two months later. We were flying from Bombay to Mombasa. We had spent a week on an ashram where Kitaj was known. He had spent that week in meditation and discussion with young people whose eyes were as bright as his. I had felt out of place. "You see," he went on, lightly, with a half smile,

"I began to realize how much I missed your dour Scots serious-ness. I got worried if I left you to your own devices much longer you might turn into a fanatical Puritan pulpit thumper, or some-thing dire like that."

I was angry. Insulted. Almost ready to go back to Scotland.

"And you, what are you turning into?" I exclaimed bitterly. "One month you're publicly taking baths in shit, the next you're acting all spiritual. Where's the connection? Where's it all going?"

He raised eyebrows. He was relaxed, healthy. We'd done a lot of traveling since I got his call; he was up and about twenty hours out of twenty-four, meeting so many people, doing so much and setting so many different schemes in motion that I couldn't keep track. I'd begun to realize he was *managing his vision*, he had an inner program and the flexible perspective to deal with and interrelate several thousand different details at once . . . though you'd not have known it if you met him only briefly: you'd have seen whatever you related to best, for by this time he had mastery of all the different masks and speeds he needed. He could relate with anyone and anything that moved. "Patterns dancing in the One!"—he had central purpose which often to me seemed like no purpose at all. Round the world in his jets we jumped so fast through such different situations that after two months of it I was emotionally exhausted and ready to quit. For I could not integrate it. From presidential palaces to shady backstreet meetings with radical healers. Always the security problems. And I did not think I had a real function. I was there because he'd asked me along, but I didn't then see this as function; I was in cautious reverse, immensely suspicious and increasingly surly . . . essen-tially because I no longer had any handle on him. I thought him beyond me; I felt demeaned. Unconsciously competitive think-ing. I'd been trained to win over others, to relate not vertically but horizontally.

So had he, once.

But now I could no longer read him. And unspoken in my attitude was my sense of failure from the hilltop. Rigidity and reaction which he'd begun to needle.

That day coming into Mombasa he'd arranged for the chauf-feur of his hotel car to be a man he didn't want the press or The Club to learn he'd met. Then a meeting with the Kenyan Minister of Finance, followed by the press, and lunch with Marvin Caide, a Hollywood director wanting to make a big-budget movie about

Kitaj's early life. Kitaj wanted to check the man out. Then Isma'il, joining us from Durban, where he'd gone to see some friends of Kitaj's there. After Mombasa, Kitaj said, we'd fly over Ruwenzori on the way to Monrovia, which was being overthrown by Muslim revolutionaries: there was a young woman there he wanted to meet and pluck from danger. She was a telepath, he said. And he smiled, but I did not. . . and that's how we started arguing about pulpit thumping and baths of shit.

"I don't get you," he answered. "What's wrong with shit? Are you saying that shit isn't spiritual? Because that's it!" He grew animated. "That's the essence of the Black Hole Joke! Our sense of the Fall, of guilt, of false division! And nowhere more clearly than in shit as money. Filthy lucre! I mean shit is mine is money and the earth, right? But why money? What *is* money? I guess you know that most money substances are distinguished by their absolute uselessness for any other purposes. And that the first money was issued by the temples. It was sacred. Holy. Symbolic. Gold and silver, sun and moon, their value ratio stable at 1:13½ since classical times at least. Why? Because it's an astrological ratio, expressing sun-moon cycles which influence us, which structure our lives, and so it's sacred when expressed as money value because it's functional in reminding us what and how and where we are. Hah! But we forget. It's all there, but we don't notice. Take a look at the back of a dollar bill. What's the eye in the pyramid doing there, and the Novus Ordo Seclorum? What do they mean, these symbols that we put on the shit that we have in our wallets. Think. Because that eye in the pyramid's on the dollar bill, that makes it the most commonly transmitted symbol throughout an entire continent. Communication. Evolution. Triggering symbol. See the heads of gods on ancient coins, distributed as material reminders of the gateways to the soul. But we forget it's a god reminder, we see only the bread and stuff it buys, the desire and the false security, the domination and the power. We've got tyranny of false money-concept speared right through our collective heart, and people use money to fuck each other over, to keep their ego-armor tight. Anal arrest. Too bad. It's like spiritual glaucoma. I should know."

I found this a bit much to buy.

"Okay," I grumbled. "Shit is spiritual, like the earth is spiritual, the holy physical root of creation, substance transformed into fertilizer—but why money as shit? Money's called a million other things, like bread, and . . .''

''Bread's the same thing, just the other side of the same basic physical associative process. Money's a symbol-carrying arche-type for expressing ratios of value. Bread and shit are different sides of our basic bodily currency of exchange . . . what we first know to give or sell or keep, consume and expel. Shit is our first experience of exchange value. The money-concept is also about transformation.'' He grinned. ''Or do you think this is all bull?''

But I never answered.

That was when we were buzzed by a UFO.

I was about to tell him what I thought when my eye was snatched past him through the window to the strong violet dot coming at us out of the sun. For an instant I thought it was just the blind spot in my vision—then the dot expanded, the field of violetness seized the plane; everything shuddered, and shook, and we went into a dive; with electricity running through me I slid steeply down the sudden deep angle of the aisle, fetched up against the cabin door as the plane's electrics shorted out. The lights went. But in the instant that they did, I was jolted round, with vision running and crawling as though everything material was dissolving. And I saw Kitaj, sitting.

He hadn't been moved at all by the plunge of the plane. He was sitting where and as he had been sitting—at his ease, as though everything were on the level or in zero gravity. And he was looking up and out, with a childlike smile of sheer delight.

Then the lights went.

Kitaj's corona blazed. In the violetness everything danced; I struggled nauseously with lost orientation. The plane still plunged.

It was then I heard the Voice. It sounded pained.

''Relax. Enjoy it. It's what you make it.''

Then the UFO swept away, leaving sparklings and confusion in me as the plane righted itself, and the pilot came in, looking as white as I did.

But Ed Zimmer was laconic. He'd been flying Kitaj for over a year.

''Rafe, you want me to report this one?''

Kitaj, still unmoved in any direction but his own, was grinning hugely.

''Those were the good guys. Yeah, sure, tell the *National Enquirer*.'' Then he sobered, shook his head. ''No. Not yet.

Maybe in six months we can start opening up. Maybe longer. Maybe shorter.''

"Well, I wish you'd tell your friends to come a bit less strong when they wanna talk with you!" Zimmer growled, and went back inside to take us into Mombasa.

My sense of humor must have been out of gear. That thing shook me so much I didn't get on a plane with Kitaj again for another two years.

The UFO was seen and reported from a ship on the sea underneath. Also from the ship had been seen a falling blip of silver violet light.

"UFO?" Kitaj later answered a gentleperson of the press. "You trying to pull my leg? You asking me if I really believe that sort of stuff? Do you believe that sort of stuff?"

"I've covered a lot of these stories," said the reporter. "It's my guess there's a psychic-physical correlation, you know, like something is really happening, but what people see isn't necessarily what's really happening; they try to interpret it in terms of what they know already. So, yeah, I believe that sort of stuff. How about you? What happened out there?"

Kitaj looked shocked, impressed, he made a gracious gesture.

"Right now I have to go and talk with a man about a fictional film," he said. "You know? Some situations no words is best. Talk to my friend here if you want to know about the flight."

He left me holding the UFO.

"Well, nothing really," I said awkwardly.

"You mean you experienced nothing at all?"

"Well," I said desperately, "I guess you can say I experienced the subjective manifestation in myself of a psychoenergetic phenomenon, and that's about all I can say, you know?"

After this I realized I was going to have to pull myself together.

"This isn't working out," I said to Kitaj. "I've got some steps to make on my own. It's true I just don't want to get back on that plane. But that's not all of it."

"What's your name?" asked Kitaj. "Hall—or something else?"

"Hall," I said. "John Hall."

I felt a great tension. But the smile grew.

"Okay," he said, and embraced me. "Relax, and take your chances."

*   *   *

It was another year before I saw him again, on the summer solstice slopes of Glastonbury Tor in England, among the great number of people there.

1989. In that year there were marked changes in the way that people applied their beliefs. The chances were slimmer and more direct. Either you did or you didn't, and no sure thing in any direction, and stand as straight as you could, because anyone knew someone who'd gone down in the flood.

Sometimes I was thinking I was one of those. Certainly for some time I got very submerged, starting in Mombasa, semiconsciously driven to retrace as best I could in my own life the unknown bleak years of Kitaj's life after Ruwenzori. I went through Kenya and Uganda, and in time I came to Ruwenzori. *Liar's Gold* had been selling well, though not under my name; I hired a helicopter and pilot and checked out the Nyamgasani region. And found the valley, the enchanted valley with the pink rock and the cave where Iloshabiet and M'Botu had lived, and Marvin Caide's movie crew there, making *Midas in Eden*. Too bad the helicopter landed right in the middle of the murder scene. Caide forgave me with an effort, wanted information he thought I might have to make it all more "realistic." He knew from Mombasa I was one of Kitaj's "associates"; maybe he thought Kitaj had sent me to keep an eye on history. He complained that he couldn't get anything straight out of Kitaj or anyone who knew him. "People want to know who this man really is. *Liar's Gold* is just a fable; it's too romantic; this is a hard-edged time . . . you know . . . what really happened here?"

"I know as much as you do," I said, and left as quick as I could.

But the fascination remained: that by traveling or fixing Kitaj's presumed past I could somehow get to grips with where he was now, and so understand the events which had thrown me.

There was trouble getting into Zimbabwe to check out the prison where he'd met Ana Kanasay; I nearly landed in that cell myself; I was police checked, identified; a proposition was put to me that I might like to slip something into Kitaj's cup of wine sometime.

"You are a man who has been seen with Kitaj. In Mombasa you left him. Why? Is there hostility between you? Would you like to see him dead? Are you going to help us?"

My questioner was Nordic, with glacial eyes. I couldn't tell if he was a cop or a businessman, but I knew there were police outside the door.

"Sure," I said, "I hate the bastard. But I can't do what you ask. That would be murder."

The man gave me a funny smile.

"Next time we contact you," he said, "you will do what we ask."

With this on my mind I flew to Europe. I had enough enthusiasm left to find and speak with the Frenchman who'd been on Ruwenzori when the botanist Barthelme died. But after picking up his threats too I decided it was time to seek health in quietness. With all the passport computerization I was getting identified and hassled—taken aside and questioned—in too many situations in Europe. I had Kitaj's marks on me, and things in Europe were tight. It happened at the police check at the Gare du Nord in Paris, it happened again at a civilian roadblock just outside Amsterdam, and again at the Heathrow Customs in London.

"What the hell's going on?" I demanded at Heathrow.

"Just assuring ourselves that you don't mean any trouble, sir. And we'd like to know how long you'll be staying, and where you'll be going."

"Listen!" I said, half-standing and leaning abruptly over the table. "I'm a citizen of this country. I don't have to tell you this stuff!"

"Very well, sir. Remember, we're watching you."

Just what I needed. I said I was going to find a hotel in London. I went straight to the Victoria bus station, thinking I was going to Scotland.

But found myself in Wales.

Clearly enough Kitaj was enraging a lot of people that year, acting with an extravagance reminiscent of the late seventies, playing through yet another of the masks which intervened between his central purpose and his public image, the Black Hole Joke mask. After I'd left him that summer he'd flown into Monrovia and swept the telepathic lady from the spears of the advancing hordes.

That's the image that got played up, and their passionate multileveled romance was the next famous event.

She was called Maria; she was Hungarian, with gypsy blood and a fiery nature which she could bring to great concentration.

Biofeedback training in Russian laboratories had enhanced her natural sensitivities: the tales of how she came to be in Monrovia were soon a numerous and varied subbranch of the Kitaj mythos. During the winter months of 1988 they were together continually; they were on talk shows, Kitaj having assured the corporations beforehand that he'd keep it cool—no blood or excremental vision—and the two of them got an act together which pressed a deeper angle. The act led to her playing the role of Atlantis Rose in the musical *Rich Man Poor Man*.

They were in California most of that winter, putting this new show together. The weather was strange there too. A series of little quakes, a continual rippling of everything, with Kitaj very busy, very watched, keeping it moving all the time, dealing with people every hour, every room he entered checked before he came, until in March '89 *Rich Man Poor Man* was completed for later release.

Then they went to Russia.

To Kiev, to a parapsychological institute.

"I want to learn how to see UFOs," he told the press before they left. "So many people hitching stellar rides these days that I'm feeling left out."

All over Russia that springtime was strange and unexpectedly beautiful, though wild, and the bells were ringing, for there was a change: the iron had cracked at last; people were walking more freely. Quite unexpectedly to most, the Russian spirit was experiencing resurgence. "Dialectical spiritualism," somebody had tagged it, completely baffling the old Marxist-Leninists. But, while the psychic institutes were surfacing again and beginning exchange with the rest of the world, Newspeak and the Ministry of Love still had some claws left, as everywhere. "There is a creature called the Org," said Kitaj in 1990 at the Ecocourt trial. "It wants to swallow all the world, and it doesn't easily give up." For Politburo officials, concerned that perhaps the wrong impression was being given, particularly to the Chinese, hinted Russian possession of a Mindwarp technology so sophisticated that, quote, We could have the whole world going to sleep at the same moment and waking up singing "The Red Flag" in our glorious language—and nobody noticing anything wrong, unquote.

This became known to White House advisers as, "The Secretary's Little Joke," and they noted with satisfaction that James

Dean movies were all the rage in Moscow, and that Colonel
Sanders had opened a Leningrad branch.

These were aberrations.

The Russians had been hamstrung by commissars, not so much
by Calvinists. Newconscious research in the west has been ham-
pered by puritan materialist disbelief, by the traditional western
emphasis on the external. But Russia from east to west had
remained full of goblins and sprites, which produced for them
few televisions in the fifties, many reconnections in the nineties.
They'd been more sympathetic to the essence; they were years
ahead in several areas of technical parapsychology.

Now they were willing to share. There had been quite a few
Russian researchers at Rio. Kitaj had taken the chance to communicate with several of them. Now they paved his way, and yet
again it became clear to the world that Kitaj's interests were other
than previously advertised.

"Strange thing," he said while in Kiev. "Here there is work
going on freely, in the open, while in the 'free west' the same
work is still being harried into secrecy and disrepute."

He was asked his opinion of Madame Blavatsky's prediction
that, "when England ceases to carry the torch of Democracy, out
of Russia will come the greatest civilization the world has ever
known."

"She was a sharp lady," he said. "But who knows?"

It sounded like he was learning diplomacy. He spent two
months based at Kiev, working with Maria on telepathic development via the biofeedback monitoring system. "Refinements of
tuning in," he said. At the end of that time Maria went to
Murmansk, a long long way away, while he stayed at Kiev. They
did a week of monitored transmission-reception tests. They got
into sympathetic alpha resonance; specific images were passed.
The tests were pronounced a success; more than could be said for
Kitaj's efforts at telekinesis—mental control over external objects.
"They put a feather in a sealed jar and told me to move it," he
told me ruefully at Glastonbury. "I managed to make it flutter
after two weeks of trying, but the effort put my pulse way up
over 200. It requires more physical input than telepathy. When I
was doing the telepathy work I was strapped into an apparatus
called CCAP—Conductivity of the Channels of Acupuncture Points.
Invented by a physicist called Adamenko, back in the sixties
anyway. It uses a strategic combination of acupuncture points to

measure changes if bioplasmic energy in the body. Telepathy comes in via the energy body—the astral body—which coexists with the physical substance. You can measure the change in the bioplasma when the thought comes through.''

But it was the telekinesis that really interested him. I was sitting with him in a field near Glastonbury in June; it was a hot, windless day; there were thousands of people quiet all about, fiddle music lilting from a small distant stage; he spent over forty minutes totally concentrated on a feather that lay cupped in his hand. Nothing happened to it. It did not move. Except once my sight of it momentarily shivered, as if for an instant it almost wasn't there.

''What are you trying to do?'' I asked him afterwards.

He smiled. ''Put it into another frame,'' he said.

When Maria and Kitaj came to Glastonbury they brought with them a blind youth, Carl Schneider, from Hanover, who could see with his hands. ''Black is sticky,'' he said. ''White is smooth. You can feel red radiation furthest of all, and it burns. When I lift up my hands to the sky I can feel what's coming from space. I'm working with Rafe on developing a language for it.''

The trip to Russia certainly broke Kitaj into a new space of public opinion. The media did their best with the new angle.

RALPH M'BOTU KITAJ—ASTRAL POLITICIAN?

LOVE OF RALPH & MARIA TRANSCENDS TIME & DISTANCE TELEPATHICALLY!

''THOUGHT-FLIGHT TO STARS SOON!'' CLAIMS ZANY BILLIONAIRE.

Before Glastonbury he visited a conference of dowsers and healers at Chartres. Later he met the press in the maze in the ancient holy mound of the Carnutes under the Cathedral.

''When I was in Russia I met an old woman who said she witnessed the murder of the great healer, Karl Ottovich Zeeling,'' he told them, his voice resonant and eerie. ''One thing Zeeling could do was correctly tell scientists the sex of the last person who'd looked into the mirror mirror on the wall. He got blown out by the Stalinists in 1937. It's all politics.''

''Mr. Kitaj, be more specific. What politics?''

''Control of the energy of thought,'' said Kitaj sharply. ''The old dualism is dead. The entire Right Wing-Left Wing system. Just two monolithic lies propping each other up over a chasm.

Two adjacent fingers on the same hand, in the same game, waving at each other as though they were opposites. Likewise all the other nineteenth-century reductionist rationalist fixations we're still using as concept structure to hide in and fight about. Don't you know? Sure you do! Politics of evolution. Some want to take the blinkers off and see more. Others want to keep them on and make sure everyone else does the same. Politics. And people who try taking the blinkers off all see different things, and start arguing about what's the real description. More politics. Right now in this time we have to be asking the questions that matter— the big-time questions that'll turn us to an overall view and some plan to know what the hell to do with this planet and ourselves. Because if we don't, soon it's all jackshit.''

"So what are you suggesting, Mr. Kitaj—*practically?*"

"Well, if I were you," said Kitaj with his pagan eyes in that dark and ancient place, "I'd stop it, step off, take time out to *think* about my value as a human being—then take some chances. Nothing new in that, is there? You've heard it all before.''

This new, publicly earnest Kitaj with the Jeremiah glint in his eye was an easy target to hit, and he was hit. Perhaps because of his paranormal adventures in Russia the word began to get around that he'd been funding newconscious research for the last two years while pretending to be a ninny then a demon clown. No details, but enough to suggest he'd been playing a deep game. The Machine started to roll against him. The Club. The Org.

"Ralph M'Botu Kitaj is not motivated by a true spirit of research!" thundered the *London Times*. "He is after the ectoplasmic buck, the astral nugget of gold. His past record warns us to watch him carefully.''

"These people are crazy!" Kitaj complained, appearing on French TV in stinking rags the night before he flew into England. "They think I want more gold? They think I need it? They judge me by their own standards? Don't they know what happened to Midas?" He laughed, shakily, flinging tattered arms wide. "Since I got to be richest man in the world I haven't had a good night's sleep! People hitting me from all directions all the time. The Org wants me dead. Know what I mean by the Org? Ever see Org executives on TV trying to explain away the latest megadeath ecodisaster as though everything's really okay and under control? They're dummy vampire victims of the creature they feed; that gives them their power to screw the world. Big corporations are a biological organism with a mind of their own that swallows their servants whole. The Org. Mammon. It's not good enough. I'm a free trader and I'm resigning from all the clubs. There's too much crap and not much time and we have more important work to do than fuck each other up. Take a Chance!''

It sounded—it was—a declaration of war.

There was a near-riot outside the Paris TV studios when he left. Several hundred people, young, shouting, ''Take a Chance,'' and the police moving in.

There was common opinion among those who knew him at this time that he was making serious miscalculations, acting prematurely, arrogantly, exposing himself unnecessarily, and generally losing his grip on hard reality.

Some people blamed Maria for this apparent change in him. They said he was listening too much to her, distracting himself with her energetic and mystical charms. Maybe they meant she was where they wanted to be but weren't.

Many people also blamed him for what happened at Glastonbury.

He came in secretly. But once his presence was publicly known, ten thousand communicants became a seething crowd of nearly a hundred thousand, and there was almost bad trouble on ''the holyest erthe in Englande.''

''Everything was fine,'' I heard more than one disgruntled back-to-earther claim afterwards. ''It was a really positive situation until he came along like a vortex of famous ego to suck in people who couldn't care less.''

It was like that if that was all you wanted to see.

Kitaj came because I had told him about the festival. He'd called me from Kiev, wanting to know if I was okay, saying it was five months since I'd sent him a card, and that he sensed I was going through hard times. He was right, but I could tell him they were also positive times.

''There's a lot happening in Albion,'' I told him. ''You wouldn't know it to look at the bullshit and chaos on the surface. But it's there. It's growing. You should come and check it out.''

I told him when and where and he said he'd make it if he could, which he did.

Of course the call was tapped. I had another official visit. I was given some advice about not going anywhere. There were threats.

I must have been changing, because I went.

"He came in secretly." By this I mean his arrival in England and then at Glastonbury was not announced by press, radio, or TV. Given Rio and the Black Hole Joke, the combination of Kitaj with Glastonbury was considered politically sensitive. The state of things in Britain then was that the media denied its reality to any event involving what British OldStyle still saw as mystical pagan anarchist radical hippie drug stuff with leanings to the lunatic Celtic fringe. British OldStyle was determined to go down with all hands on deck. No matter if Russians were mindflying, if bright stars were beaming, if the world was transforming . . . in Britain the castor oil of convention was that year being forcibly applied. Decency Campaigns and soldiers on the street. But the wind of change was gusting in so many directions that no one policy seemed to last very long, and British reticence still denied the totality of a police state, though by the skin of its teeth. So that Kitaj and Glastonbury mystics, though Indecent and not to receive publicity, were not actually forbidden.

That reticence was enough to allow the birth of a new idea in Britain. A new social synthesis. The self-awareness of Chancers.

The midsummer night and half the day atop the Tor were beautiful and quiet. There were many people, from the hills and lands and cities too, and the atmosphere was good. Kitaj, with Isma'il, Maria and Carl the blind seer, had driven from an airfield near Bristol, picking up two hitchhikers along the way. I had come from Wales, taking three days about it. We met that night by the ruined tower of St. Michael's chapel on the summit of Glastonbury Tor. There was a fire blazing in the tower itself, the sparks flinging up out of it into the breezy night, and round the tower a circling weave of people, going to and fro the quickening steepness of the summit heath, laughing quietly in the darkness, greeting one another in soft-talking groups or sitting tranquil on their own with blankets round their shoulders. They were all ages there, with dogs and infants and grandmothers who had brightness in the eye, looking up to the stars which were couched as in velvet, or down and around through the summer light of the night, sighting the straight road through here to the Abbey in town and beyond, following the contours of hills, woods, and streams. "Once, a long long time ago," I heard a mother tell her little daughter, "the people who lived here shaped the land in the shape of the giant animals they saw in the sky, the creatures of the zodiac. They did this in a big circle, several miles wide, using roads and hedges and fields to make the shape of a bull, and a lion, and the other animals. They were very wise people.''

''Mummy, I've heard about that,'' the girl said. ''But Jason told me his mother says it's there if you see it and not if you don't. What does that mean?''

''Dragon energies!'' Kitaj was full of zest. He had free movement; nobody was upset or excited to know who he was, though he knew there was at least one plainclothes eye on him. He didn't seem bothered. Already since his arrival he'd exchanged a lot of energy and information with other people, while I'd met Isma'il again, gladly again realizing how unobtrusively central he was in Kitaj's affairs, and Maria, for the first time. I liked her. She was sensitive, direct, well contained, with an amused face. I remember her breaking off conversation to exclaim delightedly at something she'd heard, picked up, sensed; clapping her hands; then flinging herself round to run to the tower with a sudden burst of exuberance. People laughed as she ran through them; someone struck drama from drums. And sometime later that night I walked with Kitaj in the festival fields below the Tor. On one side the houses came quite close, on the other the land was open. We walked past horses cropping, carts up-ended with tarpaulins draped from their sky-pointing shafts to form temporary houses, lamps and candles burning but few fires in the field, human shapes nodding and murmuring by tents and high-poled tepees in the soft darkness. Then over a fence onto ground where the summer-dried mud had been rockily molded by cattle hooves, past a grove where a piper played and people moved in white-robed ritual, and a huge fire, where people danced and laughed, or stared into the flames, to the small stage near the road where a poet with the manner of wild man declaimed a mythical ode to the old gods before a crowd of about one hundred. His voice rang out, arresting us, one line. *''And before the coming of the dragon slayers there was Math, Manawyddan, and Rhiannon of the Birds!''* Kitaj stopped and turned to me, as though struck. ''Dragon energies!'' he said. ''Johnny, on the way here we picked up two hitchhikers, a man and a woman, from Wales; they said a valley near the Abergwesyn Pass. They said a lot about the dragon metaphor. *Lung mei*, dragon paths, the ley lines, the acupunctural distribution of the earth's nervous system, the energies and the interplay, the dragon associated with goddess worship, thus damned and its wings torn off when patriarchal individuality came along. The fertility energy system forgotten.''

We started back towards the Tor. Sparks flew visibly from the ruined Michael chapel on the top.

''Michael,'' I said. ''Dragon slayer. Also dragon. The lightning and the high places, and our changing attitudes to them. This part of the world is full of Michaelchurches set on the paths. In Wales they're called Llanfihangel, Church of the Chief Angel.'' There was a slight grimness in my voice. ''They're found on high places. Hilltops. Sometimes in stone circles.''

Of course he picked it up.

''Been having any trouble?'' he asked.

''Getting along much better,'' I said. ''Stopped being scared so bad.''

''Anything bizarre?''

''Yes,'' I said. ''Mostly in my sleep. Shifts of tone. Things I see and things I still don't want to see. But I've been digging ditches and working on it. Getting down to basics.'' I shot him a glance. ''I couldn't do that while I was hanging round you. I had to break that focus.''

''You're still talking in terms of personality,'' he said. ''Focusing on each other's personalities is nowhere. It's function that counts.''

He broke off and stared round the peopled night.

''There's a powerful function here,'' he said after a moment, ''but it's only half-awakened. Many people here with strong sense of themselves and the holy potent energetic world. But a tendency to the past in the present. The *old* gods! Why the old gods? Sure, we need to remember them inside us, in our earth relationship, but only so long as we need to reintegrate them. Then we make something new. New living myths of guidance and example! We make it! We take it in ourselves and do it! I think maybe something might happen here.''

''Do you mean to make something happen?''

''I don't mean to do anything at all,'' said Kitaj.

And at dawn we were all on the Tor again, many people. The midsummer sun rose in the east and there was a great indrawing of breath.

In the warm sunny fields after that there was music and meeting. Kitaj was still talking easily, casually, with anyone, and anyone with him . . . but imperceptibly a tension about his presence was growing, and arguments began to develop among people about him, and strangers eyed strangers for signs of the law. But it was not until the flood began that he was asked outright to leave by a mixed delegation, and by then it was too late, for by now the brew was beginning to bubble. Something was happening. Beginning in the morning new people started to arrive. A trickle at first, but by noon in the hundreds, and by midafternoon thousands an hour. Thousands, their minds all unexpectedly triggered by the connection, the equation, of Kitaj with Glastonbury. This was their only common denominator. They'd heard that Kitaj was at Glastonbury. How had they heard? It was vague. They'd heard from a friend. Somebody told them in the street. Something going on. Something bound to happen. So they came. A few were casual car trippers who drove away again when the police started to lean, but not many. Most of them had been traveling for hours, for a day or more in some cases, walking, hitching, on bicycles. Few could afford to pay for petrol. And they were young. Gangs of hard young street kids—Anglos, Indians, Rastas—from London, Portsmouth, Cardiff, Birmingham, and further afield. They did not look mystically inclined, not on the surface. Their eyes said they weren't about to buy anyone's false salvation. They'd come to check something out, to learn if what they might experience would measure up to the rumors. They came in loosely, in groups, at first watchful and suspicious of the unknown situation they were entering—this encampment with its horses, and brown naked children, and dogs barking, and calm-eyed, older, weathered people in their homemade clothes who'd left the cities many years before. Those fields were tranquil, almost medieval, before the invasion. Then as the afternoon wore on they became a noisy modern bustle, and there was tension, for the newcomers carried knives, not amulets, and the scent they followed fixed on a particular man.

"Kitaj! Kitaj! Where's Kitaj?"

By evening it seemed like trouble. There were police. Soldiers were standing by. There were various interests ready to turn it into trouble. The townspeople had shut up shop early, boarded

their windows, and still the influx continued. After sunset a huge
restless mass of people flowed between the Tor and the stage,
getting hungry and bored. There was little ground for communication between the newcomers and those who'd come here for
the solstice. Fights began breaking out, sporadically. The area
round the stage was a solid mass, with chants and demands for
Kitaj breaking out from time to time. The energy, undirected,
was increasing.

Kitaj was in a farmhouse discussing the situation with local
authorities and the festival organizers. One of the latter, a straight
and white-bearded old man, dedicated to the Glastonbury traditions, was insistent.

"Mr. Kitaj, of course you have every right to be here, like
anyone else. But all these people have come here because of you.
There is danger in the atmosphere. This is a holy place. We must
avoid abuse of its energy."

"Then I must speak to them," said Kitaj, "and try to integrate
this."

The police objected. So did several of the organizers.

"If I do not show myself," said Kitaj, "they will tear the
place apart. You can see that for yourself. But I think I can do
something about it." He was thoughtful, calm. "There is no
need for a riot, or for anything false, but clearly a focus has to be
brought . . . and I think I can do that."

Nobody quite trusted him. The police feared a revolutionary
rant. The organizers feared an outburst of ego that would sully
entirely the meaning of the festival. But there was little option.
The stage by now was an island surrounded by sixty or seventy
thousand New Barbarians come to hear the Word.

They got it.

Near midnight Kitaj and Maria went onto the stage. They were
both dressed in white. The sky was clear and starry, the breeze
cool but comfortable.

There was a great roar of acclamation when those people saw
the man on whom they'd put the myth.

Kitaj and Maria waited for the noise to cease. Then Kitaj stood
forward at the edge of the stage, in the light. He was small.

He pointed up at the sky.

"The stars," he said, through the microphones.

He pointed down at the ground.

"The earth," he said.

Then he pointed at the crowd, at Maria, at himself, and back at the crowd, in a wide finger circle which ended in a vertical movement, earth to sky to earth again.

"We are human beings. We are in the middle. We move between the high and the low. Stars and earth and human beings are made of the same energy, which exists in a range between the most solid matter and the most rarefied spirit. It is our task to convert this energy into the making of a beautiful world. This place is a place where the energy is strong, in each of us. There is no need to speak. The Word is inside us, and written through all the world. Now we will be quiet. We will be quiet, all together, and feel what we are, all together, between the earth and the stars."

His voice was soothing. Then he fell silent and stood utterly still, Maria joining him by his side. And the silence began.

It was over thirty minutes before it was broken.

At first, as the apparently empty seconds began to stretch, many people were restless, particularly those further away, and there were jostlings, and shouts from the distance.

But the sensation of communion spread rapidly. It developed first through the united intention of Kitaj and Maria, standing there beside each other. It spread through those with whom they first established close contact, those in the front of the crowd, seeking eye-contact with individuals until the alpha-mood was transmitted and establishing itself. "It was weird," I was later told by a youth who was there that night. "Didn't know what was going on. This guy and the woman just standing there looking at us, and he had this sort of smile on his face that kept me hooked, trying to work out what was behind it, what it meant. Then after a while I saw nothing but the smile, and the thing is, it had become my smile, and he wasn't there at all any more, there was just a whirlpool of light that all of us were in. Scary too, because for a time I thought it was some crazy psychotrick he was pulling on us. But I guess what he did—and she did—was pull us all together through them, until we were *all* doing it. Then it got like a dream, except it was a real dream which we were all making, between the stars and the earth. Then I began to understand something, about brotherhood, I guess, because we're all in it together . . . and if we can learn to work with our whole systems the way he shows is possible, then we've still got somewhere to go . . . if we take our chances."

The dreamtime. Some saw the stars come down. Some saw flashing crystalline patterns that spoke to them in geometry. Others for the first time heard voices which had always been murmuring quietly in them, unheard above the roar of the streets and the blood, and others saw themselves and everyone about them as one vast shimmering energy-body of united individualities, a glowing umbrella of consciousness latent on the earth. There were many different experiences of the same experience, and I—this time I let myself go, and when the patterns flashed I did not turn away, though I still couldn't read them. It was intense, but my trust had grown.

But for some it was too intense, because it grew, and it would have kept growing, except it had an inbuilt cut-off function. For some were suddenly startled out of reverie, flinching to feel themselves nauseously on fire with an electricity which was burning away their sense of themselves.

A middle-aged man in fawn raincoat dashed onto stage from behind, grabbed a mike while shouting out his frightened anger. In my state I saw him move like a streak of livid mercury, his shouting was a garbled warp, an ugliness and pain inside us all, a shivering rear, that could spread and envelop everything if allowed to go its course.

Then Kitaj had the microphone. His eye caught that of the frightened man, so sharp that the man blinked, and shook himself all over, and looked about, dazed and unsure where he was.

"It's all right," said Kitaj. "You're the same old you."

Before confusion could develop he spoke again. He talked us all back to the ground. "Nineteen eighty-nine," he said. "We are not the same as we were thirty minutes ago. We have all changed in relation, and something has been born. We are all different with our different functions in the same whole. It is a matter of sympathetic resonance. That is what has happened here. Sympathetic resonance and an integration. This is a good night."

The authorities didn't agree. Nobody knew what had happened except for a minister of government who said it must not happen again. Yet now there are many people who date Chancing from that night, and this is the focus and the mythreality of it. Kitaj had found a lens-role which propagated itself round the world during the next year. Sympathetic resonance. Integration. No

new ideas. But new experiences for millions of people. Kitaj a
trigger to fire their own self-recognition. "You can do it," he
said. "Make the Change, don't let it happen chaotically and
break you. You can do it—you felt something happen here,
tonight. It's not easy. You might have to work for a long long
time, and it's dangerous. Of course it is. But you can do it. Look
inside and find it and follow it, then make it in the world. We've
got science to help us now, it's not an enemy any more. Science
and magic got married again a couple of years ago. So you can
do it. Why not? What else?"

Chancing: basically a technique to make things happen by
putting yourself on the line, involving understanding of the need
to do this . . . the line being anything required to gain the
situation in which every human being knows inner function and
stands in society that mirrors and makes anew the shapes of the
heavens on earth.

Not this year, maybe.

Chancing recognizes that. Think you're doing it for yourself?
Of course you are. You and every past and future self in you
right now.

Technique and organization. From the first the Chancing consciousness had technique to apply to intuition. Many techniques
that boil down to one. Techniques of yoga, chant, symbol systems, feedback systems, poetry, ecstasy, and, overriding everything, the renewed sense of the Whole. For many years now the
integrations had in fact been taking place, human mind adhering
again after the mechanical splintering of isms and ists. But
industrial revolution and behaviorism and specializations all served
the purpose. Things had to go far apart into particular knowledge
and alienation before the new higher-level circuits could form,
mesh, fuse, come together, and get consciously functional. Evolution of necessity. The lazy man smells the smoke in his dreams
but won't wake up. Only with the house well ablaze does he
jump out of bed. Then either the house burns down with him in
it, or he invents new technique, fast.

Bootstrap survival necessity.

You recognize it if you want to. If you don't, you go crazy in
ways that are acceptable, or in ways that are not. If you do, you
take your chances and start to seek your function. What else?
Who says we're grown up at twenty-one? Our lives are at stake.

* * *

They started turning up that autumn where I was in Wales. It had been difficult since Glastonbury. I was known in the locality now: Kitaj's friend, and no police protection. It got so I couldn't go down to town without fights or threats. It got so I was tense every time I saw someone coming up the track to the house, particularly if they were in a car. But by winter many people had come and life was better, though more dangerous. For Chancing sprouted everywhere, and Wales was always a place for new radical belief, in the magic and the Fiery Word.

The people who came to visit John Hall were not fanatics. They did not elevate Kitaj as a Perfect Master. Some of them used the image of him rather as the Rastas used Haile Selassie. They called Kitaj a function, a focus, a lens. They knew that the King Must Die. They knew we each and every one of us are that King. They saw death as a gate through the black hole into the next big smile, not as a fist. They did not expect to "hold onto their personalities." They knew that energies continue in the dance, that existence happens in relationship, not in object . . . and their intentions were expressed in the deliberate terms of Rio science-magic. They were young. They were strong in humor that nothing is certain. They were people growing with a sense of relativity, not just as intellectual concept, but as gut reality. They could hear and play the music which my generation as a whole had just begun to glimpse again.

Some of them stayed for longer. Some of them stayed for shorter. They were blunt, and my reorientations increased:

"Kitaj tells the truth. No bullshit. Even the lies aren't bullshit. He's done worse than most of us and he admits it. If you're his friend, why aren't you with him? If you wrote that book for him, why isn't it your name on the cover? If you have a function with him, then do it, be it, don't hide it. You have to go down through your fear, John."

That was Kerry. She was 18. She stayed five months, then went to Peru, following a dream of Andean connection. She left refusing any money.

"No thanks," she said. "That's your problem."

Sometimes there were twenty or thirty people there. We saw the police. There were confrontations in the town. But strangely, very little real trouble. Those kids stood straight. They knew what they were doing and saying. Often the house was silent.

Meditation was as functional as cleaning your teeth. They kept themselves organized. Odd things started to happen. At the supper table, with ten people crammed round it, a lettuce leaf would suddenly twirl up an inch or two from someone's plate and do a little dance before flopping limply back. Then laughter, good-humored accusations.

I felt simultaneously like old man and child.

They used astrology to define many relationships. They talked of Sirius as extralogoidal third eye of the solar system, coded in overall stellar consciousness as an intelligent trigger of earth-human transformation to star-human. "RIGHT NOW!" they said, speaking and agreeing and harmonizing their assumptions in which I still could hardly dare believe.

So that usually it was my lettuce leaf that did the dance.

"You're Midwich Cuckoos," I told them, "Mutant Monsters," and they laughed.

Meanwhile, Kitaj went spinning on through the world, doing it, and many said he was doing it right.

But the trials were coming up.

One evening, March 1990, just after Kerry had gone, I was in my room, rather bleak, reading *The Buddha-Smile of Accelerated Protons,* an instant best seller by someone called Bob Fludd. It was a fict-fact dialogue starring Kitaj, Einstein, Messalina, Mona Lisa, and John Dee the Elizabethan magus. It was a witty extension of *Rich Man Poor Man,* which I'd seen in Cardiff with Kerry and some others, which critics were already calling the *Hair* of the nineties.

I couldn't concentrate. I was restless, a bit uneasy.

Then I saw the light in the night through the uncurtained window.

It came closer, looming, silvery, and I stared, heart thumping, the patterns beginning to flash. It flooded the outside of the window, almost too bright to look at. Then it formed into a face, very pale and languid.

Kitaj's face.

For some seconds it stared at me. My head roared. Then slowly it dissolved, and the light diminished away into the darkness.

I went out to walk in the night.

On the high slope it began to rain. It was cold. I was beginning to feel calm. Then I knew that somebody followed.

I turned round and saw the flashlight.

Heavily I waited. Patterns.

A dark-brimmed shadow fell in beside me.

"I want a word with you," it said. "CID."

Insane. I said nothing. The light shone in my eyes.

"We have this to say to you, Hall. Your boss has been getting people to do crazy things. Now he's going to be stopped. You had better get out of this country. Soon."

The flashlight clicked off. The shadow was gone into the wind and the rain and the night. When I shone my own flashlight after it, there was nothing.

But that could have been a good half-minute later.

In a state of mental suspension I went back to the house. I sat down with a whisky. Enquiring eyes, but nobody asked.

Then the phone rang.

It was Kitaj. From New York.

"Johnny. Watch out for the heat. They've put a rap on me. I'll answer it in the UN Ecocourt, next month. It means a change."

I nodded slowly, grimly.

"I know," I said. "I've felt it already."

9. SACRIFICE AND LOSS AND GAIN

That was long ago. Now is now, and it's two weeks since I wrote a word. I'm in another town. I guess it had to happen.

I went out for a walk after writing that last part. Late afternoon, when the sun isn't so hot. Absorbed in memories I crossed town without heeding the pain of my leg. When I came out of this fugue I found myself beyond the bus station amid the shanties, dogs yapping at my heels, ragged children playing. On my way back I went into Mi Rancho to get some tortillas and beans. It was cool inside the store. Flies droned. I picked up a six-pack of Dos Equis too. And it was at the check-out I saw him, watching me from the canned food section. The Org look, probably North American, hard-faced. The tic beneath my left eye started as I paid and moved out. Across the street I glanced back covertly. The man was talking with the cashier, still watching me.

There was an arrangement for something like this. Within an hour I was away from town, beneath a blanket in the back of a truck.

I didn't like it, but there you go. I have taken the precaution of sending out earlier chapters already. Now, only essentials remain.

For two years after the Ecocourt trial it seemed all over.

In April 1990 Ralph M'Botu Kitaj pled guilty to the charge of complicity in the destruction of the Amazon rain forest and its human population.

Between 1976 and 1981 he had owned a company which built and operated floating pulp mills on the Amazon and Orinoco rivers.

The connection was undeniable. The trial was a pretext. Recent studies had suggested that spoliation of the rain forest led to depletion of the world supply of atmospheric oxygen. The long term effects could not yet be estimated. The Ecocourt was newly set up, as yet unproved, with enemies who feared if it gained any power it might hit them. The prosecution of Kitaj was pressed by people who hoped that either the Ecocourt might begin Kitaj's destruction, or that Kitaj might destroy the Ecocourt.

"The trick is this," said Kitaj when I met him in New York before the trial. "The people who set this up hope I'll get scared and plead not guilty. They can then get into deeper waters which they rightly suspect, like the Cold Cure thing." And I felt the shock of his eyes. "I have to pay for all I've done—but not on their schedule. But to this I plead guilty."

He didn't look well. Something was lacking in him. Lenore was there.

"I think that's when they started sleepbeaming him," she told me in 1993.

The hearings began. There was great publicity. Kitaj, nailed down at last. Surely he would wriggle or buy his way out.

"I am guilty as charged," said Kitaj. There was a ripple of astonishment through the courtroom. "I owned AC Meier and knew about their operations, which I permitted to continue, being interested in nothing more than the immediate economic gain for myself." He paused. His face was white. "I do not wish to be represented by a lawyer or to call any witnesses."

"Is this all you have to say?" The Court was amazed.

"Not quite," said Ralph M'Botu Kitaj. "Evidently I am here as scapegoat or representative of an attitude to life which now becomes socially unacceptable, even criminal. You could as well place a million others in this dock, or a thousand million, if

intent is also criminal. I am guilty of having committed thoughtless exploitation. The country in which this court is based is built
on thoughtless exploitation. This court is on shaky ground. How
will you legislate human selfishness out of the environment? You
know as well as I that most of those who should be in this dock
will buy or blackmail their way out . . . as I could have done
. . . so that the court will be known as a corrupt farce in
the pocket of those it tries to curb.

"You have no guidelines for your authority. What are you
trying to stop? Visible ecodisasters and particular villains? That's
only the tip of the iceberg. You are trying to deal with human
selfishness. The situation which alarms us now has accumulated
through the actions of millions, not a few, and they are actions
which in many quarters are still approved and justified with all
the power of money and self-righteousness.

"This is all. I am guilty of the charge against me. There is no
excuse. I was not in my right mind. I was concerned to make
money at all costs."

It was a sensation.

He was fined fifteen million dollars, to be paid into the World
Food Fund, and auditors were sent into his books.

Kitaj? Human? Vulnerable? A loser?

KITAJ HUMBLED BY ECOCOURT!

ENVIRONMENTAL RAPIST GETS HIS!

WHAT'S KITAJ'S NEW GAME?

During the weeks that followed many people contratulated him
for pleading guilty. The Ecocourt found itself curiously endorsed.
By 1991 it was bold with success and public backing, issuing
ecological ultimatums to such effect that tree rapers and sea
killers were starting to run for cover.

By 1991, Kitaj seemed burned out.

At first the change was not very apparent. Fifteen million
dollars? The day after the trial there was a mass demonstration in
Central Park in his favor. Thousands of those now known as
Chancers showed themselves. That wasn't all. There was an
outbreak of strange events thunderously denounced by the Mayor
of New York. "This irresponsible telekinetic tampering has to
stop!" he said, showing a good understanding of the situation.
Traffic lights were going crazy at busy intersections, blipping
Morse messages on the red—KITAJ IS NOT THE ONLY GUILTY

ONE! Mysterious power blackouts hit the offices of unpopular corporations and government and UN agencies, at the same time there were unexplained surges of withdrawals of current in the public utility systems. "Kitaj is not only rocking the boat, he will put a spike through the scuppers if we let him," the Mayor went on after the demonstration, at which nothing visible or dramatic happened. "He is not a martyr, he is a convicted ecocriminal, and this should be remembered!"

Nothing happened? New Yorkers on the street found themselves drawn into the middle of it, drawn by a sort of subliminal magnetic curiosity, in among the thousands of people in the park, who were walking, talking, sitting about, some of them twirling frisbees in the sunshine. No speeches. No choked angry words. No public mention of Kitaj, and Kitaj not seen. But nevertheless it was a demonstration—a demonstration of deliberate collective vitality.

TAKE A CHANCE! was scrawled on every subway wall. Soon the official reports were flooding the IN-trays of important people. They had titles like "Countering Psychoenergetic Subversion: A Tentative Methodology," and "Towards the Generation of Philosophical Static as Negative Control Device in Treatment of Nonaligned Mentalities."

What they meant was very simple.

Get the Chancers.

Get Kitaj.

There's no success like failure. Guilty once, guilty a thousand times. Between April and September there were three attempts on Kitaj's life. Plus the Sleepbeam. Plus something else that was killing him slowly. Within a week of the trial he was banned from seven countries, including France, Britain, Australia. Shares in his interests plunged, thousands lost their jobs. The auditing revealed little—but now, for the first time, there were betrayals. Researchers on projects funded by him were identified and harassed. Some got anonymous phone calls. Some got midnight visits. There was little Kitaj could do. Doors were suddenly closed to him. He could get no one on the phone. Ruination was prescribed for anyone who dared deal with him. He was cast out.

From sun to sudden shadow.

"Fear!" he cried out to the press after the trial. "Old Man Fear! Time to call him out. Come on! Don't you see him hanging around? They say insurance companies are doing great business these days. Insurance against death? Or is it against straight vision? It's time we called the Old Man out!''

He was pale. He knew what to expect. He had made arrangements for this sudden change, this almost surreal new note of fortune—this total reversal accomplished so smoothly that it seemed like some kind of trick. But whose trick? From which direction or level?

The sickness was increasingly apparent after the trial, so much so that Lenore, Maria, Isma'il, and I agreed that he should not be left on his own. This became difficult. We were used to his wanderlust, to his sudden apparently pointless decisions which later bore fruit. But after the trial he was stalking continually round the world like a captured leopard trying to find and test the dimensions of his cage. For weeks our lives were a blur of hotel rooms, cars, planes, and walkie-talkie mountainsides. He would not slow down. He was obsessed with "seeing this," "going there," "doing that." With him in May I visited Baalbek, the Pyramids, and Machu Picchu. I thought there must be some purpose in this, but at each place he only wanted to be on to the next. He was brittle, unsure, irritable. "You look like a man who knows he's forgotten something," I told him one day.

"Johhny, I'm tired," he said curtly.

Yes, he was drained, no visions or voices, as though transmission through him, recently so intense and effective, had temporarily or permanently ceased, leaving him empty, dazed, unsure. Perhaps not surprising, given the rigors of his lensing in the last year. But there was physical sickness too, a dullness even in the eye, and his responses were slow, and he needed continual movement and company as though to fill the inner vacuum . . . which stayed empty.

"Is this part of the Joke?" I asked him in Peru.

He did not answer. We were in Lima bar, about to be thrown out because of his behavior. He sat, holding one arm in front of his face, then the other, studying them with amazement, peering closely as if wondering what they were or if they were really there at all, and this was annoying the clientele.

Later, minus jacket, which had been torn off in the fracas, he suddenly stopped in the street and turned to me sharply.

"You have it, Johnny. The Joke. Snafu, Catch-22, gravity, the Fall.''

"But you've brought this on yourself!" I exploded. "Everything gone into reverse, and you're somehow willing it. Aren't you?"

"I keep dreaming of razor blades and Hitler," he said, haunted. Then his eyes lost their light. I should have guessed. I didn't.

"Hamburg," he muttered an hour later. "We're going to Hamburg. I want to give some money away. I'll be happier without that money."

The first hit was in Hamburg. Kitaj got caught in a party full of devotees of his myth. Maria was with him. The devotees said he was a Star-Person come to enrich the human gene pool. Kitaj got angry with a woman who wanted him to give her a Star-Child right away. "So you can leave it in a wicker basket in the reeds?" he snapped. "Why confuse symbol carriers with the symbols? Don't you know you're a Star-Person too? Just give me a break." Meanwhile a bland man in a suit had come up close holding a half-open book, spine up. It was called *Invisible Aliens Among Us*. Maria cried out the instant that Kitaj belatedly sensed it too. Kitaj moved, the bullet buried itself in the wall, then Kitaj's eyes flared, briefly strong again, to grip and question the man.

"I hate you lousy Sirians!" snarled the bland man in the suit.

That was a lone operator with a grudge.

Maria tried to persuade him to go to Kiev and start real work again. So did Isma'il. So did I.

"Istanbul," grunted Ralph M'Botu Kitaj. "I must see something there."

He meant the hotel where he'd married Lenore. We got restricted one-week entry. He eyed the hotel nostalgically—then lost interest. There was a police escort to a fortresslike hotel safely outside the city. Kitaj was refused permission to address the students at Ankara. He seemed in physical pain, but would not see a doctor. That evening he sat alone in a room, tape-recording silence which afterwards he played back for spirit-advice which was not there. The three of us rang Lenore in Santa Barbara and her hints increased our concern. In the morning, feeling set-up and wrong, we left the hotel. Kitaj was brooding, arguing with Maria about going to Kiev or not. On the way to the car-park, the deadly blur of accelerated humanity burst at him from behind a fountain. Wired-up, wiped-out zombie agent with poison-tip needle gun. I

SMILE ON THE VOID 255

must have been readier than I knew. I bent and picked and threw a whitewashed stone from the border of a flowerbed. I hit, the needle went wild, Isma'il Tasered the killer who was crunching his cyanide cap even as a hotel porter just behind me cursed, grabbed his wrist, and dropped dead.

Amid all this Kitaj did not move or react at all.

"Razor blades," he said, eyeing the corpses with fascination.

From Istanbul to California. He was still a rich man; they let him in. Maria had gone to Kiev. He toyed with new movie plans, then gave them up, then spent a week with Lenore. He was in poor shape.

"Sure he was sick," she told me three years later. "But also they had a Sleepbeam on him. Very subtle. Did he tell you about the razor blades? It's a standard compulsion image. Also the Nazi imprints. They kept it low-key and continual over months. He thought he was doing it to himself. He didn't know what was happening or have any strength to deal with it . . . until Isma'il died instead of him."

Not quite true. He made the effort to break it.

"Kiev," he said, grimly. "But first, Marrakesh. I must smell more of the old world before it dies." He looked at Isma'il. He looked at me. His eyes were hooded, filled with pain. "I don't need company. These are pits I must explore myself."

We insisted. I was scared. I knew it was a gate.

"Nursemaids!" He sounded contemptuous. "Look after yourselves."

We went. A week later, in the cool of the evening, we sat at a rickety table on the porch of a cakeshop in Marrakesh. We faced an irregular sandy square with mosques in three directions. Crowds circled the stall and the entertainers. Kitaj, hat over his eyes, talked with Isma'il, who wore a striped djellabah, the hood over his head. I sat back in the shadows, uneasy with foreboding, watching Isma'il, remembering a conversation with him the day before. "It is a process," he'd murmured. "Part of the requirements of your myth-reality. When he accepted the trial and pled guilty, he made a choice. Even this sickness is a choice." Isma'il's eyes had been very calm. "You and I, we have also made a choice." And there had been something else in his eyes too. A knowledge I feared to share. Now on the porch of the cakeshop I nursed a glass of sugared mint tea, feeling opressed and threatened. Seeing Kitaj I had the image of a giant in chains. Why were we here? I couldn't quite trust my own sense of danger. Isma'il was speaking calmly. Then he sat still.

Then it happened. Kitaj glanced up.

Two grenades fell through a hole in the roof off the porch.

One bounced on the table then hit the floor. The other landed on my glass and smashed it away from me. It lay rocking on the table amid the fragments.

I stared at it in a dream.

Then Kitaj's shout. I jerked, threw myself wide of the porch, as the grenades exploded.

So Isma'il died. He had hardly ever been noticed by the world. He was not the sort. He had thrown Kitaj down, himself on top, and taken the blast.

In the hospital they sewed my left leg up. I could not walk for several weeks. The doctors showed me front page photographs in which I writhed. I was famous.

Kitaj had not been hurt. Three other people had been injured. The assassin was not caught.

Kitaj was grim three days later when he came to wheel me out. His eyes were like stone. He looked more haggard, like an old man.

"You and Isma'il took it for me," he said.

"He did. I got out of the way as fast as I could."

"You were *there*. You took it for me. You chose to be there."

I understood, and wished I hadn't. I felt bitter.

"So all you can say is Isma'il took it for you. Why? You've been acting crazy. We couldn't just abandon you."

Kitaj's face flooded with unexpected intensity.

"Just before it happened Isma'il said he was glad to know me but that soon he had to go. 'You will keep the same appointment,' he said, 'but in it must be in your way, as the patterns tell, and not like this.' Then he turned away, and immediately I knew, saw through the fog, and looked up, and . . ."

"Down came the shit." I was exhausted. Yes, Isma'il had seen it, had somehow known the score, maybe from that night in Ireland, maybe not until the last few hours when he and I had walked and talked. And maybe I had known it too, in my way. We had both chosen. But why such idiotic loyalty? Kitaj's behavior had made tragedy inevitable, and we had gone along with it. So that it was not tragedy at all. Just pure bloody foolishness. Or conscious self-sacrifice in a cause that transcended this madness. But that didn't seem likely at all to me just then. "I don't get it," I went on. "Do you mean he took your karma for you? Do you mean you're acting with purpose, not just nuts?"

His lips were tight. His eyes were fixed on face.

"Johnny," he said, "I've been proud. I thought I was following the Voice. But something else has been getting in. Someone's been pushing. Lenore suggested the Sleepbeam. I said that was nonsense, I would surely know if that was being done. But now those dreams have stopped. Nothing the last three nights." He grimaced. "Last year everything flowed, this year everything's blocked. I thought I was ready. To go through what's required. But negativity multiplies. It threw me. But now I guess it's possible . . ."

He checked. He wasn't well.

"You can start materializing the Pattern again, eh?"

I almost spat the words. Still he stared at me.

"This *is* the Pattern," he said. "What else?"

Then we flew to Kiev, and we got there.

It was hard to understand. It remains that way. Between Marrakesh and Venice Kitaj's life was such that there is still little agreement. We each have our own internal picture. It is possibly worthless to seek a set of motives that fit. Perhaps we must consider the function, not the man.

Ralph M'Bout Kitaj, lens.

All his life, the struggle to admit the power he could tap, focus, and bring to bear in the minds of others. Most of his life, with immense determination, he had avoided it. At last, the year before the trial, he had spread good seed in many places. He had poured it all out. After the trial he was an exhausted empty sack. Perhaps it was necessary. Perhaps people had to see. The error and exhaustion which climaxed at Marrakesh fertilized, did not retard, the growth of the seed. For months he had been excluded or mocked by the media. It is possible that Isma'il's act saved the myth. I believe this now. At the time, when the TV and press descended on Marrakesh, Isma'il was the hero, and Kitaj did not appear in a good light at all. Saved by the death of his faithful servant. When he refused to speak to TV about it, when people saw how sick he looked, his enemies must have thought he was through. Ralph M'Botu Kitaj, hurled headlong flaming from the ethereal sky. The Miltonic damnation in those stony eyes. So much for Taking Chances. Who loves a loser?

It didn't work out like that.

The myth no longer depended on Kitaj alone. It was already well at work, yeasting in millions of minds, stimulating changes of attitude. Kitaj as jaded pathetic victim of the hateful Org was ultimately as potent as Kitaj the born-again miracle worker. Different faces of the same process. There were many people now to appreciate that process was what counted. His enemies mistakenly thought that to the Chancers he was a god, a graven image, easily shattered, and cast out of the esteem of his "followers" by material ruination.

But they got function confused with personality.

So did some others. After Isma'il's death there were serious outbreaks of physical and psychoenergetic subversion in cities in several countries. Weird events to let people know Kitaj still had his friends. This activity was probably counterproductive. Justification for jailings, killings, more repression.

Nevertheless it is probably what got us to Kiev alive.

It wasn't the place for me. Too much intensity and genius in those institutes. Maria took over, and Kitaj started to pick up. I left to make my own way as soon as I could walk comfortably. Years seemed to have passed since Wales. It was hardly six months. I could not go back. I had come through a gate into some new space. For the first time in years I had a sense of my own destiny.

Isma'il had taught me that Kitaj was "just" another human being.

For some weeks I focused strictly on the complexities of my NOW. At the end of September I rang Kiev. "He is gone," said Maria. "He went somewhere."

Another of his disappearances.

Maria did not tell me. I did not ask.

This one lasted from September 1990 to March 1991.

During this time the message came from Sirius.

In fact it had probably been coming through a long time, but nobody had noticed it, or stumbled on the circumstances necessary to receive it.

The discovery was made by an amateur horticulturalist in Bristol, England. A retired sailor, Arthur Herne. He was interested in *The Secret Life of Plants* approach. He talked to his melons and tulips. Every night he experimented with speeded-up tapes of Bach and Vivaldi to find out which they responded to best. Late one wild January night he went into the dark greenhouse for something he'd forgotten. Handel's *Water Music* was playing quietly on a continuous loop. By torchlight he noticed that one flower—a silver-streaked rose he'd bred himself—was partly open, slightly bent in a particular direction. He made nothing of it until, two nights later, at an earlier hour, *The Four Seasons* of Vivaldi playing, he saw that the rose was now turned in a slightly different direction. He looked closer. The petals were shivering, pulsating almost imperceptibly. There was no draft in the greenhouse. The aim of the rose was south, into the open country, low into the sky.

From the roof of his house he saw Sirius, bright.

For a week he experimented. The rose-reaction, only when Sirius was above the horizon, was most energetic to the Allegro of Bach's Fifth *Brandenburg* Concerto, speeded up from 33⅓ to 78 r.p.m. He considered the rhythms of the rose.

He called the physics department of the local university.

The savants were skeptical at first. But they investigated.

Soon there were visits by a linguist, a government minister, an astronomer, decoding experts, and a brigadier general interested in possible military applications. Arthur Herne was told that his rose was now a state secret.

"Bugger that!" he said at the press conference he held.

SCIENCE TO CRACK INTERSTELLAR ROSE-ETTA CODE?

"The so-called Sirius Rose expresses a complex rhythm which automatically repeats every 23 minutes while the star is above the horizon," said an official statement. "It is unlikely that the problem can be met in terms of conventional linguistic concepts. The enigma demands serious and prolonged research."

ROSE CODE AN EVOLUTIONARY TRIGGER?

The rose did not survive the publicity, the tests. Early in March it died, even as Sirius ducked under the British horizon. By then there were hundreds of hours of rhythm recordings. Transformed into amplified sound-equivalents, the message sounded like a complex jazz bass track. But nobody cracked it.

"We *know* what it's saying!" claimed Chancers. "It's written in us too. Just sit down and *listen* to yourself!"

Then began events which reminded me of how, when Magellan's big-winged ship appeared off Tierra del Fuego, the islanders could not see it at all, even with the sailors ashore and walking among them. They couldn't see it because it was impossible: such a thing did not exist. In their sight the horizon remained unbroken. It took their shaman to persuade them that the strangers had actually arrived *in* something which could be *seen*. His mind did not reject what his eyes registered and transmitted to the brain. Yes, he decided, this new thing is really here, as real as roots and life and death.

For, throughout February, with wild storms and power failures all over the world, flotillas of flying saucers waltzed over dozens of major cities, putting on shows that had to be seen to be believed.

In March, Kitaj reappeared.

Like a phoenix—an ailing phoenix, but a phoenix nonetheless. And the Show he brought us was the Show of end-in-beginning, beginning-in-end.

The Smile in the Void.

March 1991 to December 1992. The Twenty-One Months. They flowed by like an ever-intensifying dream, and when it was all over we shook our heads and started out again. There have been many accounts of Kitaj in this time, all of them dangerous to circulate or possess. Some switch events into mathematical terms, deriving symbolic and psychologic equations. Some use the structure of Kitaj's final play to build insightful critiques of viewpoint and reality. Some seek scientific explanation; some project simple acceptance of miracle; some invoke an invisible Sirian UFO which snatched him up at the crucial moment. There are accounts comparing Kitaj with radical magical mystics from Christ to Rasputin. There are taped conversations allegedly from Kiev, from the Last Retreat, from the healer's room in Luzon, from the miracle tour and finally Venice. There are melodramas full of dramatic and staggering events: the same events have also been presented as quietist meditational parables, or as "chakra-openings," the blue star dancing. Plus all the special theories. The Cyborg-Clone Theory, that Kitaj really did die at the North Pole and his place taken by a zapped-up specially grown double.

The Multiple-Clone Theory, that after Luzon there was not just one Ralph M'Botu Kitaj abroad in the world producing clouds of butterflies out of nowhere, but fifteen, or even thirty, all of them engaged in various different activities according to the imagination of the believer. And of course, variations on the Great Fake-Out—Kitaj never did have cancer, he never even went to the North Pole; it was a put-on the way he proved medical science incompetent to cure him before going to the healer, the miracle tour and the laying-on-of-hands were just straight old ego carny hype, Venice was a trapdoor plus laser holographic illusion, and even now he is alive and well and laughing somewhere in Paraguay.

One of the most interesting theories is in a classified ISO document that happened to come my way. Dated August 1997, it considered Kitaj to be a collectively projected fictional entity which could be summoned again at any time:

I quote now from this document:

> There is acceptable precedent for this phenomenon, though never before in such developed form. In "Kitaj," we suggest, three areas of psychic-imaginative event have been integrated.

> 1. Mass Hallucination. At Fatima in Portugal in 1917 the "Virgin Mary" appeared in the sky to a waiting crowd of over 100,000 people. In the shared experience of these witnesses, the sun plunged towards the earth, and there was great heat. Shared UFO experiences may be similarly generated—projection of unconscious telepathic content onto the "outside," to be perceived as mystery or miracle. Yet it must be asked at what point "mass hallucination" becomes "consensus reality."

> 2. Hollywood Glamour. Twentieth-century humanity is characterized not least by industries of fantasy. Cinema audiences share in mass conspiracies to believe in, to identify with. Popular entertainers and actors are called "stars." In "Kitaj" we see the process carried further. He is said not only to "be a star," but to have "gone to a star." The glamour of this belief has invaded public consciousness to the level of political effect and

change. No coincidence that in 1992, the year of great-est mass emotional investment in "Kitaj," the UN Sirian planoform expedition was announced.

3. Deliberate Production of Fictional Entities. The "Philip Group" of table rappers from Montreal were well known during the 1970s for their invention of "Philip," an aristocratic Englishman who died of a tragic remorse in the seventeenth century. By calling upon this imaginary entity in a mood of jollity and joking they were able to manifest a wide range of psychokinetic phenomena. Before large audiences the "Philip" performances became more dramatic. The suggestion is that fictions consciously known as such can be manipulated to produce very real results. The human mind apparently can generate collective and effective apparitions.

Was "Kitaj" deliberately generated by a particular group of people with long-term political ends? There is evi-dence that this may be the case. We suggest that this line of inquiry should be promoted.

Towards the end of the document John Hall is identified as the author of *Liar's Gold*, and is invoked as one of the generators of the "Kitaj fiction." And so in a sense I am. But the case is overstated, and their interest in me is personally unfortunate. And the time grows shorter and shorter.

Three events are generally agreed as the key events.
The Last Retreat, North Pole, New Year 1991–92.
Luzon and the Healing on 21 March 1992.
The Smiling, Venice, Christmas 1992.
These are the visible parts.

Kiev, March '91. When the word came many gathered to meet him back, but when he came into the room there was shock.
He was hardly more than skin and bone. His eyes shone piercingly from a face like a hatchet. The hairline had receded. He walked stiffly, trembling slightly. There was a war in his body.
He refused all doctors and medical treatment.

"There's a reason." His eyes were like eagles.

Then he told us about the Last Retreat. He laid it out quite flatly, the nature of the plan, and he said nothing of the past, and I thought about patterns; I wondered if he might be mad, for the plan, though stupendous, seemed pointless. But Carl the blind seer said I was still bitter about Marrakesh. All the same, when I got a chance to walk with Kitaj in the Institute grounds, I wanted to know where all this was coming from. Because I was horrified.

"You have to see a doctor," I said. "I mean what the hell's been going on? I thought it was just energy drain, or something."

I was limping slow, and that was his pace too.

"Come on!" he said. "Don't tie me down to that hypocritic oath. Maybe I'll let them take the bread, but not yet."

"But what *is* this? How did it happen? Where have you been?"

He smiled beautifully through the pain.

"Well, Johnny, I spent one hundred and twenty days in a cave at 17,000 feet in the Himalayas, praticing *tummo*, so that now I don't ever feel cold, but," he grimaced, tapped his shrunken body, "there are prices being paid all the time. I learned some interesting things, though."

I decided to fall for it.

"Like?"

Again that painful smile. We sat down on a bench in the sunshine.

"Watch," he said. From his pocket he took a matchbox which he set on the palm of his left hand. Then delicately with the fingers of his right hand he started to stroke it, the sharpness of his smile fixed on it. I felt a brief localized warmth on my skin as the matchbox slowly began to . . . fade out. In half a minute it was a ghost. Then it was gone entirely.

Impulsively I touched his thin hand where it had lain.

There was nothing there. No matchbox.

Now he was grinning at me like a little boy.

"Useful, eh? What do you think?"

I felt fearful. I did not smile.

"Great. Where's it gone?"

"It's still there—its pattern, anyway. You could say I've shifted it up the wavelength a bit, speeded it up out of the obviously physical. Easy once you get the knack . . . though I admit it took me a long time to get it."

And he kept on grinning at me.

"Rafe, what the hell are you doing?" Angrily I turned to a safer subject. "This thing you're planning to build at the North Pole . . . nobody can see the point of it. Even Maria says you're just putting us on."

"Yes." He was suddenly blank. "The Joke. I think people will like it. I'm calling it the Last Retreat. Cost will be the major problem. There may be political difficulties too. Who gives planning permission to build at the North Pole? It's not a land surface, after all. Who claims to own it?"

"You'd better ask the Witch of the North Wind," I said sullenly. "How the hell would I know? What gave you the idea anyway?"

"You did. Science fiction story you read me in Ireland. *Tower of Glass*. About a crazy rich guy who . . ."

"Sure," I interrupted curtly, "I remember. Silverberg. Dammit, Rafe, don't you have any original ideas of your own? This is impossible! Where would you find the labor and transport? Even if you get the bloody tower built, what are you going to *do* with it?"

"We'll have a party." The smile hovered. "It isn't a tower. It's a dome, and it'll be beautiful. Can you see it? Silvery. Luminous. Glowing in the night with the aurora dancing above it, and the radiations streaming down from space. People will love it, Johnny."

Had Isma'il died for this? I nearly asked. I'm glad I didn't. It would have been a silly question, the way things turned out.

The Last Retreat became the epitome of 1991.

Look back to that lunatic year. Finally, Kitaj's dome at the North Pole was the only thing that made any sense. But that was in December. In April, when the scheme was announced, after Kitaj had carefully showed his wasted new appearance in public a few times, the general reaction was one of derision, disbelief, or both. It was so obviously ridiculous there was hardly any opposition. Had he come back with anything "sensible," involved in the world, he would have been stopped, fast. As it was, the Org just grinned collectively and let him get on with it, convinced that Kitaj was now quite insane and effectively beaten out of all the arenas that mattered. Why stop a dying man from wasting the last of his money on a senseless folly? In fact, why not encourage him, keep him out of the way. "If Mr. Kitaj can persuade any of our companies to support him in this obviously necessary venture," said the French premier, with a smile on his face and an expansive gesture, "then he deserves their help, and we should not stand in their way."

The Joke. Kitaj got all the help he needed. But perhaps he would not have done so if not for the nature of that year. The Black Hole Joke.

Pluto was busy between June and December. Vesuvius blew again; so did South Africa. There were violent rainstorms that lasted for weeks, in other regions a second year of drought. Harvests failed everywhere. And quite suddenly there were millions of starving people on the move, restlessly, out of Asia and Africa, seething west and north, particularly towards Europe, where people were already packed and hungry. Frontiers were overwhelmed, giant shantytowns grew outside Vienna, Prague, Bucharest. Massacres and mob-rule were commonplace. Plague broke out. American grain became a basic unit of exchange, also a matter for violent international disagreement, particularly after the assassination of President Patchen by an enraged Nigerian student whose father had been shot for leading an attack on a U.S. grain convoy. It seemed to make no sense whatever anyone said or tried to do that year. It was one continual booming on the chaos-gongs of uncontrollable natural change, the collapsing of structures which for centuries had been self-defined. If you could, you kept your head down and farmed your patch. If not, you took your chances, for people were starving to death in millions, very obtrusively.

Thus the Last Retreat became appropriate.

The logistics and costs were stupendous, but it was done, it was built, in five furious months, and long before it was completed it had become the somber fascination of millions, a symbol of the times, up there on the North Pole, so awesome, multifaceted, and luminous in the waste, in the night. To begin with in June Kitaj had trouble finding the labor, transport, and expertise . . . but as soon as the thing was begun it caught the general mind at the mythic level.

The Plutonian hell of death and rebirth . . . or maybe, something else . . .

For Kitaj had more than myth-games up his sleeve. Apart from two journeys to the Pole during construction he was not seen in the outside world that year. Rumors of his condition circulated in gossip. Yet, though ill, he was active. In Kiev he was working with Maria and Carl and a number of other newconscious talents on techniques of inner travel and telepathic group-projection. Yet when I met him in March, and twice later that year, we did not talk about the work. I was concerned by his physical deterioration, not understanding the cause of it, wondering if he'd live the year out. I said "doctors," and he just grinned. In September, after such a visit, I was back in Florence (where I'd lived since December '90: the city was threatened now by eastern invasion), and one night I dreamed. In the dream Kitaj appeared and said very clearly, "I've sent a letter which you'll get tomorrow. I want you to do some writing for me."

The letter arrived. He wanted me to work on the script for the TV preview of the Last Retreat party. He told me what he was aiming to do.

"The man's incorrigible," I muttered, and thought of refusing . . . but within the hour I'd called him . . . and so I started work on his end-game.

Kitaj hadn't lost his touch or taste for causing public uproar and diversion. The party preview was broadcast from a bat-winged studio in New Orleans on 31 October 1991. It started with the cartoon I scripted. We have a sexy Swedish witch fleeing nuclear hunt and holocaust, broomstick-jetting through roiling red and black cloud, hopelessly lost above the poison electric glow of polluted arctic wastes. Fiery elementals, condemned and enraged by the human failure, are trying to knock her off the broomstick. At last, despairing, she sees the bright jewel that sparkles through the cloud and thunder of the world.

A big sign appears that says: THE LAST RETREAT.

Then cartoon Kitaj with a big *S* on his chest swoops up to rescue her, and takes her down through airlock doors into sparkling cosmic geodesic dome, even as the world cracks and gouts . . . and the dome is revealed as an eggship, seeding speedily away into shock-waved rippling space-time as the fair witch from a porthole exclaims: "If I believe this, I'll believe *anything!*"

Then CUT from cartoon to real-time camera.

We track through howling artic blizzard. The storm is tremendous. How can anything stand in this? Then we see it, looming. Vast electric geodesic whiteness. The huge scale, the gleaming strong external panels, the rows of porthole windows, the airlock doors . . .

"Don't believe a thing," says Kitaj's slow and painful voice. "It's all just liar's gold unless you know it in the heart. But we'll be blasting off for a great party here on New Year's Eve . . . and if you can get here, good luck."

That did it. It really looked like a spaceship. RUNNING DOG KITAJ READY TO FLEE. Suddenly thousands of people thinking how to get to the North Pole. Propositions for charter flights. Kitaj was about to take off! Why not? He said "don't believe a thing," but that's just a con! Midway through November a UN delegation visited the dome. They came back waving statements. NO STARSHIP! NO STARSHIP! There was anger. Kitaj had gone too far this time! Or had he? Nobody was too sure any more. In fact, come to think of it, how could you be sure the Last Retreat was really there, at the Pole? Unless you went there you only learned about it from TV and the press. What was going on? NO STARSHIP! Many would not believe it. If not, why not? With the world going ape, there *should* be a starship. By Christmas, a week before the party, "no starship" had become an ugly political joke. Why no starship?

CLASSIFIED TRIPLE A. PROJECT ROVER. CRASH PROGRAMS.

Official statements were hurriedly released:

"We have problems," said NASA. "Rio integrations. It's not just a matter of blasting a tin can through space-time. This requires high high yoga."

"To reach the stars," claimed a Russian release, "involves technology of the soul as well as of machine. There are human problems to be overcome."

It was four years since Rio.

Kitaj was about to declare the end.

Christmas 1991. One of the ice-buses from Spitsbergen was lost, thirty people with it. Something deadly that busted its radio so nobody could ever get a position. The other nineteen got safely to the Pole and back. I chose that way rather than fly. Either way was rough. The buses were like behemoths, huge creatures that just kept grinding through the night, tracking a wide corridor of magnetic markers between one fuel dump and the next. Three days it took, and bad movies on the headsets, and a lot of poker and joking, much of it nervous. I played endless Scrabble with a Spanish woman, a journalist from Madrid. She insisted she liked the stark black purity of the night. I didn't look outside much at all. I slept, or read, or meditated to the endless chugging roar of the engines. There were well-known faces, but we were all the same. Going to the Last Retreat. Half the people on that bus had the look of those ready to say a long farewell. Not even the poker and joking could prevail against the deep collective silences that developed so pensively among us as the Pole and the Last Retreat drew near.

New Year's Eve, 1991. The expectancy was great. There was live transmission, despite probabilities of poor reception. In many countries it was a matter of bread and circus. Politicians found it safer to permit the show. In packed-out cities the starving people wanted to see it, hear it, know it. What is the Word? How do we get out of this mess? Is Kitaj just gonna jack off and abandon us? Or can he pull something through and get us on our feet?

Giant screens went up in the squares of many cities. The haunted crowds were forming a day and a night before, people clinging to their hard-won space in front of the screen whatever the weather did. Rough communalities emerged at some of these vast expectant encampments. The Chancers were there, organizing; there were bonfires; civic ordinances were tactily suspended, for Kitaj and his myth were now a public property, and potent . . .

The Last Retreat.

Flickers and crackling on the screens.

Blizzards of static and snow and arctic music which is unutterably cold and ancient, and Total Identification for those who can afford it.

You hook in as best you can.

It is a long journey to the Last Retreat, filmed in infrared, past endless bleak vistas of darkness and ice. And when at last you see that jewel of refuge in the night you feel so glad. Yet uneasiness grows with proximity. The spectral white of the dome is fascinating, *too* fascinating, hypnotizing, making the mind giddy. You pass through the airlocks into the vast bottom-level garages, and the music has grown so low and somber.

Transparent elevators take you, ten at a time, up through the levels, up, up, and you see into the steam rooms, you see into the gardens and the kitchens. Up through the middle mazes with their corridors of little rooms, and still there is nobody seen. The Last Retreat seems quite deserted.

But just as you begin to wonder you come up through the lowest of the party salons—a vast space, the full curve of the dome, slightly more than halfway up, and bacchanalian, with Las Vegas showgirls and a rock 'n roll band dimly seen and heard through the crowds of weird-clad drunken masked celebrants who prance through the UV light. There are gesticulations at you as you rise up the crystalline elevator tube, invitations to get off and get playful—tongues and eyes and breasts and loins—and you see frantic couplings amid the roulette wheels, but already you are entering the next higher zone.

Here amid the mellow light of a smaller area people sit in studied groups, talking quietly, sipping cocktails, divided from one another in their low open alcoves of velveted furnishing. At a piano close by, a pensive woman plays Scriabin with soulfulness which clearly penetrates the shaft up which you rise: you are torn from the spirit of bacchanal by this resonant solemnity.

So you come to the topmost hall.

The elevator cage stops smoothly. The invisible doors slide open. You step cautiously into the silent and mournful space where nothing moves.

And you see Kitaj, over there.

Against the curve of the ice-blue naked wall. There are twenty human beings in a studied circle round him. They are youthful human beings from every region of the earth. They are classically posed, standing or sitting in fixed positions, like statues, wearing dark colors, amethyst necklaces, their hair adorned with violets or grape-bunch sprays of purple wisteria, ten men and ten women, all of them Kitaj's associates who have been working with him at Kiev, though you do not know this. And their demeanor is funereal.

Your feet sink into the purple carpeting and you have forgotten your neighbors as you approach this starkness and the focus of it.

Ralph M'Botu Kitaj.

You see him better.

You stop, you breathe in deeply.

There is nothing alive in his face or appearance at all.

He lolls, loose and exhausted and crumpled, on the embroi-

dered silk of an oriental divan. His Chinese tunic and trousers are
pale yellow silk with red dragons on them. His bare feet droop to
the carpet. They look tiny and wizened, like chicken feet, and the
silk lies heavy on him. His head is propped on the Dior-black lap
of a beautiful Asian woman who supports him with concern. And
it is his face that shocks most of all. Many months since he was
last seen on TV. Your old image of Kitaj's appearance is shattered. For his face is lined, dusty-grey, with the cheeks fallen in
and the lips without blood. The skin has a flaccid sheen; it is
tight on the bone, but bagged beneath the chin and the eyes,
which are heavy-lidded and fathomless. It is the face of a human
being on the edge of death; of an old, old man; much older than
forty-nine . . . and the effect is emphasized by the pale yellow,
by the ice-blue, by the grave young people frozen all round him.

Dimly he sees you, and slowly he stirs, lifting his blue-veined
hand in the slightest motion of recognition, and his voice is a
wisp.

"Welcome. Welcome to the party. It is almost New Year now,
here in the Last Retreat . . . and I offer you a one-way journey
. . . through space and time and across . . . across the Great
Divide . . . beyond the waters of the Styx."

The effort is great. His purplish eyelids flicker. The sign is
interpreted and your camera-eye tracks the faces and forms of the
ten men and women who maintain such a distant and somber
focus round him: a focus that pulls you deeper into the center of
this ending despite your mounting horror.

"These are my friends," he whispers. "They have talents to
find . . . the way beyond . . . the way through these traps we
have set for ourselves. It would be good if you could join them
and help us all to live again. But this may never be. The state of
things is not too good."

Then slowly, so slowly, as his right hand stirs in negation, life
seems to prick him, his eyes open wider. You see those depthless
pupils, expanding from their pinpoints. Weakly he pushes himself up from the lap of the Asian woman. She supports his head
with her hand. He struggles for a more powerful expression. You
are caught, you lean closer, willing him to speak, to say whatever it is that he knows, to speak of the way out, the way through
. . . if there *is* such a way. Tense, you hear his rough and
painful voice:

"You don't need MIT's latest mathematical model to tell you!

We're screwing up beyond hope of any hope! No answers that
don't also involve utopian changes in human nature overnight!''

He falls back, fighting for breath. You stand there, confused,
your hope dashed, in the silence, until he recovers, his face now
livid and naked.

''I was known as the richest man in the world. That kind of
wealth sucks. What do you think? You think I can sit back and
fiddle up here while the rest of you burn in a world that makes no
fucking sense at all?''

He glares. You feel the waves of effort that ebb out from him.
You feel dizzy now. Perhaps you feel a roaring in your ears, and
sense the approaching abyss on the edge of which you stand with
him.

''You thought this was a spaceship? So it is. Can you feel how
everything is dissolving . . . decaying . . . falling apart? I'm
going away, my friends. It's cancer. It's excess. It's spiritual
dis-ease that drives the cells of the body wild. So now I'm going
away . . . away . . . away . . .''

The voice fades, pulling you with it, as abruptly his head
slumps. The dizziness and roaring in your ears is now tremendous, overwhelming, and as you begin to fall into the fading of
his eyes, into the vortex of the whirlpool, perhaps almost too late
you sense that all this is a put-up job, engineered to pull you in,
and that the twenty men and women round him are influencing
you, driving you into Kitaj's extinction. For an instant you have
the chance to pull back, to avert your gaze, to turn away. But
perhaps you no longer want to do that. Perhaps for the first time
in your life you realize just how truly hopeless it all is. The world
has been destroyed by everything done by man, and all that now
remains is the final materialization of that destruction. So, why
not go with him? Across the Styx. Plunge down through those
dying eyes, into the depths, into the blackness, into the nothingness . . . into the void . . .

. . . into the infinite compression of the Black Hole . . .

. . . to welcome in the New Year of extinction . . .

But there is another side. If you keep going, if you stay with it
and cross that river, you come to a strange new humor. You
squeeze through death and despair into a vast new space, never
suspected except perhaps in deepest dreams, beyond individual
lifespan, beyond historical ages. Without any longer knowing

who you are you see the planet earth below you, a gleaming jewel that spins and spirals in its web, in the mesh of energies, through the intelligence of the universe. And the patterns. The ever-shifting musical patterns behind the shape of things, the patterns that flash and weave and cast the changing forms of events and history, the patterns of which you're an integral part, the patterns of those who visit us, who wait for us to acknowledge that we are them, who wait for us to admit them in all their levels.

Through the Black Hole, into the light of the patterns.

Into the expansion of the White Hole.

Into the dance. Into the song.

Into the Smile on the Void . . .

Happy New Year, 1992. Somewhere, a voice whispers:

"Is it too late? Is it *really* too late?"

AS ABOVE, SO BELOW
OR
AS BELOW, SO ABOVE

"Myths are things which never happened but always are."
—Salustius

10. THE SMILE

Thus the last year, 1992, was begun.

For maybe half an hour Kitaj succeeded in stopping the world in its tracks. He had "died," publicly, and he was not to be publicly resurrected for another eighty days. During this interim period there was a curious yet definite global uneasiness. What had really happened? Was the man dead, or not? Mythically, yes, he was dead. But physically? There was confusion in many minds. Kitaj had pulled something off, but nobody could define quite what it was, and whenever he was glimpsed publicly during the next eighty days, there was a sense of embarrassment in those who saw him, as though he should no longer be on earth at all . . . in the flesh. The broadcast, and the manner in which millions of viewers had been pulled into his extinction, had been very effective, so much so that discussion was curiously muted, and many people preferred not to see him at all, even if he was physically there in front of them. There was very little mention of the party in the press and the media . . . but millions were thinking perhaps harder than ever before in their lives. Had they been tricked cheaply, or had they been shown something valuable? The numbers of people who had identified sufficiently to go all the way through the experience were not so great—several millions, perhaps, out of a world population of five thousand million . . . but that there had been a triggering of *something* was not in any doubt. Only . . . what was it?

Open discussion really began only after the healing at Luzon.

What had really happened? What had Kitaj and his assistants (soon to be known as the "Ten and Ten") really done?

What was the true function of the Last Retreat?

Many people who were otherwise not convinced by anything Kitaj did were willing to concede that his enticement to people to die through the Black Hole Joke in order to emerge into a wider perspective—the Smile—had been masterly. They conceded that it might even have had significant effect in toning down—at least for a few hours, or even days—the rushing madness of the world's societies. As to his activities between the Healing and the Discorporation nine months later . . . these too, they conceded, were effective in bringing many people to a fresh conception of themselves. But what rationality could not swallow was that Kitaj, as ordinary human being, could have wielded such power and psychological authority as all these events demonstrated. And so the theorizing began in earnest. With regard to the Last Retreat, a common belief that arose during the last year was that the dome must have been more, much more, than a big igloo, much more than a symbolic Plutonian temple, and that in itself it had possessed purposeful scientific function and effect. The "Starship Front," many came to believe, had been a blind to conceal the true state of things: that the Last Retreat had not been for going to space, but for space to come to earth. The Last Retreat, they believed, acted as a receiver and amplifier for an interstellar message beamed to earth probably from the region of the Great Bear (it is hard to invoke Sirius at the North Pole) . . . and that the dome was placed at the Pole precisely because the radiation umbrella round the world which blocks out incoming energy is weak above the Pole. And Kitaj, by these believers, is once again regarded as the agent for particular other worldly interests—the lens of god-energies.

Well . . . yes, and no.

Let's try to keep some perspective.

I am not aware that the Last Retreat was anything other than what it appeared to be: a large geodesic dome. It is my under-standing that the effects produced in millions by their sympathetic sharing in Kitaj's "death" were created as much by themselves, in their identification, as by the deliberate focus of Kitaj and the Ten and Ten. Nor am I aware that on this occasion any specific message came from space into the world through Kitaj, not that he was operating on behalf of Sirians, Arcturans, Vegans, Ursans, or any particular hypothesized stellar civilization with benevolent or malign interest in this planet.

Nevertheless, information was transmitted, information of the sort which can aid us in our self-evolution.

Information from the Source, which is everywhere and nowhere.

Did Kitaj have a direct channel of connection with the Source?

Sure. The same as all of us. The channel that runs all the way from the base of the spine to the brain, straight up, the flexible receiving aerial we all carry, the aerial with the head on top and the hole at the top of the head—the "thousand-petaled flower." We are all electromagnetic receivers, the spine is the aerial . . . and, in addition, up and down the spine, there are stepdown transforming centers which receive and distribute the energetic universal information. These centers—not material, not organic, though sometimes associated with the glandular system—are commonly known as the chakras, and you can find information about their system in yogic and newconscious literature. We are all at least partially open to the universe.

It is also worth noting the Huxley theory of the brain as a "reducing valve," designed to exclude as well as receive the incoming universal information—designed to exclude so that, yet again, we can concentrate on particular things and not get burned out by the total influx of everything all at once. We are vulnerable creatures; we live at the bottom of a well, protected by a series of "filters"—the planets, the atmosphere of our planet, and the set-up of our own neurology. With the information we have historically received we have created the specialist realities of civilization. But also what we customarily receive from "out there" is so filtered and narrowed down by the time it reaches us that it has led to the obsessive self-focus typical of our species on this planet. We are traditionally turned in on ourselves, with a tendency to deny whatever cannot be interpreted by the body as real.

Kitaj, and many others, have been publicly extending our range of reception. There has been a great flood of new development. But the assimilation remains incomplete; the picture remains warped; fear persists, and persecution of the new perspectives, and misinterpretations based upon our former fixed insistences. And most of the theories we have about Kitaj and his last year are based on misinterpretation, on the desire for something fixed, solid, and, understandable in conventional terms.

Which is precisely what is impossible.

The Last Retreat was abandoned within a week of the party. Nobody ever went back there so far as I know. For two weeks there were over seven hundred people there at the North Pole, with every luxury imported; then the Black Hole Joke was played, death was announced, the party was over.

Myself, I'd hovered between the bacchanalian and intellectual floors. It was only after the broadcast I sought Kitaj out. He wasn't as direly ill as the broadcast had suggested . . . but I guessed he had no more than a few weeks, a few months at most. It was no fake. He admitted as much.

"Started in the bowel," he said. "Appropriate, eh?"

Symbolic or actual, I didn't find this funny. It seemed he did.

His activities between the New Year and 21 March have suggested to many people that he was afraid of dying. Hardly. He was hosting a dramatic process which had to be carried to a conclusion. The part of him afraid of dying had already died, during the time he was in the stone circle in Ireland. After that he had chosen his direction; he was acting out a purposeful play which was internally consistent though publicly it often appeared bizarre and contradictory. I tend to believe that even the cancer was somehow induced, or permitted, as a part of the play—though I have no logic to back this up, no explanation either as to how the process was controlled. After the Last Retreat, after the "death" he underwent, the dimension of events had moved well beyond the personal; the cycle of his life approached climax; he was moving through a plan, and this plan, as well as his nature and purpose, being internal to himself and his Voice, is differently perceived by each of us. Thus every account of Kitaj's last year tends to reveal more about the writer than the subject . . . for by then he was clearly a mirror.

I have an article here that somebody gave me a year ago. It comes from a photocopied Welsh magazine, *Dragon*. The writer signs himself Peter of Dyfed, and what he says is not altogether what I remember, and I suspect he never actually met Kitaj. No matter. Truth has one source but many wells, and what people create for themselves out of the Kitaj myth often becomes a basis for their positive actions. This piece by Peter of Dyfed is called *Luzon,* and I include it because it represents a particularly popular approach to the strange business of Kitaj and the Doctors . . . also, to give perspective to my own attitudes.

Luzon

Kitaj claimed he was a Virgo. I believe he was a Scorpio. His life shows a struggle typical of this sign, between the higher (eagle/phoenix) and the degenerate lower (scorpion) aspects.

Brothers and sisters who were at Glastonbury will remember how in 1989 Kitaj at last realized his higher purpose. But he lost his grip. In April 1990 the UN Ecocourt found him guilty of damaging the Amazon jungle. This condemnation caused collapse in him. He lost coherence and went dark again. For months he went round and round the world, his sense of purpose shattered. The assassination attempts made it clear that he could not survive in public. His power was gone. So he did his vanishing act again.

He reappeared a sick man in March 1991. He had a wild scheme to build a dome at the North Pole. He spent most of his remaining wealth on this folly. It was no surprise to anyone when, at New Year 1992, he demonstrated to us that he was on the point of death from cancer.

The demonstration was excessive. The broadcast had a depressing effect on many who had hoped for better from him. It seemed that Kitaj, finally, had nothing but darkness to give, and that his humor could bring no joy.

It seemed that he was ready to die without fulfillment.

But the knowledge that he was on the brink electrified him. He joked bitterly with the world about it, pulling many into the void he created for them through the Total Identification circuits, projecting his own ter-

minal condition into common reality as though his
death meant everyone must die.

Then, in sudden panic, as if affected by the power of
his own broadcast, he began to seek a last-minute cure.

Kitaj did not want to die.

He was afraid of the loneliness.

He abandoned the Last Retreat, rejected the drugs
and many of his sycophants, went to the doctors with
the last of his money, strength, and life.

During January and February 1992 he was seen in
many cancer clinics, Ralph M'Botu Kitaj, once the
richest man in the world, now close to death, seeking
expert opinion, second opinion, third opinion, and successful operation.

But medical science could not help. Every doctor
who examined him pronounced the condition inoperable. They said he had waited too long. The disease had
grown too deep. The cancer—it was physically manifested, but chiefly a disease of the soul. The cannibal
cells that ate him were able to do so since he had lost
his central light, his sense of value. He had turned the
wrong way. In his exhaustion at the time of the trial the
disease, long latent, had "taken its chance" . . . and
Kitaj had not at first realized it.

All this he admitted—but only after all OldStyle
medical options had been exhausted. It is said that
when the possibility of faith healing was brought to his
attention, at first he rejected it violently.

He found the subject offensive. Why?

In the first place it was offensive to him to have been
struck down by this illness. It was clear evidence to
him that he had failed to channel the energies properly—
almost a sign of cosmic disfavor. Thus the strange
reports of his pleasure at the failure of OldStyle doctors
to cure him. Not only did he dislike the medical establishment, there was a strong urge in him to die. Then
again, the subject was too close a reminder of the world
that he'd touched briefly then lost again, the world of
spirit, beyond the senses. He was faced by the immediate implications of a mystery which he could not buy
off or hold at bay any more. He had never wholly

assimilated and realized the possibilities which others
had glimpsed in him. Even during his crusade of 1989–90
he had demonstrated egotism . . . which the cancer
now exploited.

For now Death was knocking, only days away. Now
he knew he'd been a loser all along. Now he could
admit it. The harsh black joke he'd toyed with for
years. The black hole joke of himself, and the light
beyond.

He submitted himself.

He gave himself to the energies of love, compassion,
joy.

With all his money gone he was taken by friends to
Luzon in the Philippines, to a man, a healer, a member
of the Union Espiritista Cristiana de Filipinas, a man
who asked for no money, though it was offered.

Love. Compassion. Joy.

Impractical concepts for times like these?

Do they in fact have any real existence?

"No, no!" Kitaj had cried for so long. "Here on
earth there is only hate, discord, strife, madness, and
the drowning of all light!"

And so cries many another in these years, focusing
on terrors that the mass of human beings continue to
make unconsciously out of themselves.

Yet the answer is simple.

Kitaj went to Luzon.

Kitaj had a cancer, Kitaj was a pauper, Kitaj went to
Luzon.

Kitaj found love . . . and it was the very last gasp,
the . . . very . . . last . . . gasp . . . of . . . his
. . . pain . . . full . . . self . . . deluded . . . life . . .

Last Gasp.

First Breath.

On the twenty-first of March, at the beginning of the
year, Kitaj went to Luzon; he was carried into a small
bare room and laid upon a kitchen table. And the
healer, a man without scalpel or degree, a faithful
loving man, put his hands into Kitaj—kneading the
skin, passing within—to remove the physical mass of
the bodily cancer. Then Kitaj was able to cure Kitaj.

New Breath. In love the latent came to life in him.
New Powers. He went to Luzon dying, he came
away from Luzon . . .
. . . a man transformed, reborn, and ready for his
final road . . .

Dramatizations. It was dramatic enough as it was. I find it hard
to remember detail of the last year; the months flowed like a fast
river, and events took place for me in a curious dream which had
elements of numbness about it. Life was surreal and unprece-
dented; it was necessary to suspend judgment and try to see
imaginatively in order to catch the least edge of what lay beyond
the appearances of this reality-show.

Yet some material fact I'll vouch for.

Kitaj was not broke when he went to Luzon. The doctors had
not finished him off entirely. He still had some credit cards.

And Luzon had been planned.

One day in February I sat with the Dead Man in the waiting
room of a chemotherapy clinic in Chicago. It was weird being
with Kitaj in public after the Last Retreat. Nobody responded to
him. Nobody saw him. Maria and I had carried him into the
clinic from the car in a crowded street; several pedestrians,
approaching, had just gone blank in the face as Kitaj came into
their field of vision. A momentary flicker of recognition, perhaps—
then the tightening, and the blankness.

Kitaj was dead, and not resurrected. He had no business being
seen on the daily street.

Even the doctors were saying he was dead, couldn't understand why he wanted to see them.

This place in Chicago was about the twentieth. We had to
wait. The room was silent and mahogany, with old copies of
Harper's and the *New Yorker*. The Dead Man was propped up
beside me, wizened and motionless, but staring at a stuffed eagle
with shriveling intensity.

Yet the smile was always hovering somewhere under the surface of pain, and whenever he spoke or moved, it was likely to
cause shock, or change.

He stirred. I felt a ripple, heard his delighted whisper.

"Look, Johnny! Look at my hand!"

I did so, cautiously. His right hand was empty. Then it wasn't.

I drew back a little at the blur of wings that formed. Then I
followed the fluttering path of the Red Admiral butterfly until it
flew out of the window.''

"Look again! Look again!"

This time it was a yellow butterfly. I could feel the energy
shivering through him and wished Maria would come back quick
from the washroom: this was more confusion of my senses—
what if he died at this moment?

"Come on, man, come on!"

The Dead Man eyed me with a sly slight smile.

"In Ireland," came his whisper, "you read me some of a book
called *The Romeo Error*. I want to hear one bit again. Find a
copy and read it to me when we're waiting at the airport this
evening."

I did so reluctantly. At the O'Hare airport I met Kitaj amid the
crowd of his young newconscious geniuses who—coming and
going at seeming random, yet always maintaining a consistent
number—had accompanied him through the month so far of this
rather grisly tour. And once again when rejoining them I felt a
sense of shock, of awkwardness, to be back among the Dead
Man's Crew, which had been through a dozen countries, and
Kitaj through hospitals and clinics and specialists, without let or
hindrance by customs officials or anyone else . . . a Plutonian
crew, moving like ghosts through the networks of the hypertense
world, ghosts with taboo on them . . . and upon each of them a
gravity, a weight of coherence, something intangible save to
others on the same journey, something that gently but firmly
discouraged casual approaches. With Maria I could talk, and Carl
sometimes, but with many I felt like last year's model, honored
for vintage of connection but hardly for my present contributions.
There was a tall Indian, Silver Bird, from one of the tribes of the
Pacific Northwest, whom once I saw teleport a heavy table from
the roadway into a removal van; I asked him once about his talent
and he started scribbling down equations, covering a page and a
half before he realized I wasn't following him. "It's simple
really," he said. "Like anything else, you know, five per cent
talent and ninety-five sweat. Matter of technique." But throwing
three sixes in a row was about the nearest I'd ever come to
success in the regions that these people roamed: I couldn't understand the things they did, even though I'd been talking about it
half my life, and up at the Last Retreat I'd felt so discouraged at

my lack of grasp on what was happening that I hadn't wanted to come on this crazy hospital tour until Kitaj persuaded me, reminding me how once I'd pushed him onto the spaces that he had been denying.

Now I came back among them to him with a book, I being the only wordy one there, and it was hard to read to Kitaj's smile what I'd read him six years earlier, what then had been easy for me to believe, and hard for him.

Easy then, I realized now, because I had not really believed it, any more or less than I really believed in Tarzan.

"You have the book, Johnny?" asked the Dead Man, from the middle of the circus, wrapped up and tiny in a chair. "We've got half an hour before the flight."

His voice was so faint I had to bend close.

"Okay, what about the guy you saw today?" I demanded. "What did he have to say to you? How much did he charge?"

The smile . . . the smile in the void of that face.

"I'll tell you when you read the bit I want to hear. Find me the bit in the last chapter about the Filipino faith healers. Start with the section about George Meek."

I struggled with my reactions. I realized he knew exactly what the passage said, for his memory remained prime. This was to tell me something . . . and that something was clear enough. I stood there. Flight departure announcements boomed. Grimly I read out aloud from Watson's book:

"In March 1973 and again in April 1975," I read, "George Meek led a team of scientists to the Philippines. These were experts in medicine, psychiatry, biology, physics, chemistry, parapsychology and even conjuring from seven different countries. They brought with them numbers of their own patients and quantities of sophisticated equipment. They saw many healers in action, and although they were able to recognize and discard several fraudulent practices, they agreed that 'the factual existence and daily practice of several types of psycho-energetic phenomena by several native healers was clearly established. The practice of materializing and dematerializing human blood, tissue and organs as well as nonhuman objects was found.' All members of the groups signed testimonies which declared that . . ."

I broke off. Grave faces. Maria's large eyes.

Unsmiling, the Dead Man made the least of gestures.

"A bit of the next paragraph." I bent close to pick him up. "The one about Donald Westerbeke."

So I mumbled my way into the next paragraph.

"One of the team was himself the subject of an operation. Donald Westerbeke, a biochemist from San Francisco, suffered from loss of vision produced by a brain tumor that was diagnosed in the United States as inoperable. He had two sessions with Tony Agpaoa of Baguio and his vision was immediately restored. On return to the States, his physicians could find no trace of . . ."

I stopped there and closed the book.

"All right. How many doctors do you have to make suckers of yet? What did that man today have to say?"

The Dead Man's smile was eternally deep, like the thinnest of veils over the face of the void, and I bent again for the whisper.

"He suggested I should try a faith healer, fast."

"PAN-AM FLIGHT NUMBER 123 TO LONDON NOW BOARDING GATE 17 . . ."

So the Dead Man went to Luzon with a sheaf of terminal verdicts to show, and I went somewhere else to relax a while, feeling that reality was somehow being cheated, in no doubt at all that the Dead Man phase, a deliberate game, was now about to end into new beginning through dramatic metamorphosis.

No. I was in no doubt at all.

I lay on a warm beach, waiting for the news, and realized I had known it all along, ever since that night on the hilltop in Ireland.

The patterns. Like dynamic blueprints, latent forms of events to come, like equations of fate which Kitaj had read clearly, and Isma'il too, while Lenore had, I think, seen them according to her own understanding of things.

I had turned away, refused to recognize, not only through fear of being stretched beyond my personality, not only through reluctance to make a commitment, but also through an obscure sense of outrage that the future could be apparently predetermined.

"It's not predetermination," Kitaj told me later in the year. "The pattern may be there, our optimum line of function or movement, but we have to choose to bring it into being, to realize it."

Also in me, I realized as I lay on the beach, was another kind of outrage, more instinctual and less personal. It was that Kitaj

should be on the point of making yet another come-back . . .
this one from the very lip of the grave, and even (in a metaphoric,
mythic sense) from beyond the grave. The Dead Man Risen. Had
the man no decency? No respect for the familiar conventions of
life and death? With the world apparently falling apart, and
thousands of millions of others forced to obey the biological
imperatives, then why not he? Why was *he* so privileged? Was
he the prototype of a new human being? Could we *choose* to stay
alive, as long as we wanted? Frankly, the thought appalled me.
My Old World conservatism was strongly afflicted by the sense
of spiritual crime, of the hubris involved in such a proposition:

"If Man was meant to fly, God would have given him wings."

The old ways were going, fast, and I'd spent much of my life
trying to identify with the new wave . . . but I still felt torn; I
still felt the sneaking masochistic urge to go down with all hands
on deck, all flags flying, and the band piping "Britons never ever
ever will be slaves" as the waters closed over our heads for the
last time. Because there was a sunken comfort in this, in the
knowledge that, after all, I did not have to choose to take
responsibility. If I really wanted, I could fail with the past and
hide from the future which Kitaj and his newconscious cohorts
seemed to epitomize with their casually factual approach to magic-
science phenomena which I, at some deep fixed Taurean level,
still wished to identify as impossible and illusory. But there you
go. If you don't change willingly, you get changed unwillingly,
and energy is wasted in the process.

So I lay on the beach, and reflected, and waited.

There had been no annoucement of Kitaj's trip to Luzon.

Yet in the months that followed the healing it became apparent
that thousands of people had known. One evening that summer I
read, I remember, a lengthy book of dreams which people had
experienced apparently during the time of the Dead Man. Some
of these dreams were very detailed and touched on a future still
unrevealed in the summer. Two or three were specific about the
event that took place in Venice at Christmas. When I read them I
neither believed nor disbelieved, but it seemed increasingly obvious that the inner worlds were breaking out in a new human
technology.

Many of the dreams were about a rising from the dead.

The strange thing was that when the Healing was announced,
when Kitaj began to appear in public again, nobody seemed very

surprised, not even rationalists or his former political enemies, most of whom faced the new situation by choosing to regard Kitaj as well beyond their sphere of action and reaction . . . at least, until later in the year, when the political effect on his final crusade became all too apparent . . . by which time there was no longer any point in striking at Kitaj personally.

RALPH M'BOTU KITAJ BACK FROM THE DEAD!

The first I saw was a television interview. Kitaj looked weak still, but he was walking, and maybe it was just a trick of the light, but his thin small frame in the sunlight seemed to have a glow to it all of its own.

I was staggered by the approach the media took.

"Mr. Kitaj, it only took Christ three days, so how come it's taken you three months?"

"Well," said Kitaj, grinning, "like a lot of us I'm a vegetation deity. I die in the winter and then I get born again in the spring."

Representatives of organized religion were the most furious and perturbed. Kitaj-myth was by now so familiar that it was beginning to undermine their ground as middlemen between humanity and the Great Spirit. If things went on like this, with people taking personal responsibility for relationship with God, then soon they'd all be out of work and in the dole queues. So they feared—as it turned out, unnecessarily, for millions of people remained unwilling to step out and do it themselves. The Roman Catholic Church in particular made every effort to prove this "miracle healing" a fraud, making much of the lack of objective evidence. For, though there had been a camera filming the operation at Luzon, the film had developed unsatisfactorily, with splotches and blurs. Shades of things to come. CHEAP PUBLICITY TRICK, CLAIM CHURCHMEN.

In fact, this failure to provide satisfactory scientific evidence was nothing new in the annals of Filipino faith healing. The problem had been exercising scientists for years, and still does, in various newconscious areas. The literature is extensive and frequently well documented. It seems almost as though there is a force or entity (manifesting unconsciously through ourselves?) which works in these areas to prevent the appearance of conventionally satisfying evidence. Specimens vanish, films fog, lights fail at the crucial moment, vital tape recordings burst into flame as they are about to be played back, crucial witnesses disappear without trace, spectacular psychokinetic effects fail completely to occur when electronic equipment is brought to record the types and quantities of energy involved. Evidence refuses to appear according to preconceptions of how it ought to appear, in a manner that relates to the bias of OldStyle materialism. "Faced with this, some people invoke the "War in Heaven" theory, of meddling extraterrestrial entities. But no sure statements can be made at this point.

Later in the year I talked with Kitaj about it.

"Will you feel insulted if I reply with a cliché?" he asked.

"Probably. What is it?"

"It's all in the mind."

Perhaps, but when I met him again in May, the evidence of my senses told me that he was not only cured but had moved into a new space that was light and very energetic. His face was physically lined with all he'd gone through during the illness, and he did not look strong, but there was a brightness that leapt out of him, out of his eyes, to embrace me before we embraced physically . . . and I felt immediately energized by the touch. His hands were dry and warm; a voltage seemed to pass into me; I breathed deeply; I felt a great peace and stillness.

Then I learned his plan.

The peace and stillness fell from me.

He told me about the tour he was setting up. The world tour, the miracle-show. The Transformed Man and his friends were going to hit the stages like a traveling circus, producing clouds of butterflies out of nowhere, bending forks telekinetically, clowning on tightropes of newconsciousness, inducing collective visions and production of strange phenomena, all in order, he said, "to send people home with something more on their minds than the price of bread and when the ax is going to fall."

I couldn't accept it. I felt he was trivializing his talents, and I told him so, bluntly, feeling once again on the defensive.

He appeared surprised. "I thought you knew me by now, Johnny. You know—Ralph M'Botu Kitaj—a new trick every year."

"But why this farce?" I demanded.

"It is not a farce. It will be Kitaj who does these little tricks. Do you remember Kitaj?—the richest man in the world, the cynic, the destroyer, the dead man? Now Kitaj has taken some chances, been through some gates, and in this particularly difficult time he wants to show the world that, if Kitaj can do it—then anyone can do it!''

"It's not that easy!" I objected angrily.

"No," he agreed, "of course it isn't. But a start has to be made somewhere. And I can stimulate in people what they don't or won't recognize in themselves. This is my function. But I am not a dictator. I cannot order them what to do. But I can amuse them, and stimulate their wonder, and turn them around inside.''

"And scare them out of their bloody wits!"

"What do you want? Should I get up on a cross for you?"

His smile made me acutely uncomfortable. It reflected inside me.

"Rafe, listen, please. There are some things I've not been able to get off my chest since Ireland.'' I paused. "I mean . . . I'm still a bit scared, and I don't understand. Where's it all going? How is Sirius involved?''

All this took place on the balcony of a hotel in Lisbon. It was a warm, sweet day, with the scent of flowers drifting up, and the city below, and the sea placid and calm beyond. He touched me gently on the arm.

"Johnny, you have been very important to me. Whether you realize it or not, and whatever you think your motives, you made a sacrifice of your interests to me, and I might never have climbed again if not for the way you drove me to it. I know you got scared that night; I know you blamed me for it; I know you lost trust in me, and in yourself. You thought that you were weak, and that I manipulated you unreasonably, and since then you've never quite cast off the suspicion that I'm just playing negative games with people. Now you ask me where it's all going. Why ask me? None of us know where it goes ultimately. We're climbing a mountain; the summit's in cloud. The thing is to keep going, do what you think and feel is right, step through those gates when you come to them. And you've been doing this, though you find it difficult. You have a conservative nature; you have intellectual prejudices. You see it and you don't. Your moon side understands all this perfectly well, but your thinking sun side gets offended at the breakdown in its value whenever you get faced by the incontrovertible proof that we are more than material machines.''

There was truth in this. But still I felt uneasy, sensing the power and love now flowing through this man, and through the sensation realizing the apparently indomitable continued existence of my own blocks and barriers.

I stared out over the sea, past the horizon . . .

"You really had terminal cancer," I muttered. "Now you've been cured dramatically in a way that makes people think, and the myth has grown very strong, and you say that next you're going round the world making butterflies appear and disappear in front of millions. But what if they start calling you Christ? What if people start coming to you, asking you to lay your hands on them and take away their boils, their scabs, their sicknesses and failures?"

He shrugged, and made a face.

"Then they will be healed," he said, "if they really will to be healed. It is no longer an occult matter, unless you want to keep on persuading yourself that it is. Many people have these abilities which I dramatize, and now there is sufficiently precise scientific research so that almost anyone who wants can develop and realize in themselves some aspect of these dormant talents—if they work at it. The stars, Johnny! Don't you think it's time we got out of tribe-blindness to learn our proper functions? Your problem is the main problem—the drag of the past, of gravity, and to defunct guilty self-image. Some part of you still doesn't want to believe that we can mutate ourselves and master these talents as a matter of course, like learning woodworking or bookkeeping . . . far less that we have to do it now, or die back into having to start all over again. We've got a chance, Johnny, all of us!"

Still I let myself feel scandalized.

"Rafe, there's a danger of elitism in all this! Not just everyone can simply get up and become an active healer or telepath or whatever. You say everyone can do these things, and gain understanding of the energy levels, of the astral, of relativity—but that's not practically true! Half the world is too busy trying to find a scrap of food to put in its mouth, trying to stay clean, trying to pay tax, trying to stay alive from one day to the next! How are all these people going to even find the opportunity to start learning all this stuff? Do you think your butterflies will persuade them?"

"If I can materialize the possibilities," he murmured, "don't you think that creates the opportunity?"

"For what? Half the world seems to see you in medieval terms as some kind of Faustian pact-maker with dark forces, and the other half sees you as an entertaining extension of Hollywood. So where does it go from that?"

He just smiled.

"We have to stimulate the development of personal technique," he said. "I mean rapidly, on the large scale, among millions of people. Last year in Kiev we came up with some new approaches. Group approaches. To produce collectively at a show the myth-reality that the aborigines of Australia call the *wondjira,* the dreamtime. We will teach people to tap their own depths. You can call it a course in biological engine maintenance, if you like . . . but naturally we'll dress it up with all the thrills and spills and fun of the fair. Why not?"

"Sure," I said, a bit sourly, realizing he'd avoided all mention of Sirius, yet intrigued by the scheme. "Let's all have some fun for once."

KITAJ'S UNIVERSAL ELIXIR & TRAVELING MEDICINE SHOW! COMING TO TOWN NEXT WEEK! PHANTOMS, MARVELS, MESSAGES FROM OTHER WORLDS! FIND THE HIDDEN POWERS INSIDE YOURSELF! LEARN HOW TO PULL YOURSELF UP BY THE BOOTSTRAPS! WHY STAY ON CRUTCHES ALL YOUR LIFE? GO THROUGH THE GATEWAYS THAT LEAD TO THE SOUL WITH RALPH M'BOTU KITAJ AT CANDLESTICK PARK, SHOWS NIGHTLY AT 7:30 NEXT WEEK THURSDAY THROUGH SATURDAY, TICKETS ON SALE AT ALL USUAL OUTLETS. PLEASE, NO UNACCOMPANIED CHILDREN . . . AND REMEMBER . . . TAKE A CHANCE!

". . . *Take a Take a Take a Chance*
It's no use if you can't dance . . ."

By early August, two months into the world tour, Kitaj-mania was rife on the popular level, the song by Jake Rivers & the Snakes hitting number one in Europe and America and staying there, Kitaj T-shirts, round-the-clock advertising and comment, the whole thing, the praise, the analysis of what it all meant, the put-downs by fundamentalists and authoritarians. "Kitaj is Antichrist! Turn away, brothers, turn away!" The Japanese soundtrack album of the first show, the Tokyo show, was on sale in forty countries within three weeks; soon anti-Kitaj broadcaster and authorities in various lands were using the brief crowd panic early on side two—especially one prolonged shrilling scream from a woman when Kitaj, onstage, shatters the gilded mirror with a silver hammer—in the attempt to persuade people to take no chances at all, to stay away from the Medicine Show.

There was little resistance to the progress of the tour. Once again Kitaj could do what he wanted so far as cutting through was concerned. Authorities maintained the tacit conspiracy that Kitaj was just a showman, that the Medicine Show was just another bizarre world superstar routine, booked and conducted in the usual way, June till the end of September. It was safer letting it happen than trying to ban it . . . especially when it became apparent that about a thousand million or so people wanted to get to the Medicine Show.

Average of seven shows a week for four months. Over a hundred.

Average number of people at each show? There were a few performances in theaters, but mostly in large arenas, or in the open. Average attendance: seventy thousand people.

About seven million people experienced the Medicine Show.

About seven million people experienced a dreamtime.

Tokyo. The first night. Kitaj appears on stage alone, insubstantial in a cotton robe, his grinning monkey face beneath a magician's hat . . . and for a moment his face is my image of Njeru's face, and I wonder . . .

He takes the mike without preamble. When he came onto the stage there was a great indrawn sigh, a gasp from the crowd, and I can feel the tremendous expectation invested in Kitaj, the dynamic atmosphere surrounding him which has developed in the public mind since Luzon. The polarity, the death-and-rebirth play of the Last Retreat followed by the miracle cancer cure, has increased the power and focus of the myth upon this slight and fragile-looking man. And we are all nervous there. Will he be able to hold it, lens it, carry it?

"It is time now," he calls softly into the vast hush, and from somewhere sidestage an invisible Japanese interpreter echoes his phrases in translation, ". . . for this human species . . . this natural transformer of nature . . . to awaken itself to the star of its purpose . . . to evolve beyond the individual . . . to evolve beyond the tribal . . . and beyond all collectivities and consensus-realities of ignorance . . . to discover true function . . . and tonight . . . here . . . what we are going to do . . . is begin to discover something of what our function should be!"

And when the words end their echoing . . . then the show begins . . .

Invariably they started out simple, a straight burlesque of glitter and lights, the conjurer Kitaj aided by his beautiful assistants Atlantis Rose and Aurora Dawn, and his friends coming on to go through their tricks—dematerializations of white rabbits, mind reading, butterfly production, drum-roll acts and minor levitations, Aurora and Atlantis being sawed in half, etc.

Soon, after the first few shows, once it was generally known that Kitaj's Universal Elixir was more than colored tap water, the audience would start getting bored. They knew there was stronger medicine to come than this carny warm-up stuff. The boos and cries to get on with it would start.

"Well, well, well," Kitaj would say, hands on hips. "You want to get into the meat of your minds now, eh? Fine. If you don't think you can take it, you had better go now. Are you all ready to take a chance?"

Usually this question was greeted by a huge roar.

"Very well," Kitaj would go on, with the lights dimming and stagehands removing the glitter gear. "Tonight we are going to dream together. It is an experiment in the power of our minds, united together. I will ask each of you soon to concentrate and to send to me mentally the images of your highest hope, your deepest dream. My function is that of lens, a focus or integrator, to gather your projections together into one experience in which we will all share. My friends here"—and then the Ten and Ten (the same people who had surrounded him during the Last Retreat broadcast) would file silently onto the stage and take up position around him, all of them grave, calm, prepared—"will direct the lens with perspective, watching especially for intrusive ego-elements and imbalances of integration. They will boost the lens in output of the dreamtime, and also comb it for emotional static and undesirably violent or negative influences. Then, my friends, we will start to build something interesting . . . something out of us all together.

"Now, please, begin to relax. Settle down, take off your shoes, focus on your highest inspiration. Relax . . . breathe deeply . . . concentrate your projection into the lens . . . quietly, now . . . relax . . . concentrate on the highest . . ."

By now, all would be dark save for a single spotlight on the lens.

Kitaj, the Resurrected Man, would stand there, and soak it all up.

But not all the early dreamtimes went so well. There were influences and unconscious elements hard to integrate. Sometimes there was trouble.

WEMBLEY PANIC AT KITAJ SHOW.
(From a review in the *Spectator*, London, July 1992)

On Saturday night at Wembley Stadium 100,000 unwary people set foot inside Kitaj's fairy castle, expecting revelations, only to find themselves drawn into a dangerous glamour-dream which masqueraded as a new reality.

Several hundred people later required medical aid and tranquilization. I am glad to report I was not one of these, yet it must be admitted that even now, forty-eight hours later, my sense of acute emotional disturbance remains. I have not slept since the show. Other reports indicate that this is a common experience.

What happened? How were the effects produced? It is said that we, the Wembley crowd, are responsible for creating the collective hallucination which terrified so many, and that Kitaj was no more than lens or the focus to bring coherence to our unconscious creation. This I cannot accept. It seems clear to me that the experience was deliberately induced by Kitaj and his assistants in order to induce conversion to his beliefs.

After the usual tricks and games and minor conjurings, Kitaj told us that the dreamtime would commence, and advised the crowd to focus their innermost aspirations onto him. The lights began to fade all round the stadium, all save for one, which picked out the little

man where he stood on the truncated apex of a silver
pyramid erected in the middle of the stadium, his assistants about him on a lower level. An earnestness of
atmosphere developed. There was a solemn chanting,
as if from all around, then a violet glow, pulsing at
slow and regular intervals, rising to produce a hallucinatory flush that pervaded the entire stadium, then
fading back to darkness. A soft gong joined the chanting voices. Somnolence invaded the crowd. I pinched
myself to stay awake. Then I heard a murmuring. I
looked towards the stage.

Above the pyramid stage I saw six figures—three
men and three women—suspended apparently in the
empty air.

Before I could believe or disbelieve these figures
began to float up, and out, one above each section of
the incredulous crowd.

My eyes followed the nearest levitator with amazement. I pinched myself, I bit my tongue, but still she
seemed to be there, a Chinese girl, apparently, her
arms and legs quite straight and still, floating closer
above our gaping faces and not for one instant looking
down.

Then I became aware of something still more astonishing. It had been a cloudy night—yet, suddenly,
looking up past the levitator, I saw the stars shining,
pressing down upon us! The stars of the winter sky!
The panic began. Vaguely through my own confusion I
heard people crying out: ''The stars are coming down!
The stars are coming down!''

It seemed indeed they were. Like giant catherine
wheels, spinning globes of light pressed down upon us,
until one in particular enveloped the entire stadium in
an eerie and painful brightness. There was pandemonium. I felt an explosion in my head. There was a
moment of total disorientation in which I lost all sense
of myself.

Then followed a sequence of hallucinations which I
cannot adequately recount. Preliminary evidence suggests that these were shared by everyone in the Wembley crowd. We found ourselves dissolved in this

starlight. We found ourselves traveling into utter emptiness apparently beyond this planet and familiar scheme of things, in a condition of physical immateriality. The hallucination went through many terrifying changes and ended with a blasphemy. For at length I (we) dreamed that I stood on top of the truncated pyramid. I realized that I was Kitaj and that he was me. The light still flooded me through. With some part of my own personality I struggled to escape this delusion. But this was not possible. Next, with perfect clarity, I heard a voice, seeming both within and without, and it is something I still cannot get out of my mind.

"This is our beloved son," it said, *"in whom we are well pleased.*

"It got a bit out of hand," Kitaj later admitted with regard to the London show. "It's not just a matter of the power in the human depths of which we're not normally aware, it's also a matter of what that power attracts when we begin to express it. When we start to go to the stars, the stars start to come to us. Certain rites and changes can be understood only with star-consciousness."

And after the Paris show it was necessary to revise dreamtime technique, to introduce more lensing organization.

Perhaps by the time of London and Paris Kitaj was beginning to feel the strain, losing control and balance just slightly. Not only was he lensing thousands of people every night, he was also dealing with the logistics and politics of the massive tour. By the time the Medicine Show got to Paris, immediately after London, there was some strain—not only in Kitaj, not only in the Show personnel, but also in the expectancy of the audience. Reports of the potency of the London show made many dubious, ambivalent, unsure if they really wanted to go through the lens. Plus the fact that in Paris at that time there was an ugly atmosphere. The French were itching for another revolution. The mass unconscious of the audience was very fragmentary, and Kitaj was not at his best.

"I had to soak up a lot of hungry discontented Gallic vibes that reminded me of Château Têtaurier and after the war," he said to me later. "I guess that threw my lensing quite a bit, and the Ten and Ten had to clean up all round me. The dream of those people then and there was revolution, not evolution. I was able to steer them into collectivity of the red rose. We became that red rose. We pulsated to a certain rhythm. In congregation we examined correspondences of relationship, sharing each other—the inner sharing the outer, the One knowing the Other—in this rhythm we approached the heart of the rose. We were preparing to continue into understanding of cross symbolism—the matter and spirit of horizontal and vertical polarities. But something went wrong. Blood began to drip from stigmata of guilt and anger, the purpose of self-sacrifice was forgotten. It was my error too. I didn't accurately estimate beforehand the revolutionary anger in the people. Blood began oozing from the collective dreamtime mind. There was a plunge into kaos-abyss. Next thing we knew we were stuck in a battlefield. Then it all went ape.''

The rioting and violence went on all that night in Paris.

Kitaj acted promptly before bans could come down. The five remaining European shows were canceled. He announced that hereafter there would be more lens control. ''I don't want to do this,'' he said. ''It reduces the possibilities. But nor do I want to invoke mass craziness. Maybe we have to bring these things out more gradually. Yet if we can't learn to come with what we are, then . . .'' he shrugged ''. . . KAPUT . . .''

Thereafter the shows grew more positive, more precise. The power beaming through the lens was deliberately stepped down, focused on more particular areas. At Seattle there was a particularly successful dreamtime. Over fifty thousand people at the Kingdome walked through an ancient America as yet untouched by Europeans. They walked the ancient land. It was envisioned in every mind via the archetypes fed through the lens by the ancestors of Silver Bird. This controlled choice of dreamtime subject was announced beforehand.

''Silver Bird wants to do this,'' Kitaj explained to the congregation. ''He wants you all to share how it is three thousand years ago in this land. By deep search in himself he has brought his ancestors to mind. They have agreed to be your guides . . . if you are willing to follow them into yourselves . . .''

Silver Bird went into deep-memory trance and his ancestors spoke through the lens. Music was played—drums and pipes—and gradually the dreamtime grew by mass focus on the lens. The deep mood was maintained and amplified not only by the Ten and Ten, but also by every one of those fifty thousand people. And so every person sharing in that dreamtime walked a bright primal world, following the stirring of the ancestor levels, every one creating this in themselves, personally developing the impetus given by Silver Bird, the lens, and the Ten and Ten. The principle recognition to arise from this exercise dealt with the extent to which the consciousness of each of us is a variable expression of many interacting and energetic natural cycles. The communicants recognized in dreamtime how their subtle body vibrations—generally unknown and unheard through the roar of blood, desire, and urban life—relate with these cycles, thus determining the health and affecting the mind. Thus for many it was a pristine, valuable experience of the cellular languages. It was an education in inner technique, an exploration of harmonies.

But three weeks later in Mexico City Kitaj tried one more "open" lensing, the audience being invited simply to project at him. The dreamtime there produced an Aztec sacrifice: there was nearly trouble again before Kitaj and Ten and Ten managed to step it down before Coatlicue and other old gods came roaring uncontrollably through. People remembering the Snuff Show back in 1988, with its bloody Aztec motif, again accused Kitaj of directing the course of dreamtime towards his own chaotic, anarchic ends. He denied this.

"Here in Mexico there's still a Spanish Indian schism," he said. "It has to come out and be resolved in the open, or soon there'll be war. This dreamtime shows it. But from now on there will be no more open projections."

In Sydney, Australia, aborigines who thoroughly understood mythreality were persuaded to lead the dreamtime there, and a group of them did the lensing.

"We have the *wondjira,* the dreamtime," their spokesman explained. "It is where we are when we are not here, though here is in it. It is before and after and in between. There was a great snake that created the world. It crawled up out of the sea. It brought the shape of mountains and plains, it brought the courses of the rivers. It lies coiled deep within us, this snake, and we can run with him now—in the dreamtime we can see the creation of the world—but take care, for the snake will swallow you if it sees you!"

The aborigine lens-group focused 80,000 people into the experience of their internal RNA movies. Through the memory cells for our race the communicants experienced the intelligence in themselves of the serpentine helix, the double spiral, of the biological code that programs us and maintains our generational continuity. The experience came in the form of subjective inner adventure, journey through the primeval world, riding with the Serpent from the High to the Low to the High again. As at Seattle, they gained knowledge of their inner biological structure, expressed as sequences of relationships keyed into one another by a central binding force—

Kitaj smiled.

"What is this force? It is the force that can travel with the stars. It is YOU! Not the you that dresses sharp, that drives cars and worries about the overdraft. You can't take earth-personality out there. So, what YOU am I on about? Ever been in deadly crisis? Ever been in a crash or battle or fall that gives you time to know that in the next second you might be dead? Remember how the personality and all your usual worries cut out and made way for the distant silent YOU that knows no emotion, knows no fear, that lives beyond your daily earthly sensation of yourself? That is the YOU that will go to the stars! The hidden YOU, just waiting for you to wise up and strip away the masks! So do it! Find your gates and go through them! What have you got to lose?"

And the Medicine Show rolled on through August and September, round the world, and everywhere the expression of dream-time was appropriate to the people and the place, nowhere quite the same as anywhere else.

"In some places," said Kitaj, "you get a very tight dream-time, especially in the older countries with the same blood-traditions that go back centuries. But there you tend to get conservatism of vision. In newer places, melting pots, you get greater danger of chaos, but greater chance of real discovery. When people come from many different cultures their middle psychic ground is diverse. You have to work harder to integrate and lens such diversity, to get through to the human archetypes which we all share. If you make it, the reward is great, the integration is most valuable. Take a Chance!"

The energy increased all the way to the final show. This was held at Timbuctoo, near the lands of the Dogon, headmen of whom came to help with the lensing. By now, most of the world was hooked. For four months Kitaj had been on the road, and the myth, realized anew in a new show every night, had moved beyond political attack . . . for now it was alive and evolving in millions of minds.

In the final show, the Dogon show, the Sirian landed.

The fishbeing, the Nommo, was hideous to see, producing unease and horror in the many Total Identifiers who were tuned into the dreamtime of the Timbuctoo communicants. The ship of the Nommo landed in the desert of the worldmind, and there might have been panic, but the Dogon lensers were prepared, had been waiting six thousand years for this inner event. And what the Nommo-archetype had to say was immensely valuable. The Voice spoke from the depths, sounding through Kitaj with information about soil fertilization—how to tap the earth's energy-nodes via geophysical acupuncture: "Drill the needles into the ground at these places. The energy will flow forth to the air and attract the rain."

The last I heard, this works. The Sahara is no longer expanding, grasses are startig to root at the edge of the desert, fertility is returning.

From Brazil Forest Rape to Saharan Refertilization.

All in a life's work for the karma of the lens.

The Smile. Smile on the void.

By then, leave-taking was in the air.

Likewise for myself.

I ventured out today and on the street I saw that man who eyed me in the store in the town I left.

He didn't see me on this occasion, but I've come straight back here, to finish this account now, and get it out, get it away. Because now I feel my time is almost all run out.

On the way back I bought a red rose. It sits in a glass of water in front of me, but it will wither quickly in this heat.

Kitaj retained his strength throughout those months. He had been calm and confident. Somehow, there was continually enough energy in that frame of his. But he was remote. Everything he had went into the shows, into the organization and the lensing. The rest of the time he slept, and he was never disturbed while asleep. He had done it. In several places he had faced angry audiences, difficult situations, but the only times he'd failed to turn trouble to advantage had been in London and in Paris.

Everywhere else, the smile was the positive agent. The energy of the smile. All but the stoniest hearts it softened, and on those it had a Medusan effect, hardening them still further. Yet, save once in the ashen lands of the Middle East, there were no threats or assassination attempts. Kitaj seemed to have moved beyond reach of human action or reaction. Many who went to the shows remained unsure as to the validity of what they'd experienced, but many more had found an inner lever to work with, and Chancing consciousness had spread rapidly. Kitaj generated such effect that decisions were made which otherwise would not have been made. In the week after the end of the shows, the tentative formation of a UN scheme to send a humanned expedition to the star Sirius was announced.

CLASSIFIED TRIPLE A. PROJECT ROVER. CRASH PROGRAMS.

"The human element is necessarily involved," read an early handout to the press, "not only as resident guiding intelligence(s) in the spacecraft, but also as integrating energy source of the propulsive, directional guidance, and life maintenance systems."

CYBORG SPACEMEN EARTH'S AMBASSADORS?

Kitaj just grinned when I showed him this headline.

"There are better ways to do it than that," he said, "and if they get there they may have quite a shock. It all depends what they allow themselves to see . . . and what they're allowed to see . . ."

"Are you Sirian?" I asked him directly.

"As much as you are," he said. "Whatever is born on earth is connected with the Sirian system."

October he spent in Kiev. In November began the laying-on of hands. It seemed spontaneous but oddly inevitable, for the power of the myth was moving us all. He abandoned the stage for the marketplace. Lenore, Maria, Silver Bird, Carl, myself, and half a dozen others went with him. Only Isma'il was missing. Rio to Madrid, Paris to Cairo, Mecca, Herat, Madras, Melbourne. It took on more and more the nature of a farewell pilgrimage. Nothing had been said, but you could see his intention in the way he looked at people, at the cities through which we passed. Lingering looks. But there was no nostalgia. There was no time for that, and nothing to be nostalgic about. On the Medicine Show tour we had been moving from place to place so fast we had hardly had any time to notice the condition of the world. Now we saw, and much of what we saw was terrible. The teeming millions of the world, the shanty-cities, the starvation, the sick thin people who always moved until they dropped, the disease, the breakdown of cities. What good had the Tour done after all? Now Kitaj made himself available to whoever wished to come to him. Thousands did. They came for the laying-on of the hands of the Transformed Man, and the energy poured out of him again, person to person, and he fed them with new life. He was tranquil, friendly, but remote. Only once I saw a slightly doubtful expression on his face, as if he wondered, *Why me?*—but in the next second that luminous smiled returned, and it said, *Why not?* And there was a night he asked me to read to him from *Tarzan of the Apes*. But I'd read only a page when he told me to stop. After that, Tarzan never came up again.

It wasn't until an evening in Istanbul (yet again, and this time no restriction on our movements) that I learned his intention.

He had been busy all day, in the great public space between the Hagia Sophia and the Blue Mosque. Patiently he had dealt with hundreds of people. To each he would give two or three minutes, stroking their heads or the affected parts of their bodies, his energy feeding into their diseases. Every hour on the hour he would withdraw into the shade, to sit quietly for a few minutes, regaining his energy, shaking the poisons out of his fingertips.

All year I had been amazed at the speed of his recovery. That evening for a while I sat alone with him in a hotel room. He was physically smaller than ever. There seemed nothing of him now but the radiance, the quiet and steady glow, of the smile. The Black Hole Joke was behind him. He'd gone right through it . . . into the Smile.

"I want to know," I said. "Where does your energy come from?"

"The energy is everywhere," he said. "Each time we breathe properly we recharge ourselves. When we learn to release ourselves properly, so that no energy is wasted and tied up in muscular knots and nervous tensions, then we need never be tired at all."

Then he looked at me, carefully, before going on:

"If I am tired, then mentally I put my feet on the ground, raise my arms and eyes up to the sky, breathe the air . . . then visualize a particular pattern that acts like a key, to unlock a gate in me. Through that gate I go . . . up a long tunnel of fire . . . to the place where the Voice is . . .''

He stopped. He was thoughtful. I waited.

"You know I'm going soon," he said quietly.

I felt the chill of incipient loss, but knew immediately I was not surprised.

"What is the Voice? Is it your voice, inside, or that of another being altogether who speaks through you? Is it Sirian?"

He laughed.

"You can call it that, it's as good a name as any other, so long as you don't take it literally. It is in me, it is our future, we are Sirians."

He appeared to be enjoying a joke which I could not see.

"Then what can we take literally?" I demanded unhappily.

"Nothing," he said. His smile grew very distant. "Johnny, we are free, we are terrifyingly free, which is why we're still shut up on this planet, deliberately ignoring what we truly see . . . because we're scared to be free. Yet we have more possibilities and powers than any of us have ever imagined. Look at history. There are natural forces from which we grew estranged during the development of the intellect. We turned collectively from the Mother to the Father and the moon to the sun, from the earth to the sky and the gut to the brain. Losses and gains, learnings and forgettings—but there has been an increase. One cycle, one age has been completed, a new spiral up the ladder is beginning, and on this one we have to take charge of ourselves. Yet still we fight against our own innate freedom and power, and people still ask to be given everything on a plate. Some of them, anyway."

The smile grew wide.

"The trouble is," he added, "that the survival and evolutionary value of a sense of humor is not fully appreciated. The sense of paradox and inner flexibility that gives us space to move in. People don't laugh enough!" He paused. I was tense. He was leading up to something. "But laughter can free us from the bonds of matter. It releases the constrictions in the body-field. And people talk of 'dissolving into laughter.' Don't you think that's very suggestive?"

His eyes, amused.

My reaction was delayed.

My mouth opened, but no words came out.

"You understand?" he asked, as the smile grew.

The smile in the void. It frightened me. I hoped he wouldn't smile too wide. Patterns flashed obscurely in me, half-recognized, and I knew I could have seen this five years earlier, as Isma'il had.

"I can think of better ways," I muttered.

I did not dare ask for direct confirmation.

"It was decided in Kiev," he said. "It will happen on the night of Christmas. At S. Giorgio Maggiore in Venice. It's time to go."

Now I had to ask.

"Do I understand you right?" I was very quiet. "You're talking of going away permanently, right? You're going to do something at Venice which will . . ."

I couldn't say it.

He said it for me.

"I intend to discorporate."

I was hot, very bothered, and I got angry.

"Rafe, this is ridiculous! Last year you just about killed yourself to put one in the eye of the doctors. Now you're talking of . . . fading out into the middle of the air . . . just to embarrass the Church. What's to be gained by it? What's the point?"

"Fulfillment of the myth," he said simply.

That stopped me. I stared.

"Listen," he said reasonably. "I have to get out of the way of the myth and let it grow on its own. My activities have been useful only so far as they have developed the myth in the minds of others. Now it's time for the culmination. It can't wait any longer. All this energy has been built up, ever since Luzon, and all through the shows—I have to use it now, and there's only one way. To vanish. In front of people. Just go. Leave a space, a gap, into which people can pour their imaginations. It has to be emphatic. It has to be pointless for any other purpose than itself. That's the point."

He said this easily, without concern. I was frightened.

"Oh!" I snapped, getting up, starting to pace. "Yes. Of course. Midas Transformed. How are you going to do it? Trick mirrors and trapdoors? Laser beams at twenty paces? An invisible UFO to snatch you up at the crucial moment in an electromagnetic net? How will it happen, Rafe?"

He was expressionless. He picked up a matchbox.

"The principle is the same," he said.

I capitulated. I had no doubt by then that he could do such a thing, and that other people could probably come up with explanations of the technique. As for me, the truth is I still can't describe how the internal combustion engine works . . . let alone how Ralph M'Botu Kitaj converted himself into energy.

"But where will you go?" I asked numbly, stupidly.

He said nothing. The smile grew again. It told me that there was going to be no point, no known destination, certainly no explanation.

Just an act.

"Okay," I said, "I'll buy it!" But my tone remained sarcastic and very discomfited. "So I guess this time it's going to be The Greatest Show on Earth, is that right? Transformation amid the lagoons of the Sinking City!" I laughed harshly. "I've heard it said that San Giorgio is the only really relevant church in the Mannerist mode! Congratulations on your excellent taste! What about the advance pubicity and the promotion? Do you want me to deal with that? Mythshow Number One! Action-packed with the New Messiah! Come see a man disappear before your very eyes, wreathed in a halo of evolutionary laughter! See human being become holy ghost! Incredible!"

"Yes," he agreed mildly, "it should be good."

And it was and is.

Very good.

Venice, 25 December 1992.

Christmas Day in the Sinking City.

I was there.

So were a hundred thousand other people.

So were you.

Such events invoke the presence of all humankind. Whether there or not in the flesh, we each carry our own images of these happenings. They are utterly public, utterly private. Our knowledge and understanding of them go beyond our consciousness of them. They belong to the heightened spheres of myth.

Venice.

Why Venice? Why not? Is that not a good enough answer? Then, examine your mental picture of the scene. Do you see the mournful beauty of OldStyle decay? The ages sinking slowly? Do

you see the mossy-dark roofs, the floodlit piazzas, the hundred
thousand flickering torches all along the slow canals and far out
in the bay? Perhaps you see—I do—the thousands of tiny boats,
bobbing up and down on the pallid waters round S. Giorgio
Maggiore. And perhaps now you see Ralph M'Botu Kitaj. He
stands now, before the classical eastern arcade of the church. See
him? The small man, almost bald, in the white clothes. Me? I'm
somewhere there in the large group of people behind him, behind
the Ten and Ten who will help him in the final act. I'm there
along with many of his friends. Maria is there. Lenore is there,
though she came reluctantly, almost as reluctantly as I did. We're
there along with all the other people who have been specially
invited—the doctors, the detached scientific observers, the TV
crews. The cameras are ready, and so are all the recording
devices, the measuring devices, the timing devices. So many
devices. None of them will work. Yes, we all stand discreetly, in
shadow beneath the arcade, shivering a little in the chill of the
evening, waiting, perhaps not knowing what we think or feel.
Some of us attempted to dissuade him; others simply nodded and
accepted. Now, we all stand and wait, and from your boat you
cannot see any of us. In any case, there's only one figure you're
interested in, and you can see him, quite clearly, though distantly, alone on the marble terrace, brightly floodlit from every side,
out in the open where there can be no trickery, no mirrors or
magical boxes or secret drops into underground cavities. Because
we are modern, are we not? We all know what this man intends
to do. He is going to vanish into thin air, leaving not a trace. And
apparently this is no longer an unscientific proposition. Perhaps
you have read articles in the Sunday papers telling you that such
strange things happen all the time. Perhaps you were at one of
the Medicine Show events, and experienced much wilder realities
than a man disappearing into thin air. Nevertheless, it is a
startling proposition, and many of us are going to demand proof
afterwards, if it happens. Proof? Well, trust your eyes. What can
you trust if not your own senses? Now, what do you see? He has
lifted up his arms. Involuntarily for an instant your eyes rise
skyward in the direction indicated by his arms. Night cloud. No
stars. Your eyes fall back to that tiny figure in white. He is so far
away from you, you cannot make out his features clearly . . .
but do you see how light and bright he is smiling? Do you see
how the white sleeves have fallen back from his arms, how they

lie bagged and crumpled round his shoulders? Yes? Yes, you do. So do I. So do a hundred thousand of us. Who are we? Why are we there? We have come from all parts of the world. We have come to say farewell. And now it is time . . . and we are aware of his smile even before we begin to notice the light which is shining all round him, apparently emanating from him, a radiance that is stronger than the drenching of the floodlighting. It is a pearly radiance, a rippling, smiling light. Perhaps for a moment you look around, seeking some explanation, some other source— but, no, it is from Kitaj that this light is coming . . . as though it pours through him from some other dimension to which he is a gate. And it is growing stronger! It suffuses him, it begins to cloak and hide the physical form of him! Within it, you sense, he is growing misty, insubstantial, and in the air above his head, violet patterns appear to be flickering. And you cannot hear it, out in the bay, but beside me there are gasps of awe, shock, disbelief. I am numb, yet there is a curious exhilaration in me, and beside me I feel Lenore staring, standing stiff and straight. The camera crews—I hear curses, I hear curses even as the miracle is happening. What's going on? A miracle's taking place and all the equipment is seizing up. Quick, quick! See it with your own eyes, know it with your own heart, don't depend on machines, don't depend on the reports of other people—see it for yourself, take the chance while it lasts. Oh, see him now! A cloud of light, incandescent, giving the certainy of a smile—the Smile—you can see right through it, though it's dazzling—but still he's there, and for a moment you seem to hear a voice, speaking inside you . . . *"I'll be back. In seven years I'll be back, and hope to find you all through the Joke. Take a Chance. Why not?"* . . . but did you really hear it? Perhaps it was just your imagination. And the camera crews and even the scientists are still struggling with their equipment as the great blaze of light glows, throbbing on the face of the bay—and there is a sudden shock, a sudden surprise—a crazed man in a fawn raincoat suddenly rushes out among us, points a revolver at the cloud of light, and he fires—once, twice, three times. But there is no effect on the dancing cloud of brilliance, and the patterns wheel and change in the sky above as the man in the raincoat turns and rushes wildly away. Did you notice that? Did you hear that? Probably not. Probably the Smile had you entranced; probably you were swallowed completely in it, in the stellar width of its

humor, though possibly you too aimed your Minolta, your Zeiss,
or your Polaroid; maybe in one moment of weakness you tried
for a shot of the Smile, hoping for evidence to convince the folks
back home, fearing they'll never believe it, not really, but crassly
hoping all the same—so you hold the camera up above the heads
and waving arms of the thousands in the little boats all round
you; you try to steady yourself, to stand straight despite the
sensation that you are being dissolved in the radiance that throbs
and expands out, wider, higher—and you press the button—you
take your picture, but . . .

it's all gone
there's nothing there
just floodlighting on empty marble

Yes, but what *really* happened?
Kitaj discorporated himself—that's what really happened. He
did it. That's all. He did it. In approximately five minutes he
transformed his solid human body into a smile of sparkling light,
a smile that then dissipated who knows where? Perhaps all
through the world.
Kitaj disappeared into thin air.
No tricks. He transformed his physical substance from matter
into energy. He employed will, concentration, dedication, and
knowledge.
He became a realized myth.
Midas Transformed.
The Smile on the Face of the Void.

Fine, but where's the proof?
There is none. It's as I said. All the equipment seized up.
None of the devices worked. Soundtracks hissed blank. Photo-
graphs fogged. Official observers refused to commit themselves.
They all said, "No comment," in public at least, meaning either
they didn't trust their own senses, or they were scared to lose
their jobs, scared for their lives, scared to take a chance.
Sensible of them.
There's no evidence, but plenty of persecution.

All right, all right, but—why did he do it?

Why not? Ask a Chancer. You'll get a laugh in reply. Or become a Chancer yourself. Then you'll be laughing.

What have you got to lose?

Now? 1999? Laughter?

Yes. Now the laughter that shakes, that dissolves, the laughter that returns the weeper to his source. The dreadful laughter of atom bombs and the laughter of stockpiled terminal jokes. Now the smile of the Cheshire Cat—it gapes through the daily naked sky. The whole world's balanced in the chiaroscuro of Mona Lisa, in the curvature of her lips, and six billion Yossarians come slouching towards the edge, hands in pockets, chins sunk into their chests, the endless line of those who are caught in the jaws of the Black Hole Joke, who believe there is no way through.

Does it have to be like this?

Does it have to be The End?

No, it need not be.

Take a Chance.

Of course you will find this personally dangerous, and not only on the inner and higher levels. In my recent experience at least seventeen countries don't want Chancers around. Chancing refines the Gross National Product. Chancing ignores the social games. Living your life by its own design has become a political offense, because the designs within us take us beyond allegiance and obedience to conventional social systems. So be careful. The Org is desperate. The Org will give you every opportunity to put your life on their line. Before you take your chances, be sure that it's all your heart and soul that's doing it. It would be an awful waste getting yourself killed just to impress the boy or girl next door. Taking Chances doesn't mean being a spendthrift fool, wasting your godgiven life on some casual impulse or impotent angry moment. It means steadily seeking your function, your destiny, your pattern, and continuing to do so despite all efforts of friends and others to dissuade you. It means seeking the inner voice and following it without expectation of any earthly or personal reward. And particular Chances you take, if you must, at a time and a place and in a mood which moves the Spirit higher through the racial energy-body, closer to the star-mind with which we'll fuse one day.

And if you need some central philosophic focus—some reason, root, goal or direction—then perhaps you can consider the mys-

tery of Sirius . . . for you may be sure that the UN expedition
now on its way to that star-system (and the new expedition now
being planned for Barnard's Star) will not entirely solve the
mystery that lies within us by going without us . . . though what
is brought back, if the expedition does return, will certainly be of
interest and value.

What will be found by the crew?

Intelligent purple ocean beneath the burning ultraviolet sky?

In recent months, despite all the persecutions, there have been
persistent rumors from many parts of the world of increasing
numbers of UFO landings and communications which governments are not admitting or reporting, of clairvoyant and dream
contacts with a particular entity, calling itself Horus, which
claims to contain Kitaj, which claims connection with Sirius,
describing itself as ''a third eye trigger for those of you willing to
admit yourselves.'' I have heard people discussing this in bars,
and lately I myself have been dreaming of many people and
friends I have known, including Isma'il and Lenore and Kitaj
himself . . . and these dreams say that the seven years are
almost up, that a new gate is about to be unlocked, and that as a
species we are already through the early days of major changes
which we must accept and make the most of if we want to move
on in the light. The dreams tell me, as does Kitaj's life, that what
we call death is a gate; that there are many deaths and many
births in the existence of every spiritual entity . . . and they tell
me that I am at last about to join my friends who have departed
before me . . . because now, at last, I am ready.

Ultimately I have no rational explanation to or conclusion for
this story, because reason is a tool dependent on the extent of
imagination, not an end in itself, and because there is no absolute
conclusion, only processes which continue. The story is always
beginning, and I cannot honestly make conclusive statements
about phenomena which I do not wholly understand. Always
when with Kitaj I had the sense of falling short, or failing to see
something essential, and when on occasion the wider situation,
normally foreign to my limited vision, burst through to be experienced as reality within me, my tendency was to panic flight.
But that is now no longer necessary, and, though I know that
ultimately All is One, it would be the worst kind of lie to pretend
to you that I possess any special insight. I was present when

strange events occurred; I have tried to report them, but my
report is the vision of a blind man, and so I have not attempted
too much by way of explanations which, being so partial to my
own limited views, would only create prejudice and misinforma-
tion. I know only that we have still a long way to go, that we are
at present in great peril from ourselves, and that we are all much
more than most of us will admit to ourselves.

Yet I believe this: whether or not Kitaj came from Sirius in a
literal sense is thoroughly unimportant. The main thing is the
useful metaphor of something beyond that is also within us.
Sirius . . . perhaps, any mystery might do . . . but few can
tempt the mind so far, and few incur such a variety of approaches.
And increasingly, as the old models of reality dissolve, leaving
us with myriad personal passages through chaos, ''Sirius'' provides a beacon. The idea of the silver star can shine through the
chaos, providing a light to guide us on. You may argue that its
importance lies ''merely'' in our minds . . . but all the time the
evidence mounts to suggest that this external reference point in
some crucial fashion relates with our internal human make-up
. . . and many more of us every year are seeking the connection,
no matter what the Org may say.

It is as if like lemmings we have collectively brought ourselves
to the very edge of the abyssal ocean, and only as we find
ourselves forced into the freezing waters do we realize the light
that hangs low and distant before us. So instead of trying desperately to turn back we can summon a little hope, to swim out, and
on, with that light as a guide, not knowing what it means or
betokens, not knowing if we'll get there, nor what we'll turn into
if we do . . . but with a sense now of holy quest rather than
mere desperate animal flight, with a sense that we are like holy
grails, regirding ourselves to receive more potent brew which in
our former condition would only have burned us out. In truth it
seems to me that this species is engaged in rewiring itself,
forming new circuits to carry greater and more complex voltages
of meaning and interconnection. This is an agonizing and difficult task, and especially hard to do in the darkness. But we have
gained much new light already, and we can begin to see to do our
work. There are OldStyle agencies in the world which put up a
final brittle resistance to torture and incarceration, trying to force
people to remain within the old molds . . . but already many of

us have gained, if not a return of faith in the old external image of God, at least the realization that it is we who blow our own fuses when we try to carry new power on old circuits . . . or put new wine into old skins. The Argentum Astrum shines in our history and in our present, meaning precisely we know not what as yet, and the connection with the future realization of that meaning, our meaning, our star-meaning on this earth, is pointed out by the acts of demonstration and sacrifice which Kitaj performed. For at Venice he closed old circuits, demonstrated the opening of the new, leaving it to us to decide for ourselves, and acting in such a way that the myth was realized and accelerated, so bringing a new power into world even as he went out of it.

May we acknowledge the light within us.

Amen